Winter's war

Aaron Cowan

Authors Note.

The Rushing Winter series of books do not stand alone like some novels may. In order to fully enjoy the arc of Rushing, it's important to start at the beginning and work forward. I have intended the story to be followed in this way, and because of this there is very little reexplanation on previous events, characters, plot points or environments aside from the conversations that exist between characters and Rushing's offered recollections. While this may bother the casual reader who wants to jump in to the middle, I don't write that way, so I apologize in advance if I just gave you homework. If you've read this note before, you are already following along. If you haven't, you have skipped ahead.

Start at the beginning. You'll thank me at the end.

-Aaron Cowan

For my father.

A man who left this world with no regrets.

I

One month before Resolute.

Nobody gave a shit about Sudan, least of all Darfur. At least, nobody gave a shit enough to do anything more than donate money, maybe go to a benefit concert or sit through a documentary. Sure, the UN, Red Cross and a slew of non-government organizations collected millions, hell even billions in aid that was funneled towards Sudan. The money bought rice and medical supplies, provided health services and kept the refugee camps running, but what this country needed was a professional military to move in and put rounds in bad guys until the bad guys were gone.

That wasn't going to happen.

Way too little interest in creating a way too big political quagmire.

Master Sergeant Tony Card wasn't a fool. He'd been promoted. He spent some time as an idealist, now he was just a cynic. He didn't give a shit about Sudan either, so the feeling was probably contagious. Yet, here he was, laying under an Acacia Senegal tree, one liter of water away from being *out* of water, three days into a two-day op. Master Sergeant William Toomby was right next to him, both of them not giving a shit about Sudan, only about what was going on *in* Sudan. If Card was in a better mood he would admit that he did care, but Toomby wouldn't have cared even in the best mood.

Three days ago, they rode a CV-22D Osprey out of Al Hudaydah, Yemen, punching out over the Red Sea. Just outside of Eritrea airspace off the coast of Africa, they topped off on a KC-135, then went to the deck to hide in the clutter, navigating Eritrea's archaic radar network. Card slept for most of the trip. It was his first ride on a CV-22, but far from his first ride with the 58th Special Operations Wing; all in all, it wasn't a bad trip. The Osprey didn't vibrate his teeth nearly as bad as a C-130, and the Air Force sticks kept the ride as smooth as possible. The trip was somewhere around 1,300 miles one way, figuring that they would have to give natural terrain features and urban areas a wide berth to avoid detection; A straight shot would have been just over 1,100 miles. Toomby did the math on the tarmac before they took off, said it would be a four-hour flight, Card was cool with that.

Once they violated Sudanese airspace, the pilot rode the desert floor like a wave, Nap of The Earth. He pushed the Above Ground Level limits, skirting along at what Card figured couldn't have been more than 50 feet. Card knew that pushing at max flight speed at fifty feet was going to move the fuel gauge along pretty quickly. He was sure they had enough gas to get them there but wasn't so sure about the Air Force boys having enough gas to get back to their air-conditioned hotel rooms. The last thing Sergeant Card wanted was for them to have to ditch the bird. If that happened, he would have to baby sit four crew members and keep Toomby from leaving them in the dirt. Toomby wasn't big on interservice cooperation. Card knew it was out of his hands, so he didn't worry about it. He had bigger concerns.

When they passed over the White Nile River, Card could see the glow in the night sky to the south, Khartoum. The city was mostly asleep at this hour, plenty of extremists dreaming of American soldiers, wishing they would fall from the sky like a check waiting to be cashed. He found irony in flying over, silently forsaking their dreams. The crossing point was tricky. Sergeant Card knew that a few hours of deliberation had gone into picking the precise point that the Osprey would hop the river. The river was life in Sudan, especially in the north where the desert owned more real estate than the Sudanese did. With so much of the population crowded along the river banks, the decision was made to hide in plain sight. The Osprey, running with lights out, crossed the river just south of the Wadi Sayyiduna airport. Card had to smile at the giant balls the Air Force displayed with that move. Wadi Sayyiduna was home to a good deal of the Sudanese Air Force, including a wing of hand-me-down Russian fighters. With the low flight altitude and the droning engines of two Shaanxi Y-8 transports loitering before takeoff on Wadi Sayyiduna's tarmac, the Osprey slipped through without any official notice, though Toomby swore to Card that he saw a *dirty goat herder* with a cell phone to his ear looking up at them as they zipped across a fallow field just west of the airport. Card kept primed for a few minutes, expecting something to happen. Nothing. They had slipped by clean.

An hour later, one of the flight engineers signaled that they were ten minutes out. Card and Toomby slugged on their gear. Each of them would be humping 75 pounds without the weight of water and weapons. Once they hit the ground they would have three hours of darkness to move five miles.

Cake walk.

The flight engineer gave the word, the Osprey got loud, fast. It vibrated so bad, footing was precious with a 75 pound ruck on one's back. The engine nacelles tilted up. Card had been warned that the transition from plane to helicopter would bring a sudden altitude drop. It did, more falling-off-a-ladder feeling than anything else he could compare it to. The Airforce sticks brought the bird into a hover in a depression that had probably been a flowing river a few millennia ago. The ramp came down, Toomby lit out like he was wearing flip flops chasing an ice cream truck. Toomby was a fit man in a pudgy man's body. He carried 20 extra pounds on his body that he shouldn't, despite that, he never failed a PT test and regularly ranked in the top percentage of whatever unit he was in at the time. He also flaunted the fact. Even owned a T-shirt that read *Kinda Fit, Kinda Fat*. Card was humping the drag bag in addition to his ruck, so his sprint off the ramp was a little slower. He had barely hit the sand when the Osprey went ramp up and nose down, fading off into the night. The two Sergeants went back to back, waiting on bent knees for any signs of hostile locals drawn to the sound of the aircraft. Five minutes of listening and scanning the night through white phosphor tubes resulted in nothing but some indistinguishable live stock down the shallow valley.

Card consulted his GPS, found their path, and got moving. The terrain was soft sand called *Goz,* with scarce vegetation and just enough rocks mixed in to roll an ankle. The land was mostly flat, slight rolling hills with the occasional dry creek or river bed and a few seriously deep wadis. Northern Darfur was probably worse off than most of Sudan. Once rich with wildlife, woodlands and villages, the north had seen too much population growth and too much war to sustain, it had become a sad carapace of tribal life. Deforestation for fire wood to feed the red brick industry and for basic cooking increased the open desert land by hundreds of square miles a year. Hunting and poaching saw the game population decrease to dangerously low levels. The second civil war, maybe it was the third, between the Sudanese Government, Janjaweed militias and the rebel forces of the Sudan Liberation Movement Justice and Equality Movement ravaged the region further, seeing over three hundred thousand killed and millions displaced into refugee camps or neighboring countries before a tenuous cease fire was declared in 2010. After that, Sudan became two separate countries, then warred its way back to one. Now maybe it was working on being two again.

Card traded point with Toomby after the first mile, wary of patrolling Janjaweed technicals in the area. The technicals were little more than light and medium sized trucks with either DShK heavy machine guns or Type 67 machine guns mounted in the rear. The DShK, or *Dushka* was uncool, Card didn't like the idea of coming under fire from a heavy machine gun that spat 12.7mm rounds at 600 a minute. He had seen firsthand what a Dushka could do in Afghanistan, it was a death machine. Card had a satellite high overhead dedicated to seeing him and Toomby make safe passage to their hide point and avoid the Dushka wielding locals.

Every so often a sweet sounding southern accent would whisper updates in his ear. She was steering them clear of the patrols with veteran skill, predicting the movements of the rusty Toyota and Datsun trucks like she could see the future. They had one close call. Two Skinnies riding on horseback crested a hill off their left flank. If not for the sound of clacking hoofs on the basement rock at the bottom of the hill, the two khat chewing gunmen would have been on them before Card shoved Toomby into the dirt. Toomby was a professional and his bond with Card was as close to symbiotic as it could be, so the sudden bout of physical contact from Card didn't elicit a single complaint. He just lay in the dirt, breathing shallow until he figured out why Card pushed him down. He heard the hoof beats, heard the two men chattering on in a tongue he didn't speak. Heard their banter get close, he heard the clanking of the fasteners on the reins of the horses, the heavy breathing of the labored horses, the clatter of soviet rifles banging against legs. The sound got loud, peaked, and then faded away into the distance. A few minutes of silence and they were on their feet and moving again. Card didn't admonish his eye in the sky for missing them; he didn't want to blow a chance at getting her phone number when this was all over.

They made their hide point beneath a grove of Acacia trees atop the highest hill with a good view of their target just before day break on the first day. They dug their rucks into the sand a hundred meters from the hide, took essential gear with them and then picked out a primary and two alternate hides. Each hide was prepared with a shallow bed to lie in, fresh branches to aid in camouflage and a precise GPS fix in case they needed it. Once that was done, Card deployed his long gun, Toomby set up his spotting scope, they both dressed out in their ghillies and set in. The work wasn't done then. Toomby started ranging distances as soon as the sun revealed them. They were just shy of a thousand meters off the compound wall; the furthest building inside the compound broke even at thirteen hundred. If they had to make any shots they wouldn't be breaking any world records. They had done that four months ago in Afghanistan. Sergeant Card hit an Afghani on a motor scooter from the flank at twenty eight hundred meters. Since the Afghani was in Pakistan when he was removed from his bike by the .338 Lapua round, and neither Card nor Toomby were officially in Afghanistan, the shot wasn't an official record, but it was one seventy-five more than the current public record, and it took Card one round compared to the Brits nine. Card knew he had the long shot, that's all that mattered. Toomby was pissed that the fan boys wouldn't be talking the shot up on the internet.

When the sun painted the shadows in the compound, Card started introducing himself to the locals. The compound wall was mostly red brick, some rough lumber and crude cement mixed in to fill gaps. Various buildings dotted the interior with no real pattern; small huts, barns, brick kilns and open air canopies. The social gathering point seemed to be a semi-circle of red brick kilns that were situated in the southern corner of the compound walls. They belched smoke without pause, firing bricks and serving as a good place to cook up some lamb. Near the kilns were a number of squat huts, a few surplus tents, and a collection of odd chairs and tables that made up the dining hall for the guard force.

The *guard force* was comprised of a dozen locals, light in the sandals with a few Ak's and some older British bolt actions. Augmenting them was a team of six professional soldiers with German assault rifles and American body armor, comms and equipment. The locals either rode horses or putted around on patrol in one of two Toyota trucks. Both trucks had crew served weapons mounted. The hired help had two American Chevrolet Silverados, decked out for rough use. Toomby snapped pics of every single face using a telephoto lens, sending them on to their handler. By the setting sun on the first day, they had no intel on the locals (no surprise there) and all six Pros had been identified as contractors working for Virtua Corporation. Card and Toomby had run into Virtua contractors before. They were pricks. The fact that they were at this compound meant that they were pricks that had a very good chance of being dead in Darfur.

Night set on the first day. The two Sergeants took shifts through the night watching the compound. They reported any activity up the chain to the voices in Virginia. Sometime on day two, their target was supposed to arrive.

He didn't. They spent day two watching a number of teenage boys gather wood for the brick kilns. A larger group of Nubian women wearing colorful dresses and large hoop earrings worked a grove of Acacia trees to the north, harvesting Arabic Gum to sell. At their rate of work, Card was comfortable with knowing that they wouldn't come anywhere close to the hide for a few days. Around noon Toomby spotted a tribe of Dar Hamid moving camels south on the far side of the compound. It was the highlight of the day. Their target was due before sunset on day two. He didn't show. Sergeants Card and Toomby had been briefed specifically that their target would arrive for a meeting at the compound with an unknown third party. The compound was a neutral meeting location, unofficially authorized by the Sudanese government because they seemed to have an unknown interest in the outcome of the meeting. The presence of the Virtua security detail meant that the meeting was probably still on, just not at the expected time. Card was used to the plan changing. He was twelve years into his Army career, and four into his time with the Army Compartmented Elements, the new ambiguous name for what used to be known as the Combat Applications Group, or to the civilian world as *Delta Force*. Of course Card and Toomby were sheepdipped by who they thought was the Agency a year ago, so he wasn't exactly sure if he could count the year towards his twelve. Not that it mattered, Card would stay in uniform until the Army told him to hang it up. He had no intention of leaving a second sooner. Toomby would too, Card imagined. Ever since meeting in the First Ranger Battalion, they had gone everywhere as a package deal. Either because the universe willed it, or because they fought for the same billet. When you work as a team, you want a well working team.

The night air was stiflingly hot. Not nearly as hot as the day sun, but still hard to deal with; dry, lacking any real breeze, seasoned with a fine dust that hung in the air like a mist. The dust got into everything and got on Card's nerves. Once it stuck to sweaty skin, it hung on and clogged pours. Card knew better than to try and wipe it away, all that would get him was a rash. He stoically dealt with it, Toomby a little less so. The distance from the compound gave them a degree of movement that was welcome. They did not have to remain stone still throughout the day to avoid being discovered, but economy of movement was ingrained in both of them. An increased distance from the target just meant that they could forego the ghillie hoods during the night, the other rules remained in effect.

Day three came on hot. Toomby woke, glanced at the temperature on his Suunto watch, cussed for a few seconds under his breath before he accepted it. Card laughed to himself. Toomby could be such a baby sometimes. Toomby crawled up next to Card, getting behind his spotting scope. After a few seconds of adjusting, he settled in and didn't move again for hours.

Now they were both thinking about how much it would suck to have been born in Sudan. Card was also wondering what Kafka or Neitzche would have to say about the fatalistic attitude the world took towards a country that seemed to be firmly in God's blind spot. Humanity cared only enough to send food, doctors, perhaps a diplomat or two. God couldn't be bothered to offer a steady rain or a case of conscience to stem the simmering desire for religious cleansing. Card often wondered how God felt about being called down on two sides of an argument. Maybe, like Card, he didn't feel much of anything.

"Spotter up"
Toomby croaked. Card snapped out of his philosophical
moment, getting proper eye relief on his Leupold scope,
waiting for Toomby to call his target.
"From the south on the road, tan Rover, moving north at
twenty to thirty, range five thousand and closing."
Card moved the rifle to the right, following the road. Five
thousand meters out was a life time away. Since the only
road ran just outside the compound wall, and they were a
thousand meters off the compound, he only traversed a few
inches to the right before the vehicle fell into his view.
Once he had it, Card reached up with practiced patience,
dialing the scope to its maximum 24x magnification. He
adjusted the parallax to put the target and his glass on the
same focal plane. At that distance, in that heat, mirage was
one more obstacle to look through, a distortion that caused
his scope picture to wave and distort. They were above it,
but just barely.

The Rover carried a driver and two passengers.
"I'm up, three occupants, no ID."
Card said, letting Toomby know he had the target.
Sergeant Card tracked the dingy thirty year old Range
Rover on its trip up the road. It bounced, swayed and
sagged along on shot suspension, the occupants bouncing
along with it. When it came abreast of the compound wall,
half of the local guards tugged open a lumber gate,
allowing the Rover entrance. The gate struggled closed
behind it. The Rover was lost behind the wall momentarily
until it drove deeper into the compound, moving past the
kilns and tents, stopping outside of a low slung barn that
was dead center in the compound. It sat for a few seconds
with no movement. The Virtua contractors walked up from
the tables. The Rover opened up, three men stepped out.
"Range it."

Card said to Toomby. Card knew the range to the barn was 1,125 meters but he wanted Toomby to shoot a new range off the Rover. This far out, objects stacked on top of each other with high magnification and could appear closer to each other than they really were. Card measured the barn against the tire of the Rover with the milliradian lines on the Leupold reticle, he knew the approximate height of the tire from memory, some quick math in his head told him the Rover was sitting twenty meters off the barn. Toomby called out the range, Card's math was dead on. Toomby consulted his Kestrel.

"Wind out of the North at one, one hundred two degrees, ten percent humidity, barometric pressure is thirty even. Three degree down slope angle."

Card already knew most of that. He checked his data card on his wrist. The temp and pressure was consistent for the past few days, today was no different. A three degree down angle shot was child's play. The humidity was up from yesterday, but not enough to change his solution. A shot at this range would have a flight time of around three seconds. A lot could happen in three seconds. Card reached up to his scope, adjusting the windage and elevation. He could have simply *held off* for his shot, using the grid from the Tremor 3 reticle that offered quick alternate points of aim, as opposed to adjusting the center cross hair for the shot but Card wanted a cold zero shot, he didn't want to have to miss and adjust.

"Sniper up."

Card said, watching the three Rover occupants stretch and mil around near the barn. They were a trio of sweat stained skinnies, dressed out in khaki pants and light-colored button down shirts. Two of them were toting Uzi submachine guns, the third, tallest of the three had a battered leather brief case and a pair of aviator sunglasses. These jokers must have been the third party.

Cool.

"Toomby, get some pics of these clowns."
Toomby rolled over to his day pack, grabbing the Nikon camera off it. He made sure it was still plugged into the lap top before stabilizing the telephoto lens. He snapped off a few pics, they were transmitted immediately to a wireless satellite dish set up near their cached gear. From there they would bounce to Virginia. Card marveled at the fact that the Nikon lens Toomby was using cost more than his rifle and optic combined.

Sergeant Card waited a few seconds before reaching for his push to talk button connected to his Comtac headset.
"Foundation, this is Breathtaker."
The transmission was silent for a few seconds before the sweet sounding southern accent replied.
"Go ahead, Breathtaker."
"Third party has arrived."
"We have the faces, Breathtaker, standby one."
Toomby gave Card a gentle elbow.
"So you gonna get her digits or what? Fastest way into the panties, bro. Sure she gets all kinds of bored hanging out with the other computer geeks."
Toomby was a crass man, he meant well though.
"Breathtaker, Foundation…"
Card pulled his mind out of the Southern girl's pants.
"Go ahead…"
Man, she had a hot voice.
"Breathtaker, the man with the briefcase and sunglasses is Malusi Dosi Al Taybi. Al Taybi is an Abbala local and Janjaweed commander. Spartan is asking for termination after the primary target is down."
Card subconsciously drifted his point of aim onto Al Taybi's chest.
"Breathtaker copies."

Spartan was the call sign Colonel Wayne Solomon, a legend in the Special Forces world and Card's ultimate boss. This was Colonel Solomon's op, whatever the Colonel wanted, he would get. Solomon had handpicked Sergeant Card and Sergeant Toomby, bringing them on board with a counter-terror unit that didn't even have a name, originally Card and Toomby thought Solomon was with the Agency...he wasn't. Card didn't know the details of how the Colonel had the latitude that he did, didn't care. What he knew was after the President and most of her cabinet was killed in the crash of Air Force One six months ago, the war on terror went black, under the radar and red hot. Solomon was stopping hearts on six continents using a company-size unit that was, aside from some transportation, totally self-sufficient. Card and Toomby had been on board for a year, *officially* working for the NSA for anyone who went looking, *unofficially* getting more trigger time than they ever would have working for any three letter agency or Big Army. Whatever deal Colonel Solomon had with the new man in the big seat, it was a sweet one. Card liked nothing more than slotting honest to Allah terrorists.

"Breathtaker, Foundation, Spartan is requesting a count on the ground."
Card nodded to himself. Satellite time was lost on Card, sometimes they had it, sometimes they didn't and the whys for if or not seemed more nebulous and political than common sense. Having one on the compound would have been nice. But hey, he was there.
"Roger that, Foundation, stand by."
Toomby, who was listening to the same transmission, consulted his notebook before getting on his scope to do a fresh count. He panned from the south of the compound to the north, then back before jotting down a few lines which he showed to Sergeant Card.

"Foundation, Breathtaker. 21 armed hostiles, between 18 and 25 women, children and teenagers."

"Roger, Breathtaker, be advised, Vicious is on the ground and standing by."

Vicious was the second part of the operation, another team from the unit that had been in country for a little more than a week. They came in early to secure transportation and find a suitable location to stage away from prying eyes. Once Card eliminated the primary target, he and Toomby would provide overwatch for the ground team that was going to breach the compound and extract intel.

"Breathtaker copies. Any idea on when that will be, Foundation? We are black on water and food."

She came right back.

"Breathtaker, eyes on target currently in Kutum, moving north towards your location."

Kutum was around a hundred miles south. With nothing but dirt roads, wadis and barren desert between here and there, Sergeant Card guessed it would be sunset before the target arrived.

He could live with waiting a little longer.

"Roger, Foundation, we will advise. Breathtaker out."

Card took his hand off his radio and put it back on his rifle. The sun was high in the sky now, punishing the earth. Card could see the thermals rising off the rocks, drifting in prismatic colors into the air through the excellent glass on the Leupold scope. The mirage rise and drift told him that the wind at the target was more or less the same as the wind on his neck. It felt constant and nice.

Africa would be beautiful if it wasn't so ugly.

An hour before sunset Toomby called out a vehicle on the road. A pasty white new model Suburban that rode heavy on its shocks. The windows were tinted dark. The SUV moved fast, a plume of dust running high and far back along the road. Card tracked the run-down Suburban all the way into the compound. It pulled up behind the Rover amid much of the same fanfare. The Virtua contractors treated it differently; instead of mild curiosity they guarded it inconspicuously from the locals. Toomby went back to the camera, snapping pics. The driver stepped out, Card got a good look at his face, he was a nobody. The only passenger in the vehicle came around the back, meeting up with the driver and the six contractors. He was the primary.

Martin Heller.

Martin Heller was an international fugitive, wanted for war crimes in a half-dozen countries, suspected of war crimes in just as many and had probably committed worse that no one breathing knew about. He was a Virtua Corporation problem solver if ever there was one. Martin was arrested in the US six months ago, handed over to the US Marshal Service for transport to trial in Europe. He, four Marshals and a flight crew of two left Hartsfield-Jackson airport in Atlanta. The Gulfstream landed in BFE Spain short four Marshals. Martin had taken the aircraft in flight, forced the pilots to divert and then killed them before vanishing into the Spanish countryside. Card had read up on Martin Heller. He was a monster. Card was pretty cool with being the guy to shoot him.
"Foundation, Breathtaker, advising we have Heller on site."
"Roger that, Breathtaker, stand by."
Card pulled into his Blaser Tactical 2 rifle, his thumb caressing the safety, waiting. Heller was standing still, looking across the compound to Al Taybi. Al Taybi was waiving at him, motioning to the clutter of chairs and tables. None of the buildings on the compound had air

conditioning, having their meeting outside made sense. Martin was having none of it. He pointed to the barn. Card needed a confirmation to fire. He needed it now. Toomby was reading his mind. He set his rifle close by, ready to use it, then gave his glass a quarter turn out of focus so he could track Card's shot to target. He would call out adjustments if Card needed them when he fired.

"Breathtaker, Foundation, Spartan advises you to wait for the meeting to occur before engaging, we need to ensure intel is on site."

Card didn't know what the intel was. He figured if he needed to know, Colonel Solomon would have told him. Heller wasn't going to be going anywhere under his own power. Card could wait.

That was cool.

"Breathtaker copies, we are standing by."

Card relaxed his body, wrapping his free arm across his body and under the butt of his rifle, one finger going to his pulse. Beating steady at 50 beats per minute. Card was in peak physical shape. Missions like this required it. A lower calorie intake and minimal physical movement made the body sluggish, unresponsive. Sergeant Card had trained for years, preparing himself for the inevitable moments when he would lay in place for days in a prolonged state of physical rest before being required to act.

Martin Heller was surrounded by a loose perimeter. Six men guarding their *noun*, Heller's driver remained with the vehicle. Before Heller arrived, the six-man detail had been relaxed, indolent. Now they were alert, responsive, heads on swivels. Toomby was off his scope, looking down on the compound instead through his own rifle. Sergeant Toomby was the spotter, he didn't require the same long range firepower as Card. Instead of a bolt gun, Toomby lay behind a M110 7.62mm semiautomatic rifle. It didn't have the same punch at range as Card's Blaser, but it could still reach out and ring bells if Toomby needed it to. Of course, at their current distance, it wasn't much use for the compound.

Daylight was fading. Heller and Al Taybi were inside the barn, Al Taybi had taken his two men in with him, Heller had taken all six of his. Whatever they were discussing, it was taking time. Once the sun fell things would become more difficult. Card and Toomby would need to go to night vision. With a 17% waxing crescent moon, illumination wouldn't provide much help. Card had the option of slaving a night vision monocular to his rifle's scope, though its image quality dropped greatly over distance. Nothing Card could do but accept it if it came to it.
"We have a baby sitter."
Toomby whispered. Card scanned the horizon, back and forth, his eyes going higher with each pass until he found it. Somewhere in the neighborhood of thirty thousand feet a Reaper, or Predator drone was catching the sun just enough to show itself. Toomby didn't like it, Card was okay with it. If it was a Reaper, that meant they might be able to call in some air support if they needed it. Card needed that meeting to be over before he lost his sun.

II

There was perhaps twenty minutes of sun left in the sky when the barn door pushed open on uneasy hinges. Al Taybi walked out, his gunmen leading the way. He had his chest puffed out, arrogance in his walk. Whatever the meeting was about, he had benefited from it. The inside of the barn was dark. Card couldn't see more than a few feet into it. He saw no one.

Card keyed his radio.

"Foundation, Breathtaker."

"Go ahead, Breathtaker."

The Southern girl wasn't working yet. Instead, Card was talking to the other voice on the radio Toomby called *Sniffles*.

"Foundation, the meeting is over; Al Taybi appears to be leaving. I do not have eyes on primary. Do you have eyes on the compound?"

The radio was quiet. Not a good sign. Toomby scanned the air for the drone. It was still up there.

"Negative, Breathtaker, no eyes on station."

Sergeant Card cursed to himself. He had assumed the drone was theirs. Twenty years ago, the US was the only country that had them, now you could damn near buy one on Ebay. Someone was watching, maybe Virtua.

"Foundation, we have what appears to be a drone loitering in the area."

"Copy that, Breathtaker. We will look into it."

Look into it, huh?

"Spotter up. Two thousand to the South on the road, four arm up's headed north. BTRs"

Card got back on his rifle, panning right until he spotted the four vehicles.

"I got 'em."

They were BTR-152's, Soviet era six wheeled armored troop carriers that were mass produced in the 1950's. They were ancient by today's standards. Three of them had light machine guns mounted. The last BTR in line was an anti-aircraft variant. Four KPV heavy machine guns in a quadruple mount. The KPV trumped the Dushka as the baddest gun in this neighborhood with its 14.5mm rounds.

Each BTR was desert sand in color, bearing the colorful flag of the current state of Sudan. It seems the Sudanese Army was going to stop by. Card was tired of the surprises.

"Foundation, Breathtaker, be advised, we have Sudanese military in the area, four BTR's moving towards the compound."

"Roger, Breathtaker, will advise Vicious."

"Hey, Tony, this thing tits up yet to you?"

Toomby asked, packing away gear in preparation to move. Card had to agree.

"Yeah, the dance card is a little too full for my tastes. I was feeling pretty cool about it until the army showed up."

"Maybe they are just driving by."

Yeah, maybe.

Card focused back on the barn. Al Taybi was at his Rover, leaning against the front bumper speaking on a cell phone. He chatted for a few seconds, glancing over his shoulder towards the West wall. He was expecting someone. That someone was probably in one of those BTRs.

Card didn't care as long as he saw Heller before they arrived. Heller was the target, anyone else was gravy. The BTR's made it all the way inside the compound, still no sign of Heller.

The armored cars stopped in a straight line, troops pouring out of them. The man that looked to be in charge walked right up to Al Taybi. Hugs and kisses on the cheek were exchanged. Toomby struggled for a good face shot in the fading light. Once he had a few they were sent off to Virginia. Al Taybi and his military buddy walked towards the barn. Al Taybi's guards shut the barn doors. Back to the meeting.

"Breathtaker, Foundation."

It was the Southern girl. Nice.

"Go ahead."

"Breathtaker, your new arrival is General Waleed Abd Alraheem, commander of the 9th Airborne Division. Spartan wants you to add him to your list of priorities."

Card cursed. This place was turning into a scumbag swap meet and Spartan was seriously killing Card's cool. Card, Toomby and the four-man Vicious team were seriously outnumbered. There was a drone, possibly an armed drone, loitering under god knew whose control and four armored vehicles with around ten soldiers apiece that were now holding a perimeter around the barn. It was now dusk. Card had maybe ten minutes of good light before visibility began pulling in.

"Roger, Foundation."

Sergeant Card reached into his assault pack. He added four magazines to the two he already had laying beneath his rifle.

"Will, get on your gun, I'm going to need you."

Toomby folded up the tripod on his spotting scope, packing it away without a word. He flipped down the bi-pod legs on his M-110.

"I don't know how much help I'm gonna be, Tony, compound is outside of my envelope."

Card fine-tuned the focus on his scope, adjusting the parallax until his crosshairs were crisp against the compound.

"First round down range is going to bring plenty of targets our way."

Toomby thought about it.

"I'm going to move to hide two."

Their second hide was two hundred meters south and about four hundred meters closer to the compound. A much better position if Toomby was going to get in the fight with the reduced range 7.62.

Toomby packed up and moved out, sulking back into the trees before heading south. Card made sure his range card was in place, so he could make adjustments on the fly.

Toomby came up on the net ten minutes later.

"Breathtaker, Ruckus, I'm set."

"Roger, Ruckus."

Card opened a second channel. He wasn't supposed to contact Vicious via radio unless it was an emergency. This qualified.

"Vicious, Breathtaker."

Vicious must have been waiting.

"Go ahead."

It was Warrant Officer Three Fred Tellison, the coolest dude Card knew.

"You have eyes on this meeting?"

"Yeah, it's busy down here."

Tellison was stoic as always, ice cold.

"Recommendations?"

"Take your shot when you get it, let us worry about killing our way in there."

Maybe too ice cold.

"Roger that, Vicious."

Card switched back to his main channel, watching and waiting. All he could do was wait and hope Heller came out of that barn before Card ran out of light.

"Breathtaker, Ruckus, south east corner of the compound."

Card traversed his rifle. The south east corner had a low wall with plenty of scrub brush grown up around it. Card didn't see anything worth looking at for a second. He was ready to ask Toomby what he was talking about when he saw it. A pair of legs sticking out of the brush, a dusty AK lying next to them. Card could see blood on the sand.

"I'm only counting ten of the original twelve guards, Breathtaker."

"Roger, we have another player."

Sergeant Card knew it wasn't Vicious, they wouldn't go in without telling Card. What the hell was going on? Card followed the compound wall north, scanning for anything else. He found the body of the second missing skinny near the barn where the meeting was taking place.

"Ruckus, second skinny is down near the barn."

"Roger...Break, Foundation, Breathtaker."

"Go ahead."

"Breathtaker, we have an unknown on the field. I have two local guards down, no sign of the belligerent."

"God damn it, Breathtaker, this is Spartan. What in the hell is going on down there?"

"Spartan, primary is still out of sight, inside the barn center of compound. Sudan regulars and locals are guarding the interior. I have at least four heavy guns inside the walls and no shot."

A series of pops rolled up the hill from the compound.

Gunshots.

"Spartan, we have action, will advise, Breathtaker out."

Card got on the glass, putting his scope back over the barn. The barn doors were open, two bodies right in the entrance. Sudan regulars were putting fire into the open entrance, fighting a stonewall defense for General Alraheem. The General made it to the rear vehicle in his convoy, crouching down behind it. He fumbled a cell phone out of his pocket, dialing a number as his troops pulled back to protect him. The General was low on the list of priorities. Card had no sign of Heller or Al Taybi.

Fuck it.

Sergeant Card ranged the General at 1,175 meters. Card felt no change in the wind, the temperature was in the high 90's, not enough to change things. Card felt his pulse, checked his breathing, made a slight elevation adjustment, just .2 Mils up, centered his crosshair on the General and brushed the safety off. Card felt the trigger, waiting for his natural respiratory pause, his prime physiological condition from which to press the trigger. Between heart beats, just before his body would naturally feel the urge to draw a breath, Card confirmed his point of aim and pressed back on the trigger. The single stage action broke at 3.3 pounds, the 250 grain Lapua round left the 26 inch barrel traveling at 2,950 feet per second. With over a thousand meters to the General's upper chest, the round would be in the air for close to three and lose over half of its speed before striking him. Card worked the bolt back, coming off the scope to do it, rammed in a second round and went back on the scope. His first shot followed the arc from the elevated barrel to its natural apogee before dropping 510 inches to its point of impact. The General was hit just right of center chest while in mid-sentence, falling back into the rear of his BTR as Card fired his second shot. One of the compound guards was crouched down not far from the General behind a pile of bricks, Card's second shot hit him in the left shoulder as he spun to the sound of the General being hit. His arm and body went different directions.

Card adjusted his elevation back to the barn. The Sudan regulars were pulling back to the BTR's. The lead BTR began strafing the barn with its mounted machine gun.

Card scanned for anyone fleeing the barn, he could see no one. Dusk was becoming dark, he could see even less of the inside of the barn.

"Breathtaker, Vicious, advise."

Card keyed his radio.

"No sign of primary, we have an unknown inside the compound."

The General's men struggled to pull him into the rear BTR. A gunner popped up in the turret, spinning the four machine gun system to the rear, towards the hill.

Towards Card.

Card dialed back down. The gunner opened fire, four starbursts stacked by twos blinded Card's view of the gunner. Tracers raced up the hill amid the *thump thump thump thump thump* of the four heavy guns, hitting low and working their way up to a spot fifty yards to the North. Either he would get the gunner, or the gunner would get him. Card was cool with his odds. Card aimed between the muzzle flashes and fired. Two seconds-ish later the gun went silent, depressing down onto the rear deck of the BTR. The gunner had vanished, fallen back down inside the BTR. Sergeant Card shifted back to the barn in time to see Martin Heller, Al Taybi and two of the Virtua contractors break from the inside. Card adjusted, predicting their path, predicting Heller's path. Card was aiming for a patch of open ground, doing math on the fly in his head, using the Tremor 3 reticle to give educated guess as to the distance between Heller and where Card was aiming. No time to dial in. Card predicted Heller's running speed, chose a final point of aim and fired. Heller shifted his path, the round hit one of the contractors instead, putting him on the deck like he'd been hit by a car when the .338 Sierra Match King hit him low in the pelvic girdle.

Heller saw him go down, didn't bother to break stride, limping in a sprint on his prosthetic foot.

Card set up a new shot. He had one round left before he would be forced to reload. Heller was headed straight for the Suburban. The driver had it running, ready to go. The Blaser kicked, a round on the way. Heller wasn't stupid, he knew he was being shot at. He could guess from where. He dodged again. Card's round hit the ground harmlessly. Heller made it to the Suburban. Card palmed in a new magazine, working the first round into the chamber. The last contractor fell behind the Suburban, someone shot him from inside the barn. Al Taybi scampered into the Suburban with Heller. Three Sudanese regulars pulling off the barn went down like dominos.

The Suburban tore around, rooster tails of dirt, headed for the gate.

The BTR's began moving, pulling their dead General out.

The civilians from inside the compound were fleeing north on the road.

Sergeant Card dialed in the dope for the gate, did his math and fired. The round hit dead center of the windshield and stopped there. It was armored. Not cool. Not even the .338 could punch it with one shot.
"Vicious, Breathtaker, Heller is in the Suburban. It's a hard car."
Card dumped out his magazine, digging in his bag for one of two mags he brought along with armor piercing rounds, cursing himself for not being prepared. He cleared the chamber, loaded the magazine and drove in the first AP round.
"We got this."

Tellison said. Card set up for a shot anyway.
"Breathtaker, Ruckus, I'm moving down."
Toomby wanted in the fight, Card couldn't argue with that.
"Roger."
The Suburban smashed through the gates, spinning recklessly towards the south. Card was at a disadvantage, he wouldn't be able to predict the exact location of the Suburban when he fired because he had no idea what its rate of acceleration would be. It was armored so he guessed slow, that was as good as he could do. He fixed a point of aim and fired. The round hit just behind the passenger side front door, breaking through the leading edge of the rear passenger door window. Card worked the spent casing out, loading a new one. The Suburban accelerated. The BTR convoy came through the gate, all four vehicles were strafing the hill with heavy fire. Tracers flying through the air like supersonic flaming arrows, some were way off, many more were much too close for Card to be comfortable. He should have moved. He never had the chance.

Vicious team announced their presence from the low land, three distinct muzzle signatures and one smoking trail of an anti-tank rocket, most likely an AT-4, in flight. The AT-4 hit the Suburban broadside, lifting it onto two wheels. It coasted for a few feet before bouncing back down on all four wheels, continuing down the road. The BTRs hesitated; gunner's adjusted fire to the roadside. Card calculated a shot for the lead BTR gunner and fired. The Sudan regular vanished in a flash of pink mist. The convoy of BTRs broke left at the edge of the compound, headed out into the desert, tracer fire peppering the flat lands and back up the hill towards Card.

A second AT-4 rocket was fired, hitting the tail end of the Suburban. It sheared the rear door clean off, bent the rear roof up like it was made of tin foil, yet still the Suburban accelerated. Muzzle flash directed at the Suburban continued. Card attempted a shot, but the Suburban was moving far too fast, he would have to rely too heavily on luck for a hit. A few seconds later, the Suburban was lost in a trail of dust. Card searched for the BTR convoy, they were well over a mile out past the east compound wall, still firing in random directions.

Shit.

Card pulled back off his rifle, collected his gear and sprinted back towards their cache as fast as his heavy ghillie pants would allow him to move.
"Vicious, Breathtaker, I'm rolling up here and moving to you."
"Vicious, Ruckus, same traffic, popping IR."
"Foundation, Breathtaker, primary has escaped, secondary has escaped, tertiary target is down. Primary is headed south."
His Southern girl answered.
"Roger, Breathtaker, we have satellite coming on target in ten, we will attempt to re-acquire."

Darkness put its hold on Africa. Card made it to the ruck sacks, dumping his rifle on top of them. He stripped a satchel charge out of Toomby's ruck, pulled the pin on the delay fuse then tucked it between his rifle and the two rucks. No need to hump the gear out. Card pulled on the bump helmet for his night vision, fitting it to his head, activating the IR strobe on the top. The sprint back to the first hide was quicker without the long gun, he had left his M4 at the hide, picking it up as he went by. Card hoped the intel in the compound was worth all of this.

When Sergeant Card reached the road, Toomby had already rallied with the four men of Vicious team. Toomby stayed behind off the far side of the road near the compound wall to meet him, Tellison and his men breached the compound to collect what they could.

"Jesus, this is fucked."

Toomby said, jogging with Card into the compound. Card agreed. They reached the barn. Tellison was standing just inside the doorway with a dim red lens light, reading something. Warrant Officer Hollic stood next to him, on the radio, speaking with Foundation, arranging exfil. Card and Toomby reached the barn. Up the hill behind them the satchel charge blew. Tellison motioned inside the barn.

"Blood bath in there. See if you can make heads or tails of it. We need to be gone in ten."

Toomby didn't care to look. Card wanted to know what screwed his chance to get Heller.

The barn was much larger than it looked from the hill, and not just because of distance. It was one large room with a few low walls built off of support columns to break it up into different sections. Hay stalls lay empty. The largest section was just off the door, holding a hand-built log table with hand built chairs strewn around it. One body lay on the table, one of Al Taybi's guards. He had been struck in the chest by what appeared to be an ax or hatchet. Four of the Virtua contractors lay in random places on the far side of the table, killed while advancing on their threat that appeared to have made entry through the rear of the barn. In the rear corner Card found Sergeant Finn. Finn was standing over Al Taybi's second guard. He was face down in front of a gap in the barn's siding, a wide gash in the back of his head. It was a clean, sharp blow that probably killed him instantly. This was the entry point.

"Hey, Tony. What's missing?"

Card looked around the barn, his night vision was grainy in the immense darkness. Even the multitude of holes opened in the barn siding by the BTR's machine guns didn't let in much light.

"The aggressor."

Finn flipped his rifle mounted light from IR to white, pulling off his NV so he could see. Card did the same, looking everywhere Finn looked.

"What you think?"

Finn asked, producing a digital camera. He began taking methodical pictures from the entry point to the table. Card bent over, picking up a 7.62 shell casing, there were plenty of them, mixed in with 9mm brass from what Card assumed was the Uzi's that Al Taybi's stooges were toting. He dropped it in a pocket.

"I think someone wanted these assholes more than us, came in here right under our noses and almost killed all of them single handed. I also think that same person, or *per-sons* is now gone."

Finn nodded, snapping away with the camera.

"Looks that way..."

Finn rolled one of the Virtua contractors over with his foot.

"What the-"

Card saw it too. A battered Browning High Power, the slide locked to the rear on an empty magazine, was sticking out of the man's chest just above the top of his plate carrier. Card bent down, gripping the pistol. It slid out, welded to the underside of the pistol was a blade, about four inches in length. It was razor sharp and expertly crafted.

"That's some crazy shit. Imagine the derp boy validation for pistol bayonets if that ever made it online."

Finn said, snapping a photo of the pistol. Card admired it for a second before tossing it back on the body.

"Have a look at this, then."

It was Madeline O'Neal. She was in the corner opposite the door, digging through Al Taybi's brief case. Madeline was the only civilian on the op, an Irish/English/American chick that worked for Virtua once upon a time. Card didn't know much about her except that she and the Colonel went way back; she worked just about any weapon with trained skill and her ass looked amazing in just about anything. Card was all about equality, especially when it let him work with quality.

Madeline was reading over a piece of carbon paper, a small light held in her teeth. Card and Finn joined her. What she had was an export receipt for a shipment from Doraleh, Djibouti, bound for the New York Container Terminal. The gross tonnage was in the single digits. Not much for the size of the container listed on the receipt.
"Spartan, Knight, I'm looking at a shipping receipt. Al Taybi shipped something to the US, cargo is listed as Arabic Gum, bound for New York. According to this, the shipment should be at sea now."
Madeline looked at Card and Finn while she waited for a reply. She was already thinking ahead to hunting down each and every container. No small task.
"Knight, I copy. Collect what you can and get to the exfil, the SFA just put two Hind's in the air, headed your way, you have about ten minutes."
No one needed any motivation to want to avoid two Russian made gunships.
"Time to go!"
Tellison yelled from the door. Those inside moved out, white lights were extinguished, night vision turned back on. The team moved back through the destroyed gate, heading north through the desert. They were over a mile away when the oppressive sound of two sets of five bladed rotors powered by Kilmov turbines filled the night air. The beating rhythm was arrogant in its volume. The two Hinds landed at the compound without searching the surrounding area. Everyone breathed a sigh of relief for that. This

operation was not supposed to be the production it turned out to be. First the Sudanese Army showed up, then an unknown individual or individuals ruined the party and with it, the ability to eliminate Martin Heller. Heller escaping was unacceptable.

Early the next day Sudanese police would find Heller's Suburban, and the body of Al Taybi in a wadi not far from Nayala. Al Taybi was missing most of his skull due to a .338 AP round that entered through his cheek. There was no sign of Martin Heller or the driver, not that the Sudanese police knew to look, or would have bothered if asked.

The killing of a Janjaweed commander and Army General was blamed on the rebel forces, threatening to reignite a civil war that didn't exactly end to begin with.

Solomon's team was extracted, riding the same CV-22 out of Darfur that Card and Toomby rode in on, using much the same route back to Yemen that they had taken in. Once in Yemen they *went civvy* and took the first flights out, traveling in twos. Over 30 hours travel time each from Aden to Sanaa to Frankfurt to Washington DC. The intel they had gathered secured safely in zip lock bags, divided up and secured with medical tape to each team member.

The intelligence collected revealed that Al Taybi was an aspiring terrorist with America as a target. Heller was facilitating his aspirations by providing logistics and equipment. Al Taybi was due to sail out of the Port of Sudan on a Russian owned freighter flying a Bahamian flag sailing for an American port in South Georgia. His cargo was supposed to beat him there. Customs and Border Protection working with the Coast Guard boarded the Maersk Global Horizon twenty miles off the coast of New York. The container was gone, unloaded in Algiers. The trace for where the container went once it was on the ground in Algiers was nearly a dead end. Three ships were in port when the container was unloaded. It was loaded onto one of them, the question was, which one?

Other documents found pointed to Al Taybi's plan.

Al Taybi appeared to already have assets in place in the US, there was just no mention of where Al Taybi's people where or who Al Taybi was ultimately working for. There was also no mention of a target. The containers were still headed for the US; there was no doubt about that. Solomon needed to find it before Martin Heller found a replacement for Al Taybi.

1

Four days before Resolute

I hadn't said a hand full of words to him yet, and I had already lost his attention. His legs were crossed at the knee, one on top of the other. More feminine than masculine in its form. A yellow legal pad poised on his lap, the pen busy at work. He wasn't taking notes. The elongated vertical curves the 200-dollar Cross pen was making told me he was drawing, the picture in my mind as I watched the pen move was one of a quickly materializing duck. Without breaking his concentration from his doodle, he asked his first pointed question.
"How was your relationship with your mother?"
No eye contact, flat in tone, not accusatory, not even really inquiring, just words that on paper would have a question mark at the end...black ink, conservative font, no emotion. I leaned forward, rubbing my face in my palms, regretting even thinking this would work.
"I can see this was a waste of my time."
The thought of one less troubled soul paying him three hundred an hour got the pen to stop and pay attention.
"Excuse me?"
This time his words carried a little emotion. I must have been giving him one hell of a blank stare because his face flushed, consternation ebbing to the surface.
"Look, I know you are used to a number of certainties in your line of work, I can't even begin to guess most of them, but I'm pretty sure the majority of the people who come in here and sit on your couch are easy to read and probably easy to fix, if they need fixing at all. My problems are not so inconsequential, nor my intellect so dim that I don't recognize a question tailored to address a broad range of personality hang-ups found in a disproportionate amount of

people that would grace the doorstep of people in your line of work."

The consternation was joined by annoyance, like I was wasting *his* time that *I* was paying for. I shrugged.

"Let me see if I can get us to the same place; you asked your question in the past tense, not the present, making the assumption that I no longer have a relationship with my mother. Now, right or wrong, your Freudian assumption that all my ills stem from my mother would be insulting if it wasn't completely irrelevant. I'm sure plenty of poor bastards can sit on this side of the coffee table and drone on about their mother for weeks and talk themselves into a better place without you ever really having to exercise your jaw, but I'm not that kind of person, doc."

His eyes scrunched up at the edges staring back at me with a frown, like a person gets when they are trying to work a problem with no context of what the end result should be. The legal pad went to the table beside his chair, the pen was capped and placed in the pocket of his Egyptian cotton shirt, and then his fingers intertwined and made a neat little hat for his knee. I guess I had his attention now.

"I suppose I could apologize, Mister Winter, but I hardly think the offense was so to require it, and I don't think you are a man who ever really needs to hear one. You made some correct observations, but the question is a relevant one, it helps me to get a feel for a person. Mothers are a wonderful starting point in my line of work, the source of either great love or great pain for many people, and for some a great deal of both. You don't have to answer, but it will come up again if we continue this…more than once I'm sure."

I gave him another shrug, leaning back into the voluminous cushions. I decided to give him an answer and see where he went with it.

"Not helpful."

A furrowed brow.

"Excuse me?"

"My relationship with my mother was not helpful."

His eyes lit up like he won the teddy bear with the first ring toss.

"Interesting."

I chuckled, almost convinced at that point that it really was a waste of time. With him, with anyone in his field, with help at all…if I even needed it. My chuckle earned me a tilt of the head, he waited for me to fill the air.

"*Interesting* is a non committal statement, and observation of opinion that really does nothing for anyone. Of course my relationship with my mother could be interesting, but you have no way of knowing that yet. You used the word because it sounds thoughtful and intelligent and insightful to a layman. Most people would have asked me to elaborate, or questioned my choice of an answer all together. Of course it's interesting."

Now he looked offended, annoyed, and wary. The eyes darted once around the room before locking onto mine, his posture straightened a little, a slick shine was showing just at the edge of his well maintained hairline, I was making him nervous.

"I think we may be off on the wrong foot, Mister Winter."

I nodded like I never agreed with anything more in my life.

"I'm not here to make you comfortable, doctor, but for the sake of discussion, and to help me decide if this is a complete waste of my time, let's see if we can find a good starting point."

I let him have the air, seeing what he would do with it. He leaned in, interested. I doubted he had ever had a session start off like this.

"How do you purpose we do that?"

"Do you consider yourself a smart man?"

The questioning look again, trying to see where I was going with it. I didn't get an answer, so I helped him through it.

"I would guess you're pretty intelligent, a PHD isn't easy to come by if you're a dimwitted bastard. It takes a confident and comfortable grasp of learned knowledge that can be demonstrated and quantified. Of course, common sense isn't necessarily an ingredient, and life experiences aren't required; just a strong ability to retain knowledge and understand concepts. But its academic, more theory than application right?"

"I suppose one could put it that way..."

There was a tremble at the back of his voice, announcing unfamiliar territory. I kept him off balance, not on purpose, not caring either way.

"Armed with an intelligence like that, with a proven ability to learn, a person such as yourself could feel confident typing people. Identifying their issues in an academic way. Cataloging their emotions, responses, gestures, comparing them to memorized mental states, disorders, whatever...You are coming from a professional view point where your intelligence is sought out by others to help them reassemble their lives or find closure. Which is exactly why I'm here I guess, but in order to do that we need to see eye to eye on something."

I left the bait, he took it.

"What's that?"

I leaned forward, letting my knuckles tap gently on the table between us. He hid his startle well, he was so focused on me that the sound much have been as loud as a gunshot in his ears.

"That, while your intelligence helps you professionally to help others, you have the advantage of being objective, which more often than not gives a person a *strong* advantage. Being objective while someone else is emotional can make a guy feel more powerful than he really is. The problem with that state of mind is that it won't help you when dealing with people like me, so when you ask assumptive questions about my relationship with my mother, I see chinks in your armor that I could exploit if the situation was different. I'm a pretty smart guy myself, and I am absolutely sure of this because I can sit here and have a conversation with you that's bordering on semantics...as opposed to being dead."

I let the words sink in, watching him for any sign he thought I was crazy. I would think I was crazy, he apparently did too.

"Context is everything, isn't it? Let me clarify. I'm still here, others aren't. My intelligence has literally kept me alive, while yours has provided you with a well paying job, a three bedroom condo in the Garden, a winter home in California, three high end cars, a trophy wife and two kids doing well in Ivy League schools, but I seriously doubt it has ever prevented someone from stopping your heart." The good doctor jolted slightly with each mention of his personal information. He began to perspire, a light sheen on the forehead under his fifty dollar haircut.
"Don't get me wrong, doctor. I have just done my research. I pass your office nearly every day, have for the past six months. I just wanted to know who I was dealing with before I decided to stop by for a chat. I have no idea if you can even help me, but right now my only escape from depression is physical exercise and that is temporary."
Doctor Breaux relaxed some. His body language read as weary of me but he resisted the urge to flee if only out of curiosity. He removed his glasses. I saw the rim of a contact in his eye when the light caught it. He probably wore the glasses for a bit of theatric gesture.
"Mister Winter, you make me a little uncomfortable. I would prefer if you came out with whatever it is you want me to help you with, otherwise I would rather put an end to our session and not schedule another."

That seemed fair.

"A woman I loved died, she was killed and I feel as if it's my fault. I know it's my fault despite the fact that I didn't have a direct hand in it and didn't directly cause it. I just set forth the motions that lead to her death."

Breaux held his first comment before it left his lips. He contemplated, finally speaking.

"I am tempted to ask a number of questions; the first would obviously be about the circumstances of her death. I don't feel like I should though. I feel like asking such a question would either force you to lie, or force me into a position where I would have knowledge of some criminal activity. I am in a business where people tell me their secrets, and those secrets stay with me so long as they are *legal* secrets. I feel like we can continue, however I think it would be best to avoid specifics. Specifics I don't need to help you, Mister Winter."

I could live with that, I had no intention of giving him specifics anyway. A nod from me and the Doctor continued.

"Responsibility requires conscious thought. We are programmed to accept responsibility because it's the very nature of social interaction. Those that shirk responsibility are doomed to being placed beneath their peers either overtly or subconsciously. We are raised, at least some of us, to take responsibility for our actions. For you, your feelings lie in those actions. We may not take a life, but can be complicit in it being taken all the same. To share responsibility in this regard, you need negligence, malice or indifference to act. Inability to act or unintentional consequences of your actions remove you from responsibility as far as psychology is concerned."

He was making more sense than I expected him to. I allowed myself to relax, leaning back in the ornately plush chair. I considered his words before I spoke.

"I know, at least intellectually, that her death was not my fault. But I feel guilt, I feel responsible. I feel as if I should have predicted it and stopped it, or kept her from harm's way."

Doctor Breaux put his glasses on the table on top of his note pad. He leaned in, speaking softly.

"I will make a few assumptions for the sake of this thought. Is the manner in which she died a violent one? If she was killed at the hands of someone else the answer is probably *yes*. Was she competent in the skills of protecting herself? I have a feeling that the answer to that is also *yes*. Were you negligent in a way that directly attributed to her death? I will assume that the answer to that question would be a matter of perspective."

"I made a mistake-"

He interrupted me with a raised hand. I let him speak.

"That's the crux of it. Your guilt is written on your face, a guilt I have seen in the faces of countless patients that come through that door. New Orleans after Katrina saw many seek my help, and me just beginning my practice at the time. I have counseled, and continue to help rescue workers, police officers, every day citizens and even a few politicians with Survivor's Guilt all these years later. You blame yourself for not being able to prevent her death and you blame yourself for surviving when she did not. Time and acceptance are the only cure, Mister Winter. I don't think, given the nature of her death and my reluctance to know specific details that I could be of much help to you. Your peace of mind will come from gaining closure."

I didn't know what to say. I just sat there, hoping he would fill the silence, unintentionally playing with the St. Jude necklace around my neck. It had once belonged to Katie Pepmode. It was one of the few things of hers I had left.

Pepper, as Katie was called by all who knew her and I shared a unique relationship. I realized I loved her far too late. Before either of us were able to explore that love, she was killed and her death was my fault. Not just Pepper, but two other good friends died because I failed to prevent those who wished us harm from finding us. I had led them right to us.

Doctor Breaux realized I had nothing to say, so he spoke. "Violent death is often the hardest to accept, especially when that violence is not accidental. Even hardened soldiers throughout history have known the depression and helplessness that comes from not understanding why you lived and others died. Some might even say it's an emotional self-destruct we all have built into us; without our loved ones, what purpose do we serve? I can tell you that closure is illusive and that there are no easy or certain fixes. The more someone meant to you, the harder it will be to move on."

"I don't want to move on."

Breaux frowned.

"Of course you don't. You are perfectly capable of spending the rest of your life reliving the moments you were with her. Feeling as if she's just around the corner, feeling like letting her go will diminish what you felt for her when she was alive. The truth is, moving on is harder than living with the depression. The human mind is at its worst when it can simply adapt to the most deplorable circumstances imaginable, and much worse than that. We are literally capable of getting used to anything and living with it. But it's not healthy. You have to find a way to move on, not just *deal*, Mister Winter."

I sighed. He made good points, as much as I didn't want to admit it.

"So how do I do it?"

I needed an answer like a magic snake oil even though I knew there was no such thing.

"You don't. There is no conscious thought that can get you past this. You simply have to keep living, every day trying to accept that what is done is done and culpable or not, the death of your loved was not your fault through any intentional way. You may never truly let it go, many don't. But you can get to a point, with time, where the beast on your back isn't there every day."

Sometimes hearing someone else say what you already know to be true can be cathartic. Doctor Breaux was not at all what I saw him as when I walked in the room. He was not the self-important, shallow prick I expected. Instead, he was an insightful man with more experience in dealing with the type of trauma I had than I had expected.

"So what exactly are you telling me, Doc?"

Breaux sighed. It was not a sigh of annoyance; maybe he simply didn't know how to elaborate.

"I'm not sure I can tell you anything you do not already know yourself. I think the most important thing you can do to help reach closure is to avoid situations that are emotionally stressful. Healing takes time, Mister Winter."

I didn't think I could do that, but I was willing to try.

"I can try."

Doctor Breaux smirked; his expression told me my answer troubled him. He smiled like that when he was uncomfortable. I could tell he wanted specifics but was either afraid or unwilling to ask. The silence between us approached uncomfortable. It was time to go. I stood a little too fast, my chest strained at a not so fresh wound.

"Are you okay, Mister Winter?"

Breaux asked, rising to help me if I needed it. I waved him off.

"I'm fine, Doc. Still healing."

I said too much, even if he would have been able to figure that out all on his own. Breaux avoided asking the obvious question. If he had, I probably would have told him that six months ago I had been shot in the chest. The bullet had gone through the costal cartilage connecting my 9th and 10th rib to the sternum, missed my pancreas and spleen, drilled through the bottom of my left lung and shattered the seventh rib before it exited my back. My wound was *fixed* by a surgeon who no longer had a license to practice, in a room that served as an operating room and a place to keep his car. All in all, he did good work, given what he was able to do. I was still healing. Sudden movements tended to strain the muscle around the wound, threatening to tear the entry and exit wound open.

Breaux gave me a stiff nod.
"You are a curious one, Mister Winter. I have many questions I would like to ask, but none I am comfortable with. If you wish to continue sessions with me, please tell Susan on your way out. I would be happy to do so, of course."
I shook the Doctor's hand.
"Thanks, Doc, but I don't think that will be necessary."
Breaux held my grasp.
"All the same, Mister Winter, I think it would do you some good."
Maybe it would.
"I'll think about it."
He smiled, genuine. A hand on my shoulder.
"All I can ask. Have a good day, Mister Winter."

2

I let myself out of Doctor Breaux's office, walking down the stairs to the street. As soon as I hit the sidewalk, the sweet summer smells of New Orleans surrounded me. I smelled the wet musk of the tree bark, a fresh rain still evaporating. I could smell beef cooking, drifting up the street from a po' boy shop not far away; I could also smell flowers, but I had no idea what they were. It was a spicy smell, strong and pleasant. Down south just before the river, summer smelled pleasant, a distinct dichotomy from the smell of the French Quarter in the summer which was often pungent with alcohol and cooking grease. I would take the scent south of St. Charles any day.

The Doctor's office was on Amelia Street, a block-ish south of Touro Infirmary, Kindred Hospital and Community Care Hospital, in a mixed use neighborhood that held many homes that were converted to private practice offices. The neighborhood was well kept; postage size lots holding single and two story homes and offices painted in the earth tones popular in the middle class neighborhoods south of St. Charles. Fences weren't as popular here as they were further east in Garden District proper. The neighborhood had a more friendly feeling.

The Street was lined in Southern Red Oak, casting long hands over the sidewalk, shading halfway to the center of the slim lane where they met with the trees from the other side. It was hot, just after ten in the morning and already pushing ninety degrees. I walked north, mindful of everything that was around me. Every car, every person, anything that looked out of place, this was my life. I mutli-tasked, enjoying the sun, the smells and the generous shade as I used reflective surfaces and innocent glances to check alleys between houses, side streets and occasionally behind me. It was five blocks to St. Charles, I made good time.

When I hit St. Charles I went west a few blocks, pretending to admire the rich real estate tucked away behind ancient oak trees and walled or fenced property lines. I crossed to the north side of the street, pausing to let the trolley pass before making it to the north sidewalk. From there I cut up and over a few blocks, coming to the intersection of Barrone and Peniston where I had parked my car. Before I came to New Orleans, I drove a muscle car that was all horse power. It was loud, fast and it stood out. Nothing Like the Honda Accord that sat in front of me now. It was used, two years old, forest green and about as plain as they came. Perfect for blending in, the kind of car I should have been driving all along.

I popped the locks and climbed in. With the AC on full blast, I pulled off the curb, busted a U turn and headed east. I had to be to work by noon, so I drove straight home. I lived in Bayou St. John, just off Orleans Avenue in a *shotgun* house, a style of home that was traditional and common in many neighborhoods within New Orleans. It wasn't much, just like I wanted. A blue plank paneled house that was 12 feet wide and four times as long with a simple veranda porch on the front and back. The trim was white and freshly painted, simple, single pane windows lines the sides, facing out either direction on nearly identical shotgun houses. Most of the neighborhood was the same house with different colors and a different address. Yards were the two feet of grass between the sidewalk and the stairs, maybe a few more feet in the back before you hit a fence. The shotgun house was common in New Orleans, favored because the rooms did not feed off of hallways. Rooms simply opened up into rooms, allowing good circulation and a favorable breeze if you opened the front and back doors. At the end of the Civil war, the shotgun house was the most popular style of house in the south.

More survived and thrived in the Big Easy than in any other city.

Anonymous.

I liked anonymous.

I parked on the street, sitting in the car, reading the neighborhood. My neighbor to the right was an artist. She wouldn't be up for hours. My neighbor to the left was a nurse, he left for work before the sun hit the sky. I looked for cars or people out of place, I didn't see anything that jumped out at me, so I opened the door and stepped out, my hand brushing the 1911 in an inside the waistband holster on my left side. It was cocked, safety on. A nonchalant walk around my car to get a full view of my surroundings…It looked clear. I moved up the stairs, one hand on my gun, the other held my keys. There were two tell tales in place on my door. A piece of hair stuck with saliva above eye level, a small piece of folded matchbook tucked between the latch bolt and dead bolt in the seam of the door. They were still in place. I keyed them open, then pushed the door open and followed it in. The 1911 came out of its own accord, going where my eyes went. Thirty seconds later I had searched the house. It was the same every time I came in. I checked the tell tales on all the windows and back door. Satisfied that I didn't have any unwanted visitors, I got ready for work.

My house was spartan. A bed, a dresser, a small table with two chairs, a growing stack of read books that lined the wall near the front door, and a huddle of kettle bells and other exercise equipment on the floor. A small TV I hardly used. All the furniture was in the bedroom, the largest 'room.' Every other room was bare. I spent my free time training, healing, and gathering knowledge. I had taken numerous firearms classes from professional trainers within driving distance and read every book of interest in the closest libraries, so I was forced to buy them after that. I had no need for anything that did not involve these things. Likewise, my personal belongings were few. I prepared a small Camelbak backpack for my trip to work, inside was a pair of work boots, socks, coveralls and work gloves. I filled the water bladder, dressed out in running shorts, a tank top and a pair of running shoes, then tugged the back pack tight on my shoulders. Before leaving, I slipped my 1911 into a waist pack along with my wallet and cell phone, snapping it around my waist before I left the house. I locked the door, replaced my tell tales then hopped down to the sidewalk, stretching before I began my four mile run to work.

I never really cared for running. It always struck me as primitive growing up, an inefficient way to get from one point to another at a rapid pace. I still felt that way, though running was therapy to me. Exercise was therapy. I stretched deep, palms flat on the warm cement, legs straight. I let the burn in my calves build up, walking my hands backwards slightly between my legs before letting off gradually. Movement next door caught my attention, Cynthia, or *Cyn* as she signed her oil paintings, was awake and watching me through her living room window. I stood straight up, stretching back, bending until my back was in full arch and my hands touched the cement behind me. Cynthia gave a little wave, her other hand at her mouth, biting the tip of her finger. I held the stretch before waving back. She smiled, content to stare.

Cynthia was in her early twenties. An LSU grad, she bucked the traditional route her degree offered her and opted instead to become a painter. Her paintings were landscapes and human form in rich oil, capturing New Orleans as if taken with a camera, though often they were of moments in time when cameras had yet to be invented. Her skill amazed me, the colors were vibrant and precise, setting a mood to tell a story, the plots of her painting were intricate, freezing moments like the first Mardi Gras, Pirate ships docking off the Mississippi, Voodoo ceremonies in the slaves quarters on a plantation and a recent painting of the Joan of Arc having coffee at the Café Du Monde during Hurricane Katrina. Cynthia worked nights as a bartender on Bourbon Street to pay the bills until her painting career took off. To my knowledge, she had only sold five paintings since beginning her painting career; I bought four of them anonymously. Her work captivated me.

I slowly lowered myself into the splits, politely ignoring Cynthia's admiration while I worked my legs forward and laid my chest to my knees. My abdomen burned, my ribs protested. I ignored the pain, it was the only way to convince it to leave my body. I needed it gone.

Satisfied, I came to my feet, got a mouthful of water, started the timer on my watch and started off, keeping to the edge of the narrow street. I had four different routes I could run to work, today I was taking the short one.

I cut through the neighborhood until I hit Esplanade Avenue, maintaining a strict seven minute mile pace. My lungs protested, but I pressed on, forcing them to work as I wanted them to. The first half a mile always reminded me I was six months past nearly dying. By the first mile, the fog of depression would begin to lift. Endorphins would hit my blood stream and burn off the mist in my mind, make thinking clearer, more objective.

Objectivity was crucial.

Six months ago, I had left Katie Pepmode's funeral and ended up in New Orleans without really meaning to. As far as humans are concerned, six months isn't a long time. Objectively, it certainly wasn't. As far as my heart was concerned, six months was but a day. I missed Pepper every waking moment. I could still feel her, smell her, hear her giggle. She was the first real intimate connection I ever had outside of Stewart Garitty's *School* where I grew up. She was the first woman that I was myself with, as opposed to being forced to lie about who I really was and what I really did. Her love was my rebirth, and I shuttered at the thought at living life without her.

And yet I did.

Mile two approached. I increased my pace, moving up to six minutes thirty seconds. The longing for Pepper held on, even though thinking at this speed became labored. I concentrated instead on my surroundings, watching reflections, people, traffic, predicting the movements of pedestrians in my path, listening in on snippets of conversations as they touched my ears. Somewhere, those that wished me dead were still out there, I was dedicated to being ready for them when they came. I ran twice a day, five times a week, two hours a day with weights, agility exercises and mental preparation that would leave me in a heightened state of awareness, ready for the day that they found me.

When I heard that Martin Heller escaped custody, I expected him to personally track me down. He worked for

Virtua, and Virtua wanted me deceased. Virtua, after a fashion, created me. Stewart Garitty raised me, trained me, and sent me into the world to do their collective dirty work. I found my conscience, and since that day I was a target. Being a target got Pepper killed. Being a target caused the death of friends. I wouldn't let that happen again.

Mile three, North Robertson Street, I sped up to a six minute mile. My legs ached; my lungs burned and sent their protest up my throat in the form of bile that seared my throat. I continued, less able to concentrate on traffic, people and conversations. My left hand instinctively hovered near my waist pack. A nylon pull tab yanked straight down would tear open the pack and give me instant access to my 1911. The faster I ran, the more primal my defensive posture. A six minute pace always put me at a heightened state of readiness, an attack always felt imminent. It never came. Eventually it would.

Mile four came on without me noticing. I ran at least a quarter mile past my landmark before I realized it. I slowed my pace. Seven minute mile. Eight minute mile. I broke to a quick walk before finally coming to a gentle stroll across Poland Avenue. I was a few blocks from work. Sweat flowed freely off my tanned skin, the humidity pressed against my labored breathing. I touched my watch, letting it take my heart rate while I sucked down water. 150 beats a minute. Not bad. My vision opened up, my senses taking in more of what was going on around me. I was close to water again, approaching what was once a thriving center of shipping and industry perched on the banks of the Industrial Canal that cut the line between the lower and upper 9th Ward and New Orleans Proper. The Industrial canal connected the Mississippi river to Lake Pontchartrain. Enlarged several times over since its construction in the early 1900's, the last of the enlargements took place in the 1960's in expectation of a heavy increase in traffic that would come and go via the industrial canal to the intracoastal waterway. The project intended to move all major shipping from the port wharfs along the river to the Industrial Canal, but like many grand dreams, it failed. When it failed, the property value went through the floor and many industrial size warehouses built in expectation of business were either abandoned or sold on the cheap. Most of them would never see renovation, some of them didn't survive into the new century, more didn't survive Katrina. The neighborhood backing up to the Industrial on the west side struggled to stay above the poverty line, it was an uphill battle.

I worked at a former dry storage warehouse where North Villere Street hit the canal. It was more rust than metal, the center of the pitched roof caved in, the fence more down than up. I could smell the metal and rust in the air before I rounded the corner to see it. The weed covered lot was alive with activity, small bob cat tractors ran mazes of discarded scrap metal from flat bed trucks, piling the confused balls of bent and torn metal into a growing mound of multicolored hazards that would soon surpass all surrounding buildings in elevation.

I walked off the street, stopping just inside where the gate used to be, stretching out the run. A few of the dusty men lounging around the camp trailer that served as the yard office watched me from the disappearing shade. I knew none of them, not by name, didn't care to. Faces around the lot changed constantly and I was not there to make friends anyway. I was there to work, not because I needed the job, just because I had never actually had one. I finished stretching and walked to the trailer, taking my work clothes out of my backpack. I would sweat all day, a shower would be a waste of time. I changed my shoes for boots, left the waist pack on and then pulled on my coveralls. I left my bag on the table next to lunch pails and paper bags full of fast food lunch.

"Oi, you bracque runnin' in dis heat fo' shor."

I turned to face Manny Orry. He was the only man on the lot with a baritone voice that fired out English/Cajun at a rapid pace like he was always in a hurry to get the words out of his mouth. Manny owned the lot and the scrap metal *business* that occupied it. He was a Houma, Louisiana native, coming from a long line of Orry men that stretched back to Lezine Orry who was the first of the line to set foot on Louisiana soil in 1765. Lezine Orry led a storied life that included captaining a pirate ship under the Jean Lafitte armada, sailing around the Gulf of Mexico attacking Spanish ships. Lezine later threw in with Lafitte in his battle against the British during the battle of New Orleans.

The story of Lezine Orry was well known to anyone who came within ear shot of Manny. He loved his family's history. Every single one of them a pirate in their own fashion, and Manny was no different. Manny ran a scrap business that trucked in tons of dilapidated metal a day, all salvaged from hurricane wreckage still not cleaned up all these years later, or debris dredged from the river. Manny, in turn, sold the very same metal either back to where it came from in a recycled form, or to local ship builders. He owned the tractors and the trucks, but they were crewed by men that worked for the New Orleans Department of Public Works. Manny's cousin, Louis, was more or less in charge of all public works in the city and allowed his people to double dip while working for Manny so long as he received a kick back. With no subtle audacity, sometimes the trucks that hauled scrap and the tractors that moved it belonged to the city whenever Manny's substandard equipment broke down. Manny received the best scrap available with a cousin in the Department of Property management, and a brother that captained a river dredge for the Army Corps of Engineers. The Orry family business ran in wide and confusing circles.

"Afternoon, Manny."
Manny gripped me in a hug. I could smell Tabasco sauce and cheap cigarettes on his dingy coveralls.
"An aftanoon to you, pardna. We got work today, dit mon la verite!"
Manny pointed a grubby glove towards a row of trucks idling on the north side of the lot.
"I'm showt a tracta so we emptin them cassie's slow, bu' you can werk the hand pile by ma' patrack."
I looked over to the large mound of scrap made of man sized pieces next to Manny's truck. I knew the drill, I would take a magnet with me and separate the ferrous from non-ferrous metal. It wasn't a bad assignment to have. It sure beat appliance detail, which entailed digging any and all appliances out of any load that came in, running them to an extension cord and plugging them in to see if they worked. If they did work, they went on a load down to Houma to be sold in Manny's sister's junk shop.
"I'm good with that."
Manny slapped me on the back with one hand, wiped the crumbs from breakfast out of his moustache with the other.
"I knew ya would be, you see me fo' leaven, no?"
I gave Manny a nod. He responded with his usual large and friendly grin before moving his rotund frame off towards some of the day laborers that were hiding out near the warehouse awning. Manny was a crooked businessman to be sure, but a hard worker who expected the same out of anyone who worked for him. He wasn't a con man, or even a crook, he just had a view of commerce that wasn't shared or celebrated in any other city. New Orleans was honest about its corruption, and without that corruption, the city probably wouldn't run very well.

I found a large, ruler sized magnet hanging off the trailer and set off to work. The job was about as simple as they came. I held the magnet to a piece of metal on the outside of the pile. If it was ferrous, the magnet would stick. That piece went into one bin, if it was non ferrous, the magnet wouldn't stick and that meant it went in another bin. Manny liked to give this job to the men who actually worked. It paid the same as every other position except for tractor and truck drivers, but was much easier. I had been working for Manny for almost four months, and working this position for about three of them. Five days a week I separated chunks of metal into two bins, some of them were thin and small, weighing in at only a few pounds, some were large and jagged and weighed more than me. It was exercise, I liked that. It also let me blend in, I liked that more. I could work a twelve hour day, or show up for only four and Manny would be just as happy to have me toiling away at a pile of twisted steel and aluminum that never seemed to get any smaller. It was real, honest work that paid a good wage, all under the table with no questions asked.

The humidity was high and abusive as the day wore on. I lost water as quick as I took it in, fighting my way through sharp, cumbersome pieces of metal one at a time. As I labored away, the activity in the lot hit its peak. Trucks sped in and out, dodging other trucks, tractors, and workers as they moved about. Curses were thrown about in English, Spanish, Cajun and sometimes a bit of all three. Manny was everywhere at once, often with a sandwich in one hand, directing the dysfunctional symphony that was his business. Occasionally I stopped and watched; only interested in what was going on outside the lot. The surrounding neighborhood was similar warehouses and a few streets of shotgun houses. Some occupied, some not.

Street traffic was intermittent and usually consisted of commercial vehicles or cars, trucks and vans that belonged in the neighborhood. What stood out was a dark blue Chevy Tahoe, an aggressive bumper and brush guard on the front. The SUV sat low on police suspension. It looked familiar.

I was pretty sure I had ridden in it or one like it not too long ago.

I stared at it, parked alongside the curb of one of many streets that ended at the canal lots. The windows were tinted dark; I could see a set of hands on the steering wheel and little else through the windshield. The Tahoe's roof displayed a number of different antennas and the front bumper carried no plates.

Government.

Maybe.

I zipped my coveralls down, my left hand hovering close to the waist pack holding my 1911. I stared at the Tahoe. Someone inside was staring right back at me. The list of people who knew I was in New Orleans was pretty short. It had one name on it, Madeline O'Neal. I took my gloves off, walking across the lot towards the office trailer. I watched the SUV while I pulled off my coveralls, changing my boots out for my running shoes. I stuffed everything into my backpack. Manny came out of the office, the trailer nearly tipping over when he came down the stairs; he considered me through squinted eyes.
"You leavin'? I got ya' piastres if you gimme a min, weh? Manny climbed back inside the office, he was inside for a few seconds, I heard the clatter of dishware and a few swear words, then Manny squeezed back out, a grease

stained stack of bills in his hand. I took my two week pay from Manny with a customary handshake.

"Ah see you on Monday, af you workin, or not, bon ami." Manny slapped me on the back as went back in his office. I tucked my pay into my backpack, turning my attention back to the Tahoe without looking directly at it. The SUV sat still, nothing had changed.

A duel axle flatbed had just dumped a load of cut I beams and was headed back out to the road. I hopped up on the passenger side running board as it passed by me, riding the side of the truck out onto the road out of view of the Tahoe. The driver, oblivious to me hanging off the side, picked up Manuel Street so he could double back across the Claiborne Avenue Bridge to pick up another load. I jumped off the truck as it crossed Kentucky, letting it pass by before I started south. When I made it to the corner, I could see that the Tahoe was still sitting in the same spot, watching the yard. I crouched down behind a discarded refrigerator that was making a long term home out of the sidewalk. I had to admit to myself that I could have just been paranoid. The Tahoe was definitely a LE vehicle, maybe even NOLA's finest out on a stakeout. It probably had nothing to do with me.

I believed that about as much as I believed white people can dance to anything but techno.

I could see nothing through the rear of the Tahoe's tinted glass. The body carried a lot of road grime, lots of travel and few washes. Not very uncommon in New Orleans, the summer humidity, pollen and dusty streets made keeping a vehicle clean an exercise in futility. The grime had a red tinge to it. Red clay. Not common to New Orleans. There wasn't a plate on the rear of the Tahoe either. That was a little strange. Even undercover government vehicles used sterile plates. The lack of a plate drew attention. I was curious about that, thinking it might be a good idea to go and ask the driver. I was about to do just that when my cell phone vibrated in my waist pack. I ducked back down behind the refrigerator, digging the phone out. The screen told me it was a blocked number, I answered it anyway.

"Hell, Rushing, will you stop pratting about and come have a chat?"

For some reason my mouth went a little dry, my heart rate jumped up a few beats.

Madeline O'Neil.

3

I hung up the phone. I hadn't seen Maddy since Pepper's funeral in Montana. I had spoken to her a few times. The conversations had been uncomfortable, filled with long periods of silence. After the obligatory *how are yous?* there was not much said worth mention. There were things left unsaid, I just didn't know what they were. We had not spoken for a while since the last call. I was in New Orleans, blending in, healing, and waiting. Maddy was out doing what Madeline did best; hunt. She was working with Colonel Wayne Solomon, that much I knew. Any other details I would have to get straight from her.

I tapped on the passenger door glass. I heard the *thump* of the electric locks. I climbed into the passenger seat and shut the door. Madeline was behind the wheel, Oakley sunglasses hiding her eyes, her fire red hair tied back into a pony tail behind her head, her usually pale skin held a deep tan, the light freckles normally visible around her nose were invisible under the bronze. She was as beautiful as ever.

Pensive as ever.

It was just me and her.

Maddy faced me in her seat, pulling off her sunglasses to reveal her green eyes. She looked concerned.
"Working the docks these days?"
I shrugged. Not really interested in giving her an update on my life.
"How did you find me?"
Madeline folded her glasses up, putting them on the dash.

"A bit of dumb luck. I just came into the city, stopped off for gas. You ran right by me at a light. I followed you here. I was just about to call you when you hoofed by."
"And what? Just watched for the past few hours?"
Madeline showed me her palms.
"Give over, Rushing, I waited because I needed to know you were better. You seem healed up."
I thought about the implications of the question...healed body, or mind?
"I am, more or less. Hurts in the morning, hurts when I bend the wrong way."
Maddy reached out, touching the right side of my neck where the shot after the one that had pierced my lung had carved a deep and long gash. It had healed too, leaving a shallow scar that was a few shades lighter than the rest of me. Her touch was cold, it felt good against my sun heated skin.
"You look well."
I pulled her hand off my neck. She grasped my hand for a second before letting it go.
"Thanks, Maddy. Why are you here?"
She frowned. It came out like an accusation, I didn't exactly mean it that way. Madeline softened when she figured that out.
"Hunting a shipping container, actually. We had a line on Martin Heller, a meeting not far from the middle of bloody nowhere in Sudan. Heller was financing an aspiring terrorist. Before we had a clear shot at Heller, someone else effed in and made an awful mess of things. We managed to scribble the terrorist, but Heller got away. We found documents on the ground, one of them pointed to a container being shipped out of Africa. It was bound for New York, we dropped a tip to Homeland Security, they boarded the ship, container was gone. It was off loaded in Algiers, Three ships were in port. Bloody likely it was loaded onto one of them.

Those three ships made port in various parts of Europe, turning three into eight, and then eight into fifteen. Have no idea what's in the container, just that there is some sort of terrorist cell on the receiving end of it that is probably eager to have it."

Bile rose on my throat. I hated the name Martin Heller. Him being involved in supporting terrorists meant that whatever they were planning, it was in the interests of Virtua Corporation. The interests of Virtua Corporation seemed to be directly aligned with the interests of the sitting President, who just happened to be sworn into office after the last President was assassinated in grand style by a man named Robert Wigglin, who was working for the Corporation. Of course there was no proof of this.

"You don't know what's in it?"

Madeline raised her eyebrows.

"We haven't the foggiest. Been running leads to ground while following the bloody ships all over the world. The shell game was set up months in advance to take the container completely off the grid, overwhelm any search. Would have worked out nicely considering the official paper trail ends in New York with a container that never made it there. Now all we have to go off is a list of ships that can be tied back to the first ship. Only three of those ships have the US as their final destination. One ship is headed for Los Angeles, one for Houston. The last ship is due into New Orleans. All arrive in the morning. It could be on board any of the three, or none. We sent men to each port, but we are stretched thin, still pulling in assets from the ports were those other ships went. It's just me for New Orleans."

I really couldn't care less about a shipping container goose chase. I did care about Martin Heller though. We had unfinished business. The bile burned low in my throat, filling my mouth with an uncomfortable heat.

"Heller?"

Maddy shook her head.

"Absolutely nothing. He killed four Marshals in order to escape, that makes him a pretty popular topic with all the federal yanks. I seriously doubt he could find a way back into the US if he wanted to."

I couldn't argue with that. All entry points into the US were staffed with federal law enforcement. If Heller attempted to re-enter the US and was recognized, he would go straight to a holding cell. Of course there were ways around that. The US's porous border with Mexico was certainly one of them. A slim chance of Heller being involved made me lose interest. But Maddy had come to me; I didn't see any reason to not hear her out.

"So what's your plan?"

"If we can put a set on the container, we will follow it to the cell. The terrorist, a Sudanese militia commander named Al Taybi, had people in place somewhere in the US. We don't know how far Heller's relationship went with Al Taybi besides logistical support, but I reckon he at least knew of Al Taybi's people. Killing Al Taybi may have stopped nothing."

The accepted model of a terrorist cell, based on countless terrorist cells that had been stopped or investigated after they had committed an act of terrorism, said that the cells are usually small, consisting of perhaps a half dozen or more men on the ground. Small teams within the cell were responsible for different aspects of the plan such as initial surveillance, equipment, logistics or execution. The smaller teams had no knowledge of each other and were often redundant to other teams conducting the same task. Sometimes the leader of the cell had no direct involvement in the operation, they served as a conduit for information and made targeting decisions. If a plan was in place when Al Taybi was killed, then it was very possible that plan was being carried out without him. I was left wondering why

Madeline was talking to me about this. I wasn't an anti-terrorism expert, or a member of Colonel Solomon's unit. My only interest was against the Corporation and as it stood, the Corporation didn't seem very involved.

"What do you need me for?"
Maddy considered her words before she spoke.
"We want your help, Rushing. Colonel Solomon had an agreement with the last President. She's about as dead as one can be, the current chap in the White House doesn't even know we are out here. Solomon leaks intel to people he can trust, which is a quickly shrinking list. President Allister didn't waste any time shaking things up when he was sworn in. He replaced the head of the NSA, FBI and Homeland Security among others. His appointees replaced a number of senior officials below them, all loyal to the Allister White House. With these people in place, our internal support structure is small. Our ability to bring in new shooters is hindered by that fact. We need about thirty more bodies for this operation alone, we have no way of getting them."
So this was a recruiting visit. Madeleine had a way of making me feel used and appreciated at the same time.
"Is this you asking, or the Colonel?"
Madeline seemed offended, though I had no idea why she would be.
"Are you asking because my answer will help you in your decision, or because you are just curious?"
"I'm just asking."
I wasn't just asking, I wanted to know where Maddy was in all of this.
"It was my idea."

I heard honesty in her words. I never doubted she would tell me the truth. Me and Madeline had an interesting relationship. Each of us had nearly killed the other not too long ago, before I had my change of heart. Even then we were honest with each other. I looked through the windshield while I thought about the implications. I could see Manny moving around the yard, directing his laborers, dodging traffic, all the while eating a po' boy. I had the feeling I had just worked my last day for Manny. I was about as healed as I was going to get. Physically I was in the best shape of my life and I was tired of waiting for the Corporation to come find me. Madeline's offer would let me take the fight back to them.

"You hungry?"

Maddy cocked her head.

"I could eat."

I belted in.

"Off we go, then."

Madeline considered me for a second before she put her sunglasses back on and fired up the Tahoe.

"Where to, Rushing?"

"How do you feel about Creole food?"

Maddy turned the block., her eyes wide, wheels turning.

"Howsit? I don't even know what that is."

"Great, Creole it is then, I'd like a shower first though, if you don't mind."

I gave Madeline directions to my house. On the drive, she filled me in on specific details regarding Al Taybi and their search for the container. I was especially interested in the unknown third party that attacked Al Taybi and Heller while they were in a protected compound that was being watched by Solomon's unit. Maddy only knew what she saw, and that was someone, perhaps a small group, had infiltrated the meeting and eliminated a number of security personnel without taking any losses. That same someone, or *someones* escaped before Solomon's people made entry. Heller, maybe Al Taybi, had other enemies. Those same enemies were likely to follow the same clues Colonel

Solomon was. Madeline told me what she knew of the unknowns, which wasn't much. The only real clues were the evidence that they had been there in the fact of multiple bodies, shell casings, and a single firearm left behind. The casings were fired by a Fabrique Nationale Fusil Automatique Léger, or FN FAL. The FAL was almost as prolific on the African continent as the AK-47. The firearm found was a Browning High Power, almost as popular in Africa as the FAL, the photo Maddy had showed a tarnished and used pistol that had a straight, drop point blade welded beneath the frame. One hell of a close quarters weapon. I had seen bayonets on rifles, never on a pistol that anyone had a serious intention of using, mostly just foolish internet nonsense. A tinge of blood on the blade told me it was used. So, not the crap gear groups on social media.

Pretty serious business.

We made it to my neighborhood. Maddy pulled the Tahoe in behind my Honda. I was out of the Tahoe and half way to the door before she even shut off the engine. Satisfied that no one had been through my door since I left, I drew my weapon and went in. Maddy was right behind me, gun in hand. The house was secure. I didn't bother giving Maddy a tour, she could see the back door from the front and there wasn't much in between. I grabbed a fresh set of clothes and set off for the shower. She busied herself thumbing through my book collection while I showered.

When I came out of the shower, Madeline was admiring one of Cyn's paintings, the only wall decoration I had, mounted above my bed. It was a painting of Jackson Square with the sun rising from the west, morning sunlight touching the sides of buildings, statues and objects it never touched in morning light. If one looked hard enough, they would find the visage of Andrew Jackson hidden amongst the rays of light, looking up at his own statue.

"You don't care much for decorating?"

Madeline said, looking at me as I left the bathroom.

"What's the point? Last time I tried to make a home it didn't go so well."

I regretted the words as soon as they were spoken. My comment hurt her as much as it hurt me. I had to remind myself that I wasn't the only one who lost friends.

"Quite right."

Maddy said, dropping the subject.

"I'm sorry, Maddy. I-"

Madeline put her hand to my lips. Tears strained at the corners of her eyes. She was just as emotional about things as I was.

"Don't, Rushing. I know you didn't mean it, not like that. Let's just go get something to eat, okay?"

A deep breath, a forced smile. I nodded in reply. We left my house, back into the Tahoe, and back out into the city as the summer day ran into the evening.

We drove into the French Quarter, Madeline concentrating hard to navigate the wide bodied American V8 through the narrow streets and tight corners. I guided her onto Rue St. Louis where she managed, against my belief, to parallel the Tahoe between a set of scaffolding and a waiting limousine. Three things were common to take up parking spots in the Quarter; scaffolding, Limos and garbage trucks.

"Where are you taking me, Mister Winter?"

Maddy asked when we hit the sidewalk.

"Antoines, one of the oldest restaurants in the country, been around almost two hundred years."

I said, heading up the street.

"Two hundred years? Well, I hope they keep current on the health laws."

Maddy was skeptical. We took the short walk up St. Louis to the main entrance. Antoines was two floors, occupying much of the building it called home, tucked into the city on a one way street. The second floor boasted a wrought iron balcony common in the city that provided an overhang for the ground floor entrance. As it was summer, many of the street side double doors were open, giving the first floor the breeze from the street. The sun was still high, but it was dinner time and the main dining hall was filling in. We asked for a table for two, and were escorted right in. We ordered drinks, I took the liberty of ordering an appetizer, *Huitres Bienville*, Louisiana oysters baked on the shell with a white wine sauce.

Madeline took in the room while we waited. The main dining room was ivory white with high ceilings and an open floor plan with well spaced round tables for four. White linen table cloths, gas lamp chandeliers, open back wood chairs with plush cushions; it looked every bit as it did in a photograph on the wall taken in the fifties. Antoine's had many dining rooms, including four ornately decorated rooms that were each dedicated to different Krews of Mardi Gras.

When our appetizer came, Maddy brought her attention back to the table, staring at the dish, then me.
"What the bloody hell is it?"
"Baked oysters, I thought that was obvious."
I took one and ate it. With trepidation, she did too. Convinced that she liked it, we polished off the dish in short order while we talked. Maddy seemed to want small talk.
"How do you like New Orleans?"
I wiped my mouth, actually having to think about the question.

"I love it, actually. This city is pretty honest with itself. You have hustlers running scams on the street, and if you call them on it, they are all smiles and friendly. Try that in Detroit, or LA, or even Atlanta, you might get punched in the face. This city takes natural disaster standing up and keeps right on moving. I admire that. Decades of liberal government running it into the ground and they keep on." Maddy poked an oyster shell around the plate with her knife.

"Good on them, I say. Home sounds like a wonderful thing to have. Not quite in our future though."

She had a point.

"I guess not..."

She waved her hands.

"Rushing, we aren't built for standing still. Both of us are better off not trying to pretend we are anything other than what we are."

Point two. The waiter reappeared, ready for our order. Madeline hadn't even glanced at the menu so she trusted me to order for her. I ordered the *Gombo Creole* for myself, and the *Poulet aux Champignons* with *Pommes de Terre Soufflées* on the side, basically chicken and mashed potatoes. New Orleans, if nothing else, was a place of amazing food.

With the waiter gone, I felt it was long past time to ask Maddy a question about her past. A question I should have asked her six months ago. Something I had been thinking about since then.

"How do you know Martin Heller?"

I might as well have slapped her. It would have gotten me the same response. Maddy flashed ten shades of red, bent her knife in half, fought to maintain her composure. I was convinced she had less than no intention of telling me. She stalled, drinking down her iced tea, thinking over the question. To my surprise, she answered me, speaking like I wasn't even in the room.

"I was a squaddie of Martin's. Actually, he was my boss, my first operation with Virtua as a shooter. Martin was pulled out of Iraq to run the lot. We were in Syria, protecting one of Virtua's people who was working a deal to supply the Syrian military with weapons. Virtua was always eager to sell when there was a customer. The conflict was simmering again. Virtua wanted a way to move it along, to provide a more desperate need for their weapons. Martin Heller was that motivation."

Madeline took a moment, collecting herself, trying to keep her emotions under control.

"Martin had intel on a Syrian Special Police unit that was due to move through a small town on a routine patrol. Virtua provided all of us with Syrian Special Operations uniforms. We dressed out and were inserted into the area. I thought we were just going to agitate the conflict by roughing up a few locals. Instead, Martin moved into the town market and started shooting."

The tears fell. Memories prevented them from being held back any longer.

"I tried to stop him. All I managed to do was get a rifle to the stomach and a boot to the mouth. I had to watch, helplessly as he and his men massacred anyone in sight, maybe twenty adults, a few elderly..."

Madeline choked down a sob. I was regretting asking the question. I pushed out dishes out of the way and grasped both of her hands. She refused to stop once she started.

"Martin found a young boy, maybe ten or twelve hiding under a stall. He drug him out, barefoot, held him against the side of the wagon and shot him in the h-head."

Her voice cracked, low so no one near us could hear the story. I knew she was reliving it in her head. I was sorry for causing that. I was also sorry for asking the question in a public place. We had the attention of a few other diners, concerned looks on their faces.

"So that's how I know Martin Heller. He told Virtua I didn't have what he was looking for, and I was sent off to another team. The worst bloody part is that the attack was totally unnecessary. The Raqqa Massacre happened the same day, the media didn't even pick up the attack on the village, the world only cared about Raqqa."

I remember the Raqqa massacre from TV years ago during the opening days of the second Syrian War. The US had struck an airfield in retaliation for the Syrian government using chemical weapons. Syria had doubled down and gassed entire neighborhoods in Raqqa attempting to kill US troops. It didn't work because, despite all US servicemember moaning to the contrary, their chemical gear worked and all the training on it saved thousands of American lives, though the locals weren't as well off. It lead to an overwhelming response from the US that made the Shock and Awe of Iraq War II look like a rifle club shoot.

Maddy leaned back in her seat, breaking my grasp. She dried her eyes on her napkin as our meals arrived. The waiter put the plate down, giving her a concerned look, and me a stern one before he departed. Man, if he only knew. I didn't know what to say, I couldn't think of anything that would make Madeline feel better. She saved me the trouble.

"I actually feel a bit better. I haven't told anyone about that. I was involved in a lot of dirty business when I worked for Virtua, but that was the worst. I should have quit right then. I would have ended up buried in Syria if I did, maybe that would have been better."

How do you respond to that?

Martin Heller was not unique as far as I knew. Mankind produced many monsters, either by mistake or by design. One more in the world usually gathered little notice save for those whose lives were touched, or destroyed by them. In that sense, Heller had much to answer for. Something bugged me about him though, and it was more than what I knew of him personally. Rather, it was what I didn't know that bothered me. Martin, for all intents and purposes, did not exist prior to 1989 when he showed up in Angola working for the Russians. I had searched for any mention of him prior to that and found none. It was like he materialized and went right to work. Anyone, especially a purported westerner like Martin Heller, would need to have a resume to work for Russia when the hammer and sickle still flew over the Kremlin. Getting hired on as an outsider required a resume, which meant training. Training back then was almost exclusive to nation states. No such luck. If Martin Heller was the product of a western, or any government, they had gone to great lengths to hide that fact. Add that to his varied employers over the years; Angola, Liberia, Sierra Leone, Mozambique, Rwanda, Chechnya, Somalia, Afghanistan, Algeria and Congo all before his first known job working for Virtua in Uganda. Far too many conflicting political ideologies for Martin to have been working for anyone other than himself, or a private party, maybe the only person who really knew where Martin came from was Martin himself.

"Maddy, where in the hell did Heller come from?" Madeline found a bit of her appetite, cutting into her chicken. My *Gombo* had cooled enough to let me start eating as well.
"Search me, Rushing. I didn't have much time to chat shit with him when I met him. Sonya knew more about him than anyone and she couldn't trace him any further back

than Angola. He has been using the name 'Martin Heller' for long enough that it is either his real name, or has become it. No idea how old he is, I figure in his late fifties, sixties maybe, at this point, or his nationality, though he sounds enough like a Yank to make no difference."

Madeline pointed to her plate, seeming to signal she agreed with my choice in dinner.
"Why are you so interested, Rushing? Heller is god knows where and not bloody likely to show up anytime soon."
"Because it doesn't make sense, I guess. Heller works for Virtua, right? Well, it looks like they are on their way to getting what they want. Allister is now President. The investigation into the crash of Air Force One is going nowhere, which will probably continue. If Robert was telling the truth, Virtua needs a catalytic event to occur within the next three and a half years to convince both parties that Allister is their only hope for salvation. This Al Taybi nut may have been part of that plan. Since he's dead, that leaves Heller, if only because he logically is the best choice from a knowledge standpoint to step in and run the operation."
Maddy was listening, seeing my side.
"Six months ago, Virtua had prepared a group of unwitting Iranians to take the fall for killing the President on her visit to Atlanta. Al Taybi may have been the same type of straw man. You are assuming that Heller will stay outside the US because he killed four federal agents. I say with Heller's history, it would be unlike him to *not* come back. He is the very definition of an international fugitive, has been for over a decade and he still carries on like it's another day at the office. Besides that, no matter how secure the US borders are, and we both know it's not very, Martin has more than enough experience and sense to get into the US without much effort. The Feds catch terrorists entering the country because of solid intel, human and paper trails,

money transfers…Heller may still be working for the same corporation that has carte blanche to move about as it pleases."

Madeline suddenly seemed more concerned with the thought. Not because she feared Martin, rather because she had not considered it. It surprised me that no one in Colonel Solomon's unit had. If Virtua was willing to create ghost terrorists in the past and it worked, well, if it isn't broke, don't fix it.
"I think I need to run this by the Colonel."
I couldn't have agreed more.
"I think that's a good idea."
The waiter returned. He was less stern on this visit, as Maddy had dried her tears and he could tell whatever caused them, it was not me. A refresh on the drinks and he was off. Madeline changed the subject, asking me what I had been doing since I got to New Orleans. The answer was pretty short; healing, training, trying out working for a living and mourning. When I told her I saw a psychologist that very morning she seemed shocked. Madeline was brought up a hard girl, trained as a young adult by tough men, and went into dangerous situations with the same kind of men as one of their peers. Despite never serving in a traditional military, Madeline Charity O'Neal was a solider through and through. Psychology for soldiers was a fickle beast. Some sought help, some shunned it, and other treated psychologists as they would a prostitute; they may see one, but they aren't going to tell anyone about it.

Madeline didn't press the issue; instead she changed the subject and told me about her last six months, as much as she could in a public place. I began to get a picture of what Solomon was doing. Incidents I had heard about on the news; terrorist camps destroyed, terrorist financers found dead (no less than three Saudi Princes) and of course the bits of news about terrorist plots being foiled by *bad luck.*

We ordered dessert, *Peche Melba,* I was well on my way to taking in more calories in one meal then I had in the past week. Inevitably the conversation turned to Pepper. We shared stories about her, facts that the other did not know about her, and memories that brought out the best in the woman I loved. The night wore on. I offered Madeline a place to stay. She declined, if only because I didn't have a couch to sleep on. Instead, she offered me a ride home.

4

Tony Card hated LA. When he was young enough, he was enamored with the *idea* of Los Angeles, the idea that money could be made simply by pretending to be other people. As far as work went, it seemed to be the most could be gained by the least effort. He had the looks for it; more than one woman in his life had called him handsome. Acting needs all types, Card once thought of himself as the dashing action hero type. He had eyes like blue flames and a nose of a Greek god, at least that's what his ex-wife used to say. Maybe still would. Sergeant Card grew out of it of course; otherwise he would have ended up as a waiter slipping headshots to dining directors. Instead, he joined the Army for lack of a better idea and started doing headshots for a living.

His hatred for LA was born when he first visited on vacation with his first wife. He quickly found that the clamor of residents that spent most their time sitting still in traffic while in a hurry, the smog, and the literal indifference of man towards his fellow man-made Card wish he never bothered wanting to see the Pacific from a little further down the coast. Card was from Portland, Oregon; his first wife was from Wichita. She wanted LA, so they went. After they divorced, Card didn't think he would ever need to go back to LA. No such luck. Card didn't hate much when he thought about it, but he did hate LA. Card was unapologetically American, where LA apologized for America even when no one bothered to ask for it. Card wasn't cool with that.

He and Sergeant Toomby were running in six different time zones when they went wheels down in LA. With no support on the ground in Los Angeles they were forced to rent a car. Since it was LA, they ended up with a hybrid

Toyota that Toomby was convinced would kill them. Every few blocks he would do an *emergency brake check* to ensure the brakes worked. Card didn't bother telling Toomby that the Toyota brake recall was over a few model years back. They made it to their hotel, the Hyatt Regency in Long Beach, without much trouble aside from Toomby nearly shooting a homeless guy who wanted to clean the windows at an off ramp traffic light. When they got to the hotel, they didn't bother unpacking. They went right to sleep, Card did so fully dressed without even bothering to take his sidearm off.

When ten PM rolled around, so did Card. He fought fatigue all the way to the bathroom. Some water on the face did him good. Card stared into the mirror. He wasn't one to worry about his looks, but he could see middle age coming. His chin was still strong, his eyes still bright and recessed in his skull that gave him a perpetual inquisitive look. His skin was tan and smooth, with the lines of a mostly worry free life, based on acknowledging that much was out of his control, fair and only beginning to appear at the corners of his eyes. Card considered his hair. With most of his professional life spent in the military, the business suit cut he wore bothered him. If Card wasn't trying to blend in to some third world country with scruffy hair and a beard, he preferred the traditional high and tight. Since he was working on blending in with the civilian world, the Wall Street look favored him better than the boot camp look. All in all it was cool. Card would be thirty six years old at 11 PM, Pacific. Aside from some aches in the morning he didn't have when he was twenty six, losing a few seconds off his normal twenty one minute three mile run, and less longing looks from college girls, Card didn't have any real complaints. He was still at the top of his game, keeping the sheep safe from the wolves. He would gladly put wolves down until it killed him.

78

No better way to die than protecting the sheep, whether they appreciated it or not. The Sheepdog thing was corny, cliché out loud. Card kept it to himself.

Card changed into a new suit, ran a brush through his Wall Street look, found his credentials, grabbed his backpack and hit the hallway. Toomby was waiting by the elevator, not much better for the rest. He didn't bother to change his suit, nor comb his hair. Toomby wasn't really cut out for the soft clothes approach to things. He was also not too hot on working stateside. William Toomby was on a short list of men to have in a fire fight, he just wasn't programmed for social niceties. Card didn't have a problem in the world with Will, he just knew that eventually Toomby would have to learn to adapt, or he would become extinct. The mission for *Tier One* counter-terror units had changed. Nothing illustrated that more than two shooters waiting for an elevator in Los Angeles, dressed out in off-the-rack suits acting in a law enforcement capacity when ten years ago, it would have been impossible.

Driving a rented Toyota, no less.

The last President, during her short time in office, had passed the Manifest Homeland Protection Act. It was her largest, most controversial and really *only* major action before being murdered. The MHPA allowed active duty military personnel to act in a law enforcement capacity for an indefinite period of time as deputized United States Marshals. The President reasoned that military operations against terrorist organizations need not be restricted by borders or Posse Comitatus when those restrictions could hinder hot pursuit of terrorists and a continuity of pursuing unit made more sense than the hassle and ineffectiveness of passing along hunts from military to domestic law enforcement. Pervious to MHPA, the President could authorize military action on American soil under the Insurrection Act, but the scope was narrow and was situationally specific, such as riots or terrorist attacks. The President wanted a more general and longer lasting exception, and she got it. To placate the opponents of MHPA, the bill's major caveat only allowed for a set number of active duty military personnel to be deputized at one time. Solomon's unit was part of the MHPA authorization, hidden in plain sight. Solomon's unit existed because of a Presidential Finding and that Finding, if ever made public, would be legal because of the MHPA authorizations. Knowledge of the unit outside it didn't extend beyond the former President and former Chief of Staff, both of whom were deceased. They were as *off the grid* as you could get.

"The hell is taking this thing so long?"
Toomby said, staring up at the elevator. They were on the sixth floor, the elevator light showed that the car was sitting one floor down and not moving. Toomby looked at Card. "Stairs?"
Card nodded. The two men hit the stairwell and ran down. It wasn't much of a workout for either of them. Better than nothing. The next few days could be very boring, or much too exciting.

Toomby and Card couldn't be more different and still get along. Tony had a great respect for Will, more than was acceptable to talk aloud in the alpha male circles of professional soldiers. But Will was a caustic mix of brave and violent, with a sense of humor reserved for only the darkest jokes. He grew up in the rust belt of Pittsburg to a perpetually out of work father and a mother who filled in the gaps as a welder when there was paying work. With five bothers and him the last, Toomby grew up on the losing end of fighting for hand-me-downs. He was a mechanic that stumbled into a recruiter at a mall and joined the Army before he was sober enough to realize it. When he went to basic, he was the man who embodied the myth so common in men who never had the nerve to join. *I couldn't be in the Army, if a drill sergeant yelled at me I'd have to hit him.* Toomby did. Week three of his stay at 30th AG waiting for assignment to a training cycle, Will had put fist to face of a DS who had singled him out for ridicule over Will's weight. Somehow, he managed to stay in, and use the anger from his life to drive him to become the professional he was, with the occasional reduction in rank because of his temper and poor choices. It wasn't until he took a chance at becoming a Ranger that Toomby calmed down, at least enough to not get kicked out. Card and Toomby met in Battalion, attended sniper school together and had been a shooting team ever since.

As far as drives to work went, it was a short one. They took Shoreline to Queensway, passing the premium summertime beach night life. Beautiful women, seeming to outnumber the men three to one, moved with purpose along the sidewalks in front of trendy restaurants and nightlife bars. Toomby drove with the windows down, letting in the cool night air that was full of ocean salt. Card loved the salt air. They passed a large aquarium, moved over the long Queensway Bridge and drove into the Port of Long Beach. It was only a bridge away from 20-dollar drinks and late night hook ups, but was worlds apart.

Toomby gassed the little compact onto West Van Camp, following the commercial lane until it took them around to Pier F Avenue. From there it was a lazy drive to their destination. Card scanned around them. Nothing seemed out of place. Trucks hauling intermodal trailers moved in all directions, cranes and mobile container stackers milled about, hauling tons of cargo effortlessly, smaller service vehicles passed occasionally, or could be seen driving by through gaps in the massive stacks of cargo boxes in a hundred different colors that reminded Card of Legos; all under harsh sodium lights. They passed a plant complex that featured a literal mountain of white salt before the road curved to the left.

"Left here."

Card said, pointing to the entrance of one of the many container ship receiving areas. Toomby cut the wheel, pulling up to a comically small guard booth with a disproportionately large guard somehow inside it. Will rolled down his window, badging the guard.

"We have a meeting with CBP."

The guard looked at the badge, looked at Toomby, checked his clip board, gave Card a quick glance then waived them in.

"Where the hell is the office?"

Toomby asked, peering over the steering wheel, craning his head as they drove into the container farm. A super stacker with tires larger than their compact cut them off, a container held high in front of it. Toomby slammed on the brakes.

"See? Brakes just saved our lives."

Toomby just shook his head. He started moving again, giving the super stacker a safe lead.

"There."

Toomby said, pointing to a building with a number of Customs and Border Protection patrol vehicles parked in front of it. Toomby headed for them. As soon as they parked they left the car, backpacks in tow. A CBP officer sat on the front of his patrol car, near the entrance to the building. Stenciling and a logo on the double glass doors announced it as the CBP office. When they walked past the officer, he stood up.

"Help you guys with something?"

Card stopped and looked at the man, a kid really, he couldn't have been far enough out of high school to have forgotten his gym locker combination.

"We have a meeting with Captain Antere. Where can we find him?"

The young officer straightened up a little.

"He's out on the yard right now, should be back in ten or twenty minutes."

Toomby looked at his watch and shook his head.

"Our meeting is now, you think you can radio him and let him know we are here?"

He looked at Toomby, looked at Card, thought about it for a second.

"And you are?"

Card pulled out his credentials, showing the officer his badge and ID.

"Special Deputy US Marshal Card, this is Toomby."

He examined the badge for a few seconds. It was the traditional five star Marshals badge, though the ID card was different from a traditional US Marshal's. The young officer knew it was different but couldn't spot the difference. Card grew impatient, holding his wallet out while the kid tugged on it to see it better. Just as Card was convinced he would start asking stupid questions, the officer let go, keyed his shoulder mike and requested his supervisor at the office.

The Captain replied he was in route.

Five minutes later, a slick back Dodge Charger squealed into the lot. It parked a few rows down. A CBP officer in the traditional navy-blue uniform walked up the row of cars, studying Card, Toomby and the junior officer.

"Cringle?"

The kid motioned to the two Sergeants.

"These gentlemen say they have a meeting with you…"

Captain Antere looked confused, he opened his mouth to speak before recollection washed over his face.

"Oh damn, I'm sorry Marshals, I forgot you would be out here tonight. We're good here Cringle, you can hit the pier."

The kid gave his Capitan a nod, hitched up his duty belt and headed out for his patrol car. Toomby watched him leave.

"Little young, isn't he?"

Captain Antere scoffed, nodding in agreement with crossed arms.

"Yeah, seems like it, he's a few months out of FLETC, seems bright enough though, but the young ones either get in too much shit or not enough. I'm Captain Antere."

They shook hands.

"Tony Card."

"Will Toomby."

The Captain motioned to the office.

"You guys wanna cup of coffee, sit in the AC?"

Card shook his head.

"No, Captain, thanks, we'd rather get right to it."

Captain Antere was indifferent in his tone.

"Sure thing, Marshals. If you like, I can give you a ride out to the pier."

Toomby looked at the rented Toyota, then down the row of American V8s to the Captain's slick back. It wasn't a hard choice for him.

"Yeah, we can leave this piece of shit here?"

Captain Antere laughed.

"Another sure thing. I can't have it down on the pier anyway."

Card and Toomby transferred their gear from the Toyota to the trunk of the Charger. The three men loaded up, Antere driving, and drove into the pier yard. The main road in was wide for trucks, passing between manmade canyons of intermodal containers, stacks of eight through 56 feet long containers sat and waited to be unstacked and loaded on a never-ending stream of truck traffic. The Captain hooked a wide left out of the canyon of containers. Ahead of them was nothing but open pier and the monolithic 15 story towers of Pier F's Super-Post-Panamax gantry cranes.

The SSP gantry cranes were a boon for Long Beach, and essential to unload the newer breed of cargo ship. The Panama Canal was becoming less and less critical to shipping. Companies today were floating larger and wider ships carrying more cargo than the Canal could let slip through its narrow, though less so than they used to be, locks, all in an effort to generate more business. With a width of up to 24 intermodal containers, these ships could carry twice or more than that of a canal-wide ship, sacrificing the speed of delivery the canal offered for gross tonnage and a larger profit margin. These wider ships needed super cranes, and Long Beach had them.

"Your ship is due in at six AM, gentlemen, she'll be right under those cranes there."
The Captain said, pointing to the red and white crane super structures that sat at the edge of the pier. There was currently a ship under them, its deck nearly cleared of containers.
"If you don't mind my asking, Marshals, but why are you here to pick up a warrant? CPB snatches them up for you all the time and all you have to do is pick them up from us."
The Captain wasn't stupid. Not that Toomby or Card expected him to be.
"We aren't that kind of Marshal, Captain. We're with the JTTF. Our subject is a Level One with NCTC. We are going to put eyes on him and follow him to wherever he plans on going in the US."

Captain Antere nodded, his face shown serious as it was illuminated by the dock lights that flashed the interior of the car as they drove under them. Sergeants Card and Toomby were officially deputized under the Joint Terrorism Task Force, because it was easier to put in plain words than explaining they were deputized under a counter-terror unit that didn't exist. As far as Customs and Border Protection knew, they were there to observe a Level One, One being the worst, terrorism subject that the National Counter-Terrorism Center had identified and discovered was planning on entering the US as a member of a cargo ship crew. Colonel Solomon's computer geeks had put it to the CPB as two JTTF members coming in for a surveillance, somehow CBP got their wires crossed and thought it was a warrant pick up. Not that it mattered. There was no Level One that they knew of coming into Long Beach. Card and Toomby were after a shipping container that may or may not exist, much simpler as far as they were concerned. The hard part was knowing which container was which.

"Oh, well, I suppose that changes things a bit. This guy dangerous?"
Toomby was riding up front; he glanced back at Card as if to ask *is this guy serious?*
"Yeah, Captain, you don't get on that list for watching Al Jazzera and driving a cab. All we need from CBP is cooperation. As soon as we pick him up and he leaves the pier, you can go back to business as usual."
Toomby was abrasive as usual, his tone didn't escape Antere.
"With all due respect, Marshal, until seven AM, this pier is mine. Anything that happens on this pier is my responsibility-"
Toomby cut him off as the Captain pulled the Charger up to a row of yard tractors.

"Captain, we aren't here to ruin your night or your career. We are just going to hang out in the shadows for a few hours and be gone before you know it. Just do us a favor and keep your patrols from poking around in our business and we will leave a light footprint."

The captain sat on the brake, not yet putting the car in park. He mulled over his options, made a decision and put the car in park, his hand lingering on the shifter like he might change his mind. Card waited in the back, curious to see how the rest of the conversation would go. He almost wished he had popcorn.

"Look, Marshal, we don't have a habit of letting other agencies do things in our jurisdiction without our involvement. A warrant is one thing, but this is different." Toomby tried to remain civil. It didn't come out as civil at all.

"Captain, no one ever said anything about a warrant. You dipshits at the CBP snatched that out of thin air. We can settle this as simple as you like, either between you and us, or between you and your supervisor. I'll call him right now and hand you the damn phone if you like."

Card's head bounced back and forth between the two men. Toomby was as calm as he could be; the Captain was a different story. Thoughts of dealing with an irate supervisor steered his decision.

"Fine. You guys can have run of the pier, just don't get run over and don't count on me giving you a ride back up, now get out of my damn car."

Toomby was out the door before the words left the air. Card followed behind. Antere was nice enough to pop the trunk and let them get their bags before he sped away.

"You are ever the diplomat, Will."

Toomby smiled.

"Thanks, Tony. Now where in the holy fuck are we going to hole up?"

Card looked around the pier. He had studied the pier with a map program on his phone while reading up on just about everything that had to do with it, including the stats on the Officine Meccaniche Galileo-built cranes above his head. Card pointed to one of the last containers being stripped off the ship. It was snatched off the deck by an adjustable hoist, drawn up to the gantry runway and pulled over the pier by the trolley. The container was then lowered to a waiting intermodal trailer that would tow it into the stacks to be stored, or take it directly to a holding lot to be picked up for transit.

"According to Gianna, this ship is carrying over two thousand containers, all of them properly papered with legitimate destinations, for what that's worth. There are three containers on deck that were loaded last minute, paperwork is supposed to meet them here where they will sit in customs until they are cleared. I have the BIC numbers for those three containers, so if they are pulled from the ship and go anywhere but customs, we track it." Toomby sighed as he opened his backpack.

"Is that why I have a jumpsuit an orange traffic vest in my bag?"

Card chuckled.

"Luck of the draw. I'll call them out, you tag them."

Toomby accepted his fate.

"You get Gianna's phone number yet?"

He asked, stripping down in the shadows to pull on his coveralls.

"And when, Sergeant, would I have had time to do that?"

Toomby laughed.

"Jeez, you spend so much time with me, she probably thinks you're gay anyway."

The OOCL dry goods freighter, Tianjin was due into port at six AM, and she didn't disappoint. Card was high above the docks, watching the white behemoth slide up to the pier under the guide of a pilot boat, pushed into place by dirty tugs. Sergeant Card knew the measurements of the ship, had visualized them, studied pictures of the vessel, but it didn't prepare him for the sheer size. Card had stayed in towns smaller than the Tianjin.

As soon as the ship was tied off, the cranes went to work. Sergeant Card lay on a narrow service catwalk on the first crane half way up to the gantry, covered in a simple white nylon fabric to blend in as much as possible with the crane. The summer heat was coming in off the ocean with the sun. Card didn't expect to be in place long. Toomby was somewhere below him, lost in a small crowd of men in coveralls, hard hats and orange vests. Card figured clocking the containers coming off the ship would be easy. How fast could they possibly unload them? He should have known it wouldn't be that easy. The cranes worked fast, the ground crews faster. Card watched each container, searching for BIC numbers that matched the three he had memorized. Each intermodal container had a unique serial number issued by the International Container Bureau. The container serial would tell anyone who knew how to read it who owned the container, the origin and the cargo. The number was simple enough and was printed in multiple places on the container. Time, wear and damage made some numbers all but impossible to read. Gianna had gone over the entire manifest, just as she had with every other ship. Containers without paperwork weren't uncommon. Each ship out of the fifteen had cargo on board that was suspicious in the fact that some or all of its paperwork had not yet made it into the hands of the CBP. As Card had found out in his research, that was suspicious, but not uncommon. Card and Toomby had been tasked with other work until now; this would be their first time running down containers.

The first container was unloaded right off the top stack. Card called it out to Toomby below. Toomby waited for it to be lowered onto a waiting yard tractor and tagged it with a magnetic GPS as inconspicuously as possible. The second container was an hour behind, Card nearly missed it, only deciphering the badly damaged serial number as the metal box was locked down to a trailer. Toomby got it tagged before it was driven away. The last container was at the bottom of a stack, coming off the ship as noon rolled around. Toomby tagged it as well, announcing to Card over the radio that next time, he would be the one to lay on his ass all day. Card didn't antagonize him with a reply. He stripped his cover, packed up his gear and made the long and narrow climb down to the ground, dressed in coveralls toting a tool box. He blended in and no one on the dock so much as gave him or Toomby as second glance as they made the long walk back to their rental. The best way to get away with anything is to act like you are supposed to be doing it.

Sage advice.

Toomby took the wheel, Card rode shotgun.
"Look at this fuckin' guy."
Toomby said, pointing to Captain Antere as they pulled out of the pier. Antere was leaning against the hood of his personal vehicle, still in uniform, watching them leave, a look of satisfaction and possibly distain on his face. Toomby rolled down the window as they drove by him.
"Hey, Captain, stay in your own goddamn lane."
He gave the Captain the bird and peeled out of the lot with all the chirp the hybrid engine could manage. Card laughed.
"That would have been a lot more dramatic if we had rented a V8."
Toomby rolled up the window.

"Tell yer damn girlfriend when you talk to her that real men don't drive windup toys. If she wants me to do my job driving a fucking car that doesn't know if it wants to be a lawnmower or an electric razor, I'll replace her computer with a legal pad and a crayon and see how she gets along." Card ignored him, dialing the number to Virginia while he booted up his laptop to check the GPS locators. The phone rang its customary single ring before it was answered.
"Gianna."
There was that sweet southern accent.
"It's Card. We tagged all three."
Card's statement was confirmed when the three GPS locators began pinging on his screen.
"I have them. You and Will are flying out on Delta in two hours."
"Where are we going now?"
Toomby asked.
"New Orleans. O'Neil had some interesting developments this morning. Solomon wants you two there."
Toomby smacked the steering wheel, his disdain for the hybrid quickly forgotten.
"Bourbon Street? Hell yes."
"Yes, Sergeant Toomby, y'all can have a drink or two while you wait for the others. O'Neil will pick you up at the airport. She enlisted some local help, just so you won't be surprised."

5

Three days till Resolute

I was up before dawn, dressed out in running gear
and hit the streets. I took Orleans Avenue East, keeping
my speed steady at a seven-minute mile. I ran this route
once a week, always before the sun, always before most
joggers than ran the straight and level avenue took to the
pavement. A few still ran this early, familiar faces. Some
kept pace for a mile or so before slowing or breaking off on
their own predetermined route. I pushed on and by the time
I hit Canal Street, I was always alone. My head was clear,
focused on the rhythm of the run, too busy with
maintaining my pace and my breath to drift into painful
thoughts of the past.

Canal Street was narrower, older than Orleans, if not in age
than at least in care. If the sun was in the sky, I would have
appreciated the near total canopy of trees. Without
daylight, all the trees did was trap the night air close to the
earth. My lungs were filled with the sticky sweet mist. I
overcame the familiar urge to gag and drove on. Always
pushing forward. Canal Street west took me to North
Carrollton. I hung a right, willing my lungs and my legs to
carry me through to the end. Muscles burned, breath was
deep and even, endorphins flooded my mind, showed me
clarity in its most simplistic form. I slowed my pace,
gradually coming to a walk as I crossed the five-mile mark.
I cooled down on the short walk back to my house, arms
above my head. I checked my pulse; a rock solid 150. The
sun was breaking. I checked the time. Madeline was due
in an hour. I spent the next thirty minutes off the front of
my house working with kettle bells. Using a 25 pounder, I
did figure eights through my legs, then hand-offs behind
my back, starting at my ankles, going all the way up to my

head. Next, I did ten reps on each arm of the Turkish Getup. I finished with a 30 pound medicine ball in a sit up position. Each time I rose I would throw the ball high on the side wall of the house. I would catch it, go down and repeat. After one hundred reps my abs strained and burned, protesting further punishment. For once, I listened to them. I went through a series of stretches to prevent cramping before heading in for a shower. The sweat on my skin was sticky in the humidity. It was going to be another hot day in the Crescent City.

I showered, hot water keeping the ache out of my body before it could take hold. I stepped out into what many would consider to be a comically small bathroom. I was among them. Nothing more than a claw foot tub as old as the house, a shower head with exposed plumbing and a curtain rail added later, a toilet and a pedestal sink; all dressed out in white subway tile that was ivory with age. It served me just fine. I stared at myself in the mirror, brushing my wet light brown hair off my forehead. I looked at my scars, as I did each time I showered. The tight pucker at the bottom edge of my ribcage, it was pale with the texture of scar tissue. The most important scar.

The one that should have killed me.

Yet I lived.

The scar on the side of my neck. A shallow trough carved by the same gun that should have killed me. Under the furled scroll tattoo on my chest, an intricate lined banner carrying the word *Invictus,* lay a scar from a knife. Once my most cherished scar, when I still carried such things as medals, from a blade wielded by a clinically insane Turkish man who wished me dead as quickly as possible. He came close to seeing that wish granted.

I stared into my own eyes, always trying to figure own what color they really were. Trying to see past them. It never worked. I left the bathroom and dressed, opting for desert tan 5.11 pants, a pair of Merrell ankle high shoes designed with rough terrain in mind, and a muted blue short sleeve button up shirt. I took my 1911 out of my waist pack, dropping the magazine. It was a Wilson Combat CQB model, the slide flat black, the frame olive drab. The finish was scratched and tarnished, out of use, not abuse. The Trijicon sights were in perfect condition despite rough use. Internally, the 1911 was still a finely tuned pistol. This Wilson Combat once belonged to Pepper, once was held in the hands of my *Sister* who tried to take my life with it and nearly succeeded. An inanimate object, designed with a purpose, guided by the will of whoever held it.

Indifferent.

I replaced the loaded magazine, grabbed four more from my dresser and put the weapon on with my belt, tucked securely into a Raven Concealment holster. It supported my 1911 with a Surefire light mounted on the pistol's rails and kept it close to the body, as flush as possible to conceal the weapon. The four spare magazines went into pouches against my right side. My shirt concealed them and the pistol well enough. A trained eye might be able to spot the pistol printing against my shirt if I bent or turned the right way but that was true of any concealed weapon. I slipped an Emerson Commander knife into my pocket, four more magazines into a sling pack with other items I might need, grabbed a hat and a pair of sunglasses and left the house.

Madeline was just pulling up to the curb. She popped the locks. I hopped in. Maddy gave me a welcome smile and a cup of coffee.

"Morning, mate."

"Good morning, Maddy."

I stretched out in my seat, shifting my weapon forward on belt to keep it from digging into my side. Maddy pulled off the curb, flipped a U turn and headed east. We hit North Broad and followed it down through Mid City, under the Ten until we reached Washington Avenue. Washington Avenue ran towards the river, Toledano Street on the other side of the median ran away from it. We passed neighborhoods of row houses, shotgun houses and the occasional ranch style home. Varied flavors of decoration care and property value flashed by in color contrast. More of New Orleans character. Washington turned into Toledano. We passed newer construction consisting of apartment buildings, single family homes and new age façade businesses. Toledano became Louisiana when we crossed South Claiborne. Louisiana Avenue was the border between Central City and Freret, then the Garden District and Touro before it spilled us out on Tchoupitoulas Street along the river. The Tahoe carried us east through commercial warehouses, vacant lots and businesses closely tied to the shipping industry.

"You know the docks, Rushing?"

"One of my running routes takes me by here, other than that, not really."

Maddy watched me out of the corner of her eye.

"You trot all the way down here?"

"Once a week."

"A bit out of the way."

Madeline dodged potholes for four miles, running along the concrete flood wall that surrounded the Napoleon Avenue Terminal. Intermodal trucks passed headed in the other directions or crossed in front of us at traffic lights. Traffic was light early in the morning, it would pick up steadily throughout the day. When we reached Felicity Street, Madeline pulled off the road.

She took a black wallet out of the inside pocket of her suit coat. It held the five star US Marshals badge and credentials in her name. She was dressed the part in a white blouse, a light weight pant suit with razor sharp creases complete with a pair of black kitten heel shoes. I had avoided on commenting on her attire. It was the first time I had ever seen her in anything other than utility pants, boots and either t shirts or body armor. Her fire red hair was slicked back into a pony tail, a splash of makeup peeked out from underneath her Oakley's. She looked good.

"Right, then. I'll badge these blokes to get in. The plan is pretty simple. The Wayward Slip will be docking in thirty minutes. There is one container on board without paperwork. Customs thinks I'm here to talk to one of the crew about one of their family members."

It seemed like a good reason to get into the terminal as any. Specifically vague, it left plenty to the imagination, which was usually more exciting than reality. Usually.

"How do we find the container?"

I asked, watching traffic pick up on the road, it looked like the morning rush hour was starting. Madeline took a slip of paper from her wallet.

"Container serial. All we have to go off. The Wayward Slip is a Panamax, carries up to 512 containers, more if they are under forty feet. So, we watch the containers come off and tag the one we want with a GPS."

That was the plan?

"Then what?"

Madeline gave me a hard look.

"We see where it goes, Rushing. Without paperwork, they are going to hold it. Someone will have to come pick it up and provide the required paperwork when they do. Either the blokes on this end do things the right way, or they nick it right off the dock. We need to know where it's going regardless."

"Okay. What do you want me to do?"

"Watch my back, Rushing. Al Taybi's people, if this is the right container, will be about to pick it up. I can think of no one better to keep me from getting slotted."

"As long as you promise to do the same."

Madeline put the Tahoe back in gear, pulling onto the road. The two-lane path of thick concrete led west on the opposite side of the flood wall. The history of the river was right there next to us, dilapidated wood planks, warped and abused, made up what used to be the primary dock separated us from the river. I imagined they fell out of use about the time diesel replaced steam as the primary power source for cargo ships and barges. The entrance point was just inside the wall. A small booth with hardened concrete Jersey barriers angled out into the road to create a choke point and slow traffic. Three uniformed Customs officers lined the road. Two were busy with a tractor trailer in front of us; the third walked back the length of the trailer to Maddy as she lowered the window. He glanced down at the front of the Tahoe, Madeline had put the Government plates back on. I had been meaning to ask her why she took them off in the first place.

"Help you, ma'am?"

He lacked interest, it was evident in his voice, his body language and in his physical appearance. He was about 30 pounds overweight, his uniform needed a press and he was far too lazy. Maddy held her badge up.

"Madeline O'Neal with Marshals. I'm here to speak with a crew member of the Wayward Slip, due to dock at nine."

The officer glanced at the badge then at me. He didn't even take the time to consider the situation before waving us through without another word. He walked away, back towards the air conditioning in his booth.

"Well, that was a little too easy."

Maddy nodded, pulling around the truck.

"A bit. You would think things would be tighter. Even after Nine-Eleven, the ports are still vulnerable. Only about ten percent of the cargo coming in even gets x-rayed. Man power is higher, considerably so, but the weakest link is always the human element. You put a man on a checkpoint five days a week, eight or more hours a day; he's bound to lose interest in short order."

The sentry could be blamed for countless failures and victories throughout history. One man's complacent guard was another man's way in. Ports were a major security concern for the US. Customs and Border Protection was born after 9-11 and despite its monumental budget, the increase in shipping in and out of the US was outracing the CBP's ability to keep up. The fear of someone slipping a nuclear weapon through the ports had become the largest security concern after the theft of nuclear warheads in Nevada nearly two years ago and because of that, radiological detection scanners absorbed much of facility budget's that instead could have been used for more man power, x-ray machines and anything else that would help raise the ten percent benchmark. The major ports were all equipped with the scanners, as were major interstates and highways into metro areas. Perfect if this container had a nuke in it. Since there wasn't a single nation in Africa known to possess a single nuclear weapon, let alone a spare to sell, I doubted nuclear was on the table.

We passed by a row of long warehouses, spread out along the older parts of the terminal. Forklifts bounced in and out of open doors toting pallets, boxes and bags of grain and flour. The thin sliver of land between the flood wall and the river grew wider, traffic picked up and we passed the first row of intermodal containers. I could see a rail head behind the container lot, locomotives towing flats and spine cars into place to be loaded for shipment. The terminal widened more, a switching yard twelve tracks wide filled up the right side of the road as we snaked in between it and the walls of containers. It was occupied with a rainbow of box cars, hoppers, tank cars and well flats. Some were freshly painted with company colors and logos; others also freshly painted with graffiti, both murals and words in elaborate designs. I recognized tags from local New Orleans, Whole Car pieces in Wildstyle, I also saw a Married Couple piece from an artist in Los Angeles and a few amateur pieces by artists called *Toys* by the more experienced set. Trains were free advertising for graf artists.

"Here we are."
Madeline said, pointing to a row of inspection lanes that faced Felicity. Ten lanes, most already occupied with trucks waiting to clear paperwork. The road looped around behind the waiting lanes, leading to another guard booth. Madeline rolled down her window, the badge came out again. This time, the CBP officer that walked up to the window was on his game. Even though he saw a badge held out the window of a government vehicle, he took a proper position off the B pillar, just behind the driver's side door, making Maddy hold her credentials out and back at an odd angle.
"Where you headed, Marshal?"
He asked, handing the ID back after a close examination.
"Wharf C. I'm going to have a chat with a crew member off a ship."
The officer tapped on the passenger door window behind Maddy.
"Put this down, please?"

Madeline lowered the window. The officer peered in at me.

"You here for the Wayward Slip?"

His question seemed routine, like he had been directing people to the ship all morning.

"Yes."

Madeline said.

"They towed her in this morning, you are a little late for the party, I've had FBI, Coast Guard, and Homeland Security coming through for about an hour, I guess adding some Marshals to the mix won't hurt."

I didn't know what the hell he was talking about, if Madeline did, she hid it well.

"We were a little late getting word."

He didn't seem to care.

"Take a right here, then a left. Follow the signs down and keep out of the way of the stackers and cranes. You shouldn't have any problem finding it."

Madeline rolled up the windows without another word and pulled through.

"It's nice to see one of these blokes is green eyed. Even if it was a bit inconvenient."

"What the hell is he talking about?"

"I have no bloody idea."

Madeline said, speeding down the service road. We drove for maybe half a mile before we saw the first police car. An unmarked Taurus with its blue lights dancing in the rear window posted at the corner of the wharf C warehouse. Madeline made the turn, revealing a sea of marked and unmarked cars from half a dozen federal agencies. Uniformed officers and federal agents in polos, suits and street clothes dotted the landscape. Crime scene vans and coroner vans were backed up against the river, doors open, awaiting work.

"Fuck all."

I couldn't have said it better.

6

The Wayward Slip was a Ceres freighter, a battered black beast the length of two football fields that sat low in the water under the weight of its cargo, bobbing up and down with the rhythm of the river. It was moored beneath two of the wharf's gantry cranes. The cranes were stationary. Whatever happened on the ship, it was preventing them from unloading containers. I didn't have to be a genius to figure out that what happened on the Wayward Slip, it had to do with the container we were looking for. Coincidences did not exist in my world.

So.

Madeline hit her lights. Blue LED bars mounted in the grill and where the headliner met the windshield inside the cab began flashing. A few agents took notice of the newest government vehicle to join the crowd, but the interest was short lived. Maddy's blue Tahoe was one of many similar vehicles. Most of the feds just went about their business of standing around or interviewing people who appeared to be crew members off the Wayward Slip. Maddy threaded through haphazardly parked cars until she decided she had driven close enough. She stopped and looked at me.
"I'm going to see if I can find out what the bloody hell happened, why don't you do the same?"
Rushing Winter, always ready to adapt to a new situation.
"Sure."
I said, choosing a course of action. We left the vehicle. Maddy headed straight for a small knot of suits that were dressed nice enough to be supervisors of some sort. I walked the other way, towards the wharf warehouse. Stevedores, or longshoremen or dockworkers, whatever they were called in New Orleans were gathered around the entrance to a roll up door. Some leaning on the wall

sipping on coffee even with the heat, some lounging on buckets or fold up chairs. All watching the drama playing out around the ship they were supposed to be working. Every one of them looked annoyed, inconvenienced and bored. I was somewhat rusty in the casual interrogation department, but I didn't have anything to lose in asking questions. I scanned over faces as I approached, searching for the alpha of the pack. Some might go for a straggler or outsider, the man on the edge of the crowd. The outcast was usually easier to gain information from, as they were more likely to offer information willingly. Unfortunately, by being the outcast, the individual was unlikely to have critical knowledge, either because they were not in on the gossip, or in a position of authority to receive it.

I preferred to go directly to the dominant personality, if only because they were the holder of any information I might need. Since this was just going to be a friendly chat about whatever was going on with the ship, and because the ship being a crime scene that was preventing these men from working, I could gain more information by letting the man vent his frustration about not being able to work. Besides, it wasn't like I was going to be trying to talk a nun into a spring break trip.

This group of men was hard to read. They were all dressed out in Carhartts or coveralls, safety vests, hard hats, nothing to signify a supervisor or alpha dog. A simple salutation would tell me who to talk to.
"Mornin', guys."
Three sets of eyes immediately went to the tallest man in the crowd. Probably six inches short of seven feet, a face that made me think his skull was a football helmet. A jaw best suited for digging ditches was hidden behind a briar patch beard that held the remnants of breakfast in a firm grasp.

"Fuck ya' want?"

Yep, this was the guy.

The others didn't so much as mutter a response. I held my hands up.
"Hey, easy. Just want to ask a few questions."
He came up off the bollard he was leaning on, spitting out a mouthful of caramel colored tobacco spit.
"We don't know shit about nothing happen'd on that ship, and we sure is fuck don't want to talk to any damn cops."
I shook my head.
"Not police."
I purposely averted eye contact, choosing a space off over his shoulder to stare at. Consciously or subconsciously he took the bait.
"Who tha hell are ya?"
His tone dropped a degree from hostile to pissed. The men around him stiffened as I reached the edge of their comfort zone for outsiders.
"Name's Jake, I work for Freeport, down on tha Isle. We got a box on tha ship I'm suppose to pick up. Just want to know if I'm gonna be able to git to it today with all this business."
I threw a little accent into my voice. I couldn't do a Manny, but I had been in New Orleans long enough to fake a native who worked up from the sidewalk to an office job. The way I was dressed, these men would, hopefully anyway, peg me for a supervisor. I tossed them the name of Freeport Sulphur Company down on Grand Isle. I was playing local working man. It would either work or it wouldn't.
"Well, Jake...Don't know too much. The Wayward got towed in this mornin' by tha Coasties, found adrift off tha Southwest Pass. Looks like she's hit by pirates. Heard one of dem docs talk'in, few crew were killed. These feds got

'er locked down until they finn'sh pokin' around. You might like try back in the afta'noon."

I cursed for show, gave a shake of the head while staring at the ground.

"Pirates?"

The shovel jawed giant gave me a nod and a raise of his coffee cup.

"Sure 'nough. You know well as I, pirates neva' left tha Gulf. I got kin down in Port Fourchon that were out for shrimpin' fore' dawn, saw it happen near Mud Bay. Coupla' ribs threw on to the Slip as she was waitin' on a river pilot. Say's they saw gunfire on the deck. Somethin' was lowered onto a rib."

Piracy in the Gulf of Mexico was sporadic, but it still happened. Usually the pirates went after luxury sails or yachts, hardly ever was a commercial ship hit, especially so close to the River mouth.

Coincidences grew.

"Where do ya think they went?"

Shovel jaw spit out another mouthful of tobacco juice.

"Wha? Pirates? You thinkin' they took somethin' of yours?"

It was the only response he could think of given my question. Easiest line of thought to form when he thought he was talking to a man there to pick up a container.

"Might have,"

I said, looking back over my shoulder at the Wayward Slip as if to look for my container.

"Just curious, really."

Shovel jaw laughed. Everyone around him did a half beat later.

"You from tha isle?"

"N'sir. Born and raised in Belle Rose."

Another group laugh. My fake family home wasn't water front.

"Too far off tha river to know, Pirates most come out of Timbalier Island. 'Sept my cousin said they went 'round the pass across East Bay towards Redfish, maybe Blind Bay. No pirates out that way I know of."

I had a vague idea of where Timbalier Island was, South of Montegut, the largest island between Terrebonne Bay and the Gulf. From what I knew it wasn't much more than a ragged crescent of sea shore and swamp land barely above sea level. Redfish and Blind bay were on the east side of the Mississippi River Delta past the South Pass to the river, names for two of but a few mouths that led into region between the Delta National Wildlife Refuge to the north and Port Eads to the south; dozens of small islands, fingers of land off of the river levees bayous, wetlands, sea marshes and shifting sandbars covering hundreds of square miles in Plaquemines Parish. I did some more head shaking for show, hands on the hips.

"Your cousin gonna tell them?"

I motioned to the growing crowd of federal officers and agents behind me.

"Ah doubt it. Down that far, he could be rattn' on a cousin or broda of one of his friends."

I couldn't argue with the logic. He told me about as much as he could without me asking suspicious questions.

"Many thanks."

Shovel jaw chuckled.

"Think nothin'."

I wandered back towards Madeline's Tahoe, thinking over what I had just learned. I could see Maddy near the side of the ship, standing at the gangway, looking up towards the deck of the ship while an olive-skinned man in a three piece suit spoke to her. It took me four more steps towards them to realize who I was looking at.

FBI Supervisory Special Agent Dominic Hijazi.

Dominic was dressed out in a summer weight charcoal suit with faint white pin stripes, his black wing tip shoes glinting brightly in the sunlight. Dominic was as I remembered him the last time I saw him, his black hair trimmed close to his head, the edges razor sharp without taper, as if his hair was painted on. I couldn't hear what he or Madeline was saying, but I could read body language. They knew each other and were on friendly terms. Dominic was just inside Maddy's comfort zone, which meant she trusted him.

Hijazi was gainfully employed in seeing how many licks it took to get to the center of a Tootsie Pop when I walked up. He saw me, recognized me and choked a little on his candy.
"Mister...Winter?"
I read him. He didn't expect to see me. I didn't see fear, just confusion.
"Agent Hijazi."
Madeline looked at him, then me.
"You two know each other?"
Dominic shrugged, looking at Madeline.
"You could say that."
Then he looked at me.
"Mister Winter, I feel as if I need to make you aware of a few things that happened last time we met..."
I held up a hand to cut him off.
"You mean that you were working with Colonel Solomon and that show in the hospital room was all about getting me to play on your team?"
He was genuinely surprised. The last time we saw each other, I was in a hospital bed. Hijazi had me under arrest and was the man who told me Pepper had been killed. He made a show of having a clash of conscience over letting

me go or putting me in prison for the rest of my natural life. Colonel Solomon showed up and after a spirited argument on my behalf, I was left in the care of the Colonel, who quickly pointed me in a direction he wanted me to go and let me loose.

"Yeah, Hijazi. You may be an excellent investigator, but you aren't much of an actor. I saw recognition on your face when Solomon walked into that hospital room. You hid it pretty well; I didn't even realize it until later."

Madeline watched the exchange, a bit of nervousness in her face. Dominic took a step back, probably just in case I lunged for his neck. I thought maybe I would be mad when I saw him. I wasn't. I didn't even know if I had the ability to *be mad* anymore. Not at anyone but Martin Heller.

"I feel like I should apologize all the same, Mister Winter." The words were genuine. Not that hearing them changed the dynamics of what had happened last time we met. Hijazi and the Colonel had played me, or at least they felt that they had, into leading them to Robert Wigglin and Robert's program, Auger. I produced results, just not the results they may have wanted.

I had a bad habit of doing what *I* wanted.

"No need. I would have done what I did without you and the Colonel involved. Just to be clear, though-"
I said, stepping into Dominic's face.
"You try to run a game on me again-"
I looked at Madeline.
"and the only solution will be a violent one."
Madeline was calm. Dominic opened his mouth as if to say something, thought better of it and shut his mouth. He considered his thoughts before he spoke.
"That seems reasonable, given the circumstances.
However, Mister Winter, I do not take threats lightly."

"You can take them any way you want, Hijazi. I don't do appeasement."

"Right, then."

Madeline said, heading off what could have become an argument.

"If you chaps are done comparing your naughty bits, we have a bit of a problem."

I ignored Dominic's stare, focusing on Maddy.

"What did you find out?"

Dominic took the question, unwrapping a fresh Tootsie Pop.

"The ship was boarded last night while awaiting a river pilot to bring them up here to the terminal. Around four AM, between six and ten armed men came on board and went directly to one container. One of the deck hands stumbled upon them, he was shot and killed. Apparently, the crew of this ship take the threat of piracy very seriously and maintain a small armory on board the ship, illegally, of course. They armed themselves and engaged in a running gun battle. For their troubles they lost two more crew members, with an additional two wounded and only managed to kill one of the boarding party. Whatever the men came for, they most likely got. They left the ship disabled in the water and sailed off into the night."

Although I was pretty sure of the answer to my question after talking to shovel jaw, I asked anyway.

"Local pirates?"

Dominic scoffed.

"No, Rushing. The dead man on the deck has no eye patch, nor parrot, cutlass or wooden leg. He has all his teeth, shows no signs of a vitamin C deficiency and is in the possession of equipment usually reserved for professional soldiers trained in maritime boarding operations. These men were not local pirates, nor pirates of any kind."

Dominic pointed to the deck of the ship, taking a quick look around to insure no one was in ear shot.

"The FBI is running the dead man now, we shouldn't have a problem accessing the information they turn up. This isn't being seen as anything other than an attempted hijacking. Local FBI is looking at things small picture right now and probably will end the day looking at it the same way."

"What was in the container?"

Dominic popped his lollypop out of his mouth, it clacked against his teeth as he did. I hated that sound.

"We don't know, at least not yet. It's stacked full of 55-gallon drums, all contain Arabic Gum powder as far as I know. One barrel was opened on the deck, something inside was removed, a cylinder of some sort. The powder around where the cylinder lay still retains an impression. Whatever it was, it was perhaps a few inches in diameter and maybe two feet in length."

As if on cue, two FBI techs dressed out in blue tyvek suits wheeled a black 55-gallon drum down the scissor walkway of the ship. The drum's lid was in place, the entire drum wrapped in air tight plastic. The two agents were taking special care to not bump or jostle the container on the way down. An FBI van was backed into place to receive it.

"Did you find out anything, Rushing?"

Madeline asked. I told her and Dominic about the dock worker's cousin, the shrimper, and what he saw near Mud Bay as we walked back towards the Tahoe. Dominic had his phone out, using a map application to visualize what I was talking about. Madeline peered over his shoulder to do the same. When we reached the Tahoe, Dominic opened the passenger door. He pulled a laptop up and out of the center console mounted on an articulated bracket. He swiveled it towards him, opened the screen and woke it from sleep mode. He pulled up a satellite map of the Mississippi Delta. He scrolled back and forth, zooming in and out of the menagerie of islands off the eastern side of the Delta.

"Jesus. We need to move on this fast. Whatever is in that cylinder, it will not be in the swamp for long."

He picked his phone up off the seat and made a call.

Madeline went to the back of the Tahoe, raising the hatch. She took out a second laptop, hopping into the back seat to work. With nothing to do, I leaned against the side of the SUV, burning slowly in the searing sun. Humidity was beyond ridiculous. It came in waves, like walking through endless sheets of tissue paper soaked in hot water. I watched the docks, the activity. One of the terminal cranes came to life, quickly digging its way down to the breached container. Once it had it, the container was lowered onto the deck of a step deck trailer pulled by a CBP truck. The container was secured and towed out under escort.

"Watch the crowd, will you, Rushing?"

Her thinking that someone from Heller's group or Virtua Corporation might be watching was my own thought as well. The fact that she felt the need to mention it bothered me.

"Not my first rodeo, Maddy."

"I know, Rushing,"

She said, peering around the open hatch at me.

"Sorry, mate."

I regretted my tone, she, her reminder.

The thing about watching crowds was to not watch them. With hundreds of moving parts, twice as many varied colors and irregular objects and shapes coming in and out of view, watching a crowd as a whole was an exercise in futility. Crowds always had a purpose. This crowd's purpose was focused on the ship, the container, the evidence, the investigation. Any part of the crowd that didn't fit into that focus was either an onlooker, or something that didn't fit. So I, out of habit, looked for what didn't fit. It didn't take very long for someone to stand out, actually, *two* someones.

Tucked into the man-made shadow of a stack of containers stood a man as indescribable as one could imagine. He was wearing jeans and a green t-shirt fitted tight against his skin by sweat. Sunglasses shielded his eyes; baseball cap protected his head. His clothes would be far more memorable than him. It was almost like I was looking at myself…Someone who just *blended in,* on purpose. He was just watching, a cell phone clutched in his hand down by his side. Officers, agents and dock workers moved past him without taking notice. I noticed him. So did another man. He was opposite me, leaning against the tong of a forklift as if he was tired. His clothes were wrong. An all black suit with a black shirt frayed at the collar. His black hair shaved close on weathered skin. He was focused on the man in the green t-shirt, seeming to see only him. The look on his face told me all I needed to know.

He intended to kill him.

When he moved, so did I.
"Maddy, now!"
I said, walking across the terminal towards the man in the green t-shirt. She hopped out of the Tahoe and fell in beside me without question. I trusted her to see what I was seeing. It didn't take her long.
"What the hell is this about?"
The man in the green t-shirt disappeared into a forest of stacked containers, his phone going up to his ear as he made a call. The man in the dingy black suit was just ahead of us, on track to follow him into the container farm.
"I have no idea."
I said, brushing my side to check the condition of my weapon.

"But I'm willing to bet one of these guys knows something about what was on that ship."

The man in the suit disappeared into the containers. I saw him take a right just before he went out of view. As soon as we entered behind him, I drew my weapon and thumbed the safety off. Madeline did the same. We took opposite sides of the corridor, watching angles. I motioned to where I saw the man in the suit turn. Maddy nodded, she had the best angle on it, so she sliced the corner wide with me right at her back. We made it around the corner, into a jagged canyon of closely placed containers in stacks of varied heights. The noise from the dock dropped away. It was quiet.

Cozy.

Perfect conditions for an uninterrupted gunfight if it came down to it.

The intermodal corridor seemed to stretch on forever, the two walls of corrugated metal going off into the distance until they appeared to merge into a point. We quickened our pace, searching out the two men.

"There."

Maddy whispered, using her off hand to point to a drop of blood at the corner of a narrow gap between two container stacks. It was only a drop of blood. A single oblong splash on the concrete no larger than a dime, fallen at the base of one of the containers. From its shape and position, the drop was under centrifugal force when it fell, as if it fell from a bleeding wound when the injured person turned. The person was either turning left or right. Since right would have taken them into an uninterrupted stack, left into the gap was the obvious choice. I had the best angle, so I took lead, slicing around deliberately a section at a time until I could see the narrow path was clear. Madeline fell in behind me. I kept my weapon tucked close to my chest, aimed ahead to keep my field of vision clear. We emerged on the other side into another seemingly endless row of containers. I searched but could find no signs as to which way either of the men went.

"Fancy a guess?"

Madeline asked, watching the direction I wasn't.

"Listen…"

The faint sound of a scuffle. I heard the specific sounds of deliberate movements, the thud of something being bounced off a container.

"This way."

We moved fast towards the sound. It was ahead, to the left, behind another stack. We were not going to find a gap to the other side quick enough.

"Find an alley, I'm going over."

I broke into a short sprint towards a stack of containers only two high, holstered my weapon, jumped and kicked off the container beside me, pushing towards the opposite side. A hard kick off the other side, shoving myself up as hard as I could, I was just able to get a hand hold on the top of a badly rusted intermodal box. I got both hands on it, set my feet for a push and vaulted up to the top. The stacks to the left and right were much higher, my only choice was straight across to the other side. I heard Madeline curse something as I moved to the opposite edge in a crouch. I got there in time to see the man in the dingy suit bounce the big man in the green t-shirt off a container. T-shirt man rebounded with a jab, his arm was trapped expertly, spun against the natural rotation of his shoulder and hyper extended. The man in the suit landed a devastating knee to his stomach and still with a grip on his arm, went for something under his jacket. I took two steps back, ran and jumped. I hit the container wall on the other side low enough to keep me from serious injury as I ricocheted off, landing in a crouch. My weapon came out just as the man in the dingy suit pulled free a pistol. A glint of light told me there was something under the barrel. The blade of a knife. It made contact with the green t shirt at the bottom hem. The pistol was pulled up the front of his shirt, a thin line of flashing red following it up. The man in the suit saw me out of the corner of his eye, he pulled the other man into my line of fire, I saw the pistol come clear of his neck, a spray of blood following it in a wild arc. He took aim over his human shield. I was in the open without cover, trapped in a funnel. I stayed low, trying to put his head in my sight picture.

"Drop him."

The man in the green t-shirt was pressed against him, face to face. He was fighting. Judging by the amount of blood I could see pooling under him, he didn't have much of a fight to offer.

The man in the suit fired a pair of rounds so close together, the clap ringing off the metal walls sounded like one. I rolled to my right, his arm was blocked by his shield's neck, making tracking me difficult. He twisted his shield. I slid onto my shoulder, found a target, before I could fire, Madeline appeared between me and him. She held tight to a corner for cover.

"Drop it!"

Yeah, I tried that.

I got my feet under me. With nowhere to go but forward, I advanced. Dingy suit man dragged his shield further back into the corridor.

"You can have him."

He said, pushing the man towards us, blocking both our shots as he ducked into a gap between containers. I rushed right past the wounded man, following the shooter into the gap.

"I got him!"

I yelled. Madeline went to the man on the ground. She may have been able to get something out of him before he died.

This day was off to a spectacular start.

The shooter couldn't have had more than a two second lead on me but by the time I came out on the other side he was gone. I listened for footfalls. The ringing in my ears from gunshots made that difficult. I ran to the right on a guess. There was yet another gap between containers. I went through, weapon ready. I came out on the other side. Scanned left, right. My eyes locked on a fluttering suit coat as the shooter went over the top of a fence. He came down on the other side favoring his right leg and sprinted into a large warehouse, dodging forklifts and yard tractors as he went. I sprinted after him, running up a flat deck trailer backed against the fence. I cleared the fence behind it, came up and ran as fast as I could through the same door the dingy suit ran through. Right inside were two confused dock workers.

"Which way?!"

One man looked at me like he didn't speak English; the other raised a hesitant arm and pointed. I followed his direction, running through random stacks of dry goods, boxed appliances and bolts of fabric. The warehouse was immense. Sprinting though it in the uncooled air sucked away my energy but I pushed harder, determined to catch him. I reached the far wall, an exit door was wide open. My weapon came up, I moved towards the door, watching the corners. I gave my eyes a few seconds to adjust to the bright light then went through into a thin patch of abused grass that ran the length of the warehouse between the building and the floor wall. Directly in front of me was a thin ribbon of blood half way up the wall, still wet, rolling down the concrete. It glistened in the sunlight. He went over. I climbed to the top. On the other side was a two lane road, beyond it the rail head. He had disappeared into the train cars.

Injured and bleeding, he had outrun me.

His voice.

An accent. I had only heard a few words, it was hard to pin. The *e's* were sustained, drawn out. The *h* almost cut off the word *'have'*. French, maybe? But not natural, like it was picked up along the way. I replayed what I saw and what I *thought* I saw in my mind. The black suit. The black shirt. A black shirt with a Roman collar. A clerical collar.

He was dressed like a priest.

That was interesting.

7

Dominic was with Madeline by the time I got back to the body. She was on the phone, with the Colonel by the sounds of it. Dominic was crouched over the body, hands covered in blue nitrile gloves. He was going through the man's pockets, finding nothing but a set of car keys and a fold of cash in his back pocket.

"Madeline said he had a phone."

Dominic said, almost to himself.

"He did, the man in the suit must have taken it."

Dominic frowned, sucking air over his teeth. He pulled up the green t-shirt to look at the wound. It was an impressive wound, separated wide at areas of elastic skin, his entrails and the pinkish-white of his ribs visible.

"Clean cut, probably three inches deep, from the waist line to the neck, right up the middle."

Since the shirt was cut from hem to collar, Dominic folded it back on either side of his chest. The large man was indeed large. It took dedication and repetitive lifting of heavy objects to produce a chest like that, for all the good it did him. He was well built in proportion to his chest, his face a simple oval with thin lips, a generic nose and unimpressive brow line. Other than his size, he could blend in almost anywhere those of Anglo-Saxon decent could be found.

"This gentleman is completely unremarkable."

Dominic said, turning one of the man's hands, then the other. He had thick calluses at the top of his palms, just at the base of fingers, except for the index fingers.

"Pull ups, free weights perhaps."

I picked up the set of car keys Dominic had taken off the body. One ring, a BMW smart key and a padlock key. Not a whole lot to go on. Dominic dug into the pocket of his vest, producing a thick but small device with what looked like a touch screen; a row of buttons below the screen for imputing commands. He turned the device on and once it booted up he selected a program. He grabbed one of the man's hands, pressing and rolling his fingers one at a time onto the screen.

"The latest in technology, Mister Winter."

I didn't say anything; I just let Dominic do his thing, searching the ground for shell casings. The man in the suit had fired at least twice but I could only find one casing. A single 9mm brass, the headstamp on the casing read *PMP 9mm P*. PMP was South African ammunition, not too popular with Americans because it was corrosive and Berdan primed, making reloading difficult. The primer was coated with a red lacquer to prevent oil or moisture from entering the casing, common on African and Eastern European ammo.

Dressed like a priest.

South African ammo.

A pistol with the blade of a knife welded beneath the frame.

Dominic came to his feet, having scanned all the man's prints.

"We can't sit on a dead body, I'm afraid. We should probably tell the locals about this. I'm quite surprised no one heard the shots."

I tossed Dominic the shell casing. He looked it over then dropped it on the ground.

"It was over there."

I said, pointing to a spot behind the body. Dominic frowned, kicking the shell casing close to where I found it.

"Anything else?"

He asked, glancing around the body.

"The runner left a trail of blood."

Dominic perked up.

"Where?"

He dug in his pockets, pulling out a yellow capped sterile tube used to collect blood evidence. He seemed happy he thought to bring it along. I gave him directions to the rear wall where the priest went over.

"I'm going to go see if I can get a sample of the blood then chat up the locals about this, I suggest you two make yourselves scarce."

Dominic pocketed his fingerprint scanner, unwrapped a new Tootsie Pop and headed for the back wall where the blood was, whistling *A Pirates Life for Me* as he went.

Madeleine finished her call, walking back to where I stood.

"Hijazi is going to point them to this body, we need to go."

She led the way without a word, I fell in beside her.

"Got away, did he?"

It sounded more like a playful jab than an accusation.

"Yeah, I don't think I've seen anyone run that fast outside of the Olympics. Did you get anything out of the dead guy?"

She scoffed.

"Yeah, he told me to go fuck myself then carked it. What about you?"

Cheeky girl.

"As unbelievable as it sounds, our runner was dressed as a priest."

She gave me a sideways glance.

"What!? Are you sure?"

"Well, yeah. He didn't have the white tab collar in, but he was definitely wearing the shirt and jacket."

She laughed, guiding us out of the container farm.

"That's ridiculous. Are you having me on?"

I laughed in spite of the situation.

"I wish I was. You think this is the same guy from your operation in Sudan?"

We reached the Tahoe. Dominic was headed in the other direction, a small group of FBI agents with him. He gave

Madeline and me a nod before passing. Madeline buttoned up the rear hatch before we climbed in. She started the engine but didn't put it in drive. Instead, she just sat and ran over things in her mind.

"I reckon it has to be. He used the same cute gun, didn't he? Pistol with a welded blade. I've been doing this for more than a while and I don't think I have ever seen anything like that."

"Ammo was South African."

I said, watching the docks.

"More coincidences then. No, somehow this is the same bloke. Jesus, this is going pear shaped straight away. Whoever this guy is, he's a smashing escape artist."

She smacked her hand against the dash, frustrated.

"We have prints on the dead man, provided they come back with anything, and we have the vague direction the hijackers went after they got what they came for. That was-"

She paused, looking at the Chase Durer UDT watch on her wrist.

"Almost eight hours ago. It's bloody likely that the package is on the mainland and on its way to wherever they want it, and the dead man's phone went with your murdering priest."

I thumbed the BMW keys out of my pocket.

"We have these."

I handed her the keys. She didn't bother looking at the BMW key fob, just the padlock key. It was for a generic Master Lock, shiny brass with not much use. Convinced it wouldn't tell her anything, she changed tactics.

"Fancy a scavenger hunt for the car?"

"Sure."

Madeline drove, I worked the key fob. We drove down the water front, passing close by any group of civilian vehicles. Nothing. We made it back out to the main access road, turning in and out of parking lots both purpose-built and impromptu dirt lots. Nothing. When we approached the main entrance, I had a thought. Economy of movement. Criminals favor convenience just like anyone.

"Turn around, head for the truck exit. This guy wouldn't have parked at the main entrance if he didn't come in that way; he would have wanted the car close to where he was." Madeline didn't argue with the logic. She flipped around, speeding back down the access road, headed for the CBP exit on Napoleon Avenue exit. She blipped her lights to get through the line of trucks waiting on the scales and X-ray lanes, turning out onto Napoleon. I had my window down, pressing the alarm button on the key fob. When we crossed the double set of freight tracks outside the gate I heard the faint beeping of a BMW's panic alarm.

"Over there, somewhere."

I said, pointing to a parking lot of a supermarket just across another pair of tracks off Napoleon Avenue. We homed in on the sound, a blue five series BMW with tinted windows and Mississippi plates parked between an ancient station wagon and a work van. I killed the beeping alarm, Madeline blocked the BMW in and we got out. I hit the unlock button and popped the trunk. The trunk lid opened easy on hydraulic arms, revealing nothing but gray carpet and an emergency roadside kit. I took the driver's side, Madeline the passenger. We started at the back seat and worked forward, overlapping in the middle as we tore the car apart. The car was sterile. Completely clean of any of the personal items you might expect to find. No drink cups, food or gum wrappers, not even so much as a crumbled receipt.

"Car is clean."

Madeline said, standing up from the passenger door. I stood by the driver's door, wiping the sweat from my head, thinking. I sat down in the driver's seat, inserted the key fob in the square ignition slot and turned it to the accessory setting. The car chimed on, the navigation screen mounted in the dash came to life. I played with the controls until I got the hang of them. Madeline climbed back into the car, watching me.

"Navigation history."

I said, selecting the last traveled route. The destination was the container terminal, the origin was somewhere without an address out on US Route 90, Chef Menteur Highway on Bayou Maria according to the map on the screen. I scrolled to the next trip. It was a residential address in Slidell, across Lake Pontchartrain from New Orleans. A house on Wyndemere Drive, tucked into a subdivision just off the Ten. The rest of the navigation history was blank. It looked as if the driver made a habit of deleting the history and just hadn't gotten to the last two trips. I checked the odometer; just over ten thousand miles and nothing in the car told me it was a rental.

"Well, that's something, I'll get these addresses to Gianna, see what they can do with them."

Madeline said, pulling out her phone.

"Fine by me. Where we going to first?"

She held off on dialing when she responded.

"The colonel is sending us help. I think we should wait until they get here before we do anything."

I wasn't thrilled with the idea of losing momentum. The thought of being close to Heller made the back of my neck hot. Tension snuck into my jaw, I had to fight the urge to not grind my teeth when she told me we would be waiting.

"Did you tell him about my theory?"

I asked, resigned to wait. Madeline cocked her head, poking a number into her phone.

"I called him after I dropped you off last night. He doesn't exactly agree with you, but he doesn't disagree either. Al Taybi was a simple fool in a third world country. Without Heller, there was little chance he would be able to organize an operation on US soil. The shell game with the container, professionals boarding the ship and stealing whatever was in it, our dead man and this car, that's way beyond a third world outfit."

History has shown us that complex operations can be planned by candlelight, in a cave or hut or tent, but planning and implementation are two different things. Terrorist organizations have proven that they can go low tech and produce results. This operation wasn't low tech. A ghost game designed to hide the container, then a professional boarding party to remove whatever was in it prior to the ship making port. A man posted at the terminal to watch the ship come in. And of course, one can't forget the wildcard; a gunman with unique weaponry and expert training in close quarters combat.

"So, the Colonel does think Heller is still behind it?"

She shrugged.

"He thinks the Corporation is. We know Heller is still out there, but there's nothing to suggest he's in the US."

"And nothing to suggest he isn't."

Madeline didn't respond to that. It was hard to argue my point and she knew it.

I left the key fob in the BMW but pocketed the padlock key, someone would find the car and get some use out of it. We got back in the Tahoe. Madeline made her call, speaking to whoever Gianna was. She gave her the GPS coordinates for both addresses and the Mississippi plates from the car and rung off.

"Where to now?"

I asked when she started the engine.

"The airport. Two of our men will be wheels down in an hour."

She turned the Tahoe around, headed for the street.

"What about Hijazi?"

Madeline chuckled.

"Dominic has his hands full taking the piss with the FBI."

"Wha?"

She shot me a smirk.

"Keeping the suits out of our way, that's what he does best. He will probably convince them to be on the lookout for a wooden legged Englishman dressed like Edward Teach, all the while feeding us information they turn up. If this is a Virtua operation, they have people in the government that will be pleased to see the official investigation going nowhere."

"While we work it from the outside?"

She shot me the smirk again.

"Only way to get results in this strange world, Mister Winter."

8

We made it to Louis Armstrong International Airport just in time to pick up two serious looking men from the curb. They were dressed to blend in, screen T's, cargo shorts, flip flops and baseball caps. I recognized both of them from my last visit with Colonel Solomon six months ago; Mr. Goatee and the computer geek that rode shotgun in Solomon's Tahoe. Madeline stopped in the second lane, the pickup lane was stacked full of cars, vans and cars. The two *tourists* tossed duffels in the back then climbed in. Maddy pulled away, headed for the Interstate. The two men settled in, both looking right at me. It was quiet. Madeline broke the silence before it became awkward.

"Warrant Officer Fred Tellison, Sergeant Tom Finn, meet Rushing Winter."

Mr. Goatee was unreadable, just a single bob of the head. Finn extended his hand. I shook it.

"Nice to see you guys again."

I decided diplomacy would be best if I was going to be working with these men. Not that I cared about their opinion of me, but I could live without alpha posturing for the duration. Finn smiled. Tellison was unmoved.

"Likewise. You did one hell of a job on that warehouse in Atlanta."

As if on cue I could feel my chest tighten around my wound. Not pain, just pressure.

"I did what was needed."

Finn's smile tipped up on one end.

"Don't we all. I hope you can handle team-based events as well."

He didn't have a problem with me being around.

"There's no *I* in *team,* right?"

I said. Tellison cleared his throat before he spoke, and not a word for me.

"Madeline, when are Card and Toomby do in?"

"Afternoon, earliest flight they could get."

Tellison accepted the news without comment. Finn leaned up between the seats.

"Who else do we have?"

"Porter and Hollic. They are half way across the pond right about now, due in at nine tonight."

"Hijazi here already?"

Tellison asked, tugging off his sunglasses. He carried bags under his eyes and looked like he had no idea what time it was, or day, month, maybe even the year. Solomon was pushing his people hard. Both men seemed to be no worse for the wear.

"He flew down from Atlanta as soon as news about the hijacking hit his desk."

Tellison rubbed his shaved head.

"Okay, that's good. What do we know?"

Madeline steered the Tahoe onto Airport Road, fighting the sluggish traffic to get ahead.

"Gianna and Dino are following up information we got from the docks, as soon as they have any new information we will do a full brief. Until then, I want to get you blokes a bed and a shower."

Tellison sneered, pulling back on his Oakleys.

"O'Neil, I have been in the air for three hours today, sixteen hours yesterday, and was sniffing around a dirt hut the day before that. I'm good. Give me a brief, now."

His tone was soft, direct and told me who was ultimately in charge when the Colonel wasn't around, and that was keeping with the command structure Solomon was used to as a Special Forces soldier. Solomon served as the commanding officer for his detachment (though well above the usual detachment commander rank of Captain), Tellison was second in command. I guessed that put Madeline and I at the bottom of the food chain. Madeline went into a full brief, covering the boarding of the Wayward Slip, the firefight with the crew, the drum of Arabic Gum that held a mystery cylinder, and then the man in the green t-shirt and the *priest*. She also told them about the BMW and the addresses I got out of the GPS history.

"Hijazi get anything on the prints?"
Tellison asked, referring to the green t-shirt man. Maddy shook her head.
"Not yet."
"Blood?"
Tellison asked. The priest's blood left on the wall.
"Nothing."
Tellison sighed.
"I guess I can't expect things to move as fast as I want. Where are we staying?"
"Bourbon street, right?"
Finn asked, rubbing his hands together in anticipation. Tellison shot him a sideways glance.
"I hope not. I would actually like to get some sleep when I get a chance. This isn't a vacation, Tom."
Finn put his hands up in surrender.
"Woah! It's cool. I know."
We made it to the Interstate despite the best attempts of slow cabs and wandering rental cars.
"No, Finn. We are staying at the Hilton. It's a bit of a hike from the French Quarter, I'm sure you can handle the walk if you get a chance…in one direction at least."
"Transportation?"
Tellison asked, changing the subject back to work. He seemed to have a one tracked mind.
"You are riding in it."
Madeline said, looking over her shoulder to the Warrant Officer.
"We can get rentals once we get to the hotel."
Tellison seemed okay with the idea.

"Fine. Tom, as soon as we get squared away, get over to Agent Hijazi. He has hardware for us."

I found Tellison interesting. He seemed to lack any overt signs of emotion. I imagined him to be in his late 30's, most of his adult life probably spent in the military. Despite that, his face lacked the hard definition one might expect from a senior Special Forces operator. He seemed to embody Zen, as most of the men cut from the same cloth did. Tellison was relaxed to a point where I thought he might actually be asleep behind his aggressive Oakleys. He wasn't. He was watching me.

Given my history, I'd be watching me too.

Sergeant Finn couldn't have been much over 25, and it showed. He was competent, I knew that from Atlanta, but he still had enough youth mentality in him to bother the senior men on his team. His black hair was long and unkempt, a scraggily beard adorned his face, colorful Koi fish sleeve tattoos ran from his wrists up under the arms of his short sleeve Deftones t-shirt. The last time I saw him he was clean cut, tattoos covered. Where ever he and Tellison came in from, clean cut wasn't much of an option. Neither was clean, they both smelled like wet straw and musty dirt. The hunt for the container must have taken them to some interesting places, places where running water was the closest creek and soap was a luxury.

Madeline put the Tahoe on the bottom floor of the hotel's parking garage, somehow managing to squeeze in to a spot between a concrete pillar and a Mercedes sedan. The width of the parking spot couldn't have been legal. New Orleans was a lot of things, parking friendly wasn't one of them. The garage would be better suited to park vehicles made prior to World War Two and even then, it would be close quarters. I managed to squeeze out of the narrow gap between the Tahoe and pillar, joining the others behind the SUV. Gear was collected from the back and we crossed the street to the hotel. Madeline handled the check in, I stood with Tellison and Finn in the lobby, waiting. Finn's head was on a swivel. He stared down every single person in the lobby and wasn't shy about it. It wasn't posturing or arrogance; instead it was simple professional interest. Tellison trusted Finn to monitor the lobby while he watched me, hands folded in front of him, eyes still tucked away behind his sunglasses. Maybe he was waiting for me to say something. I decided to humor him.

"We need to talk about something?"

Tellison stepped closer to me, close enough that only I could hear his words. His voice was clear and even.

"Be clear. This is my team, my operation. I have room for one civilian on my team, that slot belongs to O'Neil, so that leaves you as a tag along on a temporary basis I'm willing to tolerate because the Colonel thinks you can be of some help. You endanger my men or this operation-"

I cut him off before he made a threat he may not have been able to back up.

"Tellison, this may come as a shock to you, but I don't give a fuck what you think…"

In a situation where I once would have felt anger, I only felt indifference. Tellison was simply part of a problem that needed solving. I was here for one thing.

"I want Heller, that's the only reason I'm here. So, if you can point me to where he is, you can have this *operation* all to yourself and I'll be on my way. Short of that, I'll be around to fetch you coffee, maybe make a few McDonalds runs or iron creases in your pants while we look for whatever the hell it is we are looking for."

A ghost of a smile passed over Tellison's face.

"You got a dog in this fight, then."

I shrugged, walking away, headed for the gift shop to see about a bottle of water.

"Use whatever metaphor you want."

Tellison let me walk away without another word. Finn broke away from staring people down to speak with Tellison. Madeline was still occupied at the check in counter. I paid an outrageous price for a bottle of water, finishing it off in one pull while I leaned against the lobby wall, watching. I should have been willing to play nice with Tellison and the others. I wasn't. I was locked onto the idea of getting Heller. Nothing else mattered.

Madeline finished at the counter, handing keys to Tellison and Finn. They exchanged a few words then the two men headed for the elevators. I stayed put. Madeline walked over to me. Before she could say anything, her phone chirped. I got the international *wait a minute* sign while she answered. A short conversation, most of the talking done on the other end. She gave me a few glances before the conversation ended.

"Plates on the BMW."

Concern on her face.

"And...?"

I asked, listening for a faint drum roll or any reason for her reluctance.

"Gianna says it's registered to a dead man. An identity built around a birth certificate for a lad that died when he was a baby."

"Pretty standard for Virtua."

I said, remembering similar situations like this in the past. She was acting strange.

"Yes, it is..."

I came up off the wall, stepping closer to Madeline.

"What aren't you telling me?"

She hesitated before speaking again. I read concern and a hint of trepidation on her face. Her pulse was up. She soothed a dry mouth with a swallow before speaking.

"The car is registered to you. Rushing Winter."

9

Julian stopped running half way through the railhead. He ducked into the framework of a grain hopper that was just one in a long line of similar hoppers waiting on an engine to take them away. He compacted himself back into the cavity created by the inverted triangle shape of the car, sinking into the pale shadow. The pain in his arm demanded attention. The wound was bleeding again.

Pain was penance.

He accepted the pain, pushing it to the back of his mind, focusing on the man chasing him. He was fast...and agile, Julian would give him that much. He couldn't remember a time when he had seen someone move that fast. Julian had fired on him twice, with the intention of killing him. The man seemed to have predicted where the bullets would go and went the other way.

Impressive.

He was obviously a competent...well; Julian didn't know *what* he was. But he had almost been caught by the man. Almost been killed by him. Of course, Julian was a little out of practice, but it was all coming back to him. Whatever the man was, he was not a cop. There were plenty of them on the docks. This man wasn't one of them. He moved with an athletic grace and confidence that was unburdened by the trappings of American *due process.* Julian supposed he was a spook of some sort, maybe one of the CIA types. Not that it mattered in the end. All Julian was sure of was that this man had seen the same thing he did, the same person, and was just as interested in him as Julian was. Julian had first spotted his pursuer talking to some of the dock hands, only paying him idle attention at the time. Then he saw him speaking with the woman, a red haired bird who was attractive in a dangerous way. Later he watched him as he leaned against a police SUV, absorbing the crowd. He saw the man in the green-t-shirt. There had to be close to a hundred cops on the dock and only Julian and this enigma of a man had seen him. What caused Julian no small amount of anger was the fact that this bloke had spotted the man in the green t-shirt in a matter of a few minutes. It took Julian twice that time to pick him up. Julian accepted the situation for what it was; growing more complicated with each passing hour.

He waited, his heart rate abated, letting him listen for the crunch of feet on gravel. He heard nothing. His pursuer had given up. Julian was surprised, relieved. He eased his Browning High-Power back into its handmade holster under his jacket. It hung snuggly under his left arm. An identical holster sat empty under his right arm. He lost that pistol in Sudan. It was either leave the gun or have a run in with who he imagined to be Americans. Julian chose life. He was perfectly able in a fair fight. The bloody Americans never fought fair and at the time, he was a few seconds into being shot in the arm by some wanker with an Israeli machine pistol older than he was. So he went back out the way he came. He had what he needed. He overheard the entire conversation. He knew Heller would go to America, to New Orleans. None of that mattered at the time because Julian was convinced Heller would die in the next few seconds. He didn't.

Heller's men were professionals. They reacted fast, working a fighting retreat, buying Heller time to escape. His had missed his chance, now Julian was doing the next best thing to find him, going after whatever was in the container. It would lead him to Heller. Apparently these other people, the agile man and the woman, were after

139

Heller as well. Julian's advantage over the Americans had been hearing where the container would go and when it would get there. His head start was gone now.

Julian eased out of his hiding place, light headed. He had debrided, cleaned and stitched his own wound not long after he escaped the Janjaweed compound. The fact that he did it in the middle of the desert by weak moon light with dirty hands, a handmade needle and coat thread from his jacket was a recipe for infection. And an infection is what he got. A few more days to heal, maybe a few less drinks to put him to sleep at night and he would be as fit as a butchers dog. It would be like he was standing tall as a young, stiff lipped recruit in Aubagne, France, ready for the worst the Legion had to throw at him. They didn't disappoint. They showed him the best, and the worst that could be found in his soul. Or maybe he did that all on his own, they just provided the chance.

Julian made it out of the rail yard, getting his bearings, trying to remember where he parked. His lightheadedness was getting worse. He needed to eat. He had food in the car. If he could just find the damn thing. Julian made his way north on unfamiliar streets, averting his eyes and ignoring curious gazes from passersby. He still wore his suit. He had brought himself to removing the collar, it was stashed safely away in his breast pocket, but couldn't bear to take off the suit, no matter the undue attention it brought with it. He was doing God's work, and should be dressed appropriately. The suit was his armor.

He would find the blasted car. Then he would use the phone he took to find Heller. Maybe in so doing he would find peace. If he couldn't find peace, he would have to settle for revenge.
He muttered to himself as he walked.

"Lord, hear your servant. I ask only for the fortitude to carry your will, the insight to see your purpose, the strength to carry your vengeance through. Lord, I ask of you to help me remove from your world a daemon son and I give myself to you to do as you see fit as payment for the sins I have committed, and those I intend to commit."

10

Coincidence.

New Orleans. Me. Heller.

Madeline might as well have hit me in the face with a bat. The car was registered to me.

Imagine my surprise.

"I would ask if you were sure, but that would be an insult." Madeline gave me a sad look, said nothing. We got on the elevator. Once the doors closed and we started up, she asked a question. I could read concern on her face. Whether it was concern for me or for something else I didn't know.
"How in the hell would they know you were in New Orleans?"
I didn't say anything. I didn't have an answer. I was not going to start guessing just yet. She let the silence go for a few seconds before speaking again.
"I guess that removes any doubt about Heller being involved."
I gave her a raised eyebrow and an ironic smile.
"I never had any."
As is common with the human mind, tangents are often born with total disregard for more pressing issues. Instead of breeding thoughts designed to glean what Heller was planning by tying me to the BMW, the only question that came to mind was; *I have a birth certificate?*

My past before becoming one of *The Children* was like tuning an old radio, a ghost of fragmented sound that couldn't be reconciled. Just bits and pieces I couldn't quite remember the words to. Suddenly the elevator was much smaller than it should have been. My chest ached. I knew very little of my past before being kidnapped. For all of my adult life until that point, I was okay with that. Suddenly, I was not okay with it.

"Rushing, are you alright?"

Madeline asked as the doors parted on the fifth floor. I walked off into the hallway shaking my head. She followed right behind me, a reluctant hand to my shoulder. I spun on her, perhaps faster than I should have. She startled, just barely. I saw it all the same. I had that effect on people.

"Maddy, I need you to follow that trail back. I need a copy of the birth certificate."

She stared at me, a dozen questions flashed over her face. She didn't ask any of them.

"Okay, I will ring Gianna and have her track it down. She's working the information right now to see if it spiders into anything else, or just this car."

"As soon as she can."

I said, more aggressively than I should have. Madeline gave me a concerned nod.

"Sure, mate. Are you okay?"

I broke from her concerned stare, looking down the narrow hallway. I could see Finn standing near a door halfway down, smoking a cigarette. The room may have been non-smoking, but I knew the hallway was.

"I'm fine. It's just not every day you get a shot at finding out who you are, where you came from."

She sighed. An apology not needed on the tip of her tongue. I cut her off.

"Don't. Pepper and I tried to track down my birth certificate once. I knew Rushing Winter was my birth name. I was old enough when my mother abandoned me to remember that much. I was also pretty sure I knew where I was born. We found nothing. There aren't even any records with the state of Idaho of me ever having been in the foster care system. When Garitty took me, they were all erased."

My words were heavy on my heart. Heller was fucking with me. I had to give him credit, it was working.

Madeline risked grabbing my hand. I let her. She gave it a squeeze; just enough to let me know she was there for me then it was gone, back to her side, fidgeting with the corner of her slacks pocket.

I decided to avoid further conversation on the topic by walking down the hallway. Maddy stayed by the elevator, her phone back to her ear. Finn watched me approach, not once breaking eye contact or staring at a neutral space as people are prone to do. Some might call it arrogance; I like to think it was confidence.

"It's good to see you still breathing."

He said, ashing his cigarette in a disposable cup half full of water. I listened to the ash hiss as it was extinguished. He had changed into OD green cargo pants and a pair of desert tan boots. I saw the soft bulge of a sidearm under his Deftones shirt.

"I try."

Finn laughed.

"You are one strange dude, you know that?"

I gave Finn a pat on the shoulder as I passed by him, inviting myself into the room.

"I've been told."

It was a double. Two queen size beds, flat screen, a table not much larger than a trash can lid, two mass produced poster back chairs upholstered in a Fleur Di Lis pattern that matched the drapes and the bed spreads, and there was a door that led to an adjoining, identical and just as hideous room. Tellison was at the tiny table, eating an energy bar while he flipped through the complimentary visitor's guide.

Tellison had changed too. Utility pants, a button up shirt over his T, left open to access his weapon.

"You sleeping here?"

He asked without looking up, jaw working lazily over a mouth full of protein and carbs.

"Not really tired. When I am I'll probably go home and sleep in my own bed."

Maybe he had a sense of humor, maybe he didn't. Either way, he didn't respond or look up.

I went into the bathroom, taking a minute to collect my thoughts and wash my face.

Madeline was in the room when I came out. Tellison was into a second energy bar, almost done with the visitor's guide. Finn had finished his cigarette and was hooking his laptop up to the room's flat screen.

"Right then, Finn, Gianna is sending you everything she's got on the two addresses we have. She's also sending what the official investigation has turned up so far and what Hijazi got."

Finn nodded.

"Get your keys, Maddy? I need to go meet Dominic right now to get gear."

Madeline handed over the keys to the Tahoe.

"Off you go then, Finn."

Her words were playful. Finn pushed her out of the way with a smile.

"The rhyming…reeeeal cute."

"Hold on, Finn."

Tellison said, finally looking up.

"Rushing, go with him."

It sounded like an order. Part of me wanted to use Tellison to break the same window I would throw him out of. The other part of me realized that was just the way Tellison was. Cold. Monotone. His personality was direct. Conservative in speech was a good way to describe him. I

wanted to get my mind off of Heller. A drive with Finn
might help.

"I suppose I can do that."

I said, adjusting my bag on my shoulder. Finn seemed cool
with it, giving me a tap on his way by. Tellison gave me a
single bob of the head. Madeline offered a raised hand,
still unsure of my mood or my thoughts.

"Thank god. Even with GPS this city confuses the fuck out
of me."

Finn, on the other hand, was far more extroverted. Maybe
in ten years, Finn would be like Tellison. Maybe ten years
ago, Tellison was Finn. The life they lived did strange
things to people. I knew a little bit about that. I put my
thoughts of my birth certificate aside and followed Finn out
into the hall, heading down to the street to reach the Tahoe.

Finn fired up the Tahoe and backed out with a small squeal
of the tires. He slugged the gear selector down into drive
and tore out of the garage with more protesting rubber and
two trails of white smoke. He broke left at the exit, not
even stopping to watch for cross traffic. A few horns
blared, Finn flashed the blue lights on the Tahoe and gave a
quick succession of chirps from the Whelen siren box in
response. The V8 growled as we went up through the
gears. Dust and debris from the streets whirled in the air
behind us, usually undisturbed by vehicles moving past at
the posted 25 MPH speed limit. We were doing nearly
three times that before Finn let off the gas and found a
more sensible speed.

"Man, I fuckin' love these Tahoes. Sorry, dude. I had to
blow the carbon out of her."

"Crowded city streets are always the best place to do it. If
you want, I can give you directions to a few elementary
schools. There's a preschool not far from here too."

I said. Finn laughed.

"Maddy said you could be a bit of a wise ass. Me and you should get along just fine. Now, if you don't mind, tell me where the hell I am and how do I get to the Lakefront Airport?"

I looked for the closest cross street. We were in the congested Central Business District, passing side streets in a blur. I locked onto one ahead.

"Left on Julia, then left when we hit Saint Charles. Pick up the expressway then hit Ten east."

Finn followed my directions, driving like a cross between Mr. Magoo and Ken Block. He wasn't big on signaling lane changes or looking in his blind spots before doing it, didn't mind cutting off other cars and maintained a speed well above the posted limit like it was a mere suggestion. We made it up Interstate Ten, crossing the Industrial Canal then took the Downman Road exit. This surface street was home to strip malls, strip clubs, and stripped car bodies. Finn finally let off the gas, falling in with the natural flow of traffic.

"We almost there?"

I checked my surroundings, only somewhat familiar with the area.

"A few more miles, take a right on Stars and Stripes."

I spotted a driving school as we crossed Morrison Road. A sign in the window announced that a new class was starting on Saturday. I pointed it out to Finn.

"Fuck you."

He said with a smirk.

"I drive just fine."

I stared at him for a second.

"Do you even have a license?"

Finn shrugged.

"Used to."

Finn turned onto Stars and Stripes Boulevard, passing by the main entrance to the Lakefront Airport. Instead he turned into an empty parking lot, crossing it to reach a side entrance that led to one of the private aircraft tarmacs. The gate had no guard and appeared automated, a keypad was mounted on a post near the driver's side. Finn dialed out on his cell phone.

"Finn. I'm here."

Finn listened for a second then hung up. He reached through and punched a code into the keypad. The gate slid open gracefully. We pulled through, Finn guiding the Tahoe to a line of parked planes that ranged in price from a simple 1960's Beechcraft Musketeer to a factory new Cessna Citation CJ3. There were a few Pipers, Cessna props and even a P-51 Mustang on the line. Finn stopped the Tahoe close to the end in front of a sleek single engine jet prop, white with a thin blue ribbon running down each side. It looked new and expensive. I had no idea what it was. Dominic Hijazi came around the side, a white cloth in his hand, wiping down what appeared to be a carbon fiber fuselage. Dominic saw me sitting in the passenger seat, offering a sardonic smile. Finn left the engine running and hopped out. I joined him.

"Mister Winter."

Dominic said, draping his cloth over one of the blades on the five-blade prop.

"We meet again so soon."

Finn shook Hijazi's hand, ignoring his comments. He looked at the plane with a low whistle.

"What the hell is it?"

Dominic beamed like a proud father.

"This, Mister Finn, is an Extra EA Five Hundred. A masterpiece of German aeronautics, Extra specializes in acrobatic aircraft primarily; the Five hundred was their offering to the business class crowd, it's since been discontinued. I have logged eighty hours in her thus far, and don't think I will be looking for another plane for years to come. She's a dream to fly."

He sounded like a proud father.

"You buy this on a fed salary?"

I asked, looking over the plane. It was at least a six seater, high wing with a fluid and aerodynamic design a far cry from the stiff lined and stodgy aircraft sitting to either side of it.

"No, Mister Winter. I, as they say, *come from money*. This plane is a gift from my father, who is finally convinced I have turned my life around after disappointing him by not attending some Ivy League school and going into law as he did."

I was afraid to ask how much the plane cost. Dominic's father must have been pretty sure he had to drop what was easily in the high six figures, perhaps more.

Finn snapped his fingers impatiently, playing a tune.

"You wanna get this over with?"

Dominic nodded, leading us to the left side of the plane. He popped a recessed handle. The door split horizontally, half lifting up as a hatch, the other half folding down with a set of stairs. Inside the plane was carpeted with a rich burgundy color, accenting the dark cherry wood and tan leather seats. Directly in front of the door was a two by two stack of Pelican cases. What we came for.

Instead of helping us with the cases, Dominic went back to wiping down his plane.

"Do be quick about it, Sergeant Finn. Some of the locals are nervous enough having an Arabic looking man with his own plane loitering around. They see this, they're likely to call the police or just shoot us dead on the tarmac."

"Sure thing, Mustafa."

Finn said, tugging on the first container. He pulled it out far enough for me to get the back handle and we took it to the Tahoe, loading it on the rear bench seat. We made three more trips to load the others. Each weighted more than a hundred pounds. When we had them loaded, Dominic locked up his plane.

"Always a pleasure, gentlemen. I would risk a ride with you, Sergeant Finn, though I have my own car and value my life, so I will just meet you back at the hotel."

Finn didn't bite on the semi-playful insult.

"Suit yourself."

We loaded into the Tahoe. Finn spun around on the line, laying two black lines of rubber on his way back to the gate. Finn didn't seem to need directions back to the hotel, so there didn't seem to be much to talk about. I sat in the quiet with my thoughts. Thinking about Heller just made me angry, yet I couldn't help it. It was an anger that didn't burn away the heavy depression, it just made it buoyant, bringing angst to the surface. I thought about what Doctor Breaux had said.

Time and acceptance are the only cure.

I couldn't really get a firm grasp on the truth in his words. Intellectually, they made sense. Emotionally, I disagreed to the core without any control over the feeling. I seemed to have no say in the argument I was having with myself. I was effectively removed from the human condition.

"Madeline told me all about you."

Finn said, breaking the suffocating silence inside the SUV. I was glad for it.

"Really?"

Finn wagged his chin.

"More or less. I gotta say, when Solomon put her on the team, I didn't like it at all. I mean, she's a civilian. Sure, she did some time as a LEO, but her having worked for Virtua didn't sit well with anyone. None of us trusted her, despite the weight that the Colonel's word carries. Well, that lasted about three weeks. We put some work in with her over in, uh, let's just say she's earned our trust. Last six months, Maddy has been relentless. So, when she tells us about you, we listen up. The Colonel backed the idea and here we are."

Finn said a lot. He also didn't say anything at all.

"You have a point, Finn?"

He took his eyes off the road to look at me. He was driving like a normal person at the time so it didn't make me as nervous as it could.

"You gotta carry your own water in this unit. Solomon recruited me right after my Robin Sage. I literally went from Q course into the unit. Every other shooter on the team has years of operational experience. I had two combat deployments with a line unit when I showed up, which in their eyes meant I hadn't done shit. Took me a year to get some of these guys to feel I deserved to be here, some still don't."

I wasn't able to relate.

"Finn, you will have to forgive me for being crass, but I don't give a shit if I'm one of the boys. I'm not joining Solomon's unit. My interest is in Martin Heller. My loyalties are to Madeline. Me and Heller have a history."

Finn wasn't offended. He actually appeared to see where I was coming from.

"I can appreciate that, man. I'm just giving you a friendly warning. Tellison isn't happy about you being here."

I had a dry laugh.

"Finn, I feel like I have had this conversation before."

He didn't get it at first.

"Atlanta...yeah, I guess maybe you have."

Finn was there when the Colonel used me to get at Robert Wigglin. It didn't end the way the Colonel wanted it to. Not exactly, anyway. His demeanor seemed to change, as if remembering the conversation between me and Colonel Solomon changed his opinion of me.

"I guess you aren't interested in the bigger picture. I am. We are out here in the wilderness, man. Completely off the grid. We have been fighting non-stop since Air Force One went down, I mean, they *assassinated* a sitting President. I can say with no hyperbole that our way of life is at stake here and it sure as fuck seems like we are the only one's out here fighting the fight. The enemy isn't just some dirt farmer with a rusty AK and nothing better to do than sit around and hate America over Coca Cola and porn. The enemy is right here in America, born, bred and educated. The enemy is our own people."

Finn was passionate about what he did, what he was involved in. He was also worried. It was in his voice, subtle cracks hidden under the words. My focus on Heller was singular, narrow and maybe even selfish. I wanted revenge. Revenge as an ending.

Closure.

Nothing else mattered.

"You don't really care, do you?"

Finn asked. His voice was grave. I could have lied to him if I knew the truth.

"I don't know, Finn. That's an honest answer."

He accepted it as the truth.

"You should care. If we don't find a solution to this, we lose. If *we* lose, then your personal vendetta against Heller is going to seem childish in comparison."

The Sergeant was quiet again, but I could see thinking on his face. He spoke again after some time.

"Heller is the hand of Virtua, right?"

I had to nod in agreement. He may have had his own plans, but Virtua steered him to do work on their behalf.

"So?"

"*So* have you thought about why a man like Heller would risk coming back into the US? He's an international fugitive, which wasn't a big deal to the US until he killed some Marshals. Now he's on the mind of every federal agency in the law enforcement business. Heller has to know that. This isn't some jerkwater African nation, or some toothless European country that hardly bothers with keeping up with ICC warrants. This is *America*. Despite Virtua's influence, they can't keep Heller out of a body bag or a jail cell if he pops. So then you have to ask yourself, what is so important to Virtua that they would risk leaving it to a high profile dickhead like Heller?"

Finn had a point, one I had not considered. I wasn't on top of my game, that was for sure. I used to be more calculating, analytical. Now I was becoming reckless. Virtua was taking a serious risk leaving anything to Heller. Six months previous in Atlanta, Virtua had acted nearly as reckless in their pursuit of me. I discovered it was because my *Sister* was more or less in charge. At least that was what she had told me. The truth was somewhere mixed in with the lies…where it always was.

"I didn't think of that."

Was all I could think to say. Finn grinned.

"I am just guessing, but whatever Heller is doing, it's some sort of catalyst. Any one of a hundred things could have been in that container. Hell, dude, *everything* in Africa can kill you; the water, the grass, the insects, the politics…everything. I'm thinking biological. Africa was never able to scrape together enough cash, or had many nations that were stable enough to go nuclear. So that means chemical or biological. A bio weapon makes more sense. So then, what's the target?"

Sergeant Finn had undoubtedly put some thought into his theory. Everything he said sounded plausible, almost like he was speaking in hindsight. There was more to Finn than met the eye.

"What did you do before the Army, Finn?"

He didn't answer at first. Perhaps he was weighing how the information pertained to the conversation, or maybe if he was willing to part with personal information. He decided to tell me in the end.

"Me? Well, I was born Tom Finn. My mother read Mark Twain growing up and was both in love with Huckleberry Finn and had the fortune to carry the same last name. So she named me 'Tom' because Huck was based on a childhood friend of Twain's of the same name. I was off to a pretty eccentric start. Stranger than that, my mom moved us to Hannibal Missouri, which is a whole story in itself. I grew up waiting to be grown up, just to get away from home. When I finally did, I was putting myself through college delivering pizzas in Springfield. It wasn't college that gave me my future, it was delivering pizzas."

He took the inevitable pause people always do when they are leading up to something. When he spoke again there were memories in his voice.

"I killed my first man delivering a pizza. He tried to mug me; just popped out of the darkness like a bad movie scene. I was stupid and went for the gun. Ended up crushing his windpipe just trying to survive. I didn't feel anything. Nothing for him."

He paused, staring down before continuing.

"I realized then I had a gift. I dropped out of college the next week, was headed to basic training by the end of the month. I guess you could say I didn't do anything worth anything."

I could relate to that. I spent some time not doing anything worth anything, only it was for someone else and not my choice. Finn grew up an American. I grew up between the lines. *Patriotism* still seemed like a foreign concept to me. I hadn't even considered that fact that I was just as

American as Finn. I had as much to lose as he did if Virtua succeeded. I just didn't realize it because I spent most of my life not allowing the events in the world to effect how I saw it.

"Me either."
I said.
"What?"
Finn asked.
"I didn't do anything worth anything either. That changed when I met Madeline. She introduced me to Pepper, I guess you could say. Pepper showed me life. Then she died, much too soon. Heller shares some responsibility in that."
Finn was empathetic at my tone, my words.
"Who was she?"
I guess Madeline hadn't told him everything. I considered the question, careful to answer it correctly.
"She was everything."

11

Finn left me alone for the rest of the drive. I didn't complain about the solitude, lost in my own thoughts as I was. When we returned to the hotel, everyone that was coming had arrived. Madeline met us at the door, introducing me to Tony Card and William Toomby. The former struck me as a jam band following backpacker that probably didn't own more than a Bonsai tree and a yoga mat to put it on, the latter was a salty slab of a man with a permanent sneer who moved around the hotel room like he was looking for the source of a bad smell. Besides Tellison, Dominic was in the room, lounging on one of the beds flipping through the channels with the TV on mute. I wanted to know how in the hell he beat us there. Tellison was all business.

"Sergeant, we have all our gear?"

Finn nodded.

"In Madeline's Tahoe."

"Good. We brief and then roll as soon as we pick up Porter and Hollic. They can be briefed on the way. I spoke to the Colonel while you two were gone."

He looked at me and Finn.

"He wants us to hit both addresses at once. If there is any chance that the item in the container is on land, we want to maximize our chances for getting it while it's still in Louisiana. Dominic, if you don't mind, will you cover your information?"

Hijazi nodded absently, engrossed in the muted QVC channel. Tellison went right back to it, grabbing the remote to switch the TV over to its auxiliary setting then went to fat fingering keys on Finn's laptop to bring up a satellite photo of a house with identical houses on either side, tucked into a subdivision.

"Alright, listen up."

Everyone in the room except for Hijazi, who was disappointed to have Tellison switch the TV over to display the computer screen, gathered around to watch. Hijazi already had the best seat in the room.

"This is the Slidell address, not much to see. A three-bedroom single story with a decent sized yard, two car garage and neighbors too close for comfort. We don't have time to collect specific intel on the ground and don't know the floor plan. Gianna is trying to get time on a satellite, but I wouldn't hold your breath. We are going to have to go in blind. Property records on the house show it as a rental, one of those app properties you can rent on your phone."

Someone with enough money to have a second home or someone who traveled a lot could simply offer their home to a complete stranger for as long as they liked for a fee, and that person could rent the property using a phone app. What a time to be alive.

"The neighbors are all taxpaying citizens, nothing outstanding. As for the other location, the best we have is a set of GPS coordinates. It looks like nothing more than a lot at the end of a dirt road according to Google Earth, which is as good as we are going to get. We will run on that address blind as well. Gianna tried to pull an owner, it looks like the property was more or less abandoned after Hurricane Katrina and has been for sale ever since. Its previous life was as a decent sized home and a single slip boat dock. There isn't much left standing now. The closest occupied residence is at least a mile in either direction. Traffic on Ninety is usually light."

Tellison looked over those in the room as if trying to make a decision.

"Sergeant Card, you will lead the team on the house. Toomby, you will go with him. Porter and Hollic will join you once they get on the ground. Hollic has rank, but Card, it's your show. I'll lead the second team on the highway address with Maddy, Rushing and Finn."

Tellison looked at Dominic, who looked right back at him like he was crazy.

"Oh no, Mister Tellison, I will not be going with you. It is hard enough for me to maintain a cover with the JTTF without being party to the situations you get into."

Tellison simply shrugged at Agent Hijazi's refusal, moving on without further discussion.

"Agent Hijazi, please tell us what you learned."

Dominic moved off the bed, taking a flash drive from his pocket which he plugged into the laptop. He opened a series of files off the drive, pulling the first one up onto the screen. The photo was of a man not long out of his teens, maybe still in them, wearing a Navy Service White uniform, an American flag in the background, it was a posed photo.

"Meet former Navy Petty Officer First Class, Ron Stillwithe. Stillwithe served eight years in the Navy. For five of those years, Stillwithe was a Special Warfare Combatant-Craft Crewmen with Special Boat Team Twenty Two. SBT Twenty Two is based in Mississippi and specializes in Riverine Warfare. As a Swick, Stillwithe was trained in a number of skills that made him quite competent as an assault craft crewmen with specific focus on inland waterways. Stillwithe cross trained extensively with Navy SEALS, as well as other maritime SOF units. Two years ago, Stillwithe was court marshaled along with another Swick named Alavoza, both charged under Article Ninety of the UCMJ. They were convicted, did a year each in the Navy Consolidated Brig, Charleston and were then dishonorably discharged. Stillwithe is our body from the ship. I suspect Alavoza was on board with him as employment opportunities for men like this with their skills are few with dishonorable discharges on their record."

I seemed to be the only person in the room that didn't know what an Article 90 was. Dominic brought up a second picture, this one of a Latino man in the enlisted whites, narrow eyes, narrow nose, a strong jaw and dark skin. "This is Petty Officer Second Class Alavoza. Last known residence was Charleston, last employment was as a deck hand on a tour boat. The FBI is currently trying to track him down. As for Stillwithe, his last known residence and employment is the same as Alavoza's, adding further credence to believing he was part of the boarding party. Nothing incredibly remarkable or suspicious about either man, which is to say, they still exist in every database they were ever entered into. More than I can say for this guy-" Dominic pulled up a photo of the man in the green t-shirt from the shipping terminal. He was very dead in the photo, it looked to be taken hours after his death. If it were possible, he looked even more unremarkable as a deceased man.

"We know exactly *nothing* about him. He is not in a single system accessible to the Department of Justice, which is a nearly exhaustive list. The FBI will run his DNA, which will take time. I imagine we won't find out who he is that way, either."

Agent Hijazi closed out the three photos.

"The blood from the wall is not very exciting. It's A Positive and contains antibodies consistent with someone who had yellow fever in the recent past, a nasty strain found in Sub Saharan Africa."

Dominic gave a knowing look to everyone in the room but me.

"So, and I don't think this is a great stretch of the imagination, I surmise that the gentleman who killed our friend in the green t-shirt also spent some time in Africa in the recent past. Perhaps you have already met him."

Tellison cleared his throat. Dominic's tone was bordering on sarcastic and it appeared to be bothering him.

"Anything else, Hijazi?"

Dominic didn't bite on Tellison's condescending tenor.

"Not much, really. The weapons and gear we removed from Stillwithe's body were dead ends, as was the clothing from Mister green t shirt. The FBI does not know about the BMW that Mister green t shirt drove to the terminal, however they may eventually discover it and connect it to him. That is, of course, unless you would like to go blow it up…"

There was no love lost between Hijazi and Tellison.

"That will do, Agent Hijazi."

Dominic wasn't bothered either way. He plopped back down on the bed, remote in hand until he realized the TV was still in use by Tellison. He tossed the remote, pulling out his phone to play a game. Tellison ignored him.

"Whether this is the same guy from Darfur or not, doesn't make a difference. We have a few hours lead on the FBI at best and we can't afford to let them bury this. We proceed."

Tellison looked to Sergeant Card and Madeline.

"Recommendations?"

Card shook his head.

"I'm cool."

Maddy did the same.

"All right here, Tellison."

Tellison closed the screen on Finn's laptop.

"Pack it up then."

He said, looking at his watch.

"We roll in ten."

There was a mild flurry of activity, all except for me and Dominic. Hijazi wasn't going, and I didn't need to change, I just waited while everyone else changed. Dark colors, no uniformity in their attire besides dark shades. Eight minutes later, we were in the lobby headed to the parking garage. The last flight in, Porter and Hollic, would be on

162

the ground in 45 minutes. I didn't even know the guys and I felt for them. They would get off an international flight, receive an incomplete brief based on spotty information and be expected to go right to work. For most of these men, and Madeline, that was probably normal. I guess it was for me too, in a way.

Card and Toomby had rented a car, a big body Nissan SUV in a conservative shade of green. Madeline got her keys from Finn, unlocking the Tahoe. Finn opened the rear door, tugging out one of the hard side containers, I helped him set it on the ground.
"Did we get four-man packs?"
Tellison asked.
"Looks like it."
Finn said, entering a four-digit code into the container's cipher lock. It clicked, there was a small hiss of air then it beeped. Finn glanced around the garage to make sure there were no bystanders watching out of curiosity. He opened the lid with some effort. The container held four handguns; Smith and Wesson Military and Police model 9mms, secured to the underside of the lid. Laid long ways were four FN M4s with 12-inch uppers. Each weapon had a Surefire Socom II suppressor fitted to the muzzle device. They were more submachine gun than assault rifle in appearance, at least as far as length was concerned, having the maneuverability of a sub gun with the lethality of a rifle chambered in 5.56mm. The detachable carry handles had been removed, replaced with Aimpoint Micro red dot optics. Finn pulled one of the weapons out, working the bolt to check its functionality.
"Looks like we are good...how long were these in storage?"
Tellison took the rifle from Finn, setting in back in the box then closed the lid. He was in a hurry.
"A few months. Load these into your vehicle."

Tellison said to Card. The Sergeant nodded, opening the hatch on his rental. Card and Finn lifted the box into the back, Maddy and I joined in, helping transfer all four boxes from the rear bench seat of the Tahoe to the back cargo area of the Nissan. Now we could ride in the back seat of the Tahoe.

"Card, Toomby, follow us to the airport. Once we pick up Porter and Hollic we will find a spot to stage and gear up. Let's move."

Madeline, thankfully, took the wheel. Tellison rode in back with me. Finn was in the front passenger seat running the computer. When we pulled out of the parking garage, Agent Hijazi was across the street, leaning against the wall with one foot up, eating Milk Duds by tossing them in the air and catching them in his mouth. He gave us a hearty wave as the two SUV convoy went by. I wondered if maybe sitting it out alongside him might not have been a bad idea.

Madeline navigated without any help from me, I was happy for it. I sat in the back next to Tellison. He didn't talk, I didn't want to, it worked out pretty well that way. I just thought. I moved to New Orleans to heal. I came to New Orleans because I knew Virtua would come and when they did, I wanted it to be on unfamiliar ground for them.

Well, they did.

Only it wasn't how I envisioned it. I expected more of the same, some sort of organized overkill in silver Audi's. Men dressed in next generation combat suits, hell, maybe even a guided missile strike on my house. Instead, it looked like I was being set up to take the fall for something. Something to do with whatever they brought in on the container ship. I expected Heller. There was little doubt he would want to get even with me after basically handing him over to the police. He might even be a little upset about his entire operation in Atlanta being destroyed. If he was anything like he seemed, every bit a sociopath, then there was no way he wouldn't come for me. I had counted on it, waited for it. As usual, it was not going to be simple. If I didn't know better, I would be inclined to think that they knew I was in New Orleans the whole time.

Perhaps they did. When I found Heller I would have to ask him.

The airport was the same as before. We pulled in, two men, one exceedingly large dressed like he was headed to the gym, the other a light skinned black man one genetic roll of the dice away from a professional running back were waiting at the curb. Light baggage, impatient and tired faces. I didn't get a chance to meet either of them, they jumped into the Nissan behind us and we pulled out of the airport. We moved back into the city, Finn and Madeline up front having a friendly argument over American versus English cuisine. Tellison spoke for the first time since we left the hotel.
"Where can we stage?"
He was talking to me. I thought about it, trying to think about a secluded spot close to the Interstate and Chef Menteur Highway.
"Take the Almonaster exit, follow it, you'll know it when you see it."
Maddy followed my directions when we came upon the exit. We passed through a semi-industrial, semi-commercial area that still hadn't quite recovered from the hurricane all these years later. The road was in grave disrepair, barely pavement anymore. Street lights once lit served only as *somewhat* vertical silhouettes in the darkness. The sidewalks had lost their way, straying in broken ribbons into the road as if the earth beneath them

had changed positions. Passing under Alvar Street, the night became total. Not long ago the road would have ended there. Katrina had leveled everything within two hundred yards of the Industrial Canal on either side. Whole slabs of roadway and entire buildings pulled out into the water with the storm surge. The Almonaster Avenue Bridge over the canal sat for years unused by vehicle traffic. Only recently repaired, the road leading to the bridge was in better condition than that west of Alvar Street.

New pavement was about all that had returned though. Aside from a construction firm with a barge dock, there was little along this portion of the canal. Surely no one with honest intentions was out at that hour along the water. We pulled off the road, sliding behind an old rail box car that was probably left over from the hurricane. It was settling in and I didn't think it was high on anyone's list for removal. Madeline killed the lights, the Armada behind us did the same. Doors opened and closed softly. Everyone gathered around the back of the Tahoe, the four cases were laid out and opened up. Two contained weapons, the other two were loaded with body armor and other equipment. I watched Madeline release the cummerbund on hers; she slipped it over her head, fastened the cummerbund then took her 1911 off her hip, sliding it into a Safariland holster mounted on the chest of her plate carrier above a double row of magazine pouches. She then took an M4 from one of the weapons cases, tossing it to me before she took her own.
"You remember how to use one of those?"
I felt over the familiar weapon. Collapsible six position stock, red dot, flip up iron sights if I needed them, two-point sling, select fire from semi-auto to full, five pound two stage trigger, Surefire Scout with pressure pad and a BE Meyers MAWL IR laser for use with night vision.

Yeah. I didn't have much time working with IR lasers or night vision, not nearly as much as those around me, but it wouldn't be my first day, either.

"I think I can manage."

I saw her grin in the dim light, filling her plate carrier with magazines from the bottom of the weapons case.

Tellison handed me one of the plate carriers, I set the rifle down, using the same technique to put it on that Maddy did. Two flaps in the front, secured by hook and loop pulled upward, the cummerbund secured underneath, then the flaps were folded back down. It really was only a plate carrier that also offered side protection under the arms, not as large or cumbersome as other armor I had seen and even worn in the past. The MOLLE real estate was limited to slightly more than the 12x14 inch level IV Polyethylene plates and that on the six-by-six-inch level IV plates under the arms. The carrier had four magazine pouches attached over the abdomen, four pistol magazine pouches on top of these, all empty. I slung the rifle, digging in a weapons case for rifle magazines. I found four, topped off my pouches then dug into my own backpack, putting the four spare 1911 magazines I had into the pistol pouches. When I was done I had added more than a few pounds to my torso. I loaded my M4, chambered the first round turned to the others who were just about done prepping their gear. Madeline helped me with the radio attached to the back, checking to make sure it had a fresh charge and was on the correct channel. Then she handed me a light Kevlar helmet with attached head set that went with the radios, a Peltor Comtac that served as ear protection, sound amplification and communications all in one package. The helmet was a high gunfighter cut, night vision shroud and arm already attached up front. Madeline handed me a set of PVS-31s to clip in when I needed them, giving me a super fast crash course on how to run them.

"You good, Rushing?"

Madeline asked, bumping me gently. Her tone was one of concern.

"I'm fine."

I wasn't. The more I thought about Heller the angrier I became. She must have been able to see it, but she didn't push.

"Right then."

She had more to say, Tellison spoke up before she could. "Alright, stow these boxes. Card, Toomby, brief Porter and Hollic on the way. Card, Gianna will be on for support, call her as soon as you hit the road. I want you to stand by until we get in position on our location, we will hit them at the same time. The Colonel wants as many live bodies as we can get but don't let that stop you from ghosting anyone who shows the least resistance. Our package is an unknown object that is highly portable and should be considered priority over everything else. The FBI isn't very far behind us on the intel, maybe a few hours, so we need to be dynamic. I don't want us on site over fifteen minutes on either location. The primary fallback point will be right here; secondary will be the south entrance of the Metairie Cemetery. The go code is 'Redundant,' abort code is 'Columbus.' Everyone frosty? Good, mount up."

No conversation, questions or clarification, just eight armed individuals loading into two vehicles heading for potential firefights. The seven of them were well used to this, having worked together more times than I knew. I was just along for the ride. There was a time when I wouldn't have given it a second thought. Now, I had a foreboding feeling that we were either moving into a trap, or the situation was far more complex than anyone imagined.

I clutched Pepper's St. Jude necklace around my neck as Madeline steered us towards US Highway 90, thinking only of Martin Heller and what he really knew about me, where I came from and just how deep the rabbit hole was.

12

Slidell was a major New Orleans Suburb situated across Lake Pontchartrain from the city proper. Founded in 1883, chartered in 1888, fed by the river, brick, lumber and space industries, Slidell had little of the *Laissez Faire* attitude of the bigger city across the lake. Slidell left the parties and parades mostly to New Orleans, preferring a quieter life in trade. The predominantly middle-class population was reflected in the neighborhoods and streets. Respectable brick and vinyl sided homes, fresh store front facades, green lawns and well-lit streets. Card liked Slidell. It reminded him of parts of Portland. He didn't like that dangerous men were nestled into a neighborhood here, risking the lives of innocents around them. That wasn't cool.

Toomby lost a coin toss on the flight into New Orleans, which meant he had to drive. Even after insisting a new coin toss was in order when Porter and Hollic arrived, Card was adamant that he honor his loss and drive, he mumbled obscenities but drove anyway. Card thought about Rushing on the drive. He had heard about him from Madeline and had heard him mentioned by the Colonel not too long ago. Madeline had described him as '*A solid, dependable shooter, more dangerous than anyone I have ever met.*' Sergeant Card didn't know how to take her words. They were delivered with what Card felt was reverence, perhaps complimenting, but it was a tall statement. *Dangerous* to Card meant *unpredictable*. There was something about the man that made Card uneasy. Tony was no stranger to dangerous men. He sat within arm's reach of two of them. Hollic on the other hand, was a combat virgin as far as Card knew, which made him just as unpredictable as Rushing could turn out to be. Rushing was a different kind of dangerous. He had a sharp sadness in his eyes.

And death.

Tony knew what the wish for revenge looked like. Rushing Winter personified it. There was an ambiguity to that man, like he existed somewhere Card didn't. Card had read his face, his scars, his dedication to physical ability and his calm. His calm bothered Card the most. Grenades were calm too, until you pulled the pin. Part of Card was glad Rushing went with Tellison; another part wished he was going with Card.

"This our exit?"
Card looked up at the approaching exit, then at the GPS. "Yeah."
Toomby nodded in the ambient light, steering the Nissan into the exit lane. Card used his fingers on the GPS's touch screen to zoom in on the surface streets off the interstate. Little pop up icons shaped like gas pumps, dinner plates with silverware or shopping bags told him where the major businesses were. Card's watch told him which ones were likely to be closed. He double tapped a food icon. Tellison and the others had a much farther drive, Card figured it wouldn't hurt to get some food while they waited.
"Anyone else hungry?"
He asked. An affirmative from everyone. Hollic actually used the word *affirmative.*
"Burgers and fries it is. Only thing open within a mile."
No one complained. You eat what you can, when you can and pay for it later.

Toomby parked the SUV in one of the stalls, he seemed confused by the carhop theme of the restaurant. A bored looking teenage girl coasted over on skates, tapping on his window. He rolled it down. She gave a plastic smile and asked for orders. Everyone rattled off requests for food that would be quick to eat and had the least number of excess calories. Card was mildly surprised she didn't comment on all four men wearing body armor adorned with magazines and handguns. Each plate carrier was marked US MARSHAL by an olive drab green panel with black lettering. Sergeant Card imagined she had peered into vehicles to take orders and seen worse.

They received their orders, Card paid cash. Toomby backed out of the stall into one of the parking spots close to the street. All four men watched traffic while they ate. When they finished, Toomby rolled out of the lot, driving the short distance to a right turn onto Bridge Water Drive. A squat stone frame around an artistic plate announced they were entering Berkley Estates. The drive was narrow, manicured grass and fresh fences on either side. The street ran on into a T intersection, all the homes Card could see were new, well maintained and stereotypical in their suburban appearance; landscaped shrubbery, basketball hoops off the sidewalk or hung above the garage, two stories, one stories, well positioned fire hydrants and well-lit sidewalks.
"Not ideal for us."
Porter said from the back.
"No, it isn't."
Card said. Toomby turned left, he could have turned right. Meadow Lake Drive encircled a large portion of the subdivision. The target house was on Wyndemere, more or less half way between the entrance and where Meadow Lake met itself in the back.
"I bet we can get one or two roll bys before someone calls the cops."
Toomby said, watching an older lady walk a trio of nervous terriers. She stared at the SUV as they passed, suspicion written all over her face.
"Probably right."

Card said, watching for the turn. It approached; Toomby guided the SUV onto Wyndemere, slowing to almost an idle. The address they were looking for was dead middle of the street on the right; a smaller single story with a two-ish car garage splitting the tiny lawn, a palm tree sprouting from the ground on either side. The front door was set to the left of the garage under the awning coming off the pitched roof, a curving flag stone path leading from the concrete to the single step to the door. Tall cascade style double hung windows were to the left of the door, partially obscured by shrubbery and a palm meadow plant, semi-transparent curtains drawn closed inside. Wood plank fences ran off either side of the house, connecting with the neighbors to the left and right, a gate to the back yard was set on the right. The driveway was empty. There was a light on inside, dim and somehow low to the floor, not quite filling the tops of the windows with illumination. The neighbors were home, a work truck in one driveway, a minivan in the other. The lights inside extinguished except for the blue glow of a TV from the house on the left.

Toomby drove passed the house without comment, turning onto Meadow Lake. He went up one street and turned right, checking the approach from the back. The house directly behind the Wyndemere house was live with activity, some sort of party. Guests milled around inside an open garage, cars lined the street, more party goers on the sidewalk, sitting and leaning on cars. Approaching from the back would be out.
"Jesus Christ, we are going to have to park in the damn driveway."
Toomby said, heading out of the neighborhood. He pulled the Nissan into a semi-deserted strip mall parking lot a quarter mile away to wait.
"Recommendations on entry?"

Card asked, absently checking the condition of his M4. It felt light and fragile compared to the bolt guns he was used to humping.

"Not knowing the floor plan, I'd say front door. With the door next to the garage we are looking at a corner-fed room, probably right into the living room. That's where the light is. I can probably slip the lock, we go in stealth to contact. No good walking in, have to park short."

Porter said from the back. Sergeant First Class Andrew Porter was a certified master breacher, certified by more than one authority to carry the title, including the US Army, US Navy, Israeli Defense Forces and many private schools including TEES. Porter had mastered every technique for both dynamic and surreptitious entry, Card knew his favorite was an unlocked door, closely followed by a shape charge cut through an exterior wall. If Porter wanted to pick the lock and go soft, Card was not going to argue.

"What do you think, sir?"

Card asked Hollic. Danny Hollic was the ranking person on their stick, a newly promoted W2. That meant normally he would be in charge, but Chief Tellison had given Card operational control. But Hollic was not SF, he was a 351Lima, Counterintelligence. Prior to going Warrant, Hollic had been a Counterintel Special Agent, one of two *gold badge* agencies in the Army. Hollic specialized in human intelligence and espionage investigations. Not much of an operational resume compared to the others. Even Hollic knew that he was only being asked his opinion out of politeness. He had been extensively trained by Solomon's unit in small unit tactics, mostly by Porter and Sergeant Bosmino, but that was a few months training experience against the wealth of real world experience in the vehicle with him. Ironically, Hollic was the best pistol shooter in the unit, by a matter of fractions of a second, though he had yet to fire on a live target.

"I appreciate the consideration, Sergeant Card. I will defer to you on this."

Card nodded.

"Alright, sir. Porter, take point, Ill fall in second, Toomby then you."

'Fine."

Hollic said, slightly nervous with the very real prospect of shooting in his near future.

The night wore past the top of the clock into early morning before the call came over the radio.

"Redundant, Redundant, Redundant…Good hunting."

Tellison's voice was ice as usual. Sergeant Toomby pulled out of the lot, accelerating quickly for the turn. The tires squealed faintly as he powered down the straightaway, the veered left so he could approach from the garage side of the house. They gained speed on the straightaway before their last turn. There was no clack chambering rounds or clatter of magazines being loaded. Everyone was ready, hands where on door handles, thumbs riding on safeties, ready to flip weapons to fire. Toomby killed the lights around the last turn, hopped two tires onto the sidewalk and coasted to a stop just out of view of the front windows of the house. Doors opened quietly, closed quietly. The four men fell into a greased stack, going to the garage side of the house to avoid the front windows, pinning close to the wall. Heel to toe, fast and quiet. Toomby reached up and yanked the power line for the garage flood light, leaving them in darkness. They snaked to the door. Card kept his weapon on the door while Porter worked a composite plastic lock pick gun on the dead bolt, Toomby covered the windows. The composite gun was not nearly as durable as the metal alternative, though it was nearly silent, its silence was mostly not needed. The pounding bass from the party behind the house was masking their sounds perfectly. Five seconds and Porter signaled with his hand he had the lock open. He took another five to unlock the door handle. He waited for the squeeze up before initiating entry. Hollic gave a gentle squeeze to Toomby's thigh, the signal was passed forward. As soon as Card touched Porter he pushed the door open silently, his weapon coming up to confront any threat he saw going in. Card watched his shoulders, when his left dipped, Card knew he was going straight in. The four men pushed into the living room, no more than six feet into the room forming an arc from the right wall to the exterior wall.

The living room was basic furniture liked you'd see in a furniture store display, the only lamp in the room lay against the back of the couch, it had fallen over. The reason it fell over was evident; a body lay half hidden by the couch, the legs most likely laying across the lamp. Blood had long since soaked into the vanilla carpet around the head of the body.

"Hallway front, no angle on the kitchen."
Porter whispered. Card weighed the options three dimensionally, a decision in less than a second.
"Porter, me, kitchen. Toomby, Hollic, hallway."
Card said. The four split into two. Card slipped behind Toomby and Hollic, stacking close on Porter as he sliced the angle to the kitchen partially obscured by an interior wall, he kept a weapon on the body until the passed it even though he was pretty sure the man wasn't going to be a threat to anyone. Toomby moved into the dark hallway, stopping at the first closed door before he fell out of Card's peripheral as they crept into the kitchen. The other side of the interior wall held the stove and a section of the wrap around counter. A second body lay crumpled in the corner near the stove; the cause of death was evident, two gunshot wounds to the face, the man's nose was split in the middle by the figure eight pair.

"Clear."

Porter said. They backed out. Porter provided cover while Card checked the first body. No pulse, a close-range gunshot wound to the back had blown a sizeable hole in his shirt, the edges of the hole were frayed and burnt. Just under the dime sized entry hole was a horizontal stab wound, perfectly in line with the bullet wound, just right of the spine. Card shook his head *dead.*

They pushed into the hallway. One door on the right, into the garage, two doors deep past the kitchen, one at the end of the hall; the garage door was open, so was the first door on the left. Porter flashed the garage door twice with quick bursts from his weapon light, letting Toomby and Hollic know they were coming if they were in there. They pushed passed the garage, Porter flashed the door on the left just as Toomby appeared. He nodded, hooked into the hallway and stacked on the second left side door with Hollic right on top of him. Porter pushed past him, going to the last closed door at the end of the hall. Porter and Toomby made entry at the exact same time, going soft.

The room at the end of the hall was the master bedroom. Drapes at the back of the room to the right of an air mattress fluttered in the wind, a sliding glass door, the glass was gone from the frame. Card peeled to the right, Porter skirted the wall.

"Closet, bathroom."

Card said. Porter covered him while he pulled open the bathroom door. Clear. He backed out to the closet door, a large walk in, also clear. Two flashes of light from the hallway just before Toomby and Hollic filed in.

"House is clear."

Toomby said, disappointed.

"We got a body in the garage, GSW to the head."

Card shook his head.

"Another one in the kitchen."

"Back yard."

Porter said, leading the four men through the sliding glass door frame. The yard was small, filled with nothing but lonely grass. They stood in the darkness, letting their weapons hang on slings, catching their breath, wiping away sweat in the abhorrent night heat.

"Look at that."

Toomby said, pointing to the ground next to the sliding glass door. On the grass was the pane of glass from the frame, shattered, held together by top to bottom and side to side strips of duct tape. Whoever came in through the door had taped the glass before breaking it, then simply laid it aside like a stiff blanket. It would have been a quiet entry, quick if the shooter knew what they were doing.

"Anyone else have that feeling?"

Porter asked, looking at the sheet of spidered glass. He could see the break point, a small impact in the lower right corner, probably a spring-loaded glass breaker.

"Yeah,"

Toomby said.

"I woulda' done the same thing."

Card sighed.

"Secondary on the house, let's see if there's any intel here."
The four men moved back inside. Hollic headed directly for the garage.

"Computers in the garage."

He said. Card motioned behind him to Porter.

"Go with him, will you? Ill toss the bed room."

Porter followed Hollic out. Card and Toomby slung their rifles onto their backs and went to work on the bedroom, gingerly searching the mattress, the few boxes in the closet and the single dresser in the room. They found nothing but clothes and a large stash of Pop Tarts and energy drinks.

"Check the bodies?"

Toomby asked.

"Might as well."

They passed the garage. Card took the first body in the living room, Porter went into the kitchen. Card pulled a passport and a set of car keys from the man's pocket. A holster on his hip was empty, so was a cell phone pouch. Card was tempted to roll him over. He resisted the urge, it was a crime scene and since they weren't going to cover it up, it was best to disturb it as little as possible. Sergeant Porter walked out of the kitchen carrying a wallet.

"Holster with no gun, no phone, no keys."

Card held up the keys and wallet.

"Plus one, for a Ford, an older one."

The key ring was three keys; two for the ignition, simple metal keys without the plastic coating or key fobs that came about after this vehicle was show room new. The other key was smaller, like a padlock key. Identifying markings had been filed off it.

Toomby poked his head around the corner.

"We got a locked van in the garage."

Card tossed him the keys.

"Try those."

With no reason to stay in the living room, Porter followed Toomby back into the garage. Card looked over the body at his feet. He didn't know the man, didn't know what led him to die on the floor, shot in the back. He didn't know why he wasn't able to face whoever killed him before his life was taken. Sergeant Card tried not to think too much about the existential nature of it. The body didn't bother him, Card had seen dead men before, he expected to see them again. What bothered him was how the man died. Card didn't want to die not knowing who, or why, or how. Maybe the fact that Card had killed men in the same way caused him to think about it. Maybe it was just his humanity. Maybe it was a silly, fleeting thought brought about by one man seeing another man dead, glad it was not him, and feeling slightly guilty for the thought.

We all make our own choices.

The garage held an early 90's Ford Econoline van along the outside wall, a plywood and saw horse makeshift table holding a blur of paper and a few chairs. One chair had a body in it, rolled in the mass produced office chair against the exterior wall, just behind the van. A neat red hole just below the right eye.

"This doesn't make any sense."

Card said, thinking about the three bodies.

"Our shooter came in through the master bedroom, shot one in the living room, one in the kitchen and one in here. All of them looked like they died without putting up a fight. I didn't see any stray shots, no signs of a struggle, nothing. How in the hell does someone come in here and shoot three men without one of them shooting back?"

He got a collective shrug.

"Number three is missing gun also."

Porter said. Toomby slipped the key into the back door of the van, it didn't work. He tried the other, it turned. He yanked the doors open.

"What the fuck is that?"

Card pushed in next to him. The van was a cargo model, nothing but the exposed skeleton, two seats in the nose and a sliding door on the side. Bolted dead center to pallets in the back of the van was a long cylinder, filling most of the cavity with only a few inches clearance on the top, maybe a foot on either side. The cylinder was stainless steel or aluminum. Along the sides were a number of small boxes, a series of smaller cylinders attached by metal tubing were arrayed in any spot they would fit. Toomby walked to the side of the van, keying open the sliding door. Card followed him. Attached to the side of the giant tank was a laptop, attached in a vertical position, the screen and key board facing out.

"Is that Russian?"

Sergeant Toomby asked Card, pointing at the keyboard. Hollic answered the question.

"Cyrillic, yes."

Toomby had a deep-seated mistrust of anything Russian. Since he saw Cyrillic as Russian, he was immediately on edge.

"Okay, sir, what the fuck is this thing?"

Just below the screen a little green light flickered, showing activity. Hollic tapped the spacebar to wake the computer. The simple tap spooked Toomby like hitting the spacebar would set off a bomb. The screen flickered and came to life. On the screen was a cluttered array of gauges and bar graphs. All the readings looked to be at zero except for one meter that appeared to measure the power to the cylinder. Hollic shook his head, stepping back to get distance between him and the van. When he spoke he seemed to be in his element.

"I want photos of this thing from every angle, get them to Gianna. Sergeant Card, roll these bodies, look for tattoos. Anything you find, you photo."

Sergeant Porter fought a digital point and shoot camera out of his admin pouch, going to work on the inside of the van, Card and Toomby looked at each other, shrugged, and yanked the body in the garage out of its chair. They laid the man flat on his back with some effort. Rigor had begun to set, making the task difficult. His right hand was stuck in an eternal clutch, like he had been grasping something when he died. Toomby didn't bother being gentle once they had him on the floor, he simply got two hands in the collar of the body's shirt and pulled, ripping it right down the middle. Card ignored the smell of evacuated bowels, concentrating on what he saw. He knew what he was looking at as soon as he saw it; he just didn't know what it was called. Intricate star tattoos adorned each shoulder, a bluish ink that lacked fine detail but was complex in its

design, a four-point nautical style star set over a second
four point star that was turned so all points were visible.
The middle of his chest was tattooed with an ornate
Russian cathedral, six *onion dome* spires atop it. Lower on
his chest was the tattoo of a group of cats, to the right of it
was a crude tattoo of a religious figure.
"Christ..."
Hollic said. Toomby shook his head, shaking a finger at
the tattoo.
"Nah, I think it's Saint Peter."
Hollic just stared at him.
"Roll him."
Toomby flipped the body over. The back was covered in
dozens of tattoos; swallows, spiders, Cyrillic writing in
quotations and a large tattoo of an executioner in the
middle of his back.
Hollic wiped sweat from his forehead. The tattoos had his
attention.
"He's a *Vor,* Russian Mafia. According to these tattoos, he
is a rather nasty one. Photo all of this."
Hollic bent down, looking closely at the man's arms. They
were free of tattoos and showed no signs of tattoos being
removed. That was something Hollic had not seen before.
Vor were not shy about their tattoos, always the opposite.
If this man avoided tattooing his commonly exposed skin,
he did it for a reason. Possibly being able to blend in was
reason enough.

Porter finished taking photos of the van, Toomby pointed to
the body.
"He's next."
Hollic motioned to Sergeant Card with his chin.
"Help me with the others?"
Card walked with Hollic back out into the house. Hollic
was relaxed and excited at the same time. He was
completely oblivious to the environment, focused on the

183

bodies. That bothered Card. He watched the windows, the doors, listened to the bass of the party thumping though the walls.

Parties brought cops.

A glance at his watch told him they had been there for fifteen minutes. That was five minutes too long as far as he was concerned. Hollic reached the body behind the couch. He used his Paragon stiletto blade to cut the shirt off with a mechanical *snick* and a quick swipe, the back was exposed. No tattoos. Hollic got a grip on his shoulders, Card took the cue, helping the Warrant Officer roll the body. The shoulders each had epaulettes tattooed, detailed skulls at the points, adorned in tassels tipped with smaller skulls. "Hell."
Hollic said, seeing the tattoos. He didn't bother to explain that skulls marked the man as a murderer, the number of skulls meant he was not new to it. The only other tattoo was one of a crucifix in the middle of his chest. On a hunch, Hollic cut his pants down one leg to see the man's knee. A crucifix with a star centered over the intersection. His other knee had the same tattoo.
"Never bow to another."
Hollic muttered hardly loud enough for Card to hear. He headed for the last body. This man wore a long sleeve shirt. Once it was removed, it was obvious why. He was covered in a dizzying array of tattoos; stars on the shoulders, a crucifix on the chest, a group of cats at the waist, broken shackles around the wrists, the Madonna with child on his side, a nine spire cathedral on the back with the German phrase *Gott Mit Uns* across the bottom, Cyrillic quotes in random spots, a caricature of Vladimir Putin, called a *grin,* in a compromising position with a goat and two skulls with crowns, one beneath each nipple.
"This guy was in charge."

Hollic said, as if Card should have known it by seeing the tattoos. Card recognized many tattoos for what they were, but the Russian ink was all mystery to him. It was obvious to Card that Hollic knew what he was looking at. That alone made him being on the team worth it to Card.

Toomby and Porter joined them, Porter going to work with the camera. Porter went straight for Hollic.
"What do we got here, sir?"
He seemed slightly annoyed that Hollic had yet to reveal what he knew. Hollic heard it in his tone.
"This guy is a *Obshchak,* like and advisor, uh…a right-hand man to the boss, the *Pakhan.* You don't see Obshchak …ever…outside of the organization. This is big. Whatever is in that van, my guess, the Russians are selling it, or assisting Heller in whatever he is doing. The other two are *Kryshas* or *Byki,* here to protect this man."
"Pretty obvious they failed."
Toomby snorted. Hollic frowned.
"Wrap up the photos, we need to go."
Card said, looking down at the body in the living room. "We just screwed up a crime scene, the least we can do is not be here when the cops show up."
All the sudden, Card didn't like Slidell anymore.

Toomby collected the wallets and passport they had found, photographed the contents of all of them, then left them on the couch in the living room. They did one final check of the house to see if they missed anything, any bit of evidence, any clue that would point them somewhere. Hollic was the only trained investigator, unfortunately he hadn't worked a *traditional* crime scene since his Warrant Officer Basic Course at Fort Huachuca, and then it was a staged training event.

What they missed was what was *missing.*

13

US Highway 90 was a stretch of road that spanned the state of Louisiana and then some. It had been called other names in the past, but was now the Chef Menteur Highway, at least the pavement we traveled on was. Running parallel to the Interstate in the south, US 90 saw more local traffic than it did interstate travelers. Like much of the land near the gulf, the locals had not returned to the population levels prior Katrina, so traffic was merely a visage of what it may have been years before. Michoud was the last suburb before the highway began its cut through the bayous, swampland and fragile woodland that maintained a tenuous hold on what little land it could keep from the ocean. I was sitting in the back with Tellison, watching the night go by. We would pass the occasional business; gas stations or small grocery stores, a casino and a number of businesses, already closed for the night, which catered to the marine vessel community. The lights shining in the dark were few and far between as we pushed further out of the city, the water closer to the road on both sides. Eventually, we saw no more lights at all besides the occasional car headed in the other direction, announced miles away as a speck in the distance that would inevitably grow into two specks, then the rough halo of light giving me some idea of what type of vehicle they belonged to. The light would then fill the cabin and the car would pass and be gone, the night filling in behind it.

We saw signs of civilization again where US 90 met US 11, the road swerved south then east once again. We passed through the small community of Venetian Isles at Fort Macomb, across the Chef Menteur pass and onto the thin finger of land that separated Lake Saint Catherine from Lake Pontchartrain. The same finger of land that was home to the address we were heading for. Two miles out of

Venetian Isles, the GPS showed the address approaching. I watched between the seats; the remains of a reflective driveway marker, twisted and bent towards the road, partially hidden by low lying plants glinted at as, showing where the entrance was. Madeline dropped ten miles an hour off the speedometer as we passed.

"Can't see anything."

Finn said, head against the glass.

"Bollocks."

Madeline accelerated, watching for a spot to turn in and stop. She bypassed a few overgrown driveways before turning off half a mile up the road. She hit the surveillance button in the Tahoe, killing every light in the vehicle, even the brake lights would not flare when the pedal was pressed. She drove in on the rough path, risking ruts and washboard against the lowered suspension until she found a spot to turn around. Once she got the Tahoe faced back towards the road she stopped and put the SUV in park.

"Anyone expect anything different?"

Tellison asked. No one answered.

"Didn't think so."

Tellison popped his door open, stepping out. The sounds of nature poured in. Crickets and a symphony of other insects I couldn't identify seemed obnoxiously loud. We stepped out with him as one, doors shut softly behind us. Everyone gathered on the left side of the Tahoe.

"Finn, what's the terrain like between here and there?"

"Unforgiving. Best guess we would be at least waist deep in water for a few hundred yards and swimming the actual bayou for about the same distance. I don't think we could cover it without making a good bit of noise with any speed."

Finn whispered in reply. He had spent the drive studying any maps he could find and any that Dino was able to send him on short notice. Tellison must have trusted Finn's word.

"All right...We aren't really equipped for that and I don't want to risk the time it will take to do it right. Recommendations?"

"Walking in means using the street. From here that's about a six-minute walk on the road. A little too much time exposed for me."

Madeline said. I readily, silently agreed with her. Finn didn't have an opinion that he voiced. Tellison considered his options. I grew impatient with his considerations.

"Okay."

He finally said.

"We drive in. Maddy, I want you to do it. I'll ride shotgun. Finn, Rushing, you fill in the back. We push in until we have eyes on structures then block the road and go in on foot. Rushing, no offense, but you need to keep to the rear of us. The rest of us have worked together, we know how to move as a team."

"None taken."

I lied. It wasn't that him not trusting me bothered me. It was that I was drug out in the middle of nowhere in spite of it.

Tellison looked at his watch, then up at the sky. The moon was low over the gulf, nothing more than a crescent. It wouldn't do us any favors, either to provide light to move by, or hide us from alert eyes. Before long it would sink into the salt and be gone. Tellison knew that as well as I did.

"We will hold here for an hour. Finn, move out to the road and get an idea of what traffic is like. You see anything, let us know."

Finn nodded in the dim light. He didn't seem to be bothered by being volunteered for a walk in the dark by himself.

"Will do."

And he was gone, moving up the dirt path to the pavement. He got a few steps away from the front of the Tahoe before I couldn't see him anymore. A few more after that and I couldn't hear him, either. Maddy climbed back into the Tahoe. With nothing to do, I joined her. Tellison remained outside, walking a distance to the rear, far enough away that I couldn't see or hear him, either. I wasn't in the mood for quiet.

"What's the deal with Tellison?"

I asked. Madeline shrugged in the darkness. I couldn't see it, but I could hear her body armor shift when she did.

"I hope he hasn't hurt your feelings, Rushing. He treated me much the same when I came on."

I thought myself a fool to think she knew me better than that.

"Not really what I meant."

I heard her body armor shift again. I could just make out her face as she turned in the seat to look at me. I was reminded of a time not too long ago sitting in the back seat of another SUV when we sat like this, only then she had every intention of killing me. Not this time.

"What, then?"

Well, what then? I didn't exactly know but I had the outlines of an idea.

"Tellison doesn't trust me. Fine. That makes me think either Solomon doesn't trust me, or Tellison doesn't trust Solomon. You have to see it, too. So if you can see it, I have to wonder, who is trying to play me this time; you, or him?"

I made out what I thought was genuine hurt on her face.

"Oh, come off it, Rushing. Tellison doesn't trust anyone he hasn't worked with."

Defensive.

There was an edge to her words. Like I was close to some sort of secret or detail left out that I wasn't even trying to discover because I didn't know I was supposed to be looking for it. Now I was.

"Okay."

I said, thinking about the day.

"You either tell me what the hell is really going on, or I am going to walk, literally."

I didn't have the time or patience to try and drag anything out of her.

"Are you mad? Walk? Seriously?"

I considered the distance back to the city.

"I would run, probably. Fourteen hours back to my house I think. Now, talk."

She looked as if I had asked her to cut off her own finger.

"I'm not going to sit here and wait forever, Madeline."

More silent resistance. My imagination provided me with many reasons for her to be keeping secrets. Of course, none of them explained the coincidences that continued to pile up. It had something to do with Heller, or the Colonel, that much I was sure of.

I thought I was sure, anyway.

Madeline wasn't talking. I put my hand on the door, dead serious about walking away.

"Wait, Rushing-"

I turned my head and stared through her.

"Maddy, you need to talk to me."

She took a deep breath and let it out in a thoughtful sigh. Either the temperature had gone up, or the uncomfortable atmosphere in the back seat was making it seem ten degrees hotter.

"I can't answer your questions-"

I opened the door, one foot on the ground. Maddy grabbed my shoulder.

"Wait!"

A yell in a whisper.

"The Colonel can."

She said, softer. She produced a cell phone. I pulled my foot back in and shut the door, if only out of personal curiosity. Madeline dialed. It seemed like forever before someone on the other end answered.

"Colonel…"

She spoke softly, respectfully. It was a few seconds before she could speak again.

"I know, Colonel, this is important. Rushing needs you to answer some quest-"

A tiny Colonel Solomon boomed through the phone, cutting her off.

"*I don't give a damn-*"

I snatched the phone from her hand, cutting him off.

"I *do* give a damn, Solomon. You have me out here in the fucking sticks risking my neck for you. Tellison has a problem with me that's becoming contagious. I can't but help thinking that you have something to do with his attitude problem. So either you tell me what's going on, or I'll go back to my life and you can go fuck yourself."

I could literally hear Solomon suck all the air out of the room on the other end. When he replied, his tone was lower than I expected it to be.

"Are you always this difficult?"

I didn't bother answering. He didn't expect one. Madeline just watched.

Tense.

"Rushing, I'm not going to blow smoke up your ass by saying how glad I am that you are helping us. Fact is I have no real reason to trust you. Now, I have no real reason *not* to trust you, which puts us on *indifferent* terms-"

He was speaking through clenched teeth, biting back something. It wasn't anger. It didn't feel like fear.

Then what?

"For both our sake's, I'll just be blunt. In the past few months I have lost men to your brothers and sisters. Every operation that even smells of Virtua involvement that we go after seems to end in my people getting killed by your people. So I thought to myself, *why not bring you in?*"
I wasn't really surprised that my former brothers and sisters were out working on their own. With the death of Stewart Garitty and my sister, Rose, there ceased to be an organization to direct them that I knew of. They may have been free to do as they wanted with Garitty and Rose gone, of course they may have not known what *free* meant. OR it could have been something else.
"So, what is it, Solomon, you thought this information would somehow be of no use to me? That knowing it might somehow endanger you and your people?"
The Colonel actually laughed. It had a tinge of being forced.
"Nothing so complicated. Madeline suggested you might be willing to help. I agreed that bringing you in would be smart. I am short manpower and not in a position to recruit given the current political climate. Madeline didn't give you details because she was not in a position to. My team doesn't trust you in varied degrees, Tellison being the most extreme. If you want to know why, I suggest you ask him yourself."
The truth was in there, mixed in with the Colonel's apparent tendency to lie when he felt it suited his ultimate goal. His explanation was neat. Nothing was neat anymore.

I had a decision to make.

I could see by the brooding look on Madeline's face that whatever the Colonel was keeping from me, he was keeping it from her too. I wanted to get to Heller. I *needed* to get to Heller. Solomon would help me do that if I was willing to let him lie to me. If I wasn't, I would have to call him on it. If I did that, there was a good chance he would not react kindly. As important as stopping Heller was, I wouldn't put it past the Colonel to do anything in his power to achieve that goal.

Even if that included killing me.

I couldn't blame him, even if I didn't like it. What I could do was play along.

"Fine, Colonel."
I said. Madeline let out a sigh. She must have been holding her breath, waiting for me to speak.
The Colonel seemed relieved. His relief made me more suspicious.
"Good. Let me speak to O'Neil."
I handed the phone back to Madeline without further comment, thinking about the short conversation.
Madeline's conversation was one sided. The Colonel spoke for a few seconds, the call ended. Madeline's look didn't change. She was still pensive.

She knew as much as I did.

"He's lying to me, Maddy."
She gave a slight nod, eyes downcast.
"I reckon so. Lying to both of us."
Honest.
"What now?"
I asked, watching her closely.

"First thought? We snatch Tellison up and have a hard chat."

I liked her idea.

"Of course, we do that, we run the risk of having more enemies than we can handle; just the pair of us."

I still liked the idea. She must have been able to see that, she started shaking her head.

"No, Rushing-"

"I get it Maddy, we need to play nice. I'm good with that."

I wasn't. She knew it, but she decided to leave it alone. I heard the crunch of gravel outside of the vehicle. I looked over my shoulder; Tellison slowly emerged from the darkness, no hurry in his walk. He went to his door and opened it. I could see a faint glow coming from the admin pouch on his plate carrier; rectangle and ghostly white. It was gone as soon as he climbed into his seat. A cell phone. I would bet a ridiculous amount of money that Tellison had just gotten off the phone with the Colonel. Our conversation hardly seemed worth mentioning. Tellison was probably not going to mention his either.

He glanced back at us for a second, no expression on his face before keying his radio.

"Roll it up, Finn."

Finn replied by squelching twice.

"Maddy, drive please. I'm tired of waiting, we roll as soon as Finn gets back."

Madeline left the back seat, climbing behind the wheel. I stayed right where I was. Before long the crunch of gravel could be heard. Finn glanced into the vehicle through the window, saw the empty seat in the back and took it.

"Finn, anything?"

He shook his head.

"Road traffic. No one showing interest in the area."

Tellison seemed satisfied.

"We move now. Maddy, get us back out on the road, keep it blacked out."

Tellison switched channels on his radio. He took a deep breath before keying his mic.

"Redundant, Redundant, Redundant…Good hunting."

Tellison switched his radio back, cradling his weapon with the barrel at the window, ready to exit the vehicle.

Madeline made it back out to the road, lights off, navigating by the ambient light alone. She kept the speed low, watching for the turn.

"Take hostiles alive if possible."

14

My understanding of team assaults was somewhat limited. After all, my life of violence had been mostly solo and generally disguised as something other than what it was. However, I liked to think I had a good degree of common sense, and that made me worry about the plan.

Let's walk through it.

Drive in to a largely unknown property with an unknown number of likely hostile individuals, block the only road to prevent any vehicle escape and then advance on any and all structures, if there even were any, as one of four shooters while making an attempt to take said hostiles alive if possible. Seemed like a bad plan.

But what the hell did I know?

Well, for starters, I spent a lot of time whishing I was wrong in situations like this only to be proven right. I was hoping this wouldn't be one of those times. The problem with people is that it's only natural to lay traps, and it's only natural for other people to fall into them.

Maddy broke loose of the pavement, rolling onto the unfamiliar dirt road at a coast, getting her footing before touching the gas again. I couldn't see inside the vehicle, but heard rifles adjust against gear.

"Go green."
Tellison said; Finn snapped his dual tube 31's down over his eyes. I did the same. The world came back to me, but

it wasn't green, it was shades of light blue, nearly white. Night vision was traditionally green, but white phosphor had become more popular in years past, something to do with greater contrast versus the venerable green. I supposed the *green* term came from the days when green was the most common type.

The interior was blurry, but the world outside was clean and in focus. I made some final adjustments to my focus rings and a quick test tap on the MAWL to insure the IR laser was functional. I set the output for mid-range. Finn had told me that all the rifles were zeroed to 50/200 yards on the red dot, the lasers slaved to that zero with a parallel zero to minimize parallax as distance increased outside of the zero distance. I had a basic understanding of what that meant; my rounds would hit right of the dot consistently to distance. Holdovers on the laser would be the same as on the red dot optic. Best I was gonna get.

The road remained one lane wide, but the foliage crept in on the sides, leaning over the road. Young saplings, long dead branches from long dead trees, Black Rush and Sea Blight failed to stop the Tahoe from pushing through. The sound against the metal was high pitched and continuous. I was hoping the road would dump into an open area, and just when I though it wouldn't, we rounded a slight curve. A brief glimpse of some structure, back into the foliage and then we broke free onto open, flat and tenuous land. Water stood on the road, tugging at the Tahoe's low, two wheel drive chassis. A tired fence holding up a sagging gate blocked the road. It was chained. The lock stood out against the chain and fence under IR. We coasted to a stop.

I fished the padlock key from my pocket, fairly sure it would fit the lock.

"Pretty sure I have the key."

I was out, Finn stepped out with me, he did a quick check of the gate for tricks or traps then gave me a thumbs up for the all clear. The padlock was new, the chain wasn't. The key slid in and popped it open.

"Well how about that?"

Finn whispered as we climbed back in the Tahoe. We started off, leaving the gate open behind us.

"Structure Left."

Tellison said with a chin point in the dark. A hundred yards ahead was a large rectangle of a building sitting above the ground on thick, round stilts, not an uncommon sight at sea level in Louisiana. It backed up against the edge of the property, plant life sucking half of it into its embrace. I wasn't surprised that it couldn't be seen from Google Earth. What had been a house was a dead husk, the far end collapsed on broken stilts, the roof sagging and hanging off the side closest to us in some places. The entire structure leaned towards the highway, having been perpetually smashed by hurricane winds for as long as it had been there. I didn't see any standing stairs, no way obvious to get inside. Cross beams were more missing than present, windows were shuttered or missing altogether.

"Structure ahead."

Maddy said.

"Back it up O'Neal, turn us out."

The Tahoe stopped gingerly, then we reversed back to the point where the overgrowth stopped, she kicked the back in towards the stilt house to block the road then put it in park.

Engine off, doors popped then were shut silently. We were maybe seventy-five yards from the stilt house on our left. Directly ahead, forty or fifty yards past the stilt house before the road faded into the grass was a shed of some sort that sat low on the ground, too low for a full-grown man to walk in upright, it was as wide as a three-car garage. The metal siding reflected gently under NV, showing much lighter in color than whatever the roof was made of. It appeared new.

Everyone gathered on the far side of the Tahoe. Finn laid in over the hood, watching.
"No vehicles, no activity."
Finn said, although it was clear without his report. Tellison motioned to the stilt house.
"Whatever that thing is, I don't see a way in, no stairs or ladder."
His support hand adjusted a setting on the MAWL, then he painted the structure with IR, like using a flashlight, a wide beam that only we could see thanks to the night vision. Extra light on the structure punctuated its dilapidation and lack of access. It looked like it would fall over at any moment.
"We can't afford to split and hit both structures, even if there is a way in there, its large and would require all of us to clear it. I'm hedging on it not being occupied. That shed looks recently built. Rushing, your only job in life is to keep eyes on the stilt house while we go for the shed."
I was cool with it. I even gave him my most polite nod to let him know I was a team player.
"Finn, move."

I imagined that normal operations would not have left us having a quick meeting *on the objective* before taking action. With a lack of intel or even an idea of the property before we arrived, it seemed unavoidable. Finn was on point, Tellison and Madeline slightly behind with double the distance to the left and right. I watched the stilt house, silently wishing for it to show me something. As we neared its flank, it was pretty clear that nothing as large as a vehicle had been near it, though foot traffic would have been hidden by the combination of shin high grass and standing water. The road surface had a few dry spots higher than the water, there were fresh tracks. The tread was thin, but a wide wheel base, street tires on a van maybe. Moving past the stilt house, I rotated around, walking backwards. The windows were motionless, a gentle breeze rattled bits of the failing roof. It would have been easier to check the stilt house first, if only so I didn't have to keep an eye on it. I wasn't in charge, so walking backwards for what would probably turn out to be no reason was my life. We neared the shed. The road ended. Swallowed by the grass and time. I moved so I could watch the stilt house and see the shed at the same time, pulling out beside the others. The shed sat over the water, a boat slip. A set of stairs to its right; simple, no railing, just steps down under the canopy. Finn crouched low, to see underneath as soon as he could, leading the three of them down. Our comms were switched to Vox so I could hear them talking freely. A few seconds after they disappeared from view, Tellison spoke first.

"We got bodies and boats; dig those corners."

Bodies, huh? Color me surprised.

"Boat clear."

Finn called, Maddy repeated a second later.

"Rushing, pull it in."

Dutiful as ever, I watched the stilt house until I hit the stairs, up until the last second it was blocked from view by the shed canopy. Underneath was a wooden deck, narrow, surrounding open water on three sides. Three Rigid Inflatable Boats were squeezed into the space, tied off to the dock and to each other. Even before I left the stairs I could see the bodies; strewn about the boats and dock; seven in all. Finn was with the body closest to me, male, athletic, dead.

"This that Alavoza guy?"

There was a dim red light overhead, Finn had his goggles up. I flipped up mine to get a look even though he wasn't talking to me. Madeline left the body she was checking.

"Quite."

She said, comparing the face to one on her phone.

"Well, solves that."

Tellison moved over from the far side of the slip. I looked around; the walls were adorned with fishing gear; the slip didn't appear new from the inside, but it looked maintained by someone who used it for recreation, not terrorism.

"Seven down, looks like they were unloading kit from the boats and someone stitched them all."

I had to agree, from where I stood near the stairs each body could be seen. A handful of shell casings lay at my feet. 5.45mm by the looks of them. I was sure more ended up in the boats and in the water. The shooting looked clean, precise.

"Well, let's roll 'em for intel and get the hell out of here."

I rolled my rifle to my support side, wrenching the sling down. Tellison moved back to the other side of the slip where three bodies lay. I figured I'd give him a hand. All three were dressed more or less the same, dark clothes, utility pants, dry suits under. All three had died roughly where they stood, hits to head and chest. If they had weapons, they were gone now. The first body I checked had its pockets turned out. Tellison spoke my thoughts. "Someone sanitized these guys. But why leave the bodies? O'Neal, Finn, anything?"

Both replied in the negative. Maddy had moved onto the first boat, checking the deck. Finn hopped onto the middle, doing the same. Tellison took the third, so I walked the dock, looking for anything that could be helpful. I wasn't much of a detective but in my head, it was pretty straightforward; these were the same dudes that boarded the ship, snatched what was ever in the container, and then came here. Whoever they worked for then retrieved whatever it was and tied off the loose end. It was tidy except for the bodies. They had to have been left for a reason; someone other than us would eventually find them and whoever, most likely Heller, had left them as they died. It would look to any investigator just as it did to me. There was more here than we could see.

"Got something."

Finn said, holding up a phone. The case was slick, glistening in the red glow. Blood.

"They must have missed it."

Finn bagged it and dropped it in a pocket. Maddy was busy scanning prints with a device like I had seen Hijazi use, maybe it was the same one. Tellison was back at the center of the deck, standing at the front of the center boat.

"We have seven bodies, eight counting the one from the freighter, but three boats? Rushing, only two boats seen by your local?"

I shrugged.

"He said *a couple* which means two, but some people use it for any number more than one but less than a bunch."

A scoff.

"Okay, so assume he meant *two*. We have three, but only a crew for two, realistically. Eight men for three boats is bad math. So, either we are four men short or one boat plus. The Navy SWCCs use this same boat, Willard Marine; I'd be willing to bet more than one of these bodies are former Navy or were trained in vessel boarding elsewhere. All that leads me back to a firm head count of at least four per boat. Assuming boat three is a backup; the entire boarding party is likely accounted for and deceased. Why are these boats here? Why are these bodies here? Not smart to half finish tying off loose ends."

His line of thought was hard to argue with. Not that it was helpful to any of us at the moment.

"Over here, chaps."

Madeline stepped off her boat, a timid hop as it rocked in the water. She had a piece of printer paper; unfolded, it looked like it had been folded and un folded more than once. She held it out, so we could see it. I didn't have any idea what I was looking at other than the fact that it was a picture of some kind of cylinder. The mind, as its able to do, made a quick mental connection; whatever had been on the freighter, this was it. The picture had been given to the boarding team at some point, so they knew, without a shadow of a doubt, what to grab. As if there was some risk of snagging the wrong smuggled cylinder of whatever from the same container on the same boat. Of course, given the nature of the world and the bad people in it, better safe than sorry.

Tellison took possession of the paper.

"Anyone know what this is?"

Madeline tapped her helmet light, permission to go to while light. Tellison nodded. She flipped a small switch, a dim cable light lit up, a quick bend and it was pointed at the paper. It wasn't much but it was better than the anemic overhead red lights. The paper showed a photo and a paragraph of text, it looked to be taken directly from a website. A company called Værne in Denmark manufactured a wide array of medical sampling and transportation devices, center stage was a cylinder in the photo; an 11.5," high pressure cylinder that offered self-contained liquid nitrogen cooling for an internal sample volume of 300ccs. The cylinder boasted a cooling life of three weeks at -321 degrees Fahrenheit. The outside casing was polyamide coated aluminum, the internal membranes were detailed as *proprietary materials*. Security was maintained with a GPS real time tracker, cypher coded entry and an internal sample destruction option to prevent theft. I had not known such things existed seconds prior.

Finn peered into our huddle to look at the paper.

"So...bets on Ebola? Small Pox? Super AIDS? Yo, should we be at MOPP four right now?"

I was really liking Finn, if for no other reason that he bothered Tellison.

"Stow it, Finn. O'Neal, lets wrap this up. Check these boats for hull numbers, then we check the house to be sure."

Boats, just like motor vehicles, had identification numbers, a Hull Identification Number, it wasn't quite like the small metal plate cars had, more like a large number affixed somewhere on the hull more like a license plate. I seriously doubted the RHIBs would have them, but checking was smart.

With a quick check to confirm the boats had no hull numbers anywhere that could be found, Tellison took point and we filed up the stairs, going back into a wide V at the top. With no direction as to where to be, I filled in the right, Just behind Tellison, keeping an eye on what of the waterway I could see beyond the shed and through the foliage. We veered into the tall grass towards the stilt house, most likely on the way to a short and fruitless attempt to gain access. Once my view of the water became obstructed by distance, I rolled around in the direction of travel. We were nearing the stilt house from what appeared to be the back side, it leaned in the opposite direction, towards the road, bent by wind and time. There was a light wind blowing, nothing more than a steady brush of salted air that pushed at the grass but didn't have the heart to move the trees. It felt nice, licking up under my helmet which, while vented, didn't do a very good job of letting out the heat. It was the wind that helped me see it.

My mind was already subconsciously registering something out of place, ahead under the stilt house, shown to me in vibrant white and muted blue of the night vision. A race to form a conscious thought was taking place, spinning through my frontal lobe, neurons racing footsteps. The closer we got, the more the problem refined itself, the more those neurons struggled to formulate a conscious warning against what was coming.

15

The MON-50 was a shameless, yet well done, Soviet-era reverse engineering of the American Claymore mine. Arguments about when or how weren't important. What was important, was the MON-50 packed seven hundred grams of RDX high explosive into a small and very versatile package to propel steel rods or steel bearings, depending on variant, as deadly shrapnel. Multiple trigger options were available, including the MUV MD-2 striker, which was little more than a pin activated trigger similar to a hand grenade. Two or more pounds of pressure was needed to remove the safety pin from the striker rod, which would release under spring pressure and begin the firing chain. The easiest, and by far the safest way to remove the pin was by old fashioned trip wire; well, safest for whoever was setting the mine, anyway.

Just as versatile as the Claymore, the MON-50 could be ground placed on scissor legs or affixed to any surface imaginable with something as simple as duct tape. Since the mine was roughly nine by six inches, hiding it from view wasn't terribly difficult, either. The weak point in using them for a trap was that the trip wire was victim to the environment it was in, and the height of the mine. Setting traps is all about predicting your prey's movement or forcing their movement with some sort of bait. Without bait, you are left with assumptions, no matter how educated. Of course, the environment can be your friend, providing natural choke points or ideal terrain that any reasonable, even cautious, person would use. Though even that left much to chance, so overkill and over preparation were ideal.

What I would recognize in the next few seconds would have made Rube Goldberg proud; a complicated series of fishing lines ran from elevated MON-50 mines, carefully concealed by threading through eyelets that had been screwed into the stilts of the house. Once the line reached waist level, it spidered out to cover every conceivable path. Normally trip wires were at shin or ankle height, at least that's what the movies told me. But the high grass allowed for a much higher placement and almost zero possibility of someone winning the lottery by stepping over the trip by chance. No, the height was unavoidable.

But it was the height that caught my attention.

Cognitive interpolation, if you will. My mind picked up on the fact that some of the grass was bending with the breeze, some of it wasn't. Had it been a single wire, perhaps I would have missed it. But it wasn't one, it was dozens; presented to me from dozens of angles to cover all the gaps between the stilts beneath the house. The visual stimulus kicked around my frontal lobe, my parietal lobe factored the time I had left to figure it out; Tellison was two strides from connecting with the first wire. Cognitive interpolation is a deep-rooted self-defense mechanism; the earliest mammals had to contend with nature in a much more raw form; something as simple as mistaking a snake for a branch could mean death; so the brain hardwired successful DNA passed on to future generations to assume the worst about visages of potential danger until more information could be gained. Sometimes it was as simple as assuming a coat rack out of the corner of your eye was a person; or the shadow of a bush in the night was a dog. Or that grass not bending in a certain place was abnormal and given all other known factors about why you were where you were and for what would cause the amygdala to sound the alarm; it immediately released norepinephrine onto motor neurons, which enhanced motor performance during a state of fear. Well, that's how it worked for normal people, anyway. I didn't deal in fear. In Stewart Garrity's *School*, under the tutelage of Mr. Grimm, I, just like all the other children, learned to harness the small fractions of time that the majority of people never even notice passing. To perform in a second what some people cannot do in a few. Not superhuman reflexes, but vastly above average pre-cognitive reasoning that Mr. Grimm called Selective Sectioning; taking each bit of information and processing it all at the same time, connecting all the dots at once, disregarding information that had no bearing and making the fastest decision possible, usually with one or two alternate choices that could be used if things changed before an action was completed. Learning this technique was literally the bulk of my education from the age of twelve to twenty. Despite slacking off on my practice in the past, I was back in my prime, so to speak, and it was about to save all our lives.

Tellison made contact with a trip, between the left most support pillars not blocked by a crossbeam. Two pounds or pressure was needed to pull the pin on the mine above, but that trip was tied into other lines, connected to other pins on other mines. The aftermath would have me figuring that there was at least ten mines.

Ten pins.

Two pounds per pin.

Factor in elasticity in the lines and resistance created by the eyelets and knots, two pounds became more than twenty. Twenty pounds was nothing for the forward stride of a 200 pound man in full gear. But it was more than two, and that helped.

My hand shot out and fingers slipped under the shoulder strap of Tellison's plate carrier, a rasping yell of *DOWN!* forced out through open mouth; I pulled backwards with all the strength I had, my heels turning and pushing in deep, sinking into the saturated ground to find some purchase for leverage. It was nearly too late; the 20 pound need had been satisfied, I heard the pins sing free with a metallic twang; spring pressure was released, strikers drove downward to percussion caps. I had generated enough force to pull Tellison clean off his feet as I rotated; Maddy was in the corner of my eye, rolling to her side in a dive, she had Finn within reach and was pushing him with outstretched arms. The mines fired. Four hundred and 85 steel fragments propelled outward at nearly twenty seven thousand feet per second in a fifty four degree arc. Pillars shadowed some of the blast; coupled with my response I pulled Tellison just out of the closest mines arc, probably by mere inches. The overpressure was deafening, like someone hit mute on the real world. My NVGs bloomed, the ground reacted to the impact of the explosion, water, mud, grass and what could have been a turtle showered past me as we slammed hard into the ground. The stilt house seemed to jump on its moorings, then followed its already windblown lean as it moaned and creaked in a slow motion collapse to the ground. Pillars had been pulverized, splintered and fractured; I could feel wood in my exposed skin, but that was about to be the least of my problems.

Tellison was unconscious. No response from him as I untangled myself from his plate carrier. Finn was moaning about something; Maddy was pulling him further away from the house as it continued to lean into a collapse. Sound was coming back and for a brief moment I thought the explosion had somehow erased my ability to hear English. What sounded like Russian was being yelled from somewhere behind me, at least two distinct voices, quickly joined by two more in response. I learned Russian once upon a time; had been very fluent in it. That was ages ago and it was taking a second to come back to me; having my bell run less than a minute ago by an explosion was as good an excuse as any for the delay.

I heard four voices now, all more or less in the same direction. No more yelling, more…discussing. There was an ebb and flow to the words, like talking through a strong breeze. I thought that what it was. I realized it was because I was actually losing consciousness right before I did.

The hum of tires was the next sound I had; faint, a tickle, like concentrating so hard on a far away noise and trying to trick yourself into believing you actually heard it. But it was really there. New tires on a rough road, or old tires on a new road. Whichever it was, it was academic because the shocks they rode on were certainly old. The body of what had to be a van rolled like a staggering drunk, taking far more motion from the dips and bumps than it should, letting that energy roll through the van, loading the springs and rolling back. A boat on rough waters, it rocked me awake. Well, kind of awake.

My hands were behind my back.

Bound.

Not cuffed, some sort of plastic. A zip tie.

Interesting.

I was wedged into the back, against the rear doors. My first really coherent thought was regarding the van. Where the hell had it been hidden away near the stilt house? Of course the next question was; who owned the van, who was driving it now? I was eager to find out. A quick exploration told me my feet were free; by the feel at chest and hips, my guns were gone but my body armor was still on. Helmet was missing too; and since I couldn't see anything, the pressure around my eyes told me I was blind folded. An actual blind fold. Not a bag, which is much faster, but a tight strip of fabric. Who the hell did that anymore?

I scouted the floor with my legs; if anyone else was in the van with me besides at least the driver, they weren't in reach. Logistics told me that the chance of four separate vans; one for each of us, was unlikely. I had to admit that the possibility that I was the only one left alive, was on the table, but that also seemed unlikely. This wasn't Heller, because if it was, I wouldn't be having these thoughts. I would be dead. A few of the words I heard came back to me, the voices at the stilt house. Surprise. A few comments.

What had he said?

Who the fuck are these guys? Cops?

So.

We weren't the intended target, the US MARSHAL emblazoned plate carriers helped with that, or they knew who they were trying to turn into paste and we weren't them. Could this get any more complicated? I pushed off the wall of the van to stretch my legs; found another person; stiff, a gentle stir when I kicked. I didn't know who it was by feel; even bets that I would be Finn or Maddy. Being that me and Tellison were the most physically imposing of the four of us, smart men would not have put us together. Whoever my carpool partner was, they were now awake. The next trick was going to be getting out of the restraints and taking the van. Had there been eyes on us, someone would have said something by now. I imagined a driver and a passenger, no one in the back with us. That made things easy. The van walls were exposed skeleton, not fabric and insulation and plastic found in a mini-van or vehicle intended for rear passenger comfort. No, this was a work van. Which meant the likelihood of rear lights or windows was little. I was counting on the time of night and the lack of those two things to hide my movements.

One of my favorite *school* courses had been restraint escape. Mechanical, electronic, and fabric. Some of my fellow Children hadn't seen the point of it, though given how often I had found myself in restraints in the past few years, I was glad to have taken such an interest in it. The first rule of restraint escape was leverage. When dealing with fabric or non-metal restraints such as rope or plastic, your best bet was to either defeat the knot or use friction to cut the material. This was all academic if you had nothing to generate that friction with; which is why I always wore a good belt. I rolled my shoulders as far to my right as I could, spidering my fingers forward until I was able to release the claw buckle on my Blue Alpha Gear belt. I had maybe three inches of slack between my wrists, the feel told me I was in actual plastic restraints, not just repurposed hardware store zip ties. Because of that, they were half an inch wide and joined in the middle by a one way ratcheting lock, I had a bit of work ahead of me. Zip ties would have been much quicker.

I worked my belt loose in the back between loops, slipped one hand through the opening, synched down what slack I could with my other hand then held tight as I began working the cuff center back and forth against the stiff edge of the nylon worked against the surface of the plastic, which resisted as designed, at least at first. Once heat built, it began to scuff and finally cut into the material. The van continued along, tires hummed and I worked through the building shoulder pain. Every so often I would check my progress while I listened to the sounds in the van. My mystery car pool partner was still quiet, smart. Hopefully working out their own escape. The clock in my head put time invested at ten minutes by the time my wrists snapped apart. I rolled my right side against the wall of the van, inching my arm up between me and the wall. I poked the blind fold up. It was dark, but I could make out the shape of Finn against the left side of the van, about half way to the front captain's seats; we had a driver and a passenger. Finn looked to still be working at his restraints. No light came in through the windshield. We were still far away from civilization. A look up showed me no rear windows.

No way to know if there was another vehicle. I saw a driver. A passenger. Just shadows. No talking. I suspected the Tahoe was either in front of or behind us; it wouldn't have made sense for them to have another vehicle; despite a lack of seating, the van was more than large enough for their team and I doubted based on the mines that they expected to take passengers back. I could have been wrong though and was looking forward to finding out.

16

Sergeant Toomby was working the steering wheel like he wanted to sleep with it, gently guiding the large SUV around other cars as they pushed back into the city on the highway. Card's attention was spilt between the uncharacteristically calm Toomby and the nagging feeling that they had missed something at the house, which made total sense seeing as someone had been there before them. But it was more than that, like there was a piece to the puzzle that was there and he hadn't seen it. Card was cool with it, he knew his mind would put it together, he just wished it would happen faster.

"We are coming up on late for a signal from Tell." Porter said from the back. He was the only one who could get away with an abbreviation like that. Old history. "Hollic, Sir?"
Card said, looking over his shoulder. Hollic was ranking. Hollic could make the call. Hollic looked up from the snatched paperwork he was reading through. He found himself after a vacant stare, reaching down to his radio. He hesitated.
"Uh, Sergeant Card, what's our callsign?"
Card couldn't help but smile. The officer always the last to know anything, even his own radio name.
"Well sir, just like birth, you get your own. So, what is *your* callsign?"
Hollic was embarrassed.
"Oh, uh, yeah. Of course."
He went back to his radio. Hesitated again. Card answered before he asked.

"Tellison is always *Vicious."*

A second nod.

"Sure. Vicious, this is Neo."

Silence. Except for a stifled chuckle from Toomby. Hollic treated the Matrix Trilogy like some did Lord of the Rings.

"Vicious, Neo."

More silence. Card's cool was officially gone. He traded a glance with Toomby, who immediately searched for an exit to put them into a holding pattern.

"Fuck."

Came the muted voice of Porter. Tellison was always good on comms. And since this wasn't some backwater thirdworld hole, the chances of the radios being spotty was zero. Something was up. Card switched his radio to the command channel.

"Foundation, Breathtaker, I need a real time on Vicious, now."

His words went out, Gianna's came back. Not time to celebrate that.

"Stand by, Breathtaker."

"Vicious, this is Neo, do you read?"

Hollic was still at it, but Card knew he wasn't likely to get an answer. What was less likely was that Tellison's team was down. No, that would have been a statistical improbability given who he was with. Card was sure even the Rushing cat could work a radio, and he knew the others could. Between the four of them, there would have to be a squared number of bad guys to keep anyone from reaching a radio, that or an unlucky event.

IEDs were unlucky events.

All the training in the world couldn't save you from a few hundred dollars of explosives and a motivated Jihadi. But that was third world, this wasn't.

"Breathtaker, Foundation, Location is mobile. I'm pushing it to you now."

"Roger, will advise, Breathtaker out."

Card wanted to chat her up. Never the time. He pulled out his phone, checked the secure app. He had a realtime on the Tahoe and Tellison. He could get a real time on Maddy and Finn as well, everyone had a transponder, except for Rushing. Maybe they would get to that. Probably not.

Tellison and the Tahoe were one and the same, moving at exactly the posted speed limit on highway 90 but in the wrong direction. They were close to where 90 hit 607, close to I 10.

"Toomby, turn us around, get after it."

Card propped his phone up on the dash, Toomby frowned, shot under the highway and ran a light to get back on headed the other direction; the gas pedal soon finding the floor. Hollic made a few more attempts to raise them on the radio before he gave up, he seemed unsure as to what to do next. Card helped him out.

"Okay, sir, do us all a favor and tell us what we know from that house. All of it."

Hollic considered the question, putting things together in an order that would be efficient and make the most sense in the shortest amount of time. He also didn't want to convey suspicions, or at least, too many. There were a lot of missing pieces from the house, but some things were very clear and very strange.

"Alright, we have a house with three dead Russian mobsters, one basically middle management. No guns, no phones, but we got IDs so that may lead somewhere. The house was unremarkable, But the garage held a van with some sort of mobile culture chamber or incubator, a lab. That's a little outside of my lane, but I'd be surprised if that wasn't what was in the van-"

Toomby cut him off.

"Wait, *incubator*? Like for bioweapons?"

Suddenly Toomby looked like he wanted to wash his hands.

"Well, yes, you could use it for that. Since we are dealing with bad men, Toomby, I would assume that biologicals may be involved. Don't worry, the incubator was empty. It doesn't appear to even have been used."

Toomby had a counter to that suspicion but believing Hollic made him feel better than the alternative so he swallowed it.

Card was unmoved by the possibility. If that's how the universe wanted to kill him, he had no control over it. He just had to accept it. The puzzle nagged at him still.

"Sir, what was missing from the house?"

Hollic tilted his head at the question. Card couldn't see him well, but the dim silhouette let him know Hollic hadn't considered anything until that moment.

"I...I don't know."

Card knew, in that moment the missing pieces seem to fall into place. Some of it was speculation, but all of it made sense to him.

"There was a second vehicle, probably another van. Keyring had two identical keys, except they weren't. They were just for the same type of vehicle. Two keys per ring makes sure no one leaves with the keys to both vehicles. Two car garage, but the table was smashed up against the wall instead of the open area next to the van; because something was usually parked there. Theres no house key on the ring, because it isn't needed. Someone is always supposed to be there. Way too much food in the house for three guys, but the food got there somehow, and I don't think they would run errands in the incubator van."

Heads were nodding. Card felt good about his train of thought.

"So missing van means missing man, or men. Or women too, I don't know much about Russian equal opportunity in their organized crime. We don't know what guns they had at the house, but we know they had them. But no phones? That's a stretch."

Hollic's head bobbed along.

"I think you are right, Sergeant, but what are we looking at? Until I get more info I don't want to assume too much-"

Toomby cut Hollic off again.

"We gotta tail."

Heads turned. They had already shot back through Slidell on 10 and were making the lazy curve where 10 started going more East than North. It was two lanes carved through heavy woods with nothing much that produced light on either side of the divided highway. Given their speed, they were overtaking anything they approached, but one car appeared to be matching speed. It was too dark and too far back to make out model, but if it had been a cop their triple digit speeds would have prompted him to stop them long ago.

"How long, Sergeant?"

Hollic asked, taking out his phone. Porter rested his rifle over the back seat.

"Spotted him about a minute ago. Wanted to be sure so I played with the speed a bit. Could be some dude hoping we take the ticket, but fuck coincidences. Money says that's the dude or dudes that rolled the house before we did."

Card had to agree. He would have done it that way; wait around for a bit and see if anyone shows up, or if the missing guys returned.

"Recommendations?"

He asked, checking his rifle.

"There's a car full of new intel following us. If they knew where we were going, they wouldn't be behind us. I say we roll them."

Porter said, not taking his eyes off the sleek LED headlights behind them. Card looked to Hollic, he seemed indecisive as usual.

"Roll em."

Came Toomby's vote.

Hollic checked his tablet. He had the locator push on Tellison as well, his signal was still moving, now on 607, headed for I 10, they were already across the border into Mississippi. If they went East when they reached I 10, catching up would become more difficult.

"No, we continue."

Hollic said, even and cool.

"We don't know Tellison's status. We will just have to risk bringing our tail along."

Card liked the first part, but not the second. Bringing an unknown into an unknown was a large risk. Card thought for a third option, hoping someone else had one but no one spoke.

"Nah."

Porter said, eyes still on the car.

"We need to dump the tail, and fast. Toomby, can you slow us down naturally? Put this back window down."

Card had an idea of what Porter was going to do; he was cool with it. Porter was the only sniper qualified cat in the unit that seemed to prefer being an assaulter, despite the fact that he was the most consistently accurate shooter they had, which was measured in fractions of an inch and a well defended title.

Toomby maneuvered the SUV back into the right lane, there was an 18-wheeler ahead, another a little further up. Toomby stayed off the gas until the first swung out into the left lane to overtake the other. It would be a long process. Speeds dropped to the 70's. Toomby lowered the rear hatch window. Porter steadied his rifle, turning his optic knob until the two MOA red dot was just visible enough to use against the headlights. The road was smooth. Tires were under headlights. The headlight profile said sports car or sedan, so lower than he would like. The distance was 50 meters, maybe a few more. He settled on the passenger side tire. It was going to be a blowout if he got a hit, which meant a right-side pop could pull the car off the road, which would be ideal. He didn't know if he would get a hit, not with one round. His point of aim drifted back to between the headlights, and low, then back to where the right tire likely was. He moved back and forth between the two points as quickly as he could, getting a feel for the movement, accounting for a slightly longer time due to recoil when he went live.

"How long I got?"

He asked, settling the dot once again between the headlights. The passing truck was halfway up the length of the slower vehicle.

"Don't marinate, but you have a few seconds."

Porter practiced his transition again, and again. The road stayed smooth. The distance stayed the same. He waited for the perfect breath, the safety thumbed off. The first round would sound like the car had hit something, a loud knock in the engine compartment, provided it didn't deflect up through the hood and hit the windshield. Barring that, the driver would hopefully assume nothing was immediately wrong, because there was an infinitesimal chance that the shot would do anything besides slowly cause the car to overhead due to a punctured radiator and eventually lead to engine failure. If it was a rear wheel drive he could hope for a pully hit, killing the serpentine belt, but that was reaching. No, a slow death and a flat tire. The radiator was just in case the car had run flats, as many modern sedans seemed to these days. Doubling down on breaking the car was the best option. He could just try for the driver, but the car was an unknown quantity. No, just break the car.

"About ten seconds."

Card said calmly. Porter was an excellent shooter, and this wasn't the first time he'd done this. First time like this, maybe, but not the first time in general.

"I got it."

Porter said, slowly squeezing slack out of the trigger. All he saw was the darkness between the headlights, staring through the red dot. The shot broke, the suppressor smacked loudly in the enclosed space, the rifle turreted left and down, the second shot broke not half a second later.

Porter brought his point of aim back between the headlights.

"Punch it, Toomby."

The headlights shuttered, dipped to the shoulder and began to fall back as Toomby rode the back of the left lane truck just as it cleared the slower vehicle. Toomby put the SUV on the median shoulder to pass; both trucks protested loudly with their air horns.

"We're good."

Porter said, watching the headlights come to a stop on the side of the road. He watched anyway, just in case. After a minute of watching, he pulled his rifle back over the seat.

"Anyone else feel like we just stranded a solid lead on the side of the road?"

Porter said, swapping in a fresh magazine.

"Yeah, but we have bigger problems."

Hollic said, watching his tablet as their blue dot raced across the map towards Tellion's red dot. It was blipping along, a few miles short of I 10. Hollic figured they would be within a few miles of them by the time they reached the interstate. Which direction they went would determine how fast they met.

17

The driver was talking to the passenger now; in Russian. I was following along, dusting off my understanding of the palatal articulation of consonant phonemes that Russian was known for.

"Try Bogdan again."

The driver seemed to be in charge. I could see his right forearm, the sleeve of what looked like an olive drab combat shirt was rolled up. Very American style. The sleeve didn't interest me, but his tattoos did. Deep blue ink that used to be black, usually a sign of poorly cared for tattoos, or poor ink to begin with. What I could see when the occasional sliver of light scanned through the windshield was manacles tattooed at the wrist, two of them. Above that, a light house. There was Cyrillic writing as well, but I couldn't read it. The tattoos were too specific to be some culture fad from some militarized hipster trend. He was Russian mafia most likely and had done time according to the manacles.

The passenger fumbled with a phone. I couldn't see much of him, but I doubted he wasn't part of the club. The muted sound of a number dialed. Muted ring. It rang and rang and rang.

"Nothing."

He said. His accent was different. Northern. His *O's* were clearly pronounced. The driver carried a pharyngeal fricative on his *G's*, among other things, made me think he was from the South, maybe Ukrainian. All of that was academic. I wasn't going to talk to them; chances are I was going to kill them. But I could understand them, so as long as they were talking, I was listening.

"This is fucked, where is Vadim driving us? The house is the other way."
The passenger said, throwing his phone on the dash. So. The Tahoe was in front of us.
"Bogdan doesn't answer, we don't go back to the house."
Thrown hands from the passenger. He was far more upset than the driver. Maybe younger, or more inexperienced, or both. Maybe he was tired of being dicked around. I know I was.
"What now?"
The driver turned and looked at him. Even in the dim light I could see a look somewhere between indifference and murder.
"We see Authority, he will know what to do with these Americans. What to do at all. So shut up and let me drive."
Avtoritet was the 'Authority.' An underboss of sorts, like a Captain. I remembered that much from my time in Russia, in a previous life.
"Anton? He's not in charge."
The driver doubled down on is ambiguous stare.
"Yes, I know this. But if Bogdan isn't answering his phone still, we go to Anton because if Bogdan isn't answering, he may be dead, and if Bogdan is dead, we can assume that Makar is as well, which means Anton is in charge. So we go. That is our job. So shut up. And. Let. Me. Drive."
The passenger kicked a foot up on the dash. Lighted a cigarette. He didn't crack the window. The driver didn't seem to mind.

Finn was free. He had cleared his restraints not long after me. I was glad the Army taught him, so I didn't have to. He was motioning to me, hand signals I didn't exactly know but got the gist of. He wanted to go at both of them at the same time. I saw a problem with that, being that one of them was controlling the van and the van was moving and we were not secured in any way. A struggle could mean a roll over or a head on collision. Of course, the alternative was to allow them to get us to wherever we were going, where maybe their numbers were greater. We needed a way to take control of the van without alerting their men in the Tahoe ahead of us. I didn't see a whole lot of options. I conveyed my opinion to Finn with hand signals of my own, hoping he understood. He seemed to get it. He didn't like it, but he got it. We rambled on, bouncing on worn shocks. The windshield showed darker than light. I could see two rifles up front, tucked against the console in the passenger floor board, secured by a bungee strap of some kind. Nondescript AK variants, Short, skeleton stocks, lights and suppressors. It didn't mean these guys were professional, but it made me think they were more likely that than simple amateurs.

"It's quiet, check them."
The driver said. We had slowed a few minutes ago, dirty yellow light from sodium lights washing into the van. A right turn and an assent. Probably the Interstate. Headed East. The passenger was up, far too tall to be standing in the van, he hobbled between the seats, moving towards Finn first. Finn was ready. The passenger put both hands on his arm and rolled Finn towards him; Finn's hands snapped to the passenger's wrists, a look of surprise, but no immediate reaction. Finn pivoted on his hips, his legs came

up, ankles crossing behind the passenger's neck while his right arm was pulled into to Finn's abdomen with both hands, letting his left arm free to flail. He had a handgun at the waist, right hip. He wasn't likely to get to it. I was up, moving forward. Because the passenger was tall, he had no room to work against the triangle choke, nowhere to go besides down. The driver was still unaware. I made it to the fight, stripped the passenger's gun and kept moving. The passenger was out of gas, and Finn didn't need my help. I slipped between the front seats, plopping down in the passenger seat.

"They're good."

I said in rusty Russian. He didn't buy it, but he did buy the pistol in his face when he looked over to see who the new voice belonged to.

"Hello, I'm Rushing. English?"

A shake of the head.

"Fine. Both hands on the top of the wheel, left on top of the right. I'm going to take your sidearm. If you do anything, I will shoot you and push you out. Understand?"

He wasn't scared, but he believed me. I could see it in his face. Just a professional transaction. He gave me a nod.

"Finn, you good?"

Finn slipped up behind the driver, a hand on the seatbelt on either side of the driver's head. He pulled out the slack, up to the neck.

"Got you."

"Get his gun."

I said, thinking better of grabbing it myself. Finn slipped the driver's pistol out of his holster. He was wearing a MOLLE battle belt of some kind, complete with Safariland ALS holster for what was revealed to be a Glock 17 with weapon light, just like the one I took off the passenger. Professional kit for some Russian mafia guys.

"You speak Russian?"

Finn asked.

"Uh, yeah."

The driver scoffed. And I was sure he spoke English, but I kept it Russian for him anyway.

"You going to tell us what happened back there?"

Nothing. He would need to be motivated to speak and that kind of motivation wasn't going to happen while he was in control of the van. Which we needed to take away from him before he did something stupid.

"Okay, fine. Here's what is going to happen. You are going to leave the driver's seat and move backwards into the back of the van. If you do anything other than what I have said, I will open that window with the left side of your face."

Another scoff, but he spoke.

"Okay, cowboy."

"I need you to understand that I will kill you if you don't do as I say."

This time he gave me the stare, somewhere between indifference and murder. He was thinking, working the odds.

"I understand."

A flash of broken teeth. He wasn't going to go easy. He was going to do something stupid. I looked ahead; the Tahoe was maybe 25 meters ahead, no other traffic on our section of road. I clicked his seatbelt release. Finn let the shoulder strap go, the worn-out belt took what seemed like forever to reel in. As soon as he lifted his weight off the seat and his hands came off the wheel I shot him in the side of the head. Finn was surprised but acted fast, straining forward to grasp the wheel. I pulled the door handle and pushed him out onto the road as I slid into the seat, foot on the gas to regain the speed we lost. The door shut, I tossed my gun on the dash. My ears were ringing but at least I had a nice breeze from the permanently open window.

Finn slid into the passenger seat.

"Other guy dead?"

I asked.

"Yeah, fuck that guy."

"Well I don't feel so bad then. What now?"

Finn checked the gun he had taken, then grabbed the phone off the dash.

"See if I can get us some help."

"Uh, is that a body?"

Toomby asked, swerving around a dark human shape in the middle of the road.

"Yeah, I suppose it was."

Card said, in a bit of wonder at the sight of it.

"They shouldn't be much further."

Hollic said, watching the blips on his tablet. Ahead, Toomby could make out a set of square tail lights, high on the road. As they closed the distance, the headlights crept up the back of a van. 90's era Econoline, just like the one at the house. Toomby drifted into the left lane, the Tahoe wasn't far ahead of the van.

"Well, now what?"

Before anyone could answer, Hollics phone chirped. He dug it out of his pocket, frowning at the screen. He didn't recognize the number. He hit the receive button anyway.

"Chief, Finn, what's your status?"

Hollic hit the speakerphone option.

"We are probably right behind you, what's going on?"
Toomby wagged the vehicle.

"Yeah, okay, long story short, we got hemmed up by some
Russian dudes, Me and Rushing in the van, I think Tellison
and Maddy are in the Tahoe, but I don't know for sure. We
took the van, obviously, now we are weighing options."
Card smiled. Finn was a good add to the team, he was
calm and in work mode. He was also glad to hear that
Rushing was being of use. Hollic glanced around the cabin.
"Recommendations?"

"Be tough to hit the Tahoe moving, we need to get a status
on Tellison and Maddy first."
Porter said.

"We can creep by them like we are just out for an evening
drive, but if we do we will have to either stay up front or
hop off and back on again to keep from spooking them. I
mean, I'm all for shooting these fuckers but we need to
know what we got first."
Toomby said, eyes on the road. Finn spoke up from the
phone.

"There's two hostiles in the Tahoe, at least. Pretty sure
there were only four of them to begin with."
Card was wondering how Tellison's team got snatched, he
was eager to hear the story. It wasn't like Tellison or
Madeline to let someone get the jump on them. A new
voice on the phone. Rushing.

"Hey, new guy here. I'm sure you guys have all sorts of
experience in these things and that's great, but I'm pretty
sure we can end this by relying on human nature and
curiosity."
Hollic whipped his head around, looking for anyone who
may have understood what Rushing was talking about. No
one seemed to. Rushing continued.

"Look, if we pull off and stop, they probably will, too. We have numbers on them now and they probably won't expect us to have taken out their friends. Our other option is to let them lead us to wherever we are going, which is probably going to mean more Russians, more guns, more dead people and more problems."

No one said anything at first. Card thought it was a smart play. If they let the Russians in the Tahoe lead them, chances are it was going to end with more shots fired than answers. Card had no doubts that they would win, but you don't get nearly as much intel from dead bodies as you do from live ones. Everyone else seemed to come to the same conclusion. The tricky part would be getting live bodies at the end of this.

"Okay."

Hollic said, feeling out the fact that he was ultimately in charge.

"What's the plan, Rushing?"

"Car trouble."

Rushing said.

There was no uniform way to fake car problems, seeing as there were many ways that cars break. But most of them ended in the same way; coasting or clunking to a stop. Curses said, hoods went up and usually the person peering in at the engine would have no idea what exactly they were looking at, let alone *for*. The plan was set, now all they had to do was do it. Finn ended the call, checked his requisitioned rifle and looked over at me.

"How many languages you speak?"

I shrugged.

"All the Caucasian ones, more or less. You ready?"

Finn did a quick seating check on the magazine in his new rifle.

"Sure, how do you know the driver is the one we want?"

I shrugged again. Probability. Importance. The driver was just as likely to be in charge as the passenger; imagining that I had heard correctly and there was four of them then we only had two to worry about. Of course, I couldn't account for voices I may not have heard so the number could be higher. What was one more roll of the dice in my life?

"Alright, here we go."

I pushed the column shifter to neutral, letting the engine rev, let it coast for a few seconds like I was trying to figure it out then drifted to the side of the road. The noise was awful and was going to eventually cause real damage to the engine. The Tahoe didn't notice at first, and for a second I didn't know if they would. They pulled further and further way until finally brake lights flared. I was at a stop, Finn was already out, door shut and disappeared into the wood line. The other team had killed their lights and pulled off the road as soon as I gave them a triple tap signal on the brakes. They would be on foot and moving fast towards the van. I opened my door, stopping to lodge the gas pedal with a spare magazine from the other guy in the van. I was worried it wouldn't work but our choices were limited. My worries were unfounded, the ridges in the all-weather mat helped me get it on the first try. Out of the van I pulled the hood release, then walked around to the front, fingering the short hood up. The engine was red lining, a small amount of smoke was pushing through cracks in dry rot hoses.

Finn had found a half-used container of brake cleaner in the van. I doused it on the hot engine, the smell was toxic. The smoke was impressive.

I'm a showman.

The Tahoe was backing towards me, clumsily. Nothing
worse than trying to back an SUV with tinted windows
along an interstate with anemic reverse lights while the
occasional set of headlights sped by. One thing was for
sure, it was dark. Traffic was light, mostly 18 wheelers at
that time of night and I was glad for that; no way to really
tell how the next few minutes was going to go.

The Tahoe came to a stop a little closer than I would have
liked, about a car length. I made sure to stand out of the
way of the driver's side headlight as I began cursing in
Russian, banging on metal inside the engine compartment
with my requisitioned handgun. The high beams were on,
the driver was out, walking back. He was calling out my
name, well, the name of the man he thought I was, but I
pretended like I couldn't hear. I was turned far enough to
the side that I saw Finn and the others creep out of the
woods, moving on the Tahoe. They had a few feet of
darkness to hide in before the passenger side headlight
revealed them. I moved to the passenger side, blocking the
headlight as the walk back made it to the van. He realized I
wasn't who he thought I was, but it didn't do him any good.
I smashed him directly in the nose with a palm strike; fully
cocked and with all the hip rotation I could give. It was a
large nose, attached to a large face, which was on a large
head, atop a very large body. But anatomy was anatomy, a
sufficient blow to the face and the lacrimal glands pushed
tears into the eyes. Take a man's vision, even for a second
and you can own him. He was fast, coming in with a
haymaker but it wasn't going to help him. I ducked under

the swing, rolling around his back, trapping his missthrown right arm against the side of his head, wrenching down hard. I kicked his knees out and let gravity help. He struggled, and almost broke free, his strength was impressive, but it didn't keep him from going to sleep in the end. By the time I had thrown the palm strike, Finn and the others rushed the Tahoe. They moved as a fluid unit. I expected them to have to shoot the passenger; and had no doubt that they would have, but he didn't see them and was yanked out and put on his stomach before he could put up any fight. Two when I expected one. Nice.

I yanked the magazine off the gas pedal, the engine fell to a restful idle. It was running hot but seemed mechanically okay. Finn and Hollic joined me at the van with the passenger from the Tahoe, we loaded him and the driver into the Econoline, both wearing proper cuffs from someone's kit.
"Maddy?"
I asked to either of them that could answer. Honestly, she was the only one I had any real connection to, which meant she was the only one I had an emotional investment in. The realization was somewhat startling to me. I cared for her, but that was the first time that doing so had gravity and consequences.
"I'm good, Rushing, aside from the obvious. These cunts alive?"
Madeline said as she appeared behind us, rubbing her wrists.
"Both alive."
I said. On the far side of the interstate, two sets of flashing blues rounded the bend. They were already moving at a high rate of speed, much too fast to be stopping adjacent to

us. Chances were good that they were headed to the body we, well, I, had thrown on the road. A bit of deductive reasoning would have them coming back our direction not long after that. I wasn't the only one who figured it out. Toomby and Card raced by, headed back to get the other vehicle.

"Tellison?"

I asked Maddy. She gave me a nod.

"We all came out of that alive, though search me how or why."

"Gear?"

"All in the Tahoe."

Tellison materialized from the darkness.

"We need to move, we need a place we can take our new friends."

He was looking at me. I did a mental check of places I knew and had access to. Taking them back to the hotel room would be a problem; too many eyes, too public. My house was out as well. The only one that came to mind was Manny's scrap yard in the city. It was early Sunday morning at that point, Manny wouldn't open until Monday. That gave us some time.

"I have a place."

18

Julian had hit the house in Slidell as soon as the sun set. The party was loud and drunk long before then; he walked right through one back yard and into another. Taped the window to make it quiet then went in fast. He didn't expect Russians, not that it mattered. Heller wasn't there. Three bodies left behind. A few phones, texts. Nothing Julian could make sense of in the short time he had. He left the house more or less how he found it, crossed the street and put himself in the hedges of the neighbor's house. When the night wore on, someone else came. He knew someone would. American police, at least that's how they dressed. They hit the house from the front. Julian was indecisive; he didn't want to kill police. He didn't know much about American police, but he was pretty sure they drove police vehicles. He was also pretty sure there would have been more than four of them, or more than four of them after the fact. Five minutes. Ten minutes, no other police came. That was odd.

Julian left his hiding spot and returned to his car. He parked not far from the entrance to the neighborhood and waited. When the SUV left, he followed it. They headed for the city, then they didn't. He was sure they had *made him* as they say, but whatever caused them to suddenly leave the interstate and then head in the other direction; it wasn't him. He stayed with them. Kept his distance, and thought he was invisible. The problem, as he found out, was, even keeping your distance could make you stand out if you had to move as fast as your prey. When civilization fell away and the traffic bled off, he had to be apparent. The only car keeping up. And he was. There was a loud thump. The headlights didn't show anything in the road before the noise. Then the right front tire blew. The engine hissed. He wrestled the car to the side of the road, and a quick inspection of the front grill confirmed what he thought. A single round to the radiator. He imagined a second round had taken out the tire. At least they were nice enough to not shoot him through the windshield. It was a stolen car; taken from the valet of a New Orleans hotel. Stealing another car on the side of the interstate in the middle of the night wasn't going to happen. He was angry. Rage. His head pounded, his vision pulsed with every heartbeat.

He was being tested. The lord, if there really was one.

No. What a horrible thought. The lord was with him. Always.

Julian took his rifle from the trunk and started walking. It was wrapped in cloth to conceal what it really was, simple rope served as a shoulder strap. It would look out of place if anyone paid close enough attention, but he didn't care. He wasn't a stranger to long walks, he'd walked on five continents, the US just being added to that count. Compared to a trek across a North African desert, a walk along an interstate cut through a forest wasn't difficult at all. He was tired, but he walked. His arm still ached, he was sure there was infection. A fever would come if he didn't get better care for it. He would have time for that after. Heller came first.

His mind drifted back to his church. It seemed like ages ago, and maybe it really was. He remembered the desert in

Mali, riding across the desert in the Sahel in turret of an AMX-10RC armored vehicle. It was always loud, constant vibration, and hot. The dust in the turret never had a chance to settle because of the vibration, it would just hover in the air in a state of suspended animation until breathed in or blown away by hot breath. His neck ached, head held at the slightly awkward angle needed to stay on the gun sight for the 105 cannon. It was as if it had been designed by someone with a sadistic desire to punish people with a traditional length neck. Worse still, the brow pad that was a small part of the *upgrade* under the RCR program felt like it was filled with gravel, or at least it did after more than a few minutes of rest. But Julian had to stay on the sight, the thermal sight, an older system taken from one of France's decommissioned main battle tanks, was all they had to cut through the repressive darkness as his vehicle, middle of three, crept up a shallow ravine towards a suspected Islamist fighter encampment. Julian had deployed to Mali with *1er Régiment Étranger de Cavalerie*, and his reconnaissance squadron had been tasked with confirming an enemy position and engaging them if needed. Despite virtually no intelligence besides a vague report on the encampment location, and little time to prepare, Legionaries did their duty. Julian was still proud of that fact. The Legion had saved him first, before he found God again. If not for the Legion, he would have died of drugs, guns or knives on the streets of London long before he came to Christ for the second time.

They weren't far from the closest overlook to the location of the suspected camp when the lead vehicle vanished. There was no mystery to where it went; it was hit by numerous RPGs at the same time; all from slightly different directions, Julian saw them all bloom in from the shallow canyon walls, the lead vehicle was in the right 1/3rd of his screen as he scanned left; the black and white of the thermal imager was set to White Hot; it flashed, and then flashed again and again in a matter of a second, each blast adding to the heat that completely drowned out the archaic thermal processors ability to detect a contrast in heat. The shockwaves from the multiple rockets seemed to arrive like fast thrown jabs, pounding the hull. Julian was quick to drive the cannon up, looking for targets on the ledge above. The vehicle commander was shouting orders, the driver was complying, a screaming diesel engine began to pull them in reverse. It was too late for that. Julian found a target, a white hot shape of a man with something on his shoulder. He was joined by three other identical shapes, they pointed cold tubes down into the canyon; what could only be more RPGs contrasting against their body heat. They were far too close to safely fire the main gun; but safety was a relative concept. Julian switched from the coaxial machine gun to the 105mm. One round of High Explosive went out before the men could fire their RPGs. It was only half a victory. The other side of the AMX was struck by an unknown number of rockets from the opposite side of the canyon. He heard the driver scream through his headset; saw his vehicle commander sheared in half by broken metal accelerated to fatal speeds by the 82mm warhead of a RPG-2 rocket in the dim red light of the turret. Felt hot knives stab him in the legs and side. He was pulling left as hard as he could on the turret control, slewing around while smashing the button to switch back to the coax. The engine had died but the turret still moved on battery power. The wounded AMX was rolling blindly in reverse under the power of inertia and gravity. The thermal sight flickered; he depressed the trigger at the first human shape he saw on the canyon edge; white hot splashes of what could only be blood misted the black background of the sky; he continued turning. The turret shuttered and stopped when a lone rocket struck the hull. The sound was immense, the force rocked the vehicle up on its side. A second rocket. A third. The AMX tilted and fell hard on its right side. A fourth.

A fifth.

Julian's head smashed hard against the bulkhead. Knives in his back.

A sixth.

He crawled; calmly pawing in the darkness for the hatch handle. It became more dream than reality. Fear had been beaten out of him. Either he would survive, or he wouldn't.

A seventh.

He popped the hatch; smoke washed in as he slithered out. The sand was hot and wet, blood, diesel fuel. He crawled towards the darkest spot he could find, towards the rear. A tire popped and hissed as fire burned into its contained air. Molten rubber dripped down on Julian's back. He stayed the course. He found the dark; pulling his entire body into it like hiding under a blanket.

Yells of celebration from the canyon above. No more rockets. He struggled to find his pistol; once he did he clutched it to his chest and waited. Surly they would come.

They didn't.

Night wore on; his mind suspended somewhere between alert and unconscious. The fires died down. He heard no sound made by man. Hours ebbed by. The fires extinguished. He was alone.

No one else had survived.

Julian slept.

God found him in the morning.

God by way of Father Adama Aya.

Father Aya; his kind eyes tucked away under gray brows, guiding the hands of a man who had been a surgeon in a past life and a solider before that. God had seen fit to send the only emissary in a hundred miles that could have saved his life. His wounds were fatal.

And yet he lived.

He had two collapsed lungs; pneumothorax from multiple punctures to each.

And yet he breathed.

His legs were broken.

God carried him.

Father Aya was the first thing he saw when he awoke again. He was in a simple room; the walls were bare; the paint was old but clean. His bed was simple. His bandages fresh. An IV dripped silently into a tube that ran to his hand. Julian could see it came from a bag that declared it was long since expired, but who was he to question it? The old priest sat in the corner, reading. He acknowledged Julian was awake but didn't speak, just a curt nod and then his eyes went back to the page. Julian would come to find that Father Aya was not much of a talker outside of speaking on behalf of the lord. The stories Aya didn't tell, were told by his scars. He had seen war, it had taught him lessons that only war could. But he didn't speak of it. Julian would come to love that about him.

He took to reading the bible to him when he was awake, salient verses that helped Julian understand his pain, understand how he had come to be where he was. Hours and hours of listening, but few words spoken in conversation. Father Aya would seamlessly switch from English to French, in whichever language would best convey the feeling and the meaning of the scripture. Julian drank it in. His first life was that of an only child to a wealthy family. Money earned on the backs of the poor. Julian chose the church over the hobbies of other rich kids his age. He felt that God wanted him to atone for the sins of his family. He made it to college, nearly through college before God took everything from him. His mother lost her life to cancer and his father lost his life to the pistol in his mouth. Julian didn't stray from the path, he took a hard left turn on purpose to get as far away as he could from the Lord. Father Aya was the Lord calling him back.

Within a few days, the Legion came for him, just as he knew they would. Brothers he recognized but somehow no longer knew. He had been born English, but was now French By Spilt Blood, *Français par le sang versé*. He said his goodbyes to Father Aya but told him he would return. He was leaving Mali with other wounded. He was leaving as a Legionnaire. He would return something more.

Julian was pulled out of his memories by some activity ahead. Traffic was being diverted to the inside shoulder around a patrol car. There were flares. Julian pulled closer to the wood line and maintained his course. A few more minutes closer and he could see two police cars, one officer was crouched down over something in the road, the other was mindful of the occasional vehicle. A few more minutes and an ambulance sped by, lights but no sirens. Judging by the lack of the movement from the shape in the road, the ambulance wasn't needed. Julian's next steps would need providence.

He needed attention diverted in the right place at the right time. It happened like it was choreographed. One officer was up on the passenger side of an 18-wheeler talking with the driver about navigating past the left most cruiser. The second officer was obscured by the front of the ambulance along with the two EMTs. Julian simply stepped into the open door of the other cruiser; took a few seconds to learn the switches and then turned off everything at once. Shut the door gently, shifted into drive and steered down into the sloping shoulder. Had anyone been looking they probably would have seen the cruiser idle by, lit by the reds and blues dancing off the tree line. But no one who mattered was looking. He eventually steered back onto the road and accelerated to highway speed before turning the headlights on. At first, he figured he would only have a few minutes at most to use the car before they came looking for it or were able to locate it with some sort of GPS. One look the odometer told him that was not very likely; the cruiser was pushing 300K. A department that ran cars that long, probably didn't equip them with GPS trackers. Either he would be right, or wrong. Either way, he needed to take the risk.

19

Two days before Resolute

We made it to Manny Orry's scrap yard before 3AM. At that time of night, or morning, North Villere Street was nothing but the occasional corner hustler and light traffic drifting by silently in the river. Cars were scarcer than working streetlights and the humidity left its slick mark on any surface that would bear it.

I didn't have a key to the yard gate, but it was an open secret to anyone who knew Manny long enough where there was a spare. Tucked away inside a decades-old Red Man Chew pouch that was itself slid into the remains of a fence pole near the walk-through gate. I retrieved it, undid the padlock for the drive through then swung open the dilapidated chain link. Once the vehicles were through, I fed the chain back through the gates and locked it on the outside; just in case an observant cop and/or cousin of Manny's happened by and noticed something was different. The yard only had one building big enough for everyone to be inside comfortably, but it wasn't much of a building in the way of having the usual number of walls. It may have been built as a commercial dry storage warehouse, but it didn't look much like that anymore. The entire entry facing wall was gone, ease of access for vehicles and people alike. It wouldn't do for any sort of interrogation where someone might speak above a polite dinner conversation volume. Manny's office trailer was the best bet. It may have the thin walls that job site trailers were known for, but at least it had all four of them.

The vehicles were backed in next to the trailer on the side away from the street. I went into the office and found the best chair Manny had, set it in the widest part of the small space, then let Finn know we were ready. Tellison brought the first man in, the passenger from the SUV, a makeshift blindfold on his eyes, steel cuffs at the wrist, shackles at the feet, and a gag in his mouth. He was set in the chair, but not secured to it. Tellison left Finn inside with him while we gathered outside. Sergeant Toomby remained in the van with the other Russian. We gathered out of sight from the street, far enough away that we couldn't be overheard. "Alright, Mr. Hollic, before we try to talk to these guys, what have we learned?"

Tellison said to Hollic. He was calm. Like the explosion and his kidnapping was just part of the job. I suppose I had the same demeanor.

"Gianna has a shit load of intel for us, not really in a position to sort it standing out here. Easy part is that these guys are legit Bratva, some newer offshoot of *Solntsevskaya Bratva*. What we don't know is what the hell they are doing here or what their involvement is. Based on what you guys told me about the boat house, they slotted the boarding party but stuck around waiting for someone else that maybe they expected to be there. From the house, we know they have an incubator. Whatever was…is in that tube that was on the ship, its biological and they probably intend to cook it for more. These guys deal in all sorts of stolen property but dealing in WMD's is new territory for them as far as I know. We aren't going to get these guys to talk."

His last sentence was full of conviction. Hollic may have been new to a lot of what was going on, but he was seeming more and more a solid investigator. I could see why he was on their team.

Tellison considered his words.
"Let's work on the first guy, see if we can get anywhere with him. If not, we can toss him to Hijazi and let the white side do it the legal way."
Hollic shrugged.
"I'm good with it."

"Okay."
Tellison said, pulling off the blindfold.
"We are going to talk, I'm going to remove your gag, but you will speak when spoken to, and if you raise your voice above the volume of mine, I will shoot you in the face. Do you understand?"
The man in the chair may have, but the genuine look of confusion on his face gave even odds that he didn't speak English. I repeated Tellison's words in Russian.
A smile and a nod. The smile was one of appeasement, agreement, but his eyes told me he wasn't nearly as afraid as he wanted us to believe. Tellison's look, however, was one of surprise. I guess Finn hadn't briefed everyone on the fact that I spoke Russian.
"Okay, Rushing, I guess you are going to translate then?"
I shook my head.
"No, I'm going to talk to him, you are going to sit in the corner and shut up, and before you try to posture here, remember that I don't give a shit about your chain of command. I'm the only one here with a tool to fix this problem, so if you want it done, we do it my way."
He was unreadable. A brief pause, he responded.
"Okay, I can live with that."

Tellison shuffled to the corner near the door where Madeline and Hollic were standing, the others remained outside. I got a feel for the man in the chair, his tattoos on his forearms were the same as the others, I pulled the front of his shirt down, more *grins.* Even defeated and restrained, he acted as if it was no large inconvenience. He was comfortable with the adornments of incarceration.

"What is your name?"

"Elvis Ivanov."

What?

He sighed.

"My mother, she loved your American Elvis Presley. Since my father was one of any hundreds of customers and she never knew which, she got to name me."

I supposed he wasn't a stranger to having to explain his name. I knew the feeling. Hollic stepped up briefly to take a photo of his face, then began texting. Checking for information on him I was sure.

"My name is Rushing, so I get it, though I don't have a neat story to go with it. Here's the deal, I'm pretty good at not being lied to, in fact, I may be the best at it. If I feel like I'm being lied to, I'm going to do exactly what was already promised; shoot you in the face."

I leaned back against Manny's cheap laminate desk, pistol tapping against the front as it hung ready in my hand. His demeanor remained unchanged.

"What were you doing at the boat house?"

A laugh. A literal belly laugh, it sounded like one of those hearty, cliché laughs that comes out of a much rounder and older man.

"You are police, I will tell you nothing."

He switched to English; it was heavily accented, but correct.

"I will tell you nothing."

The Vor have a code, a literal code, the Thieves Code. I was a little hazy on some of it, but what I did remember is that helping any authority was forbidden. In America, snitches may get stiches, but in Russia, they ended up dead in a river. It didn't rhyme but was more permanent. I expected him to be resistant. I also knew that the code wasn't as closely followed as it had once been.

I continued in English since he spoke it.

"Elvis, you have a problem. You talk to us, you will be punished, maybe even killed. That's an abstract future. If you don't talk to us, you *will* be killed. Right here, in this shitty little trailer. I'm not Police, neither are they, really, but you only need to worry about me."

I pointed to Tellison.

"Him, he can't kill you, not legally. Don't mistake that for *doesn't want to* or *isn't willing*, it's just he has rules that I don't. Me, I don't give a shit. I'll gladly make you a ghost. I have no patience at all, and you are going to sit there and stick to your code. I get it, I do, but now is not the time to get yourself killed. I am only looking for Martin Heller, tell me where he is, and we can be done here."

His eyes narrowed at the mention of Heller's name.

"This man, Heller. We look for him too. Maybe we can help each other. Give me a phone?"

Tellison scoffed in the corner.

"He wants his phone call?"

Elvis shook his head, not bothering to look at Tellison when he answered.

"Heller stole from us, we can do business."

Well I didn't expect that. Tellison moved out of the corner. Since Elvis spoke English, my leverage to steer the conversation was gone. He was taking over. I wasn't happy about it.

"Alright, Elvis. Tell me a story. Then we can discuss helping each other."

Elvis motioned behind him with his chin.

"Free my hands."

A stoic shake of the head.

"Earn it first."

Another Sigh.

"I know very little. This man, Heller, he paid us to smuggle, what we do. We arrange and protect. We find what he wants, we bring in the…uh…chamber. We protect it. We bring in the...uh…tube, but before it gets to us here, he steals it."

I couldn't tell if he was speaking broken English on purpose, but I got the feeling he was smarter than he was letting on. He most certainly knew more than he was letting on, he was leaving things out. Editing the information as he recalled it. Tellison was unreadable, though he had to see it, too.

"So, you went after them?"

An enthusiastic nod.

"Yes, Morozov ordered it himself, the *Pakhan,* he was very angry. We go. Find them; but no Heller. No cylinder. So, we wait. Find you inste-"

I interrupted him

"Why the trap?"

The mines seemed like overkill. Another sigh.

"Heller is dangerous man. Even Morozov has heard of him. You don't kill a man like this in his bed; you burn house down around him. When we get to the, uh…boat house, security at house…camera. Man come, kill our people."

His English sucked. Whether intentional or not, the result was the same.

"*Na russkom.*"

I said. He told me again in Russian, from the beginning. I guess I was going to translate after all. Once he'd gotten it all out, I turned to Tellison.

"The unremarkable man at the docks was their point of contact with Heller. They put some cheap mail order tracker on his car after their first meeting. The house was arranged by Heller as well. When the ship got hit, they went after the boat house. He says that they were setting the mines and had planned on doing the same to the boat house when two boats came in. They ghosted them and waited for the rest."

Tellison stroked his goatee, thinking.

"Wait, so it was three boats that came in, or two?"

I asked Elvis.

"Three come."

Tellison frowned.

"That's still bad math. We are short a minimum of four bodies. Where the hell did they go, and where the hell did their package go between the ship and the boathouse….wait, what was he saying about the house?"

"Maddy, you have his phone?"

Hollic picked it up off the desk; it was a smart phone with a touch screen. He held it up.

"There should be a camera app on there, they put wireless cameras at the house. They were at the boat house when the house was hit. Their boss told them to stay, kill Heller and then meet him across the border in Mississippi."

Hollic thumbed through the apps; the text was set to
Cyrillic, so he went by pictures alone, guessing which one
was for the camera program.

"Okay, got it. This is some cheap shit, but it records when
there is motion."

He scrolled through the videos.

"How the hell did we miss these cameras?"

The Russian chuckled.

"Small."

I walked over to Hollic and the others, he held the phone so
we could all see it, looking at the thumb nails and time
stamps. He found the first video of the priest; the front
door camera caught him heading down the side of the
house in grainy near-IR light.

"We didn't miss this dude by much."

He went to the next video, the hallway, it looked like the
camera was mounted high on the wall in the living room to
cover as much as possible. The priest entered from the
master bedroom; he moved so fast the cameras frame rate
couldn't keep up. Within a second, he had put down one in
the living room, a long shot while he was still in the hall,
then shot the man in the kitchen like he knew he was there.
He disappeared from the frame, darting into the garage.
Three dead in four seconds according to the camera clock.

Damn.

If Tellison was impressed, he hid it well.

"Who is this guy?'

He looked directly at me. I knew what he was thinking.

"Sorry, Tellison, if I'm *related* to him, I don't know him.
Seems like he wants what we want, anyway."

He didn't find much comfort in that.

"What else did the Russian say?"

"He has a name, you know?"

Tellison stared right through me.

"We really gonna do this?"

Despite myself, I enjoyed pushing his buttons.

"Maybe later. He doesn't know what was actually in the container. I believe him. But his boss probably does. I can't see them setting all of this up without knowing what they were moving."

"Does he recognize the priest?"

"No."

"Well this is proper fucked."

Madeline said, rewatching the videos on the phone.

"Well, Tellison?"

She asked. Hollic looked to him for a decision as well. I watched because everyone else was. The Russian did too because he didn't have anything better to do.

"Outside."

Was all he said, and he lead the way. Finn and Card were standing near the steps, watching the street from the shadows. Porter was talking quietly with Toomby.

"Sergeant Finn, watch our guest."

Finn broke away and moved inside. Card kept his eyes on the street. Tellison moved towards the end of the trailer, out of earshot of the van.

"Okay, we need to bring the Colonel in on this, it needs to be a command decision. If we even consider meeting these guys, we need to know everything we can about them. We've already killed two of their people, our man Elvis is playing nice because he's locked down. No guarantees at all that he's going to stay that way if we let him make the call."

Hollic opened his mouth to speak but Card spoke first, just loud enough for us to hear from the shadows near the van, his eyes still on the street.

"We got cops."

I moved for a better position to see, keeping to the shadows. A lone cruiser, still too far away to make out other than the light bar on top, crept up the street, headlights off, it idled along, but something about it didn't seem right. I watched it approach until it dawned on me; the movement was shuttering, as if the curbside tires were rubbing along as it went. A cheap trick to keep a car moving in a straight line if you didn't want to be in it while it did. Which meant it wasn't a cop.

Which meant he wasn't in the car.

Which meant he was probably already on the lot.

"Not cops, it's the priest."

I was ahead of the curve, but not by much. Hollic keyed his radio.

"Pull it in tight on the trailer, we have company."

Julian's options were limited. He could only get so close to the scrap yard without exposing himself to any potential eyes watching for just that, and he was sure that someone was watching. Or the Americans had some sort of sophisticated electronic warning and detection system in place. Either way, the closest he could get before either being forced into street light or having to scale the security fence was the shadows created by an isolated clothes charity donation bin in an otherwise empty strip mall parking lot adjacent to where the Americans had gone.

He had pulled his stolen cruiser into a crop of trees in the middle of the divided intestate where the median widened and watched the return lanes. He knew that they would eventually head back towards the city, and he was right. He had sat for less than 30 minutes before he recognized the large Nissan SUV and two other vehicles convoy by. He gave them a good lead before pulling out and stayed as far back as he dared as he followed them.

Julian knew Americans, these kind of Americans, anyway. His brief experience with these Americans told him he was outgunned, perhaps outclassed. With the time he had, and the equipment he had, he was confident that he could take one of them, two with surprise. Given the right environment, perhaps three. They were not law enforcement. Military for sure. Probably American Special Forces. He had worked with the American SF as a Legionnaire; they came in different qualities. The sort of SF that would be conducting an interrogation in what looked like a scrap yard in the early morning hours on

American soil were the very dangerous quality, the *black side of the house* as they liked to say. What further complicated things was the fact that he had no desire to hurt them. As far as he could tell, they wanted the same thing he did, Martin Heller. The first part of the problem as he saw it, was what they wanted him for. Julian wasn't interested in anything short of Martin Heller being dead. The second part was an issue of patience; Julian had none and getting on the same page with the Americans was a delicate balance of him being able to speak to them if they didn't want to listen before getting violent. They may have been his only lead at that moment, and one he was lucky to even have given how the night had gone, but he had to consider the situation before committing to a decision that could make finding Heller more difficult, if not impossible if they decided to just shoot him.

When they decided to shoot him.

Probably.

Julian had parked the stolen cruiser a street back from the strip mall, buried it in the shadows of an abandoned shotgun house. The neighborhood this…scrapyard was in; was thankfully sparsely populated and looked to be more commercial than anything else at that hour. Not that any of that was helping him. From his angle, he saw them take a bound man into the lot's small trailer. Julian figured it was one of the Russians like from the house.

Mobsters. Criminals. Sinners. Men like Heller.
Men who had been working with Heller.

Julian remembered the phones he had taken; he had them, still. He hadn't even taken a moment to go through them to see if there was an alternative trail he could follow that wouldn't include confronting the Americans. He considered it, and almost abandoned his watch on the lot to pursue it, but it occurred to him that If he could gain allies in reaching Heller, it would be better than continuing on his own.

No man is an island, after all.

He decided he needed to get closer. The longer he waited, the more he risked losing any chance he had through the Americans. The problem was geography. There simply was no concealed approach to the scrapyard short of perhaps swimming in to the water side. Julian was only a humble swimmer, and that was in peak physical condition. He could feel a fever coming on. The stale focus at the edges of his mind. The subtle burn in his throat. The sweat. He was in no condition to swim unknown waters.

Even a halfway confident sentry would spot his approach no matter how he looked at it, so he needed a distraction. Creating a distraction by yourself is problematic. Julian couldn't be in two places at once, and any distraction he created would need to get their attention and hopefully no one else's. He considered his problem. He had a police cruiser. He could use that. He had moved back to the car, idling out to the main road. He snugged the tires close to the curb to help guide the car once it started rolling. Timing was going to be an issue. Julian was a strong runner, but he wanted a head start before the car was noticed. A search of the trunk of the cruiser netted him one useful item; a small container of marking flares. They would help, but Julian needed something else. He searched the parking lot and found what he needed, a commercial size roll of low voltage wire. It was old, discarded among a small pile of scraps from a renovation either finished or abandoned, but it would serve. He tied the free end off around a large chunk of broken cinder block, then took a moment to work through his plan in his head. So far, he had killed his way through, how many? Julian considered a number, decided it didn't matter. What mattered was that the killing had so far not gotten him any closer. Martin was always just out of reach. As much as he wished, a part of him wished, that he could kill his way through these men to find Heller, he couldn't without knowing if they deserved it, even while knowing he was in no position to judge who deserved anything. No, he would hope to make it in unobserved, find a way to learn what they knew, and failing that, hope they didn't kill him before he had an opportunity to talk to them.

His final step required the officers patrol bag. Inside he found multiple spare magazines for the officer's duty rifle and a handful of restraint ties. He bound the magazines together, then secured two of the flares to the stack of magazines. Most commercial flares had a burn time of 30 minutes, which would be plenty of time. Too much. Julian had to guess the length-to-time ratio when attaching the flares. It looked right, maybe more than he needed. Julian was careful to ensure that all the magazines where facing the same way, with the ammunition aimed towards the bottom of the car as he wedged the improvised device in the spare tire well, then worked the striker to ignite first flare, then the second.

Before he started, he took his bag and rifle blanket out of the car, hiding it under a collection of siding and metal beside the road. Discarded materials maybe from the same renovation, or perhaps just someone dumping their trash. It looked as if it had been there a while. It would serve for at least the night. He lodged the cinder block under the driver's side front tire. Then he ran all the wire out off of its spool, then shifted the cruiser to drive. It rocked up on the broken block, but the idling cruiser held. He said a prayer for that, then moved, trailing out the line behind him. He reached the limit of the wire quickly. Looking back, he had perhaps 60 meters. It wasn't much of a head start, but it would have to do. The street seemed more-or-less level, so the car would idle at perhaps ten miles an hour. A quick evaluation of distances. He would have perhaps ten or fifteen seconds to clear the fence once he got to the weak point he had identified, before the car drew attention. Less if someone was watching in his direction. Less than that if they were using night vision. It would work, or it would not.

Nothing would keep him from Heller.

He reached the end of the slack on the wire, ignoring the absurdity of his simple plan. He had once heard an American say that something that was stupid, but worked, was not stupid. Perhaps this was going to be one of those things. Without looking back, Julian yanked hard on the wire as he broke into a sprint, using a small sliver of shadow between the reach of two street lights to cover the distance between sidewalks, he dodged around a harsh cone of light projected from a security light on the yard fence, then had a direct run at the spot he had chosen. The pounding in his ears was early. His fever was checking in, telling him that it was worse than he wanted to believe. He was gaining more information on the spot he had chosen as he approached it. The fence appeared to sag here, at least it had from the greater distance. The top of the fence had a standard angled three-strand topper, which can be easily defeated with patience. The sag in the fence tricked Julian into thinking that the three-strand of barbed wire would either not be there, or it would be slack and make crossing easier. When Julian was mere feet from the fence, he saw that the topper was in place, even with the sag in the fence. He had two seconds to make a decision at that point. The fence was sagging backwards, falling back into the lot at a rate measured by calendar. That meant it was likely to be weak at the bottom. Instead of going over, Julian was going to go under. He hedged his bets, sliding to a stop on his hip, hitting the fence a little harder than he would like. The sound of mass against the chain link seemed to echo and reverberate off the entire length of the lot. Julian grabbed for the bottom of the fence; he pulled upwards, ducking his head low, forcing his body under the small gap he managed to create. He could feel the bitter ends of wire grab and tear at his jacket as he slid onto the lot. He rolled onto his back, kicking his way free of the fence. On his feet, he could see the tail lights of the cruiser as it passed the lot. It had bumped off the curb and was slowly drifting to the other side of the two-lane. By the time Julian had reached the side of the lot warehouse to get a better view of the area around the trailer, the cruiser had mounted the opposing curb and stopped hard against a fire hydrant. He ignored it, watching.

They had to know he was on the lot. There was no search party. They had collapsed in on the trailer. He didn't have a firm head count, but he suspected there were at least six of them. He had seen four at the house. Two at the shipyard before that. Six seemed low. He mentally accounted for eight. Then adjusted to ten. He was viewing the small office trailer from broadside, but most of his view was blocked by the vehicles. The van and one of the SUVs were parked alongside it, the other SUV was parked at a slight angle, nose pointed towards the lot entrance. Only a single bulb above the trailer door burned, painting the immediate area around the trailer with dirty yellow light. Right as Julian concentrated to use that light to gather data, someone broke the bulb. He heard the pop of the glass; the tinkle of pieces on the ground. He heard a brief shuffling of feet; then nothing. A horn sounded across the water. A single car passed by the lot on the street. A dog barked, barely audible in its distance. Then nothing. He was effectively stuck. Again. Of course, the idea that the shadows hid him was ridiculous. The Americans had night vision. Americans always had fucking night vision. The thought that right then, he could be painted with half a dozen IR aiming lasers from rifles, made sulking in the shadows seem as foolish as it was. Julian made a decision. He stood up, raised his hands, palms out, fingers spread, and walked out towards the trailer. Within a few steps he heard movement to his left, and from behind him. Boots on asphalt. A quiet, but forceful,

"Stop."

He did.

"Down, on your knees."

He dropped, slow.

"Cross your ankles, then sit on them."

He did as he was told, still not able to see the owner of the voice. He was listening for any sound to give a location; the speaker gave none.

"If you move, I will turn you into a fucking ghost, nod if you understand."

Julian nodded.

Now he heard movement again. Approaching from his left, from the depth of the lot, and from behind him. At least two shooters. Measured, professional steps. He felt hands, they were forceful, but not brutal. His hands were pulled down to the small of his back, then the slip of something over his wrists and sudden pressure; the plastic sound of a fast ratchet; zip ties of some sort. Tight, but not cruel. A strong hand inside his arm above the elbow. He was pushed over against a knee that appeared on the opposite side, precariously close to being allowed to fall over. Kept off balance on purpose as he was searched. His remaining pistol was removed.

"Up."

The voice said, guiding him to his feet. His feet were nudged an uncomfortable distance apart, the search continued. Practiced hands missing no area a weapon could be. Search finished, Julian was guided towards the trailer.

"Just because you are bound, doesn't mean you get a pass. Sudden movements or resistance will still get you dead. Tell me you understand."

"I understand."

Julian heard nothing in his words that would give him doubt that the man meant it. As they neared the small group of vehicles, two more men moved from the shadows, both flipping up their binocular night vision. One man he recognized from the house; the other, a younger man with a slight smile, gave him a nod.

"Nice trick with the car."

His compliment got him a sideways glance from the other man.

"Stow it, Finn."

His escort said, then spoke to him again as he was pushed up against the side of one of the SUVs.

"Spread your feet. Finn, shake him down."

His one-man fan club slung his rifle to his back in a practiced motion, cinching it down tight before he began a methodical search for everything that wasn't a weapon. Pockets were turned out, his belt line was turned down, shoes removed, all fast and professional. It was a fruitless search; everything else he had, was hidden in his bag.

His escort nodded to a fourth man, Julian could just make him out, as he stuck to the shadows. The man who chased him at the ship yard.

"This your priest?"

A suppressed scoff.

"You wanna take odds on there being more than one? Yeah, that's him."

"Africa?"

The voice asked him. His shoes were dropped back by his feet, he took that as permission to put them back on. He managed to do so with considerable footwork, contemplating his answer.

"Africa. Darfur."

A statement. Julian had nothing to lose by talking to them, at least about things they already knew.

"Yes, I was there."

The voice turned him around. Emotionless face beneath a ballistic helmet. Clear eye protection covering cold eyes. "You also hit the house in Slidell."

Julian didn't know if he knew that for sure, but it wasn't a stretch of the imagination for them to assume it.

"Yes."

"British, French? I hear both."

Julian gave a shrug.

"Not important. I think we want the same thing."

"Where is Martin Heller?"

Julian couldn't help but frown.

"I was hoping you yanks could point me in his direction. I owe him a conversation we didn't get to finish."

The man looked to the one he called *Finn*.

"Let's get him inside, put the other one in the Tahoe, I don't want them in the same room. Rushing, how long do we have this lot?"

"We need to be out of here in an hour."

Julian thought about how much time had gone by since he left the cruiser. He had a few more minutes before, regardless of how the conversation went, that hour would be taken away. He needed to know what they knew before that happened.

21

I was right about him being a priest, which Madeline
acknowledged with a glance as she joined Tellison, Hollic
and myself inside the trailer after Elvis the Russian had
been moved out, careful so the two did not see each other.
He had admitted being a priest, but nothing else. Not even
a name. He was my age, maybe older. He had a pallor that
told me he was sick, a fever. Even in a weakened state, he
exuded a quiet strength. His determination was evident. I
upgraded my mental assessment of him from *dangerous* to
really dangerous. It wasn't much of a metric if I had to
explain it out loud, but I knew what it meant. In a room of
killers, he could be king, if only by fractions of a second. I
was physically and mentally back on the top of my skill,
even then, the priest was someone I didn't want to fight if I
didn't have to.

Tellison, who, I put slightly below the priest on my mental
ranking, had the aforementioned sat in the chair previously
occupied by the Russian. He was asking him about Africa,
which I thought was a stupid waste of time, so I decided to
interrupt.

"What is Heller to you?"

Tellison's glance at me was toxic, though only in the eyes.
His expression was neutral. The Priest, previously
uninterested, seemed to animate at his mention.

"He killed a friend of mine, I intend to kill him for it."

Direct. Honest. I didn't doubt him at all. Tellison decided
to go with the new line of questioning.

"How do you know him?"

A small laugh. He shifted in the chair. I knew from
experience that sitting in a backed chair with your hands
bound was no easy task if comfort was a goal.

"We didn't chum it up in school, if that is what you are asking. You see how I'm dressed? You think a priest from the Sahel would find it to be on good terms with a man like Heller?"

He let the question hang. Tellison was unreadable again, Madeline was quiet. Hollic, also in the room, was busy on his pad, running the Priest's prints and pictures, no doubt. As controlled as his emotions were, the man was holding the lid onto an impressive stock of rage and I found myself relating to him.

"I don't need to share, but Heller attacked my village, my church, and killed my mentor-"

His voice was raised, nouns punctuated with clipped vowels and curled lips.

"He killed everyone, including me. But God wasn't done with me. Third time I'd died."

He had the room, that was for sure. Emotion tells a story better than facts ever will. Combine the two, and even a basic vocabulary can hold the audience in suspense.

"They came during mass. Most of the village was at the church. Killed those nearest the doors, then put everyone else on their knees. Sent one of the boys to gather everyone, tell them they had to come to the church or they would kill everyone. Heller separated the congregation from the parish. Laid us out like luggage, he did. A building not much larger than this, no room to walk between the bodies. Once he had everyone, he made a call, got his permission, then gave the word. I was near the altar, I was supposed to give homily. I was laid to see right down the nave. I watched his men move forward like they practiced it, they killed so fast that no one had chance or thought to fight back. Lambs."

His voice caught, but he didn't break. He shifted in his seat again. I could see what he was doing. Had done. I knew his hands were free. He looked at me, seemed to look right into me.

"I watched Heller shoot Father Aya, then he did me. Should have died. I lay on that floor, blood deep enough that choking on it is what woke me up. To a child, the- *Heller* had killed every soul in ten kilometers."

He paused, taking a measured scan of the room, giving each of us a moment of eye contact.

"So, yeah, I know Martin Heller. Didn't know him by name until I had killed my way through a few of his men weeks later. I've been trying to serve him penance ever since."

Tellison, if he was moved in any way by the Priest's story, didn't show it.

"Do you have any information on where Martin Heller might be?"

He looked at Tellison, then at me, frustration on his face.

"You think I made my way in here because I had better options? I imagined we wanted the same thing. I'm starting to get the feeling from you, anyway, that may not be the case."

He pointed at Tellison with his chin.

"No?"

Tellison was unmoved. Stoic. Annoying.

"Give us what you have, we will see to Martin Heller."

Julian shook his head.

"Nah, mate. Together, or not at all. I didn't bring anything in here with me, I know how Americans like to just take things."

Tellison stared at him. Silent. He may have been considering his response. It was becoming a complicated situation. They had already brought me on board, which he was clear about not liking. Now this Priest shows up and volunteers. Not exactly how these black ops things generally went, I imagined. Madeline broke the silence. "So, you heard enough in Africa to track Heller here, we ran into you at the docks. Apparently, our chaps just missed you at the house. Now you show up here-"

The priest interrupted her.

"Ah! Yes, we are all on the same page now. I want to find Heller, you want to find Heller. I'm willing to help you. I don't seem to be getting very far on my own."

Tellison nodded thoughtfully. Not in agreement of what he said, just that natural *I hear you* nod.

"Okay. You can understand how we don't need your help. At this point, you are a complication and frankly I have enough complications without worrying about a rogue man of the cloth getting in our way. I can appreciate your grievances, I really can. But you don't have a role in this, so I'll give you two choices."

Tellison was really getting on my nerves, so I decided to say something.

"You don't think he can be of any help? Because I'm pretty sure he's a dirt-poor priest from Africa with zero logistics or support and he's made it as far as you..."

Tellison gave me the stare again. I decided to push it to see where it went.

"Further really, seeing as from what I've heard, he made it into the same room with him."

"Stow it, Rushing.

I couldn't help but chuckle.

"Fuck you. He can help."

He shook his head.

"This isn't a democracy, Rushing, and your invitation is dangerously close to being revoked."

Tellison paused, perhaps for effect or perhaps because he was making it up as he went along.

"So, as I was saying, you have two choices."

He was standing directly in front of the priest. Madeline was more or less behind him. Hollic was opposite me along the other side wall of the small office, placing him more-or-less in the same position to see what he was doing if he hadn't been buried in reading about the man who was sitting right in front of him. I had to imagine Hollic reading though a litany of facts that would immediately cause one to pay attention to the danger those facts created, right in front of them, yet he didn't. The Priest's hands were free. He had been moving them slowly to the back of the chair, gripping the cheap wooden stiles that held its single back brace. His shifting of weight in the chair would have told him how much it weighed. He knew everything about the room he needed to know, all he was waiting for was either his moment or his distraction.

Me, I had a coin to flip. Me and the priest had a lot in common. He was linear in his drive, and I was wasting time tagging along with Tellison and company in the hopes that they would let me kill Martin Heller. I knew that was wishful thinking. Whatever Solomon's people were up to, killing Heller didn't seem to be part of it anymore. I didn't know if Maddy knew that, but she had to suspect it. Everything prior to New Orleans had been straightforward with them. Bringing me in seemed to be in response to something, and that *something* had changed the approach.

So.

Let the priest do what he was about to do, and help him
help me find Heller, or stop him and play the same game
that hadn't gotten me any closer to Heller in the first place.
Tellison's attitude was pushing me to the former. I
watched Madeline. I could see she wasn't following
Tellison's train of thought, either.

"You hear me-"
Hollic interrupted, speaking for the first time.
"Julian Whent."
Tellison gave Hollic a glance as if to tell him to not
continue with a bio.
"-Mr. Whent. You either take a free trip to the country of
your choosing as long as it doesn't share a land border with
the US, or you go to jail."
Julian stared at a spot on the floor between his feet. The
weak lighting in the room left his face in a deep shadow.
He was buying time. Giving me time to make my own
decision. Quiet at first, then a low, sarcastic chuckle.
"You Americans, you always think it's you who gives
permission. Usually, you are right. It's hard to argue with
the power of a carrier group or a bomber wing that can fly
non-stop from your Oklahoma and bomb dirt farmers in
Kunar Province. But we are just men-and a woman.
Tactical, not strategic. This is about the moments we can
create to give advantage in the time between thought and
action. I do not need your permission to kill Martin Heller.
I don't want to have to kill any of you to do it, but I will if I
have to."

He looked up, watching Tellison. Giving nothing in his gaze, he was defiant, and he was right.

"Mr. Whent, that's academic, not kinetic. Ill choose for you. I feel for you, I really do, but you are going to sit this one out."
Tellison chinned at Hollic.
"We'll need local LE to pick him up, I'm pretty sure he didn't come in legally, so that should get him off the board."
Tellison was missing a singular, but important fact of reality. You only control what you can control through force or agreement. Julian was not in agreement, and he would not submit to force. All he needed was his distraction. I had made my decision. I made eye contact with Madeline, her face betrayed her feelings, she was emotionally tied to Julian through Martin Heller. So was I. Maybe neither of us were thinking clearly, but I knew the only people in that room I could trust to get me to Heller was a man I just met and a woman who I had come to trust above all else.

I looked down, hoping her eyes would follow, then gave her a simple sweeping downward palm. Hand signals could mean many things, and we hadn't exactly worked out our own personal set, but I wanted her to hear me. *Lay down.* I carried her eyes again.

Hesitation.

Then a feint nod.

"I got it, Tell."

Hollic said.

"I'll get something spun up."

Hollic moved to step outside, as he did, the rapid sound of gun fire pounded the cheap trailer walls. A few erratic pops, and then what sounded like multiple rifles at once opening up in the distance. It was inconsistent, and close enough that it got everyone's attention. Julian moved at the perfect moment, his chair came up and over his head, driven down into Tellison's shoulder and dominant arm. He carried much of the blow across the back, as he was turned in the direction of the gunfire when Julian moved. Hollic saw the motion in the dim light. A testament to his training in the unit, his hand was moving to his sidearm on reflex. I was a few steps away from him, and he would be clear to shoot before I could close the distance, so I moved into his line of fire, confusion on his face right before realization. I locked my left hand around his gun while driving my right palm hard into his nose. His grip on his gun loosened with the blow and I was able to pull it free, letting it follow gravity to the floor. I forced him down into an upward knee, I could feel the wind blow out of him as I connected under his body armor. Madeline moved at the same time I did, and her forearm slipped under Hollic's neck, she opted for an aggressive blood choke, guaranteeing Hollic would be unconscious in seconds. As her choke locked in, I spun to the motion behind me. Julian had disarmed Tellison, he was on his knees, defiant but visibly stunned.

"Don't."

Julian said, looking to me. He still didn't know my role in the last few seconds, or what I intended. Madeline moved behind me, securing Hollic's hands, pulling his radio. He would wake up on his own, in the next few minutes or hours. She kept her palms raised, working through the wreck of a room to the side of Tellison, careful to stay in Julian's vision.

"Same team."

I said, pulling a set of restraints from the MOLLE on my plate carrier.

"We won't get Heller with them, not how he deserves it. The Russians can get us Heller."

He thought quickly. A dart of the eyes from me, to Madeline, back to Tellison. The radio barked, seeming muted and far away.

"Vicious, Huck."

It was Finn, probably reporting on the source of the gunfire that had stopped seconds after it had started. Huck seemed a good choice of a callsign for him, given his history. I doubted it was his pick.

"Vicious, Huck."

Tellison gave a single *'heh'* a poison smirk on his face. He looked at me like I was the only person in the room. Like all his suspicions about me were true. Maybe they were.

"I don't answer, he's coming in. I answer, he's coming in with everyone because I won't play this game."

Julian looked to me, perhaps for suggestions. I worked around behind Tellison, he fought me, but I managed to get his hands secured.

"Huck, Knight."

Maddy said, keying her own radio. There was a brief pause, perhaps Finn wondering why Madeline and not Tellison was responding.

"Knight, our boy rigged a flare to some magazines in the car, no additional. The cruiser is fully engulfed, it's going to bring locals. We should pack it up."

Madeline was fast.

"Roger, Huck. Monitor roads and local channels, we will prep to move."

Julian had laid Tellison on his side, gagging him with a random rag he found on the floor.

"What is this, then?"

He asked, lowering the gun he took from Tellison. It was pretty clear to him that we had helped, but there wasn't much time to explain to him why. Sometimes you have to trust someone based on a lack of time to explain why you should.

"We have a lot to talk about, but we don't really have the time right now."

I said, pulling on the blinds by the door just enough to see. The path to the Tahoe was clear. I could see someone near the van, their backs to the door. The side of the lot was glowing from the car fire.

"Madeline, where are the Russians?"

She moved to the door, turned so she could watch either Tellison or the Priest, maybe both.

"One in the van, the other in the Tahoe."

"Which one is Elvis in?"

She paused.

"Tahoe?"

"Then that's what we are taking."

Madeline took on her best grimace.

"Oh, and how do we do that then, Rushing? We aren't getting out of this trailer. Jesus, how do we always get proper fucked like this? I should stop listening to you."

Julian considered her, then me.

"Well?"

He asked with a shrug of his gun.

"You have the keys?"

I asked. Madeline moved to Tellison, digging into the admin pocket on his plate carrier. His stare was neutral. Calculating.

"I do now. How's it then?"

I considered the view outside. I could still only see one body near the Tahoe, still standing near the back of the van. "We walk out like it's time to leave. Drive away. Easiest way to get away with anything is to act like you are supposed to be doing it."

Julian showed his agreement by tucking his borrowed pistol under his jacket, putting his hands behind his back like they were restrained. He would have been okay with anything that got him out of that trailer and closer to Heller. I knew that because so would I. Madeline bit her lip. Thinking. "Alright then, we don't have time to talk about what comes after. Let's do it."

I took a look around the office. Manny's office. I felt like I had betrayed the man by bringing this into his world, even if he wouldn't be aware of it for a few more hours. I rifled through the desk for a piece of paper and a pen. A greasy po'boy butcher paper wrapper and a grease marker would have to do. I wrote him a quick note, then tucked in all the cash I had on me, leaving it on the desk for him to find. "Let's go."

I pulled Hollic away from the door, putting him at the back of the room, out of view from the door when it opened just in case. Madeline hit the unlock on the key fob, and I walked out like nothing was wrong in the world, moving right to the Tahoe and opening the door. Elvis sat there, head on a swivel trying to see what was going on. "Move over."

I said in Russian. Madeline was right on my heels, shoving Julian into the now vacated seat. Finn walked up to her as she was shutting the door.

"We leaving then?"

He asked, looking back towards the trailer. She already had her hand on the driver's side door.

"We are, Tell and Hollic are still inside."

The brass balls move of not even bothering to lie to him was not lost on me. I made for the passenger side. She had the Tahoe started and rolling before I got my door shut. I watched Finn open the trailer door and go up the stairs.

"Just hit the gate, I already paid for it."

I said, watching Finn pop right back out of the trailer, he was shouting to the others in his radio. Madeline pushed into the gate, riding into it until the old chain gave up, pushing through and out onto the road.

"We breaking up with your comrades?"

Elvis asked from the back.

"Elvis, shut up for right now, yeah?"

I said, looking at him through the partition.

"We are going to need to talk to your boss. I give you a phone, you set it up by text. I want to read it before you send it?"

He laughed.

"You free hands first, *da*?"

Julian pointed across the cabin.

"Stop here, I need to get something. I'll be fast."

Madeline glanced at him, then me. I nodded.

"Sure, why not?"

Julian was out of the Tahoe and back in before it had come to a complete stop. With the slam of his door, we accelerated.

"Do you have my other gun?"

He asked, tucking what looked like a rifle into the gap by his door and the divider cage.

"In the back."

Madeline said, chirping the tires on a turn,

"Where are we going, right now?"

She asked, gripping the wheel a little too tightly. I had known her long enough to tell she had an internal battle raging. She had just thrown in on a new team by beating up her old team, with nothing more than a little bit of trust in me and a man she just met who, nearly anyone would agree, was in appearance and words, mentally unwell. I watched the passing streets, getting my bearings. Thinking of where to be.

"This thing have a tracker?"

She laughed a sad laugh.

"No, but doesn't everything else?"

"Okay, we toss phones, then head to wherever we need to be to meet Elvis's boss."

He spoke up from the back.

"You don't toss my fucking phone, it new. I pay a lot for it!"

"We wont, Elvis. Now shut up."

He sat back, quiet for a second. I worked my visor so I could see him without having to turn around. I knew it would dawn on him who was sitting next to him eventually.

It took about another ten seconds.

"Jesus Fuck! Hey!"

Elvis said, working as far away from Julian as he could.

"This *svolach'* he killed-"

I cut him off.

"So did I, Elvis. Shut up. He isn't going to hurt you."

I looked at Julian in my mirror. He shrugged at me,
looking at Elvis next to him.
"Nothing personal, mate."
Elvis shook his head.
"Zhizn' ebet meya."
I laughed.
"What did he say?"
Madeline asked
"He said 'life is fucking me.'"
She smiled.
"It is, us all."

22

Card wasn't new to being right about someone. In his career, at his level, being right about people was expected. You learned through training and more importantly, experience, how to assess a person and use your best judgment to try and assume what they were capable of. The more you knew about them, the better you tended to be at getting it right. Because humans at their basic level were motivated, as far as Card honestly believed, the desire to be happy, Card factored that into any assumptions he would make about a person. He kept it to himself, since the military and more so an SF unit, was not always a welcoming place for esoteric or *hippy* concepts like that. But he was usually more right than he was wrong. Not that he could predict a person's smaller choices. Hell, sometimes he did things and didn't know why he did them. But the large ones, the emotionally driven decisions, he had a high success rate with.

So, when Rushing helped the priest escape, and Madeline helped Rushing, he wasn't surprised. Upset, yeah. Hollic couldn't talk right after being choked to sleep and Tellison probably had a few cracked ribs on top of everything else that had already happened to him that night. Nah, he was a little pissed. He stowed it though, deciding to put that energy out into the universe and focus on the good he could do.

They were leaving the lot. Card and Toomby in the back of the Nissan. Finn was driving, Tellison was up front. Porter and Hollic were in the van with their remaining prisoner, following. Tellison didn't waste any time trying to track them. He made contact with Foundation, trying to track any phone that they could in the vehicle. Both Rushing and Madeline had tossed theirs not far from the lot. They didn't have info on the Russians phone, which they took with them when they left. The Priest didn't have one, and even if he did, they probably wouldn't have it, either. He also learned, listening to Tellison's side of the conversation, that the Tahoe didn't have a tracker, which seemed like a harsh oversight. But hindsight makes you think like that. So, they had nothing. Which wasn't much different from a few hours ago, Card thought to himself. He wasn't going to bring that up to the others, however. He was content to sit and listen, wait for an opportunity to be pointed at a target he could capture or kill. Tellison was on the phone with the Colonel.

"Sir, we are effectively blind then. Our best leads left with Madeline and Rushing. We have zero workable intel from the house or the property."

A pause. Card couldn't hear the Colonel now. Earlier in the conversation he could hear yelling, now the old man appeared to be more relaxed, which Card knew was far more worrisome in situations like this.

"Yes sir, we will be there."

Tellison ended the call. He tucked a piece of gum into his mouth, rubbing his neck. Card didn't expect him to recite the total of the conversation, but he was curious about the next move. Not enough to ask. He knew Tell well enough to not do that. Finn, of course, didnt.

"Soooo...."

Tellison looked at Finn.

"Wait for it."

His phone chimed. Tellison opened a text, clicked a few times, then set his phone on the instrument cluster to follow the navigation. A route populated, Card could see it was a 20 minute drive from the back.

"We are to meet with the Colonel and discuss our next move."

Card was a little surprised by that, he didn't know the Colonel was headed to New Orleans or had already been there. Finn turned their two-vehicle convoy around, telling Porter what the change was over the radio.

"Card, we have spares charged for the radios?"

Tellison asked, probably reminded of it by Finn's transmission.

"Roger, I have a bag- No, we don't. Spares were in the Tahoe."

Tellison sighed.

"Of course. Okay, turn em' off, save what we got. Finn, tell Porter. We can use phones for now. As soon as we get a chance, I want new fills on the radio, kill all the old channels."

Finn, being Finn, relayed the message via radio then clicked it off. It was quiet again. Card slouched down, shifting his rifle to a more comfortable position, tilting his head back to either grab a few minutes of sleep or just *be*. It lasted a minute or so before Tellison spoke.

"What do we know about Rushing, besides what Madeline has told us?"

"Fuck all."

Toomby said, from his dark corner.

"I'm sure the Colonel knows more than we do, but it's still not a lot."

Tellison considered it.

"So, any guesses as to why he would help this priest, or, for that matter, why Madeline would help him?"

Toomby took that one, too.

"No Idea. Rushing wants Heller, he's not focused on what Heller is doing, he's small fuckin picture. Emotional."

Card considered it. Finn piped up again.

"Chief, with all due respect, Rushing doesn't think like we do, neither does Madeline..."

Tellison gave him a cautionary glance but remained cool. "I'm not agreeing with what he did, but let's be honest, he could have killed you, and Mr. Hollic. Shit, Chief, he saved your life at the boat house. He sure isn't our friend right now, but I don't think we should consider him an enemy, either."

Card had to frown with his absent nod. The Sergeant had somewhat of a point. The cabin was quiet for a few moments. Finn drove. Tellison stared out the windshield. Toomby fought to open a bag of jerky. Card just *was*. There is strict rank respect in the military, but what made higher function units successful is that the very thing that most identifies the military, the discipline of rank, is often ignored to support alternative lines of thought to create solutions.

Card was 100 percent team *them* but he wasn't myopic enough with his team colors to not consider the other side of a problem. Rushing had reason to want a shortcut to Heller, he was motivated by revenge and little else. Madeline shared an emotional connection to Rushing that he couldn't quite understand. He knew that her ex-boyfriend, Robert, had worked for Virtua, had been the designer for the Auger program that was used to assassinate a sitting President in, Card had to admit, a pretty clever way. He knew that her Ex had sided with the Corporation in exchange for revenge of his own. He knew that at the time, Martin Heller was working either with, or for, another one of Rushing's *siblings* who had, Card would agree, a legitimate complaint against Rushing for dropping a burning house on her. Somewhere along the way, Heller had been involved in Rushing's lady getting killed. Madeline couldn't kill her ex-boyfriend, so Rushing did it. Card also knew that the Colonel had used Rushing to find Robert in hopes of getting control of his Auger program. Rushing destroyed it instead, as far as Card knew.

Now Rushing wanted Heller and maybe Madeline was so willing to help because she felt she owed him for the Ex thing. Thinking about it made Card's head hurt. The Venn diagram in his mind was a growing confusion of intersections that confronted the personal and the mission relationships, looking more like the donuts of a drunk teenager in a parking lot than a coherent chart of relationships. Rushing was driven. So was Madeline. There wasn't a doubt in his mind that the Priest was driven, hell, he was an ordained catholic priest killing his way up the food chain to get to the same man everyone else was after. Card didn't know much about the catholic church, but he knew that the warrior priests hadn't been a thing for a few hundred years and chances are his behavior wouldn't be officially savvy with the Holy See. Of course, Card would rather a Priest devote his time to slotting bad guys than diddling kids, so he was okay with the morality of what he was doing. Card thought about it and decided he wasn't mad at any of them, just wanted them to play on the same team for the same goal. It was obvious that they should all be on the same side, but there was something else going on that Card wasn't privy to and that had most likely caused Rushing to do what he did. Maybe now it was just going to be a race to see who could kill Heller first, and hopefully the two teams wouldn't need to fight each other in the process.

Card had his thoughts in order, so he decided to add his own two cents.

"Rushing will use whatever means he has available to complete his mission, Chief. We know enough about the sort of operator he is to know that he's been trained since he was a kid to exploit weaknesses and strengths to a goal and do it while working by himself. Hey, I'm confident in my skills, I know what I can do, I can assess how effective I can be given an environment and a goal in that environment. I'd qualify myself as professionally dangerous, within a narrow scope. But Rushing? He's the actual spook that you see in movies. Look what he did in Atlanta? Cool, I wasn't there, but between what you, Chief, and Finn have told me, he ghosted over a dozen men in a few days including at least two of his own-"

Tellison, annoyed, interrupted him.

"There a point you getting to, Sergeant?"

"-my point, Chief, is that I don't trust him any more than you do, he's an apex predator with a narrow moral compass that points in a direction we don't know. But just because I don't-cant-trust him, doesn't mean he isn't going his own way to do the right thing. The mission, as I understand it, is to capture or kill Marin Heller-"

Tellison interrupted him again.

"Sergeant Card, are you okay with his assault on your team members to *do the right thing?*"

Card considered the implication of the question. Toomby chewed nervously on jerky, eyes darting between Tellison and Card. Finn drove, but his eyes were on Card in the mirror. He was too junior to agree with Card more than he had, at least that's how he probably felt. Card had the currency to push the point with Tellison. He considered that fact and decided it was the best thing to do.

"No, Chief, I'm not okay with it, but it's not a binary situation. Do any of us know why Rushing is even here?"

Silence. Just stone faces briefly illuminated by passing lights. Card knew that Tellison had the specifics on that, or maybe he was just hoping he did.

"Well, I have a few guesses, and I suppose some of them border on fantasy, but the one that makes the most sense is a cheap sequel of us using him as a tool again like we did in Atlanta. Any thoughts on that, Mr. Tellison?"

Tellison sighed, rubbing the back of his neck. He checked the route on the phone. Still too far away from their arrival to let that kill the conversation. He seemed to consider it anyway before he finally answered.

"That's head shed level, Sergeant. Ours is to locate Martin Heller and any assisting him, ascertain their goals and stop them. Rushing decided to aid our best intel source in escaping instead of playing on the right team. Now, I don't know if he's graduated to bad guy on our list yet, but I do know that a philosophical discussion about his motivations and ultimate good intentions are not getting us any closer to a solution."

Tellison leaned back over the seat, looking at Card.

"So, unless this is going to lead to a solution, I don't see a reason to continue this mental exercise."

Tellison turned back to the front, happy to be done with it. Card let it ride. Letting his thoughts do their thing.

Tellison knew more than he said, which was normal. He was in charge, and often privy to information not put out to the rest of the team. When Card was in a line unit, it was normal for NCOs and officers to withhold information for various reasons that had nothing to do with an actual good one. In the special operations community, arbitrary withholding of information was rare, but it still happened. Sometimes information was compartmentalized for mission specific reasons, and that could have been this, Card thought. He also disregarded the thought as soon as it occurred to him because it didn't feel like that. He had to trust in Tellison, like he always did.

The rest of the drive was silent. Everyone consciously watching their area of responsibility, looking for anything that didn't fit. The address was a home improvement big box store just off the 10 in Kenner. In the early hours of the morning, the parking lot was nearly empty except for a few scattered cars and an 18-wheeler with trailer that stood alone in the back of the expansive parking lot. The truck was the unit's mobile command, really its *only* command as the unit was always mobile. In the movies it would be disguised as a freight trailer or moving truck, but in real life, every truck was subject to weigh stations and state inspections. So, the unit command vehicle hid in plain sight as a television production truck. It wasn't, but only a qualified expert could walk through the stations inside the 53-foot trailer and tell that it wasn't exactly set up to produce television remotely. It was a hardened truck and trailer with its own Secure Compartmentalized Information Facility, multi-band communications, deployable long-range drone, living quarters and armory for the crew. When parked, multiple compartments expanded to increase the usable space, but it rarely parked. The Colonel kept it on the road, mobile and hard to track. When their unit was created under the previous president, knowledge of its existence was kept to a very small number of people and only one of them, the President, an elected official. Its budget was so far buried in the morass of government spending, pulling money from hundreds if not thousands of government programs that it was unlikely even a highly motivated auditor would ever find it.

After the President was assassinated, Colonel Solomon took the unit off the grid completely. Sure, Card and everyone was still getting paid and they weren't hurting for equipment, at least not yet, but without knowing who could be trusted in the government meant that recruiting new members from the military wasn't possible and their legal movement and authority under the Manifest Homeland Protection Act as deputized US Marshals was a risk they took of being exposed any time they used their credentials.

Finn pulled their two-vehicle convoy up close to the trailer and parked. No one waited outside to greet them, but Card was sure they saw them approach on the cameras.
"Finn, Toomby, please re-up any equipment we don't have."
Tellison said as he stepped out. The side door opened, and Colonel Wayne Solomon ducked his considerable height under the doorway and stepped out onto the extending stairs. Agent Hijazi was right behind him.
"Mr. Tellison."
He said, shaking Tellison's hand as he approached.
"Sergeant Card."
Card took his offered hand next. The Colonel had a strong grip that didn't really fit his marathon build. He bit a cigar between his teeth. His smile was welcoming but his eyes

betrayed his anger with the situation. He pointed to Hollic who had just walked up.

"Mr. Hollic, we still have one live prisoner?'

Danny Hollic nodded.

"Well thank Jesus he didn't escape on the way, get him to the holding room at the rear of the trailer. Tellison, let's get everyone inside, don't want to be under the stars any longer than I have to be."

Agent Hijazi quietly led the way back inside. The inside of the trailer was mostly open floorplan. With the retractable compartments extended, there was a small conference room directly ahead with seating for eight behind a thick glass partition and door. The Colonel motioned everyone into the room and shut the door. It closed with authority and clicked. The light din of noise coming from a nearby monitor station and the two technicians manning it disappeared as soon as it closed. Sound proof. The Colonel took the head of the table, Hijazi took a seat next to him. No one else sat until the Colonel motioned them to sit. He was quiet for a second, composing his thoughts, Card figured.

"Well, what the fuck?"

Tellison took the question.

"Sir, we expected problems with Rushing, but we couldn't account for this priest, or Madeline helping him."

The Colonel took on a scowl, staring at his warrant officer for a second before responding.

"Mr. Tellison, if you had kept your personal feelings about Rushing from clouding your judgement, and by extension, the judgement of your team, we wouldn't be in this situation."

Card watched Tellison choke back a response. Agent Hijazi couldn't do the same, chuckling under his breath.

He got a sideways glance from the Colonel, but it didn't seem to bother him.

"The hunt for Heller is stalled, but the larger situation is developing quickly. You have any ideas on how to reacquire Mr. Winter?"

Larger situation? Card raised a finger.

"Sir, larger situation?"

The Colonel didn't even look at Card, he stared a hole through Tellison instead.

"Chief, have you not briefed your NCOs on this?"

"No, Sir."

Tellison was still cool, but Card could hear an edge in his voice.

"Okay, Chief. Allow me, then. Chief, get all your people in here."

The Colonel frowned while lighting his cigar. Card found himself wondering about the ventilation in the room.

Tellison stood and left the room, he returned shortly after with Finn and Toomby in tow. The Colonel waited until everyone had their attention on him before he began.

"The larger mission hasn't changed. We are still to apprehend Martin Heller, if he is in fact in the US, *and* stop elements of Virtua from carrying out an unknown attack. But there's more to this that Chief Tellison should have briefed you on. Had he, perhaps we wouldn't be in the current position we are in."

He stared at Tellison. The atmosphere in the room was harsh.

"Everyone familiar with what Rushing *is*, right?"

Nods.

"To keep it succinct, he's one of many in generations of many. There's an illuminati level conspiracy there I'm sure, but I don't give a shit about that. During the Atlanta mission, these *children* were working parallel to Virtua, but not directly with them. Virtua is their money, but they didn't create Rushing or any of his siblings. We don't actually know who did. Virtua is a customer, and a long-time customer but nothing more. Either because of our involvement in Atlanta, or because they are acting on behalf of Virtua, we are being actively hunted by them."

The Colonel grabbed a controller from the middle of the table and fiddled with it. A wall monitor powered on. The Colonel wandered the cursor around the screen until he found the file he was looking for. He clicked on it and opened a series of photos.

"The entire point of our charter was to operate independently of the larger government machine. Both military and law enforcement while not being either. Our level of secrecy extended beyond traditional or even traditional asymmetric. Which means, we aren't on any paperwork save for two copies of a Presidential order that gives us our legitimacy inside the MHPA. You remember that bank we robbed after Atlanta? That was to recover the other copy. You remember how the Vice President was suspected of being in Virtua's pocket and then became President when the last one was killed by Robert Wigglin's fucking computer program?"

He looked around the room, puffing angrily on his cigar. Nods.

"Well, we recovered that copy to prevent the now-president from learning we exist to prevent what is happening right now."

The Colonel looked up to the screen, a series of pictures appeared in a tile. Each one was a piece or a total view of dead bodies. An interior shot of an SUV, two men slumped in their seats. A hotel room, two men and a woman sprawled on the floor. A train station platform, three bodies of indeterminate sex laying in pools of congealed blood. A sidewalk, one man laying across a bench with a knife in his neck. Another car interior, two bodies. An unknown room, five bodies. There were dozens of photos. Card recognized a few of them he'd served with at times in his career. Harsh.

"What you are seeing is other cells of our unit, dead. Who killed them? Rushing's siblings. The irony here is I had a conversation about this with Rushing not many hours ago, but I'm judging by your faces that Tellison briefed you on none of this. It's his mission, so his call, at least until it effects the larger mission. What I didn't bother to tell Rushing is that I wanted him on this because, frankly, what are the odds that…"

Solomon paused, his eyes rolling up as he counted mentally.

"28 men and women of your skillset would be killed without producing so much as one dead bad guy? We have had teams in the single digits face hundreds of Muj and leave nothing but souls to Allah. One of our units was engaged by Spetznaz in Syria and they crushed them. In the history of Special Operations, we have only once taken a loss like this and that was a lucky shot on a Chinook by some dumb kid with an RPG. But this? The poster children for black side special operations being picked off by freak show foster kids who were taught to tiptoe better? As much as I don't like it, Rushing is, maybe *was,* our best chance at stopping his kind. I was using him as a canary in a coal mine and I get the feeling that Chief's animosity towards him helped the decisions he's made. That and his acute view of the situation. I have a feeling that whoever is hunting us, and Heller, are going to be not far from each other at the end of this, and I'd like to have Mr. Winter's insight for that."

The room was stone somber. Tellison had told them nothing of this. Card knew some had been lost, only because a few friends hadn't returned buddy calls over the past few months. The Colonel being upset with Tellison was something Card got. Him admonishing the Chief in front of everyone was out of character and Card could sense a frustrated desperation behind it. If Card was an empath, like his mother used to think she was, he could read the Colonel's emotions and help him navigate the stress he was clearly under. It was personal for Card to lose a few friends, but for the Colonel, he had lost men and women who he clearly felt more than just professionally responsible for. It was evident that the Chief had a fair deal of animosity towards Rushing, and Card didn't exactly know why. It was also easy for Card to see how that may have helped cause the situation they were in. What Card couldn't see was why the Chief would be so guarded about this. Only thing Card could figure was he didn't tell them to keep their heads in the game.

But it wasn't a game.

Card rolled it around, rounding the edges of the sharp thoughts until they would fit where they needed to while the Colonel continued.
"We are short on assets, men. Not just personnel but logistics as well. I pulled a personal favor for our last military air in Darfur and that's now a dry well. From here until we get to the bottom of this, we are depending on commercial availability and what covers and equipment we

have left. I won't bore you with that, and I know all of you would get it done with pistols and ranger panties if you had to. The point of everyone being here is to get on the same goddamn page and find this asshole and hopefully get Rushing and Madeline to see the goddamn light. Agent Hijazi is going to see if he can get an idea of where they are on the white side, but we have a Russian in the back that can probably get us what we need faster than that. Chief Tellison, men, I don't care what you have to do to him, get us something solid."

Card was pretty good at connecting dots, so he decided to ask the question that he hoped everyone else was considering.

"Colonel, who's the leak? Because we aren't time and place predictable and we aren't on the board. Tracking us is next to impossible. We go to great lengths to stay zero. So how in the hell is person or persons getting information on team locations?"

The Colonel's tone when he responded was guarded.

"We are exploring that, Sergeant. The leak is most likely electronic and Gianna is working to lock it down."

With that, it was over. The Colonel nodded to the room and departed, a burning cigar stub in a coke can in the middle of the table. The shift from Solomon being in charge to Tellison was seamless.

"Mr. Hollic, are you good to interrogate?"

Danny nodded somewhat reluctantly, rubbing his throat. When he answered his voice was strained but loud.

"Yeah, I can handle it, Chief."

"Good, go push buttons until you get an answer. Sergeant Toomby, gear?"

Toomby looked up from a key loader he was using to change the teams radio frequencies.

"Squared. Anything specific we need from the armory we don't have?"

Tellison considered the question, trying to predict the future.

"Sergeant Card, grab a long gun and a surveillance kit, talk to one of the techs for a portable drone in case we need it. Sergeant Finn, see what less-lethal options we have. I don't want to kill Rushing if I don't have to. Go."

Everyone more or less stood at once and bottlenecked to get out of the room, leaving Tellison behind with Hijazi, who was so focused on typing on his phone that he hadn't said a single word the entire time.

Card stood in the middle of the trailer, a blonde woman with a Crossfit build hidden under utility khakis and a tight polo was leaning over the shoulder of a smaller man at what looked like the main cluster of computers and monitors. Gianna. Cool. Card had a crush on her, her voice mainly but the package it came from didn't lessen things. He'd only met her in person a few times and briefly. She seemed to sense his eyes, turning her attention to him.

"Sergeant Card?"

Was it a smile?

"Ma'am, we need a pack drone."

Her smile turned into a crooked smirk, her cheek sucking in a little on the up side. Hot.

"*Ma'am* won't get you shit, Sergeant. You know my name. We have a few in the storage room back there."

She pointed with a square tipped manicured nail. Short. French.

"Right, Gianna, thank you."

A smile.

"Happy to help, anything else?"

Play it cool.

"No."

She kept her eyes on him a second longer then turned back to the monitor. Card wanted to talk to her, but it wasn't the time. The universe would let him know. Card felt an elbow in his ribs. Heard Toomby whispering behind him.

"Pussy."

23

Gulfport, Mississippi.

I didn't really know what to think of it. Small town. Beach
town. Casino town. Town hiding a not-small number of
Russian Mafia who may or may not kill me before the day
was over. Elvis had made good, I suspected mostly
because he didn't want to become another victim of Julian.
I didn't know if him still wearing his vestments was to
intimidate via the contrast of attire to behavior, but it
worked for him. We got Elvis a phone, he made a call.
There was a lot of rapid fire Russian profanity on his end.
A few pauses to get profanity from the other end. A
moment of calm talking, more profanity, and finally an
agreement. I caught most of the Russian. Whoever Elvis
was talking to, he wasn't the boss. He was the guy who
answered the bosses' calls. Like a secretary, but with more
time around human blood and violence. Probably less
coffee fetching. So maybe not a secretary, exactly. We
found a secluded parking lot close to the interstate and far
from the scrap yard to tuck away in and let time tick by.
After an hour of nothing, Madeline had allowed Elvis to
make his call.

Elvis ended the call and handed the phone back to
Madeline's waiting hand.
"*Da,* Okay, yes. We meet. Drive to Gulfport Miss- Missi-
."
Elvis was having a hell of a time with the word. Madeline
helped him save face.
"Right, got it."
We drove. My eyes felt like they had sand in them, excess
oil and sweat seeping in at the edges. I needed sleep and I

wasn't likely to get any, any time soon. The drive was just over an hour, west on the 10. Madeline drove like she had every intention of cutting that time in half. Not much time to decide just what the fuck we were doing. It was worth a try, anyway.

"Rushing, what the hell are we doing?"

Madeline asked. I could hear the stress in her voice. I didn't really need much time to consider my answer.

"What do we know? I may have to make a few leaps of imagination, but here it is. Heller is here, somewhere. He pays the Russian mob-"

"*Bratva,* you *hooy.* We are not spaghetti eating assholes. Don't compare to your Immigrant degenerates."

I gave Elvis a glace that said I was still willing to shoot him. He got it and shut up.

"-Bratva...to smuggle in something. Heller, probably to plan, intercepts the shipment. Julian hits the Russian house after slotting Heller's man at the docks, which prompted the Russians-sorry, Elvis, but I'm going to talk about you like you aren't here right now, okay? To hit the boat house, but they probably missed the boat that had, well, whatever, on it. But what does that deny Heller? He still has whatever was in that container, and-"

It occurred to me as soon as I said it. Had it occurred to me sooner, the past few hours could have probably been avoided. The Slidell house had been left. Whatever the machine was in the van, was still in the van.

"Shit!"

Madeline looked at me, not following at first. It occurred to her a second later.

"There was nothing stopping him from getting that van."

Madeline swerved for an exit.

"Can't use the Russian's phone-"

"My name is Elvis!"

"-We need to get a burner. Call Solomon."

As much as I hated the idea, I hated the idea of turning around and driving to some house in Slidell even more, expressly since I knew whatever was in the van *and* the van, were gone. There was no harm in her telling Solomon, even if we weren't exactly on the same team at that moment. Madeline sped into the closest gas station to the exit. Blissfully, it was a modern stop with well lit pumps and large windows showing off all the goodies inside.

"I'll get it."

I left Madeline with our guests. A cheap prepaid phone in a blister pack, an arm full of water and coconut juice. A handful of assorted nut snack packs. Small talk from the clerk and back to the SUV. Back on the road. I passed water and food to who wanted it, which was everyone. While Maddy drove, I got the phone activated and then handed it off to her. She familiarized herself with the controls and then dialed a number from memory, leaving it on speaker phone for everyone's benefit, I supposed. It rang a few times before it was answered. When the Colonel spoke, I could hear the cigar in his teeth.

"Yes?"

Madeline didn't bother with attempts at explaining her-our actions, she got right to it.

"Heller is going to need that van for whatever he is doing. I suggest you sit on it."

Solomon was quiet for a second.

"Okay, O'Neil. Now, would you like to explain yourself?"

I wondered how Madeline would play that inevitable question. She must have been thinking about it as well because her answer was prompt.

"Right, well Colonel it's pretty tidy, actually. I trust you. I trust a few of the squaddies, but I don't exactly trust Tellison and I didn't sign up so you could use my friend as bait. The mission was supposed to be stopping Virtua. It became apparent that its more than that. I don't know what you have been told, and I've not the time to correct the truth. Rushing saw an opportunity that Chief Tellison wasn't willing to exploit. So, I made a decision."

The Colonel sighed.

"You are dangerously close to being on the wrong side of this."

Madeline stared at the phone before responding. If she had any remaining doubts about picking a side, I couldn't hear it in her voice.

"Wayne, I've been chuffed to give you a lift as long as it was against Virtua, here we are not seeing the obvious play for the same goal, the one we made. That alone makes my choice the right one. You've been hiding something, from me, maybe from the other lads as well. Maybe when Heller is dead we can have a cuppa and a wag about it, but until that happens, I'm not taking orders from you."

Silence. Another Sigh. Elvis was leaning between the seats, staring at the phone like this was the most interesting conversation he had ever heard. Julian looked to be asleep.

"O'Neil, I will allow our shared past to cloud my better judgement and not have you shot on sight. You aren't thinking about the larger mission with your vendetta against Heller. You have involved an unknown and are currently working with a member of the Russian mob. If you weren't emotional, you would see the irony of me even having to point this out."

Madeline looked at me, her brow sharp and annoyed.

"Okay, Wayne. I think we have reached the end of this chat before it becomes circular. If you need to reach me, go old school, I'll be killing this phone."

She didn't bother hitting the end key before tossing the phone out the window. Elvis followed its arc to the pavement, whistling as it shattered on impact.

"I guess that's the breakup, then?"

I said with a shrug to Maddy. She gave me a curt nod.

"I reckon so."

She caught Elvis in the mirror.

"Where exactly are we going?"

"The *Bo River*...no, not right, the, um..."

I had been in Louisiana long enough to see more than a few billboards. I knew what he was trying to say.

"Beau Rivage?"

"Yes, this is right."

Okay. I assume it's a gaudy yank casino?"

I laughed.

"Is there any other kind?"

We left the 10 at the 110 and took the short drive south to the Gulf Coast. The Beau Rivage hotel beaconed to the left of the interstate where it dumped into Beach Blvd.

Madeline put the Tahoe into the parking garage, staying as close to the ground floor as she could with a spot near the elevators. She backed in and shut it down. We sat, quiet for a second. Only the ticks of the cooling engine and the distant din of traffic keeping the silence out. It was early in the morning and the sun was painting the sky a brilliant orange.

"Julian, might be best for you to stay here."

The priest nodded. He hadn't said much since we left the scrap yard and looked to want to continue that trend.

"You may need me in there."

Elvis was shaking his head violently.

"No! *sumasshedshiy svyashchennik! Avtoritet* will kill, well, all of us if he come."

I couldn't argue with his logic. I also didn't think we needed to worry about babysitting Julian. Elvis certainly needed babysitting, because there was still a chance he was leading us right into a trap. My brief experience with Russian Bratva was me killing a handful of them over a decade ago. They were organized, mostly skilled and had very, very long memories. I figured we have even odds to walk out of there alive, let alone get any real help from them. Those were good odds if I had to play them to get Heller.

"Okay, then."

Madeline said.

"We'll be right back."

Elvis nodded.

"We go, my phone?"

Madeline hesitated but handed it over. Elvis led the way while he dialed. He spoke briefly to someone then put the phone away. We did our best to look casual. No plate carriers or rifles. Shirts untucked, covering pistols only. Madeline had pulled the patches off her uniform top and let her hair down. We still stood out. Elvis didn't seem worried. He led us not to the lobby or the casino floor, but down a non-descript hallway to a row of equally non-descript elevators. A very not non-descript man waited there, probably a few inches shy of seven feet and close to 300 pounds of hard earned and hard maintained muscle. A shaven head, eyes tucked under a forehead that looked like a push bumper on a tow truck. As if for a bit of comedic relief, he wore fragile wire frame glasses with stylish round lenses. Dressed down in a tailored suit that was a rich black. A woman's face tattooed on one hand, a star on the other. Each finger carried a ruin or a ring tattoo. This was the place, then.

Elvis nodded to the large man, his demeanor noticeably more reserved in his presence. He nodded back, then stepped around him to block our path.
"Your weapons. Give them to Elvis."
We expected as much. Now unarmed, we were patted down. Quick, professional. If he was reluctant to search a woman, he didn't show it. Madeline got the same attention I did and not any more. Once he was satisfied, he slipped a keycard and held it to a black box between elevators. It dinged and one of them opened.
"Please, come."
He said, guiding us into the elevator with an outstretched arm. Up we went. The big man didn't speak, he stood at the back of the elevator. I considered my options against him if things got violent. I suspected he was the biggest of an unknown number of bad guys, sent to intimidate. Even if he was an amateur fighter, which I doubted by the story his tattoos told, his size alone meant getting caught in his paws would be devastating. The elevator continued to the top. It stopped. Dinged. Opened. The penthouse, because of course. A smaller, relatively speaking, version of our escort waited just outside the elevator in a vaulted ceiling foyer. Since the Elevator was the main *door* to the penthouse, it only made sense that the entrance would be grand, and it was. This man, unlike our escort, was visibly armed. A modernized AK variant rifle on a two-point sling, held professionally down across his chest. He

nodded, not to us, but to our escort, who was handing us off.

"Please, follow Ulf."

A nod from who was apparently Ulf. He motioned with his support hand to the left. We walked out onto the frosted marble floor, under a massive chandelier. The walls were a light honey brown, accented by ornate wainscoting. I could hear soft music coming from the room we walked towards. Elvis, still reserved, hung to the rear. He left our guns on a console table near the elevator. I took in the environment as we went. The elevator was the main entrance, but there had to be a stairwell. We moved from the foyer into a living room. It had to be 800 square feet on its own. A semi-circle couch in a modern deep purple, the carpet was a subdued gray. Chairs, ottomans and end tables. Seating for a party but it was empty. The living room ran up against a view of the ocean through floor to ceiling windows, there was a generous patio off to our right. We went left, following Ulf into the next room. I stole a glance backwards, a balcony above overlooked the living room, another suited man stood, watching with professional interest.

The next room was a dining room. An expansive dark walnut table, cleared of any settings or adornments. Chairs tucked in neatly. At the end of the table sat an older man, gray at the temples, balding at the forehead. He was working through breakfast; his eating was hungry but intentional. He wore a simple white A shirt, a prominent dagger tattoo at the collar bone. The blade disappearing at the neck and reappearing at the other side as if stabbed through his skin. I knew the dagger tattoo. It was earned by killing while in prison. He shoulders carried ornate tattooed epaulettes. His arms were also covered in various tattoos. His was a long story that probably earned him his station.

He looked up from his plate, a remote appeared in his hand to turn down the violin piece playing from unseen speakers. The look on his face was neither anger nor greeting.
"Ah, so here you are. I am Anton. Elvis, introduce me."
He said, wiping his mouth, he dropped the napkin on his plate and pushed it away, standing and moving into another room with a beckoned hand. Ulf followed him, we followed Ulf. The next room was a dark study, something right out of the 20s with green shade lamps, lush upholstered chairs and a large antique desk that was not designed with the modern computer in mind.
"Please, sit."
He motioned to the customary pair of chairs that seemed to be a staple in any executive office. I looked over the room, considering and prioritizing what would make the best weapon and how easily it could be accessed.
"Anton, Rushing and Madeline."
Elvis said, not bothering to point to who was who. Anton nodded.
"Elvis, please, stay as well. I am most curious about this."
His accent was light, but it was there. He seemed to have a good mastery of English. I sat. Madeline sat. Elvis took a seat in a chair tucked off in the shadows. Ulf stood behind the man, fading to the back of the room near a curtained window.
He leaned forward on his elbows, exhaling, a quick suck of his teeth to clear some bit of food. His eyes were intelligent and cold.
"The world, she is a different place. There was a time, not long ago, yes, when you would be hours dead by now for

what you have done. I am a businessman, but I have not forgotten what it was like to be a killer. Not so easy to be one here in America, yes?"

I honored him with a nod.

"I suppose that depends on who you are killing."

He shook a finger at me.

"You, Oh, I know you. I recognize you."

I had never met this man in my life. I was more or less a nondescript person, he was very memorable. I would have remembered meeting him.

"*Velns*. Yes, when I was in Gulag, I hear of your kind. A good friend tells me of this *Velns*, he sneaks into his Pakhan's dacha, he kills. Strong soldiers, good *Vor*, all dead. Then he kills Borya Kadishnakov. You know this man? We called him *Mertvyye Glaza*"

He laughed.

"He had dead eyes, a cold man. Which is something coming from men like us."

I could already tell he knew the answer to his question or suspected it.

"You could say I knew him, although I only met him that night."

His smile disappeared. He stared through me. Madeline shifted in her seat next to me, loading like a spring. Ulf moved in the shadows. The tension seemed to grow. Then he laughed, a slapped fist on the desk that shook everything on it. His laugh was deep, pounding off the walls. He could have been a good mall santa.

"Small world then. Borya was *scum*. Son of a *Boyevik* who fought on the wrong side in the bitch wars. *Cyka* for Stalin. Im sure it was in his blood as well."

He trailed off like I might actually know. I didn't have an answer, so he continued.

"I am recently in charge. We-"

He pointed to himself and then to us, then circled the room with his finger.

"Are in a unique situation, yes? Someone kills many of us. *You* kill some of us. We kill men of Heller's. I want to kill Heller. You want to kill Heller. I think I know how to do this. But we are few now. It is just us, you see?"

He showed his palms, closing his eyes as if all was forgiven. I doubted it.

"In exchange for not killing you, you will help kill Heller, yes?"

Madeline beat me to the nod. Then she spoke.

"Anton, that won't be a problem. But I'd like to know what your relationship is with him, first."

He motioned to Elvis as if to say *the nerve of this one.*

"Ah, well, we smuggle. Our primary business here is smuggling. Guns. Drugs. Anything except for kids and women. I am not a *pimp*. I am a killer, I am a thief. But I had a mother once. Heller paid *Pakhan*, he send us with Bogdan to smuggle in a machine and a canister. Oh, Bogdan dead, killed by this priest…anyway, we bring him his van. We guard his van. We arrange to smuggle his canister out of Africa. Tricky, that was. You see, we don't do much business in Africa. The continent has never been very friendly to us and today it's the Chinese that fill that market."

He waived off the thought of Africa. Pausing to take a pack of cigarettes from a drawer. Blue and white pack, Cyrillic writing. Belomorkanal. I remembered they smelled bad. He lit one. They still smelled bad.

"We moved the container around, hiding it. We did not tell Heller when it would arrive, or where. I think he had a tracker in this tube. He steals it."

"What's in the tube, Anton?"

Madeline asked. Anton shrugged, an apologetic smile.

"I do not know."

She shook her head.

"If you had to guess? Where did it come from, who delivered it to you?"

A soft laugh. I saw his mask of politeness drop for a moment. He was angry but hiding it well. If he was really short on men, he needed us, and he knew it, but that didn't mean he would stop being who he was.

"I think you misunderstand our relationship. I am going to help you help us, but I am not going to answer such questions. What is in the canister is of no concern to me. If you find it, it is yours. All I want is Heller. Heller and this *priest*."

A glance from Madeline.

"You, I can look past. A Misunderstanding. But this priest, I cannot, *Pakhan* cannot. When this is over, you give him to us, yes? I also want my other man returned, unharmed."

I had no intention of doing so, but I also had no intention of letting Anton know that. I was nodding before he had finished his sentence.

"Of course."

Anton considered us both for a second. His cigarette pointing at us in turn.

"This is non-negotiable. If I don't get him, I will kill both of you."

I didn't doubt he was serious. Serious about trying anyway. Madeline leaned forward, placing her hands on his desk.

"If you are done with the threats, comrade, where the fuck is Martin Heller?"

Anton erupted in his deep laugh again.

"*Zaichik*, I would enjoy your company, but work we must, no?"

I suppressed a laugh at his pet name for Madeline. *Bunny.* How I referred to her once upon a time. If she caught my sound, she ignored it.

"Yes, so howsit, Anton? Where can we find him?"

Anton leaned back into the shadows, his laugh lingering.

"At the carnival, of course."

24

The Slidell house was just as they left it. Which was to say, it wasn't a crime scene because no one had discovered the bodies and none of them had bothered to call it in. Running on zero sleep, Card and the others had been ready to catch some rest when the Colonel ordered them to get back to Slidell, verify the van was still there, put a tracker on it, then sit on the house.

It was daylight by the time they made it back and putting a tracker on the van was the riskiest part. The streets were awake, and no one on the street would go unnoticed. With everyone else waiting nearby in a shopping center parking lot, Finn had driven in and with nothing more than a clip board and a yellow vest, he made like a public service employee and ducked into the back yard of the house, made an easy entry through the broken sliding glass door, tucked a magnetic GPS to the van's frame, and then made his exit. His ditched the vest and geared back up.

Tellison spent the wait time looking for options to observe the house. The had the drone, but its flight time was limited. It couldn't loiter for hours. They had multiple batteries for it, but even hot swapping them out, they would only get five hours of flight time. Tellison found a few houses for sale in the neighborhood. Four of which were two floors and two of which, after calls to the realtor, were unoccupied and he could come by for a viewing with the realtor the next day and the end of the week, respectively. Of the two houses, the end of week house had the best vantage, so that was the one they would use. Card and

Toomby packed all their gear into contractor bags with fresh cut branches in them to break up the outline of the equipment. They dressed down in subdued work pants and long sleeve t shirts. Boonie hats and back pack leaf blowers they bought from a pawn shop completed the look. Finn dropped them off a street away from the house and they walked in. They crossed the lawn of the vacant house, a brick and vinyl sided two story that could have been dropped into almost any suburb in the US and fit in just fine. They kept to the side and went directly into the back yard. Card checked the closest window to the gate, Toomby moved to the next. They repeated this until they had seen in each room visible from the back yard. Since the house was vacant, the blinds were open and rooms were set with viewing furniture only, making it easy to see the motion and glass break sensors, as well as the alarm keypad on the wall next to a door that led from the garage. Card used a pocket monocular to get a better look at the panel. "Newer Bluetooth model."

Toomby had been waiting to hear the type, he selected the proper tool from his bag. The alarm panel communicated with the motion and break sensors via Bluetooth. Older models used more simple radio signals that were much easier to interfere with, but the Bluetooth operation was much more reliable to confront and offered more options. Toomby's handheld device was a high-end RF detector and cracker that was a design of Gianna's. She had written its programming to be simple, fifth grade level prompts and controls but Toomby was an amateur tech geek so it he was much more versed with it than Card was, which was cool. With their proximity to the signal, picking it up wasn't a problem.

"Easy."

He said, working through the screen prompts once he had identified two-way communication between the keypad and one of the window break detectors. Bluetooth, like any technology that had been around for more than a few days, was not as safe as it had been when it was first introduced. Blueborne zero-day vulnerabilities exploited the simple communication of Bluetooth, even those with encryption, allowing for third part access. Toomby could see each device that talked to the keypad, the device identified them by type. He cycled through his options and pressed a prompt to turn the alarm off. Gianna's device fooled the main keypad into deactivating by spoofing a cell phone deactivation via Bluetooth.

"Good to go."

They made their way into the house and directly upstairs, choosing the master bedroom as it had the best view of the street. The house was situated just to the left of Wyndemere Drive at the intersection. They had a good view of the front of the house, one side and the back yard. Finn had opened all the curtains when he put the tracker on the van, so they had limited view inside.

While Card rearranged furniture to suit their purposes, Toomby went to work on the windows. The sash style windows had four panes each, thin wood separating them. Toomby used a window tool to score the window casing, then a small suction cup to pull each pane free. Glass caused bullets to do unpredictable things and they didn't want it in the way if they needed to shoot. It was unlikely anyone would notice the missing windows from the street, but Toomby nor Card took chances like that. Toomby pulled a roll of special purpose cellophane sheeting from his bag and stretched it to cover the removed panes, being sure to smooth all the wrinkles out before stapling it in place. At only two mils thick, it wouldn't affect bullet trajectory in any meaningful way at the distances they were dealing with. Next, Toomby unrolled and cut multiple sections of thin nylon screen, covering each window in the room for uniformity. The screen could also be shot through and acted as a tint, making viewing into the room difficult from a distance.

By the time Toomby was done, so was Card. He had pushed a staging bed up against the wall from the windows and removed the mattress. With a small drill, Card stripped apart a large book case and desk from another room, using the pieces to build a platform on the bed frame. Because of the height of the bedroom window, and how stupid it would be to set the rifle up at the window, an elevated platform was needed to get an unobscured view of the Russian house in case they had to do more than just watch. Card set up a tripod then screwed a Hog Saddle onto it. The Hog Saddle was a wide U clamp with adjustable tension and rubber pads, designed to grip a rifle at the rail or stock for precision shooting from a tripod. In situations like this, Card preferred it to other techniques because it didn't require relying on the environment to provide a place to set up the rifle.

The command truck didn't have much on hand for Card and Toomby in the way of precision guns, but they had Card's 5.56. Sometimes you didn't need a large caliber rifle due to environment or no expectation of long distances. The 5.56 in a heavier round could easily fit that role. Card was a fan of the Black Hills 77 Grain Open Tip Match round and he had built a rifle specifically for it. A matching set forged upper and lower receiver, fit with a 14.5" 1/7 match barrel on a rifle length gas system enclosed in a MLOK wedge lock rail. Using a Leupold MK5 3-18 optic. The rifle was capable of half MOA accuracy, and that was more than sufficient, especially at the closer ranges Card built it for.

With the rifle locked down into the Hog Saddle, Card established ranges to likely shoot distances on the house, centered the rifle in the middle of his view and left the magnification at 5X to see everything at once, he could always dial in tighter if he needed to. He helped set up the tripod for Toomby's spotting scope and then set in on the rifle to watch. Toomby had found two five-gallon buckets in a closet and they made good seats. It wasn't the most comfortable hide he had ever been in, but it certainly wasn't the worst.

"How's it look?"
Toomby asked, setting in on the spotting scope.
"Not bad, Will. Max is just shy of 150 meters."
Toomby sneered behind his scope.
"I doubt we will need to shoot, anyway."
He was right, but Card didn't feel a need to respond.
"You sleep first, Will, I got this."
Both of them were going on 24 hours without sleep.
"You sure? I'm hopped up on energy drinks right now, anyway."
"Sure, go ahead and take it. I'll let you know if anything happens."
Will shrugged and ducked under his scope, keeping low under Card's rifle to find a spot on the floor near their

improvised platform. With his day pack as a pillow and his M4 across his chest, Toomby was quickly asleep.

The day wore on, hot and hotter. Card found himself wondering if turning on the air conditioning was worth the risk but figured he'd dealt with worse. By the time he started to have trouble concentrating, Toomby snorted himself awake, looked at his watch and then lumbered up to his bucket behind the spotting scope.

"Hell, man, you coulda woke me up earlier. It's been hours."

Card shook his head with a tired smile.

"I figure the longer I let you sleep, the longer I get to sleep."

Toomby laughed.

"That works, sometimes."

He rummaged around in his bag, pulling out a soda and two protein bars. He handed one to Card while he tore into the other. He chewed thoughtfully.

"Ya know, somethings bothering me, Tony…"

"You worried Gianna doesn't like you?"

"Gah! No, dude. Seriously. What Colonel Solomon showed us."

Card remembered it. Wouldn't soon forget it.

"What about it?"

"We are as close to omnipotent as you can get, all of us, and someone is working their way through us like we aren't shit. Statistically, that shouldn't even be possible. One or two guys caught unaware? Sure. But over two dozen? Nah, man. All without a single bad guy KIA?"

Card though about it. Will was a stubborn thinker who never talked much about the risk of their job. Since he was talking about it, it showed he wasn't a complete lost cause for having emotions, which made Card knew he hid away from everyone like it was a shameful thing.

He was right, of course. But what bothered Card the most wasn't the body count. It was the fact that someone inside their unit was giving information to whoever was killing them. The level of vetting that went into everyone on the team was about as strict as it could be and still allow for people to pass. Yet, someone was still talking. One team, maybe two. But multiple teams in multiple countries? The math was against it. Then there was the Colonel's vague response when Card asked about it. Card didn't need platitudes from his commanding officer, certainly not coddling, but he did expect reassurances to their operational safety and the Colonel hadn't given that at all. "Yeah, Will. It bothers me too. Maybe this is just the latest step in our journey in life, totally out of our control and only the universe can right it. Though, judging by the look on your face, I'd say you don't agree with me and its more likely that we are just finding out that we should be running scared."
Toomby wore a heavy frown.
"Tony, we are so far outside of normal that I don't know how to think about this. A few hours ago, I thought we were still on mission with a road bump that comes from involving assholes. Now, I'm genuinely worried about how alive I will be this time next week. I get what we are doing, and how we have to do it, but if there isn't a chance of outside support or replacing the people we lost, how long do you think it will be until we are mission ineffective?"
Card was quiet, thinking about Toomby's question.
"*And* by 'ineffective' I mean 'dead."

Card knew he wasn't going to die that day, wasn't going to die that year. Card didn't know how he knew it, but his life would be ended by age, not violence. He couldn't be as sure for others.

"Will, I think the universe will provide."

Toomby grunted in disgust.

"You and your metaphysical bullshit. You think this will end well just because you gonna think positive?"

Card shook his head.

"I said the universe would provide, I didn't say what it provided would be what we wanted."

25

We made good time back from Gulfport. Elvis was sent with us because Anton wanted one of his people involved and he didn't seem interested in risking more than one man. I didn't know how large Anton's organization was as far as man power, but he seemed to be short of bodies, in the US at least. I decided to give Madeline a break from driving. The Tahoe was fun. More responsive than one might expect from a lumbering SUV, and the unmarked police car look helped to clear cars out of the way as I hit triple digits headed for the Little Woods area just across Lake Pontchatrain on the 10. Six Flags New Orleans had been abandoned since hurricane Katrina. Since it hasn't been doing well before the hurricane, repairing it after the wind, rain, storm surge and flooding didn't make fiscal sense to those making the decisions. Since then, it had become a favorite for urban decay explorers, photographers, and a sliding scale of virtuous people with mundane to bizarre hobbies. It was also a regular spot for Hollywood filming. It seemed like a stupid place for Heller to be, unless he had a serious amount of manpower it would be impossible to secure the perimeter. New Orleans Police had been trying and failing to do just that since the park was officially closed. My neighbor, Cyn, had been in there multiple times to paint. She was there long enough to paint an entire painting, which was not generally a quick process, so I was convinced that Heller would need a few dozen guys at least to keep people out.

As a secret base of operations for terrorist attacks, it made zero sense. One, it was a plot from a movie. Two, it was a plot from a fucking movie. And three, well, I really only needed one and two. First, Heller registers one of his lacky cars to my name, then he sets up shop in an abandoned amusement park and is sloppy enough to let one of Anton's people follow him there. It felt like a trap, but just for me? I had no illusions that I had upset the man last time we had seen each other, but this behavior was exactly what got my *sister,* Rose killed. I mean, I killed her, but her grudge against me made me do it.

No, if Heller was using the park, there was a specific reason for it, but I couldn't imagine what it would have to do with what we knew at that point. I was the only one awake on the drive. The priest, Julian, his fever had broke and he seemed to be doing better after Maddy had properly dressed his wound and given him a lot of med from her trauma kit, but sleeping was something he needed. Elvis and Madeleine were exhausted. I was past 24 hours without sleep, so I understood. On the walk back to the parking garage Madeline had asked me if we were really going to give Julian over to them. I told her *no.* She said she was glad that she wouldn't have to fight me on the issue, then. Elvis heard me say it, and I didn't care that he did. He had his phone, was armed and was his own man again, if he wanted to raise the issue I was open to the conversation. If he told Anton, it wouldn't change anything in the near future.

I took the exit for the closed amusement park and followed Michoud Boulevard through a short stint of vacant lots and former sub divisions since demolished to a newer subdivision that sat on either side of the road until the park's former entrance came up on the right. I drove by without slowing. From Michoud it was a hundred yards or more to the closed gates, entrance and exit blocked by concrete barriers. No signs of life. I accelerated back to the speed limit and followed the road into the Willow Brook neighborhood. I understood why Heller picked the park. On the West was interstate 510, Michoud Boulevard to the East, Interstate 10 to the North and Lake Forest Boulevard to the South. There was cleared greenspace and a minimum of 100 yards of standoff between the park fence and any of the roads that bordered it. On the East, the park had much more standoff from the closest road, which was unfortunate because Michoud carried the least traffic and would be the best to approach from unobserved. The bulk of the park sat back against Interstate 510, half of the border was the old water events pond. I knew Heller wasn't an idiot, and I also knew that Virtua had a deep bench of manpower, so Heller might be able to defend the park well if he was actually in there. I pushed through the Willow Brook neighborhood, pulling into a gas station to see what I could find on the GPS. The Tahoe had a laptop so I used that instead, using a 3D map program to scour the park perimeter for weaknesses. I didn't know how recent the satellite images were, but it was better than nothing. The street view option allowed me to zoom in and out to see things at eye level, and that's how I was able to find the weakest part of the perimeter. Which meant it would probably be the best defended. So, I looked longer, trying to find a less obvious entry point. I had to wonder how many illicit activities had been planned using free browser map programs. I was too tired to do any detailed planning. My train of thought was heavy and sluggish. I needed sleep. I found the closest hotel and drove. I shook Madeline awake when we pulled in.

"I need to sleep."

It took her a few seconds to process what was going on.
"Right, let's get us some rooms then."
"I want own room."
Elvis said from the back.
"Then pay for it your bloody self."
Madeline said as she stepped out and walked towards the motel office. A few minutes, all cash, and she was back with two room keys. Elvis threw his hands up in annoyance when he saw the pair.
"I'm not sharing room with him."
Julian was just waking up, his attitude towards Elvis had been indifferent and it still was.
"Suit yourself, mate. I'm gonna lay in a bed."
"Room 202, we are in 203"
Madeline said, holding out a key over her shoulder. Julian took the key Maddy offered him and stepped out, taking his things with him. Elvis watched him go, glancing at us with an incredulous look on his face.
"Relax, Elvis. If he wanted to kill you, he would have done it on the drive back."
"Oh, fuck you. I always get shit, this is shit!"
He opened his door, cursing to himself as he followed Julian.

I caught Madeline up on what I had found, showing her various map tabs open on the laptop. We agreed to revisit it after we had both gotten rest. We left the SUV and headed to the room, which was common motor lodge fare about ten years past a need for a remodel. The room was clean, a single King bed, an old flat screen on a simple dresser. A bathroom and a small closet. No couch or anything else to sleep on, so the floor it was. I pulled my shirt off and balled it up for a pillow. Madeline laughed.

"You can sleep in the bed, Rush, my mum won't mind."
I wore a tired smile, I probably blushed.
"Ok then."
I managed to take off my shoes, gun on the night stand and then laid down. I was asleep before Madeline made it back out of the bathroom.

When I woke, the sun was on its descent, late in the afternoon. I didn't open my eyes, I could feel the sun head shot me through a one-inch gap in the curtains from 91 million miles away. It was a pleasant alarm clock all the same. My body started checking in. A headache and a neck ache from the explosion at the boat house, cuts and bruises letting me know they were there. General ache and strain in my arms and chest and pressure on my side, something warm. Madeline. She was curled up against me, her head on my chest. It felt amazing and confusing all at the same time. I couldn't tell if she was asleep or not. I concentrated, listening for her breathing.
"You got a strong heart, mate."
She said, solving the mystery.
"I don't think I can take credit for it."
She looked up at me, at the perfect distance to still be in focus without me going cross eyed to look at her.
"At least a bit, yeah?"
I didn't have an answer, so I just smiled. She sat up, a brief pat to my chest before you got to her feet.
"We are going to need clothes, food, and a plan."
I rolled my feet to the floor, ready to follow. A check of my watch. It was nearing six o'clock.
"We've burned most of the day already."
Madeline pulled on her utility shirt over her tank top.

"Yeah, but we weren't going to be much good to anyone without rest. It's probably best to have a go at this at night, anyway. Right now, I think me and you need to talk about our mates in the other room."

I tore the plastic off one of the room cups, filled it with tap water and left the tap running while I drank and refilled it multiple times. Our more-or-less team mates were a direct result of my rash decision. The calculating part of me knew that. It also knew that the events that would unfold were also because of that, at least those we were directly involved in. The emotional part of me, the part that only wanted Heller and fuck the cost, didn't really want to have the conversation. But my history with Madeline demanded it.

"Maddy, it goes without saying that my decision to help Julian at the yard was, well, without much thought. We could have probably come to this same point without him, maybe not as soon, but the same. I did it because what Solomon told me and what I saw happening are two narratives that don't intersect. If someone is picking their way through the unit, who is feeding them information? If Virtua is planning an attack and the unit is capable of stopping them, why wouldn't Virtua use its considerable influence with the government to stop you? Doesn't it seem like Atlanta part two? Like there are two different groups pushing for a similar, but not the same, goal?"

Madeline seemed aggressive at first, but as I talked she softened and sat down on the edge of the bed, her eyes never leaving me while I spoke.

"Maybe because it's easier to just kill us?"

She had a point but something about it still bothered me, like there was a detail I was missing that would explain the juxtapose. It didn't connect in my mind, and until I found that detail, I would keep rearranging the pieces in my mind until I could see the whole picture.

"Maybe…"

She continued.

"We have been looking at this wrong. We know Reno was about an attack. Atlanta was about an attack. The President was about revenge, but it was also critical for Virtua to remove the President. So, even though Virtua has been able to spin some gains out of two failures, what if the attacks never mattered? "

I couldn't see what she was getting at. If Virtua really was pushing towards usurpation of the American government and both attacks were meant to help further that goal by shaping public and political opinion to support the Vice-President turned President for a single party system as Robert Wigglin had told me before he died, then it made more sense to me for the attacks to actually happen. The plan in Atlanta had been to kill the President using Robert's Auger program, and even though it probably hadn't happened the way it had been intended, Robert's program had done exactly that. But Reno, we stopped that. There would have been no way for Virtua to predict we would have stopped them. Madeline was reading my mind.

"Reno. That's the hole, idn't? Virtua knew we were out there, but they had no idea we would stop them. They had no idea you would go against your own and help us do it. So, and bear with me a bit, maybe they planned on getting caught anyway? Think about it. The cover story was bullet proof. It was quick. Like it was ready for that exact outcome. We maybe made it easier for them to sell it, I mean, we did a bang-up job of making a mess in two different states."

The pieces were starting to fit a little better. She was coming at the puzzle from a different angle and it was helping shape the picture.

"Okay. So, Reno was supposed to fail and Atl-"

"Was only an assassination, sure they were going to make it look like Muslim terrorists did it, but it wasn't a mass casualty attack, was never supposed to be. So, what did Reno change?"

What did it change?

The puzzle was still there. It was taunting me now. I could sense the answer but couldn't quite make it out. Madeline couldn't either, at least not then.

"I don't know."

I said, getting one more cup of water.

"I don't either, so hedge our bets. If Reno really was supposed to happen and we stopped it, then Heller or whoever is going to make up for that now. If Reno was supposed to fail, then this attack was always part of the plan."

I couldn't piece that part together, but I knew someone who could.

"We should get some help on this. Call Dino, see what he can find?"

Dino Parchus was one of the smartest analysts I knew, and I only knew him because of Madeline.

"I thought about that. I haven't talked to him much since coming on with Solomon full time, he doesn't like farming out work."

I had to laugh.

"Don't seem like Solomon likes things he can't directly control."

She shrugged.

"Fair point, that. But that's later, what about our new teammates?"

I had that thought on the back burner, but I had considered it.

"Julian wants exactly what we want. Elvis is here as a baby sitter. He's Vor, but he's not stupid. He's not going to get in our way, but I have no doubt he's been told to update Anton on our movements, probably been told to shoot Julian as soon as this is over."

Madeline wore a smirk.

"I don't think Elvis is up for the job on that, he'd be barmy to try it. If we are gonna put paid to this, we need them, right about that. But I think me, and you need to be ready for either of them to do their own thing and that might mean we might need to scribble one or both."

I could see that more with Elvis than Julian. Something about the priest and his singular focus, his willingness to go against who he had become to hunt and kill Heller made me trust him. I knew what it was like to go against everything you were. It wasn't the same story, but it was.

"No argument here. I don't think Elvis will be much help, which means he's going to need to be kept away from anything we can't expect him to help with."

Before we could circle the conversation back around, there was a knock at the door. I armed myself before checking, going to the far side of the room to glance through the curtains as opposed to using the peep hole. I was a bit paranoid about being shot through one. Sure, that was mostly a movie thing, but people got ideas from movies. It was Julian. He didn't look like he had slept. Maybe he always looked like that. Elvis was with him, puffing away on a cigarette. I opened the door and let them in. Madeline went down to the Tahoe and brought back the laptop from the mount rack so we could use it to work a plan.

The plan was going to be simple. Get in. Kill who needed it. Get out.

26

Tellison was checking in. Toomby was talking to him on the phone. Card was on his scope. The house had been quiet all day. It didn't seem like the Russians who had previously lived there and were now dead there, had made friends with the neighbors. Those with regular nine to fives on the street had straggled in and either parked in driveways or pulled into garages. No one had gone to the Russian house. The mail man had come through not long after that, no stop at their box. Card couldn't see the entire street, as it curved away from him just passed the Russian house, but he could see a few kids playing with a frisbee in one yard and an old lady, the same old lady from the night before, out walking her dog. Nothing else was going on and Toomby was letting Tellison know exactly that. When he ended the call, he slid back up to the spotting scope, letting Card take a break from being on the glass.

"Nothing new, Tony. Chief is sending Porter and Finn over as soon as the sun sets to relieve us."

Card was cool with that. Finn didn't have much time on a long gun, operationally anyway, but Porter was a solid shooter and good at seeing the details some cats miss when being on the scope for a long time.

"Cool. I hope they bring some food."

Toomby nodded.

"Yeah man, I'm over gas station eating. I'd rather have an MRE at this point."

"I'm sure that's what they will bring."

"Ugh. I just cursed us both."

Card laughed

"Especially since Finn will probably rat fuck them and we will be stuck with peanut butter and crackers."

The sun was getting lower, but summer meant it wouldn't set for a few more hours. Card expected that if they were coming for the van, it would be after dark. He had already pulled an NV clip on out of his bag and checked it. Once he needed it, it would attach to the rail and co-witness with his optic. Much more reliable for longer range shooting than an IR laser. They were good for entry guns, not so much for precision rifles. Card was more concerned about the setting sun when that time came. It would be directly in his line of sight. Nothing he could do about it, but it was on his mind. The radio cracked.

"Breathtaker, Foundation, be advised, we are real time on station. Zero delay. If you boys need a break, take it." Gianna was telling them she had air overhead, either a satellite or a drone. Card figured it was a drone. Satellites could be good for zero delay in picture to reality, but they were mostly top-down. A drone could be repositioned much faster and could see the world from more than just directly overhead.

"Roger, Foundation, we appreciate it."

Toomby came off his scope.

"I'm gonna stick some rear guard while I can."

He dug in his bag, small cameras to be mounted on virtually any surface. Up until then, the entire perimeter of the house was blind to them. Set back in the room, they couldn't even see the street directly in front of the house. Toomby setting a few motion cameras would help ease Card's mind.

Toomby finished with the cameras and returned to the room, crouching back up to his seat on the bucket. He set a tablet on the platform between them, five of six squares on it held real-time images. They had the back, both sides of the house, and interior view of the front door and an interior view down the stairs. If any camera detected motion, the tablet would chirp and the corresponding camera view would highlight with a red border.

"Looks good."

Card said, checking the coverage.

"Didn't want to risk putting one on the front right now. I can get one out there once it gets dark."

"Cool."

Card said, watching what he could see with the naked eye. Toomby pulled out a second tablet, he tapped at it until he had a real-time view of Gianna's drone. He set it down next to the camera tablet so they both could see it.

"You are quite the tech geek, Will."

Toomby sneered at him.

"Don't you tell anyone. I have a reputation as a dumb ass grunt to maintain."

And they sat, watching the bringer of all life work its way down a comic blue sky. The enormity of the sun was appealing to Card. It was abstract to most people, it was there, and it was a mark of time, but not much more thought went into it. Outside the world, thinking of space, Card could see on the scale of time eternal, how insignificant they were. How what he was doing didn't really matter to the universe. He was made of star dust. So was garbage. No matter how it all played out, the sun would still be there. Uncaring, burning hot plasma eight light minutes away from decisions and actions of a sentient race it helped create but had no capacity to care for. People throughout history had worshipped the sun, and Card found it ironic that despite all the worship, the sun had done what it had always done and nothing man could do changed that. But the imaginary gods had done and not done all that man could imagine, even though none of it was what they thought it was. Card and Toomby didn't talk for a few hours, the professional roles of professional careers put them on auto pilot, but not the sort of auto pilot where you zone out. They watched, even though the drone meant they didn't have to watch as hard.

"Tony, how's your vision?"
The sun was low enough now that the light was going to create serious problems on his rifle until it fell deeper into the horizon. He could still see but getting a positive ID would be a problem.
Card was about to respond when Tellison came over the radio.
"Breathtaker, Vicious. What was your last contact with Foundation?"
Card's stomach sank. His mouth went dry. He reached up to his PPT on his chest. It was harder than usual to push.
"Vicious, Breathtaker, about three hours."
Silence. It seemed to tick on forever. Card could only think selfishly of Gianna.
"Breathtaker, standby."
Toomby looked at Card.
"The hell?"
The both looked down at the tablet. The drone feed was still live, tight on the house but clearly from a high altitude, slowly circling. That didn't mean anyone was on the other end driving it, they practically flew themselves with a few key strokes. Toomby started packing away unnecessary gear. Card did as well, if they needed to fold up, the wanted to do it fast.
"Breathtaker, Vicious, negative contact. Prepare for exfil."

Card knew that he and Toomby weren't needed for a physical check on the command truck. Tellison was pulling them because if command was compromised, so were they. They were packed and in the back yard in five minutes. Gear back in trash bags, cameras packed up. Leaf blowers shouldered. They didn't want to burn the hide if they needed to come back and running out with rifles and kit exposed would do that.

"Breathtaker, road in 30 seconds."

Toomby opened the gate, walking out casually with Card right behind him. Hollic had the discipline to cruise into the neighborhood like he wasn't in a hurry. He slid the Nissan to the curb and they hopped in. Doors closed, and he was moving again. Card and Toomby immediately freed weapons from their bags. Tellison spoke to them over his shoulder.

"Finn and Porter are looking for command now. Last contact had them set up at a truck stop North of here. There were no plans to move again for at least 24 hours."

Once Hollic hit main surface streets, he drove with urgency, pushing over the speed limit in the early evening traffic. They picked up the 10 and headed North, continuing onto 59. The scenery turned semi-rural and the bayou crept in on the right of the road. Tellison tried to raise the command truck on the radio multiple times with no response.

"Shouldn't they be there by now?"

Hollic asked.

"Huck, Vicious."

No response.

"We are five minutes out."

Hollic said, watching the GPS.

"Cut that in half."

Tellison said, checking the magazine in his rifle. Hollic accelerated, weaving though the light traffic like it was standing still. The exit was a gradual split from the main road into a hairpin curve that would put them headed in the opposite direction to enter the truck stop's lot. Hollic rounded it and the heavy body roll of the large SUV almost put them up on two wheels. Card watched between the seats. It was a spread-out dirt lot dotted with trucks, a main building with a pump canopy to the left. Despite no clear parking guide or lines, trucks were stacked orderly to the left of the building, having pulled through and behind the main store to turn around and park facing out. Far to the left, back against the wood line that separated the dirt lot from the water like a thin ribbon of dense foliage was a restaurant of some sort that had a few patrons parked out front in cars and work trucks. Card couldn't see the command truck as they left the pavement. Hollic guided them past the pumps towards the back, then he saw it, set against the back of the lot, hidden from the road by a pair of haphazardly parked 18 wheelers. The trailer's extensions were expanded, and the leveling feet were down, the cab still attached. Card could see a car, which he assumed was Finn and Porters rental. It was blocking the cab's exit just in case, not that their compact sedan would have stopped the truck if someone really wanted out. No Finn. No Porter.

"Stand us off a bit. Handguns only, keep it concealed, too many people here."

Hollic turned short, setting the SUV up to parallel the trailer's right side. As soon as he shifted into park, four doors opened and closed at the same time. There was light pedestrian traffic, a few drivers crisscrossing the lot to and

from their trucks, some close, some far. There were no signs of violence, but the trailer looked wrong somehow. Card watched as they cautiously approached the main entrance on the side. The first signs that there was something wrong was a trail of blood near the base of the door. It had come from inside, probably flowing freely until the door was sealed and cut off the supply. Since the stairs were retracted, it dripped freely onto the dirt, clumping as it did. With no windows on the trailer, there were two access points to try. The main door, and the rear. Tellison spoke in hand signals. If someone had taken the truck, any communications would be compromised. He pointed and motioned. Card and Toomby to the back. Hollic to the cab, driver's side. He would try the main door. He then nodded twice with a raised fist. Entry on two squelches of the radio. Everyone moved. Card and Toomby set up on the smaller entrance door that was set inside of a ramp door that could be lowered for larger equipment or even a vehicle if room was made inside. Card opened the keypad, the emergency entry code called to the front of his memory. He entered it and waited for the signal before he pressed enter. It didn't come.
"Will."
Card said, raising his pistol to where chest height would be if someone was standing there when he opened the door and they needed to be shot. Toomby crossed behind him, getting line of sight on Tellison around the corner. Tellison pointed to his ear and shook his head. Something was blocking the radio. The trailer could do that. *Would* do that if the emergency measures were activated. If the trailer was jamming, that meant no communication device in a square mile that wasn't a hard landline was being blocked. Comm jamming only was part of the lowest level

of emergency measures. Card didn't know what else the trailer could do, but he had an imagination.

"Comms blocked. He's giving me a finger count." Toomby said, his head tucked around the corner. "Three. Two. One. Go."

Card hit enter, gripped the door's lower handle and swung it open. No one that needed shooting, but he could hear screaming. Someone in pain. He was in the trailer, Toomby right behind them. They were in the rear cargo area, an exactly-mid-sized-sedan room that was the armory and held a small holding box. The box held their Russian prisoner. He could have been sleeping, but the amount of blood pooled beneath him told Card that he was more likely just dead. They pushed forward to the door out of the cargo area. Normally the door would be secured, and a separate code needed to open it, but the sliding door was ajar. Propped open on the head of a body. One of the technicians. Also dead by the looks of it. Toomby moved to Card's right, holstering his handgun to grip the door. Card nodded at him, keeping at a high ready. Toomby pulled, the door resisted and then with a loud pop, it released and slid into the wall. Tellison was on the far end of the room, between the two of them a scene of chaos. Another dead technician. Card knew her, Susan. The walls and monitors, as well as the glass walls of the secure briefing room were marked with gunfire. It wasn't sporadic, it was a pattern; tracking a target that was always just ahead of being hit. Finn and Porter were off to the left, between one of the work stations and the briefing room wall. Card didn't see them at first because they were crouched down, furiously working kerlix into wounds on the Colonel. Porter was holding him down, Finn was quickly unrolling and stuffing the porous gauze into a wound high on the shoulder just near his left arm. The Colonel grunted loudly every time Finn stabbed the material into the wound. His shirt was cut away and Card could see a second wound already packed and a chest seal in place in the center of his chest. The floor was slick with blood. Towards the front of the trailer, Gianna sat on her knees, covered in blood. Card moved forward for a better view. Tellison dropped down beside her, she was working on the tech that Toomby called *Sniffles*. His name was Greg and Card knew he was a cool guy. Card had played spades with him a few times; he was a former Airforce dude with a head for numbers and a 12-year-old daughter. Gianna was starting chest compressions. Greg had serious defensive wounds, hands and arms. Something sharp, straight edge. Card could trace the path of the blade by looking at the wounds, he only managed to block a few. What cuts made it through, turned into deep stabs and the knife was right back out again for another attack.

He didn't make it.

"Sergeant Card, Toomby, check on Hollic. We have this!" Card nodded to Tellison. He tapped will on his way out the side entrance, slamming the door behind them. They rounded the front of the cab. The driver's door was open. Card passed it in a wide arc, jumping up on the side to cover the inside at an angle without being right in front of the opening.
"Clear up."
Toomby took his permission and mounted the steps to access the cab.
"Two down in the back."

Toomby said from inside. The driver team were both dead in the sleeper cab.

"Where the fuck is Hollic?"

Toomby asked, coming back out of the truck. Card scanned the lot. The sun was nothing more than a sliver of burning color on a darkening sky, but it was still light enough to see fine detail. He didn't see anything out of place, nothing but their behavior out of the ordinary. Card brought his attention back to the ground beneath the truck, he looked hard towards the rear of the truck, following it with his eyes up to where he stood by the cab. The spoor told a story. Fresh tracks from the rear of the truck, in a run or jog by the stride. They met with Hollic's tracks around the front of the truck. The unknown tracks went over the top of Hollic's easily recognizable Lowa boot tread. They disappeared around the front of the truck. Then Hollic's tracks led in the same direction, overlapping in some places. Card could see it in his mind. Hollic was up in the truck when someone ran by. He jumped back down and pursued.

"This way."

Card said. Toomby fell in with him. He knew Card was the better tracker and trusting his lead was second nature. The tracks got wider, definitely running, moving off towards the restaurant at the back of the lot. Card scanned for activity as they moved. There were a few people moving to or from vehicles into the gas station or the restaurant, but no one seemed altered to anything.

"Why in the hell would he go off on his own?"

Card quickened his pace to match the quickened pace of the spoor.

"He was probably trying to get us on the radio."

The tracks veered to the left, disappearing between a
parked low boy trailer carrying a large tractor and a
traditional box trailer. Danny Hollic was between them.

He was dead.

Card wasn't a doctor. He had extensive medical training
but even without that, he would have recognized what he
was looking at. Hollic was in a clumping pool of blood
that had to be three or four liters at that point. He was
laying on his back, much of his right hand missing; Card
could see his sidearm and fingers laying around his body.
His head was laying at a strange angle, his chin higher than
should be natural. His throat was opened horizontally,
wide. Death would have been quick but not instant.
"Fuck."
Toomby said, reading the scene. He saw what happened as
well as Card did.
The radio came to life. The trailer was no longer jamming.
"Breathtaker, Vicious, report."
Card hesitated. He didn't want to broadcast anything on
the radio before he knew more about what happened.
"Vicious, we need you out here."

Six were dead. Card included the Russian in that count
because he was a human being and he was dead. Others
might exclude him from their personal count of those lost,
but Card refused to. He was sitting absently in one of the
technician chairs, they were swivel chairs that were bolted
to the floor, not much different than what you would find in
a barber shop. Toomby sat in the chair next to him. Finn
and Porter had just returned from bringing Hollic's body in.
Gianna was tending to Colonel Solomon, who was laying

on a deployed field stretcher. She had him on an IV. His injuries were bad. Tellison was crouched down next to him, talking to him before the pain killers he refused to take but Gianna gave him anyway, kicked in and he passed out. The conversation was short. When Tellison joined Card and Toomby, Gianna came with him. Both looked tired, but Gianna was pale, dried blood covered her clothes and skin. She was strong in the face of what had happened, which Card could respect in her character.

"What the fuck, happened, Chief?"

Toomby asked before Card could ask the same question. Tellison grabbed a rolling chair out of its storage cradle and pushed it over for Gianna. He grabbed a second for himself.

"Finn, Porter, join us, please?"

He asked before sitting down. Tellison was cool as he ever was, but it looked more conscious to Card than he had ever seen him. Given the circumstances, it would be hard for anyone to maintain their stoicism.

"Gianna, I'll let you give it to us."

Tellison said, leaning back in his chair. She was visibly shaken. Not in the way you would be if you weren't able to cope. No, it was more of an instant regret over not being able to do more than she did. She was stronger than Card expected, and he was ashamed of the realization of learning she was better than an abstract idea he didn't even know he had until just then.

"Greg was out to get some supplies from the store, secure protocol was observed, we locked down as soon as he stepped out. When he returned he punched his code, but I don't think anyone was on the cameras to see him. This asshole had to be right behind him. The locks popped, Greg was probably down before he had even made it all the way inside, but he managed to fight back. I was on Console Two next to Susan. The Colonel was first to engage him, the first shot got me turned around, he moved everywhere the Colonel wasn't shooting like he knew where to be. I don't think I've ever…I don't think it's possible for someone to move that fast. He hit the Colonel, then Susan. I went for the weapon locker on the wall, only reason he missed me was Andy got in his way, but he got between me and the locker. I pulled the Colonel into the briefing room and hit the emergency lockdown. Only reason we survived. He took Colonel Solomon's laptop and secure phone and went out through the back."

Card had no illusion about who was being described to him. It wasn't Rushing, but it was one of his kind, Card was sure of it.

"What was on the laptop?"

Finn asked. Gianna threw up her hands.

"What wasn't on it? Its password and fingerprint protected but I'm sure whoever wants it, can get past that or they wouldn't have stolen it."

Tellison leaned over, elbows on his knees, rubbing his neck. He was cold when he spoke, he wasn't built to offer emotional support to anyone.

"Gianna, can you explain to me how the fuck someone knew where this truck was? Or any of our other teams?"

She was wringing her hands, shaking her head before he had gotten all the words out. She caught his tone and wasn't going to let it ride easy.

"It's pretty simple, Chief. Either it's an electronic source I can't find, or someone in here was a leak. Your suspects include me and the Colonel, since everyone else is dead. Your other suspects include your men and any outside help you have enlisted."

Tellison stared at her, thinking. He had to decide if he could trust her. Card noticed his hand absently tapping the grip of his holstered handgun. The thought that Tellison might shoot Gianna occurred to him, and Card honestly didn't know how he would feel about that. The silence stretched on. The tapping stretched on. Finally, Toomby spoke.

"So, this guy, just used a fuckin' knife?"

Gianna swallowed and nodded. Remembering.

"Two of them, sort of like a karambit but much longer, and a shallower curve on the blade. A spear point tip by the looks of the wounds. He cut his way through blocks and then stabbed to hit major organs. Which brings up our next issue. The Colonel needs to be in a hospital. He *must* be in a hospital if we expect him to survive. There's a lot I can do for him, but I can't fix the level of damage he has to his shoulder or hip. He needs surgery."

"We have a plan for that."

Tellison said. Gianna nodded and continued.

"I'm sure it's stating the obvious, but this isn't some run of the mill professional. This also matches with many of the attacks on the other teams. Maybe all of them."

"Glad we brought on one of these spook assholes to help prevent this."

Porter said, more to himself than everyone else.

"Okay."

Card offered, wanting to change the energy and get pointed back in the right direction.

"What now, Chief? We still have a mission here."

"The Colonel wants us to stay on mission. Hijazi is going to get him to the hospital and help with...everything else."

"Where is Hijazi?"

Toomby asked, an edge of suspicion in his voice. Tellison stood.

"He's playing his role with the JTTF, which is going to help the Colonel get medical care and stay off the radar. As much as I don't like Hijazi, this isn't him."

"Chief is right."

Gianna observed.

"He didn't know the truck location today until I told him."

Toomby seemed to accept the explanation. Tellison stood up, checking on Solomon then turned his attention back to everyone.

"Mission is the same, Gianna is going to relocate after the Colonel is moved. We are headed back to the Slidell location. Let's get our shit together and get ready to move."

Gianna raised her hand.

"Chief, one more thing."

She said, walking over to her console. She punched some keys, moved the cursor around and then pointed to the screen. A recording of the rear cargo area came up. She moved the video forward with the runtime bar until a figure appeared on the screen. The video was from overhead, with a perspective from back to front of room. Card watched the sliding door open, watched Andy move for the door and get cut down from behind in a flash of knives. The attacker disappeared from frame and a few seconds later rushed into the room. He stopped at the holding cell, speaking to the Russian.

"We got audio?"

Tellison asked. Gianna answered.

"No, just video."

On the screen, the exchange stretched on and on. The attacker started to leave, paused, moved back to the small cage and struck through the bars with one of his knives. The Russian recoiled, put his hands to the wound in his neck but seemed to lose consciousness quickly. The attacker moved directly to the back entrance and was gone. A few seconds later, Card and Toomby could be seen entering the door. They had just missed him.

"Wait."

Finn said, looking at the time stamp on the video.

"Well, that explains how we barely missed this guy. He interrogated the Russian for damn near 15 minutes."

"Did we ever get anything out of him?"

Tellison asked Gianna. She frowned.

"No. Whatever this guy was asking, the Russian was willing to answer."

"Seems like we are the only ones they don't want to talk to. Okay, we can mourn later. Let's get mobile."

Six bodies were laid carefully side-by-side next to the crew bunk expansion. Each covered with a blue sheet. There was little time to help Gianna clean the blood from the floors. Card felt bad for leaving her by herself after everything that had happened, but she was a professional and they all had a mission. He didn't know how Hijazi was going to help keep this quiet. It was amazing that no one had called 911 or attempted to investigate the trailer. No one apparently had seen anything. They had been able to recover Hollic's body in the failing light without running into anyone. The blood was still there, but by morning it wouldn't matter. The Command truck would be moved, and everyone gone. Card didn't know a single fact about who had done this. He didn't know how he found the truck, or what his goal had been. He did know that if the universe saw fit to put him in this man within a mile of each other, Card would kill him.

27

The plan was not complex. With only four of us, it couldn't be. The former amusement park had some natural and manmade barriers that limited easy access, but no one direction was impossible. If Heller was in there, he knew it. Heller had decades of small unit experience on six continents. He could defend a position and he would have people who knew how to do the same. I wasn't going to play the *if I was him* game. None of us were. I looked at the problem like I would any; I needed to be able to move from point A to point B and encounter as little resistance as possible in doing it. The advantage was I got to decide where point A was, but point B was someone else's decision and I couldn't be accurate to a specific building where point B was. The entry into the park was also going to be recon-as-you-go. There were two really good points of entrance into the park. Directly through the front gate, and a service gate on the west side that sat middle of the park between Interstate 510 and the park fence. The service road that led to the service gate could be accessed from the south off a surface street or the North from Interstate 10 just after the merge from the 510 by just driving off the shoulder into the grass to reach the road. We had gone over the satellite map in the room. Elvis was no help and wasn't likely to be. Julian and Madeline had more conventional experience, while I had the most experience doing things like this on my own. The front entry was out. There was a massive and very empty parking lot between the drive-in entrance and the park, even at night it would be near impossible to cross the parking lot without being seen. The best option was the service gate, but a gate wasn't really needed unless we intended to take the vehicle in with us, which we didn't. No matter our entry point, there was going to be a lot of ground to cover before we reached anywhere anyone but perimeter guards were expected to be, so a distraction made sense. The problem with a distraction is that it alerted professionals to the fact that they needed to be looking elsewhere as soon as it happened and was recognized for what it was. Madeline had a plan for that. She used the rest of her cash to buy a handful of prepaid smart phones, which was a necessity because she needed to download a ride app onto each, so she could call for cars on each phone. Each phone needed an online account linked to either a bank or a payment account. She must have had enough of those to make it work, because each phone was set up and ready to go.

After we talked over the plan, I checked over my weapons. Julian brought over his blanket wrap to do the same. Elvis busied himself with daytime gameshows on the room TV. Since there hadn't been any gunfire on my part, my loaner rifle was still clean. I checked batteries on the light and MAWL, then the PVS-31s. Everything was in order. Julian watched me with a smirk while he checked his rifle. Once I saw what was wrapped up in his blanket, I was more interested in the explanation he had for just what in the hell it was.

"Probably the most popular rifle in Africa next to the AK. Always preferred it myself. This one belonged to Father Ava. I made some modifications."

That was one way to put it. Julian's rifle was a FN FAL variant. A more modern version of a rifle that had dozens of variants over it's well over half a century of service. This one had a picatinny topped receiver, and a picatinny handguard with a barrel much shorter than the standard 17-21 inches. It looked in the neighborhood of 12". The stock was a side folding skeletonized, with a long, metal spike welded to the toe of the stock, angled slightly forward so it could be shouldered without interference. It had a very old model Aimpoint optic mounted, as well as a weapon light that was cutting edge when I was a toddler.

"You know that's weird, right?"

I said, pointing to the spike.

"Here in the US, dudes who put knives on guns are generally dudes who live in their mom's basement and…wait, that belonged to your priest, uh, boss?"

Julian snickered.

"Oi, it's Africa, mate. Everyone has a rifle. Ava was not always *Father* Ava. Same as me."

I couldn't argue with rock solid logic like that.   But I had to know about the knife thing.

"So, the knives?"

Julian pressed down on the top rounds in a magazine, ensuring it was full, then loaded it into the rifle.

"Knives don't run out of ammo. World would be a much more polite place without guns. Any *pompe à chiasse* can use a gun. Knives are for people who can fight, eh?"

He checked the capacity on the other magazines he had. I noticed the ammo was steel case .308. Cheap, and inexpensive.

"Bayonets have been part of combat since the rifle came along. Not much need for them anymore in conventional combat."

He racked the first round into the chamber, set the safety.

"…But we aren't going to do any conventional combat, are we?"

"No."

I answered, holstering my 1911.

"We are not."

As soon as the sun set, we left the hotel. The drive to our first stop was short, just a few miles. Madeline slowed to let Julian out, dropping him off at the turn for the South service road. He would need to clear a fence, but it was a fence more for keeping vehicles out than people. We then turned around, drove south to the nearest interstate access and took 510 North.

"You sure about this, Rushing?"

Madeline asked as she started to slow the vehicle to let me out at the decided point.

"Yeah, too much ground to cover together."

I said, pulling my door handle. I was out before she came to a stop or could try again to talk me out of it. The truth was, I wanted to be alone. I didn't want to endanger her on what could very well turn out to be suicide mission. I vaulted the low concrete wall then rolled on my back over the sagging chain link fence, putting me on track to move into the park just above the large pond under the feet of a massive rollercoaster apogee that stretched out over the edge of the water.

Darkness was nearing absolute, I moved as quickly as I could, crossing the access road, paying attention to the time. At the park fence, I crouched down and flipped my NV down. My first sign of bad guy presence came in the form of something with an IR signature at the top of the rollercoaster track. Some asshole was up there with a cellphone. The signal was invisible to the naked eye, but all cell phones gave off IR light, usually in the form of blinking. I couldn't make him out, so I couldn't guess if he could see me. Since I hadn't been fired at, I assumed not.

We still had radios, and thanks to the trunking unit in the Tahoe, they worked. I didn't have a nifty callsign and no desire to make one up, so I just broadcast.
"Maddy, in position."
"Got it."
She replied. Now the second phase began. While I cut my way through the fence with a minimum of movement, Madeline was parked at the North end of the service road, using multiple phones to call ride share drivers and food delivery to the front gate. The first few cars would arrive in a few minutes and continue for nearly an hour. Since the gate was secured, there was little chance of any of them being in danger, but the very small chance did make me a little uneasy, so I was determined to redirect Heller's attention as soon as I could.

Julian didn't have a radio, just me and Madeleine. Not that he needed one. His part of the plan was simple; we put him on Rambo mode and let him kill his way inside until he ran out of bad guys. A glance at my watch as I clipped, Julian would wait another twenty minutes. It took me another three to get through the fence. I moved through the hole as slow as I could, watching the steady blink from the top of the rollercoaster track. A scan of the horizon didn't show anyone else, or at least no one else stupid enough to give off light. Not that I might not have been as stupid without schooling from Madeline. It was amazing how many electronic devices has IR radiation, and how many objects or garments stood out greatly under IR. Even the IR laser on my rifle could emit IR light via a small LED in the top of the unit that would be visible to the user if the laser was on. Maddy had taped over it for me and had me memorize the controls and settings, which wasn't hard. The MAWL design was intuitive. Twisting the MAWL selector clockwise past Visible to IR, I used my thumb to push the distance selector forward to midrange. I had to hold down a small spring-loaded blocker to push the switch all the way forward to the long range setting. If the man on top of the rollercoaster had night vision, he would know I was there as soon as I painted him.

I waited.

Through the buildings, rides and trees, I could just make out the occasional set of head lights pulling to the gate. Cars would sit for a few seconds, or a few minutes and then leave. Occasionally there would be multiple cars there at once. I laughed on the inside at the aggravation it was causing them. This helped me pick out a few more of the grounds guards. I had two of them in a roving patrol on my side of the park, seeming to stick to the border of the large rollercoaster. They would become my first problem after taking out the man up top. Shooting suppressed would make it harder for them to pinpoint my location, and the muzzle signature to the naked eye wouldn't be as severe, but it wasn't going to be quiet.

I waited.

Thinking I was that close to Heller made it hard to concentrate on anything but killing him. My anger rose. I fought it down. It rose again. I fought it down. Vengeance had a very specific taste. It burned, but the burning was all in your mind. It makes your teeth clench and forces hands into fists. I worked my hands, trying to burn it off.

Minutes moved slow.

"Rush."

My radio squawked.

"Yeah, go ahead."

I whispered.

"You see the vehicle in the service parking lot? Just coming out of what looks like a warehouse building?"

I turned my attention to the north, 200 yards away was a smaller service parking lot, which had probably been employee parking and the delivery entrance. The edge of the parking lot housed a large L shaped storage warehouse. Using the 3D mapping program earlier, as well as street view, I knew it had roll up doors large enough for vehicles to move in and out of. Now, a vehicle was moving out of it. It was running with its headlights off, but it was unmistakable under the light blues and whites of the white phosphor night vision. I was closer to it than Madeline was.

"I got it. SUV of some sort."

The vehicle moved to exit the parking lot. It was more likely to turn south towards me than go north. I risked a peek at my watch. There were three minutes remaining before Julian would move. The SUV turned north, then cut behind the building onto the internal service road. That road could take them into the heart of the park or across to what used to be the public parking lot.

Madeline read my mind when she responded.

"Okay, not for us."

"It will be in a minute. Get ready to kick this off."

We knew we would be outnumbered. We knew only three of us would be worth a shit. I fully expected Elvis to stay with the truck when Madeline moved. So, we planned for being outnumbered. What makes people like me and Madeline successful isn't just accurate shooting and physical fitness. More so, it was the ability to exploit time and problem solve faster than the other guy could. I had been trained to do the former faster than Madeline, probably faster than any off the assholes I was about to shoot in the face. Madeline, on the other hand, had a grace with outthinking her opponent like she was psychic. And Julian, well, a killer like that needs to be pointed at people that need killing and let loose. I just hoped he didn't beat me to Heller.

Shooting with IR was a little new to me. You don't shoulder the rifle like you would using an optic, although you could co-witness your NVGs behind most red dot optics and shoot that way as well, if you needed to. When using the laser, you looked over the top of the rifle, put the beam on what you wanted to hit accounted for the zero, and pressed the trigger. Repeat until desired results. When my watch hit the appointed time, I shouldered in and pressed the activation button. The MAWL's IR illuminator was slaved to its laser, the man on the top of the rollercoaster was instantly illuminated to my NVGs. Sure enough, he was wearing some sort of night vision and was instantly aware of me. He turned in my direction, I saw an IR laser activate and watched it sweep down and over. He was moving as fast as he could to get a shot. He wouldn't make it. Three quick presses, three loud supersonic snaps and a body fell over the far side of the tracks with a muffled grunt. He was wearing a plate carrier, and I was sure it stopped the first two rounds. The third hit him in the neck. Further to the south I could hear shouting. Then a fusillade of large caliber and very unsuppressed rifle fire. Under IR the muzzle flash was fast and obnoxious. Julian was fully involved.

I moved, sprinting towards the base of the rollercoaster. The two-man patrol was headed back around in my direction. When I saw their IR lasers dancing through the legs and crossbeams of the elevated track. Knowing they had IR, I opted to co-witness. A dropped to one knee and shouldered the rifle traditionally. My optic was set to the lowest possible setting, even so the two MOA dot was blooming to three times that size. Both guards pushed through to the outside of the track, IR lasers dancing in different directions, looking for a target. More gunfire from Julian's direction, they seemed to hesitate, the lasers danced to the south. Roughly 50 meters. A press, slight move to the right, another. Both down with shots to the head. I was up and moving again, pounding over a downed fence to cut beneath the coaster tracks. Julian was shooting again, on the wide thoroughfare near The Big Easy ferris wheel. I would run right into him soon. If Madeline was engaged, I couldn't hear her. She was on foot and the plan was for her to move directly to the L shaped warehouse and then clear towards the center of the park. We wouldn't enter any one building by ourselves. It was recon by fire; either see which building the most assholes came out of, or which one the most assholes moved to protect.

Well, you know how plans go.

"Rush, you have about twenty guys moving from the warehouse."

She was huffing, sounded like she was broadcasting at a sprint.

"20?"

I asked, pushing through a hole in the fence to the other side of the tracks. The foliage was as thick as a jungle. What was once clean and manicured was now more bayou than tourist friendly greenery.

"Was 25, mate. That SUV is coming back, too."

We had counted on men, but those numbers were troubling. I did a quick magazine change, checking to get my bearings. I was right in front of the old arcade games building. Looking around the corner to the north I could see the first of the wave of men. I did a quick mental check and confirmed that I had never gone up against that many guys at once. Either I was going to beat a personal record, or I was going to beat a personal record *and* die.

28

Julian walked North, leaving the surface road as soon as he crossed it and went into the wood line. Julian didn't know much about trees, and even less about the trees native to Louisiana. What he was familiar with was patterns and he could tell that the forest he was fighting his way through had been planted by man, at least some of it. The undergrowth was in serious need of a fire to clear it out. Insects went about their noisy conversations, making it nearly impossible for Julian to listen for anything. He briefly left the woods, crossing a manmade clearing under massive powerlines and then he was right back in the woods. With no map, no night vision and no compass, Julian was navigating with dead reckoning and memory of studying the area from above. He expected to cross a dirt road as he slowly veered to the right as he moved forward. He found the road, observed it for a few minutes and satisfied he was alone, he crossed. He hit a fence a few hundred meters after that. A simple chain link affair that was in desperate need of repair. Instead of climbing it, he found a hole and just walked through. To the right he could make out the occasional car passing on the road in the distance, keeping that road on his right helped guide him forward. When Julian could clearly see the two tail lights of the occasional car, he knew the road's angle was more going away from him than along with him, meaning he was just short of the park fence. He had done many over land missions as a Legionnaire, but nothing even close to making entry into a closed American amusement park.

The park perimeter fence was much higher, with an angled three strand of barbwire at the top. Someone had already made him a hole. The ground was well beaten, plenty of foot traffic. Too far from the city to be homeless. Probably adventure seekers and explorers looking for a hidden way into the park. Julian thanked them for making things easy as he crossed inside. His memory told him he was about to hit the South inside service road. Another minute through the trees and he was at the edge of it. He stayed low, listening for human sounds over the obnoxious sounds of the local insect and wildlife. Julian checked his watch. He had another thirty minutes to get in position. He was two hundred meters from where he would wait to set things off, according to the plan. Thirty minutes gave him time to be cautious, so he waited. The road would be patrolled, all he had to do was wait for it. Headlights were occasionally cutting through the trees across the parking lot. Madeline's distraction. Because of the headlights, two men where silhouetted as they rounded the corner in the road and moved towards Julian. One was side walking to watch the headlights, the other had his attention directed ahead. Both carried rifles and the odd outline of their head told Julian they were wearing night vision. Of course they were wearing night vision. Everyone in the US had night vision. People who didn't work in law enforcement or serve in the military had night vision. There were 16 year old kids in the US who shot each other with plastic BBs for fun who had night vision.

Julian didn't have night vision.

So he didn't move. Night vision worked by amplifying available light and showing light in the spectrums not easily visible to the naked eye. Even simple clothing dyes could cause certain garments to appear bright under NV that in natural light were dark. Julian was somewhat sure that his suit wasn't designed with low IR signature in mind, so he found himself briefly wishing for a purpose made camouflage uniform. If the sentry saw him, he didn't realize what he was looking at. When the pair was steps away and Julian was positive he would be seen if they got any closer, he moved. Coming from a crouch, he launched out of the low brush, the rifle already in a hard, underhand swing, driving the welded blade up under the chin of the attentive guard. The sudden sound of his movement had gotten both men's attention, the other was turning to the source of the noise when Julian struck his partner. At that distance, Julian was inside of his NVG focus, at least Julian hoped he was. He kicked him hard in the chest, yanking his rifle free of the first man as he did. The guard lost all his air going backwards, but he was struggling to raise his rifle. Julian was on top of him, driving the muzzle of his rifle into his face while he kicked the guard's hand off his rifle grip.

"Be still, I won't scribble you right here."

A furious resistance to stand up stopped immediately when the words connected to the pressure of the muzzle against his face.

"Nods only, mate. You have cuffs?"

A shake in the affirmative.

"Get 'em out. You go for that handgun, scribbling applies, mate."

He dug at his plate carrier, producing a pair of cuffs.

"Right, tug off them glasses, then grab your buddy."

Julian stepped back, keeping the rifle trained. The guard struggled off his back folding up his night vision, crouching over his recently deceased partner.

"Get him from the back, stand him up."

Rough math in Julian's head told him the dead man had at least three stone on the live one. Plus gear made him a fight to stand up, but he managed to do it with a bear hug under the bodies arms. Julian pulled the cuffs out of his right hand and slapped them on, tight but not cutting at the wrist.

"Right mate, here's the deal. You drop him, I shoot you. Stand where I can see you and don't talk."

Julian swung his rifle to his back on the sling in a practiced motion and drew his pistol, using its blade to cut the slings on the dead body and live man's rifle. He tossed them into the woods. Then he tossed pistols and cut the headset cords for their radios. He pulled both radios out of their gear, turning one off before throwing it in the woods. The other, he turned the volume down on and tucked in his back pocket. He reached up to the guard's helmet, feeling for the release. He found the button, held it and pulled his night vision off. It was connected by a cord to a power pack on the guard's ballistic helmet. Julian cut the cord and tossed them in the woods, also. Well aware he just threw 40K or more worth of night vision away.

"Back it up, mate."

He pushed on the dead body the live body was holding up, pushing them into the woods on the other side of the path. In the pale moonlight he could see blood still flowing freely from the wound where the chin met the neck. Julian knew what dead looked like, and this guy was dead. His partner was very much alive and very much struggling to support all of that dead weight.

"You want to sit down?"

"Fuck…yeah, okay."

"Good, so tell me a few things and I'll let you have a bit of a break."

Julian checked his watch. Still time.

His voice was strained now.

"You can go fuck yourself."

Julian poked him with a pointed hand.

"Careful. I really only have one question that I'm pretty sure you won't lie about. Are there a lot of you?"

He didn't answer right away. Hard to lie and make it believable on the spot when the question was asked in a vague way.

"Yes, a few dozen. You'll be dead before you make it to Mardi Gras."

Julian was hoping he would slip up about something. The guard assumed Julian already knew where he should be going.

"Okay, Mate. You can have a seat. Slow. I'll be gone in a few minutes so mum the fuck up until then."

One minute remained. There had been sporadic communication over the radio. They were using code words for their check points and guard posts, probably because using the names the park designers gave to the buildings would make them feel stupid. No one wants to call in from their snipers hide in Loony Tunes Village. From the communications, Julian had a pretty good idea of how many men there were, and it was more than twenty.

Julian stood up.

"Well, it's been a cracker."

The guard stared at him. Emboldened by the short passage of time.

"You think you are going to change anything?"

It sounded like he wanted to talk politics.

"I'm only here to kill a man, mate."

He stabbed the rifle blade into the side of his head, yanked it free and started down the path.

Julian heard the three suppressed shots, from somewhere near the larger rollercoaster, just barely. He was cutting through the trees, passing broken and disassembled pylons from where another rollercoaster had once stood. There was a vehicle in the parking lot, its tires were squealing, and it was turning around, headed back towards the north side of the park. He came out of the trees near some sort of amusement ride, it looked like a giant roulette table. Moving away from him in the direction Rushing was in, four men. Julian shouldered into his rifle, the lighting was too dim to be positive they were all worthy of being shot. Julian squeezed the pressure pad for his light. It was old, incandescent instead of the modern LEDs, but it was bright enough to confirm they deserved to be shot. One of them yelled something about *contact rear* the same time one of the others yelled the same thing. Julian opened up, closest to furthest, his red dot bouncing on their upper body just above the body armor and the face, four quick shots right to left, then back to reservice whoever was still standing. One of them returned fire, but his missed by a solid meter. Julian stayed on the path, giving each of them another round as he passed the bodies. The cracking concrete curved to the right, passing a bizarre looking ride that had loops and steep drops. It also had a man high on the track. Julian didn't break stride as the concrete exploded near him with a miss. He was using his fancy night vision to shoot. Julian hit him once in the leg and once in the face with his naked eye.

"Yanks and their night peepers."

Julian said to no one but himself, swapping for a fresh magazine. He moved unopposed for a while, taking the path left as it ran between midway games and the edge of the water pond. As he neared the ferris wheel, two more men came out of a dilapidated diner that was more graffiti than bright 50's chrome. They saw Julian when he was a few meters from them, bringing rifles around. Julian shot the closest man in the armor, neck and chin. The rifle double fed on the fourth round, he felt it when he pressed the trigger for the first round on the second guy. Cheap steel case Russian ammo will do that, he had already burned through his good South African ammo. He made a smooth transition to his pistol, rapid firing rounds into the second man starting as soon as he had cleared the holster. Multiple rounds hit him in the plate carrier, Julian reached out, pushing his rifle up and way, staying on the trigger until the pistol leveled off at the head. He went to slide lock, the last two rounds hit bare skin above the armor. He pushed the body to the ground, swapping in a fresh magazine, holstered his handgun and then worked the malfunction clear.

Julian followed the path to the left just past the ferris wheel. There was a figure near the arcade building. Julian could just make out the shape. He kept his rifle to a high ready until he heard a voice.
"Don't shoot me, Thorn Bird."
Rushing. The urge to shoot him for the joke was there.
"Clear to the south, more or less. Had a wag with one of 'em. Something called the Mardi Gras is the spot, according to him."
Julian said, falling in beside Rushing on the wall. He had fashioned ear plugs out of a piece of towel from the hotel.

They were working well enough, but he had a light ringing in his ears.

"Well, we have about twenty guys headed our way, so I hope you are ready."

Julian checked his magazine, then removed a second from his coat pocket and tucked it in his belt line at the front to be easily accessed.

"You have a plan for this?"

Rushing keyed his radio.

"Maddy, update?"

Julian couldn't hear her response, so Rushing filled him in.

"They are moving our way on the path, spread out pretty well. We can hit them from both sides if one of us cuts under this coaster on the other side of the building. We have about 30 seconds to make a decision."

Julian stepped back from the corner of the building. He knew from the map that the road curved behind the building, so they were on one leg of an inverted U. The pathway to the left of the building they were using for cover was the top. The search party was on the other leg. If they met them when they rounded the corner from the other side, it would be very close quarters with only the corner of the building for cover and corners only worked as cover in one direction. If they flanked, and their numbers unquestionably meant they would, then they would have no real cover to fight from. To the right of the building was a service sidewalk that lead under a water ride just behind. Julian could cut through and either hit them from the flank before they rounded the top of the U or shadow them and hit them from behind once they made the turn. Julian checked the surroundings. There weren't many other options, and that seemed to be the best one.

"Okay, I'm moving."

"Wait."

Rushing said, Madeline was talking on the radio. Rushing flipped up his nods. His face was a look of calm anger. "She's got access to the park power. Move when she lights this place up."

Julian responded with a curt nod. He headed for the side path, having to push through heavy growth and branches. It was an obstacle course of barriers and water ride track on the other side, the water was knee deep inside the ride loop and Julian found himself wondering if alligators had made their way inside it. He was thankful for the sounds of nature now, masking the sloshing sound from the water. On the other side of what had been the decorative pond, Julian had to sling his rifle to free his hands, climbing up onto the elevated slide platform. Someone had laid a ragged chunk of plywood across the top as a bridge. Julian gladly used it, walking off to the right directly onto the track, then across to the loading platform. He went back into a crouch and moved past a tangle of bollards and rope. There were bathrooms and smaller rides to his left, on the other side of them was the pathway. Julian unslung his rifle and moved low, waiting for the madness to start. He prayed to himself. He prayed that Rushing would make it out of this alive. He was as reckless as Julian was when it came to Heller, and for good reason. He wasn't worried about Madeline, she seemed to have enough discipline to realize when the fight was unwinnable, and it was shaping up to be unwinnable very soon. But Rushing, he needed to survive. You didn't throw a killer like that away.

29

They were almost back to the Slidell house when the van moved. Finn propped his tablet up on the dash so everyone could see it. Tellison, out of character, had decided to drive. Card was in back with Toomby and they could both see the small dot on the screen as it moved out of the neighborhood.

"There's a five second delay, but I think we can catch up with them. Finn, get Gianna."

Finn keyed his radio.

"Foundation, Huck."

A delay, then she responded.

"Go ahead, Huck."

Finn looked to Tellison for what to say.

"Drone?"

"Foundation, we have movement on Victor One, do we have blue air?"

Card could hear the sounds of a diesel engine at highway speed in the background of her broadcast, which meant she was driving since Porter couldn't drive the command truck. Quick math in Card's head told him that the drone still had a few hours of loiter time left in it, less if it had to actively follow a target.

"Roger, Huck. I can handoff control to you if you give me a minute. Link your tablet."

Finn dug into a bag between his knees in the floorboard, pulling out a second, larger tablet with a shock proof case on it. He woke it up, started tapping icons, typed a password and then responded to her.

"Ready here, Foundation. I'll try not to crash this thing."

"Huck, if you crash that drone, I'll…just don't crash my fucking drone."

Finn's tablet screen went black, there was a loading bar for control handshake and then the screen changed to the drone view. Smaller windows at the bottom border were for the camera controls, instruments, diagnostics and the small weapons package the drone carried. As far as technology went, Card knew it was a state of the art drone. The first clue to that was that Finn could pilot it with a simple tablet, by himself. Older drones had complicated remote piloting systems, and some required more than one operator to fly. The Rocinante, or *Roci* drone was smaller and more agile than legacy drones like the Global Hawk or Predator. It worked similarly to many commercial camera drones, with four rotor nacelles on pylons that extended from the main fuselage, allowing for helicopter flight and more maneuverability over fixed wing types. Weighing in at just over a thousand pounds, it was a quarter of the weight of a comparable fixed-wing drone and only measured 20 feet in length, with a width of just under 30 feet with the rotor nacelles locked into position. It couldn't fly as high as its heavier cousins, but it could fly longer and had a much smaller radar signature. The weapons package was small. It could be fitted with two larger anti-tank missiles on external hardpoints, but that extra weight affected flight and loiter time. Instead the Roci mostly relied on a single internal rotary launcher that held either the small F2M2 Spike missile, the slightly larger Air KAP anti-personnel cluster munitions missile or a combination of both. The drone was deployed from the roof carriage of the command trailer, where its Lithium Ion battery could be recharged and weapons refit.

Finn tapped the weapons controls, Card could see that is was currently carrying two Spike and four Air KAPs.

Plenty of firepower if they needed it. He reduced the screen, moving back to navigation, guiding the drone towards the moving van. The sunlight was all but gone, not that it would make it harder for the drone to acquire and track the van. Since the drone had already been loitering over the neighborhood, it only took it a few minutes to catch up to the van. When Finn was sure he had it, he double tapped the van on the screen. The tablet flashed from traditional view to IR to thermal, the drone memorizing the signature of its identified target regardless of camera used, and then it returned to manual camera control, still set on daytime view. The van was moving south on Interstate 10. Tellison looked over at the screen.

"Those vehicles with it?"

There were two SUVs close on the van, one in front and one behind. Same make and model, same color, muted silver. When the van changed lanes, they did also.

"Looks like it."

Finn tapped both vans on the screen, identifying them as alternate targets.

"Okay."

Tellison said.

"If that van moves into the city, burn it down. We don't know if they have already weaponized its tank or whatever the hell that thing is."

Finn nodded.

"Roger that, Chief."

Tellison accelerated, watching the tracker GPS. It was counting down the time to them intercepting the van. They were five minutes behind. Tellison would close to within a minute and then match speed. There was no reason to get closer while they had the drone on station.

Twenty minutes later, the van and escort exited to Lake Forrest Boulevard then turned left onto a service road. Finn zoomed out to see potential destinations. It was a theme park, but it didn't look open. Card remembered something about it, an old Six Flags park that never reopened after a hurricane.

"Well, that's creepy."

Finn said, reaching the same conclusion as Card. On the screen, the convoy stopped. A man in the forward vehicle opened the gate, let the vehicles through, then hopped into the rear vehicle as the convoy headed north on the access road. It passed by the bulk of the park, then pulled into a parking lot and all three vehicles drove into an L shaped warehouse. Tellison drove by the entrance, turning south the first chance he had. He pulled off at the first public parking lot he could find, a lot shared by a restaurant and a gas station. Finn was already working the drone around the park, identifying entry points, guard positions and anything else that was worth noticing. The Roci could actively track a hundred targets human size or larger, they could be labeled or self-identified by the targeting software. Even if they weren't on the screen, the Roci maintained tracking via dozens of passive cameras spread around the fuselage and nacelles. Every time Finn saw a man on the ground, he tapped the screen, zoomed in to check weaponry and then moved on to the next. There were a few roving patrols, pairs of shooters with night vision capability, and a few fixed positions he could see with either precision rifles or regular service rifles. Unfortunately, the Roci couldn't see inside of buildings unless it was angled to see through an open door or window. When Finn was sure he'd identified everything there was to see, he briefed everyone.

"At least thirty men, all NV capable, at least three precision positions on top of these positions."

Card showed the top of the largest roller coaster nearest interstate 510, which would be the highest point in the park. A second position on another elevated ride to the south, near the park's southernmost service road and a final shooter on the roof of a large two-story building with a New Orleans French façade that was just inside the old main foot entrance.

"No vehicles currently outside the warehouse, designating that as Red one. Sorry Sergeant Card, Toomby, but the only elevated position near the park are a few two-story domestics in a neighborhood to the North west, on the edge of the parking lot."

Finn panned the camera to show the McMansions he was talking about. With a larger caliber rifle, it would be a workable position for limited engagements, but Card only had his accurized 5.56. Its envelope wouldn't reach very far into the park.

"We have some decent entry points, even with their manpower, this park is huge, and the fence is in bad shape. If it has working cameras, I can't find them. We can make entry from the north or south easiest. Crossing the parking lot would be a little too World War One for me. Entering from the Interstate is doable, but a bit crazy. If we split up, we have more options."

"Teams of two."

Tellison said, almost to himself, studying the drones wide view of the park. Finn put it directly overhead to look down, currently viewing the derelict amusement park in IR. Finn was right about the cameras. The drone had sophisticated sensors in its main camera gimbal to detect electronic radiation. It picked up a lot of scatter but was sensitive enough to show the routes of power lines and help identify what they powered. It was showing plenty of live power but wasn't identifying any cameras. If there were cameras, they would likely have IR LEDs to extend their night vision range, which would show like burning torches to the drones IR. There was nothing.

"Sergeant Card, Toomby, we will drop you to insert from the south side of the east parking lot, call that Blue One. Me and Finn will come in from the North end, Blue Two. I don't know how much time we have, which means not much, so we will take the quickest path inside that still affords some concealment. These guys are NV capable, and that means it's probably better than what we have. Don't underestimate these assholes."

Card could feel Tellison's frustration. There was a time when the US owned the near-IR battlespace. Now, the major states had emerging IR and thermal capabilities and a private corporation using an abandoned amusement park as a base of operations to do whatever they were going to do was using kit beyond even what they had.

"Our goal is the warehouse, Red One. Card, Toomby, you will scout the south and either make movement along the perimeter of the park to us or be in position to draw assholes away from us. I'd rather have you with us, but without more information on what is where inside the park, having you south makes more sense."

Tellison pulled back onto the road. The night's darkness descended to stay. Card and Toomby studied the view of the park grounds, having Finn zoom in on a few spots along their path to know what they would confront in real-time. Tellison pulled off the road in a vacant lot at the intersection of Lake Forest and Michoud. A quick comms

check and they were out of the SUV. Tellison pulled off
and headed north. They were going to leave the SUV in a
clearing at the edge of the subdivision to the north and walk
in from there.

"Well, Tony, what the hell?"

Card shrugged his precision rifle onto his back and
tightened the sling down so it couldn't move.

"On mission, dude."

Toomby whisper laughed as they started into the woodline.

"Yeah, I guess."

They made good time, going IR as soon as they left the lot,
working as quietly as possible through the undergrowth and
trees. The night was loud, reminding Card of every
summer night ever he spent training in the south. From the
ranges and DZs of Ft. Benning to Ft. Bragg, the insect life
in the south was intolerable. It had bothered Card so much
as a young Ranger that he visited the post library and
poured over what few insect books they had until he knew
what made the awful, rhythmic racket. Tree crickets and
Katydids. *Katy Did. Katy Didn't.* Over and over again.
Knowing what made the noise didn't help stop it, but it
gave Card a sort of peace at least knowing what made the
din of sound that was damn near close to not hearing safe.

They only had one fence to deal with, a few feet from the
edge of the parking lot. When they reached it, the moved
to the west, following the fence to find the hole they had
identified from the drone feed. It was there, and it was
large enough to walk through, but they didn't at first. Card
crouched down, scanning the parking lot and what
buildings he could see for activity. Toomby flipped his
nods up, shouldering his rifle. He was using a Nightforce
1-8 ATACR on a 10" MK 18. He wouldn't have the same

velocity at distance as Card, but he could still hit accurately at distance. The myth that shorter barrels couldn't reach out to intermediate distances and be precise was gunshop and internet nonsense. There was enough ambient light that Toomby could see all three of the sniper positions that Finn had identified, though the only one Card would engage from this distance with the MK 18 was the closest shooter, positioned to overwatch the main pedestrian entrance. Toomby wasn't interested in shooting him, at least not right then.

"Okay, got all three."

Toomby said, dialing his magnification back out on the optic then flipping his nods back down.

"Now we just gotta wait."

"Breathtaker, Vicious."

Card keyed his radio and replied.

"Go, Vicious."

"We are Oscar Mike from the LD, be advised, we just picked up Knight."

Knight was Madeline's callsign.

"Knight has inserted one to the West of you and is now moving to the interstate. Check real-time, Huck has them marked."

"Roger, Vicious."

Toomby groaned as he unslung his backpack and wrestled out a tablet. It could monitor the drone, although it could not control it unless Finn handed off control or Toomby entered an override code in the event that Finn was incapacitated. Toomby pulled a large piece of black fabric out as well, draping it over his head before he woke the tablet up. He was under the sheet for a minute then popped out, keeping the lit screen covered.

"Yeah, we got one moving towards the park from the south. Pretty sure it's the priest."

Card rubbed the bridge of his nose, adjusting the offset on his NVGs to sit a little further from his eye protection.

"Cool. As long as he doesn't shoot at us. What about Madeline?"

Toomby ducked back under the cloth, watching the screen for a few minutes while Card kept watch on the parking lot.

"Dude, she's dumping someone off on the side of the fuckin interstate."

"That would be Rushing. Ballsy."

Card pressed the PTT on his plate carrier.

"Vicious, Breathtaker, what are we doing about Knight and friends?"

There was a delay. Tellison was probably going to play it as it went.

"Breathtaker, I'm going to try and make contact with them. Barring that, we will let this develop."

Cool. What was the worst that could happen?

30

One of the oldest clichés out there was that *no plan survives enemy contact*. It was a cliché because it was true. It was true because humans, even formed into a cohesive unit, were still human, and individual thinkers at the basic level. Subsequently, maintaining unit behavior in adverse conditions was difficult at best. I was trained to exploit that difficulty, and that was exactly what I was going to do. Heller's men, if they were Heller's men, had no idea the numbers they were facing, so they were keeping their movement cautious and spread out. I watched the first few round the corner, two men moving to the far side of the path, one hooking the edge and walking directly towards me. The distance was perhaps 100 yards. I needed them closer than that.

I waited.

Julian would be smart to wait for me to initiate, and I cursed myself for not discussing that with him before he left. Even if he fired first, I expected it would work. Because it had to work.
"Maddy, go after the first volley."
She double squelched in response. They were 75 yards away now, I could see eight more, spread out. More on the left than the right. In the back I could see two more men moving up the service catwalk on the rollercoaster track where it ran parallel to the path. Didn't count on that. Oh well, one more thing to wing.

50 yards. Any closer and I would be obvious. I shouldered my rifle, luckily the optic had a higher mount that made co-witnessing with my NVG easier. I had to be prepared to

flip them up as soon as Madeline turned on the lights, so I had already turned up the optic brightness slightly. It made the bloom under night vision worse, but I could work with it. I gave them a few more feet and then picked my first target. The body armor was problematic, but it wasn't my first concern. I slowed them down in my mind, plotting my points of aim. The dot wobbled slightly on the lead man's lower body. I pressed, shifted, pressed, shifted, pressed twice, shifted and raised and pressed again. Three pelvic shots and one directly to the face of the first man to ID my position. He had been fast. I ducked back around the corner long enough to flip up my nods, went low into a crouch and leaned back out around the corner. Julian engaged them from the flank, I watched two men go down, one of which I had already hit, as soon as I leveled off on my rifle. The park power came on and the pathway was bathed in garish carnival lights. Reds, greens, blinking white and blue. There was music too, but I couldn't hear it over Julian's rapid, but controlled fire.

Heller's men recovered quickly. I put three rounds into the next closest man to me, he was bathed in a green blinking light, the blood from his neck looked brown spraying into the air. I shifted left and up, the two men on the rollercoaster catwalk had me pinpointed and had opened fire. Julian paused briefly, then his fire resumed. Fast reload. Two men on the ground locked in on me, two on the other side of them were pushing back towards the priest, firing controlled full auto bursts. I hit the first catwalk shooter, he tumbled out of sight. The stucco wall next to my head shattered, I went lower, settled on the second shooter and dumped the remainder of my magazine into his chest, hoping at least one round found its way around his armor while I ducked back around the corner to reload. More rhythmic pounding from Julian's rifle, with the occasional suppressed snap from Madeline. I didn't have her location, but I expected her to come in behind them from the west side of the path to be clear of my line of fire.

They were getting organized now, our initial advantage was gone. It had earned us about ten down, but even some of them were still fighting. I came back around the corner standing, a few of them were using a midway game building as cover, stacked up professionally on the corner. No, not cover. Concealment. I tracked my point of aim to the left of the muzzle flash and shot them through the wall. A quick five rounds and the fire stopped. More rounds stuck near me coming from two men prone near their dead buddies. I hit one in the face. The other was stopped by Julian. I still couldn't see him, he was working from the trees underneath the arc of the water ride track overhead and they were more worried about him than they were about me at that moment. His rifle fire stopped, all the motivation three of them needed to push into the wood line. I had a decision to make. I could hold my cover or help him. I decided to help. I dropped my partially expended mag, slamming in a fresh one and came around the corner. Press, press, shift, prespresspresspress, shift, press press. Three more down. More muzzle flash from the corner, I fired back through the wall, walking forward, resisting the urge to run. A man came around the pathway corner and went down face first, a hit from Madeline. I didn't see any other bad guys so I quickened my pace.

"Rush, they are pulling back to a large building on your left, you'll see it as soon as you round the corner. I'm on the building on its north end, getting hot up here."

I could hear a dramatic rate of fire coming from around the bend. I cut to the right, pushing into the trees to find Julian. At the edge sat a few circular picnic tables, a fence to the right of that to keep guests out of the water ride. I could hear grunting and cursing. I could see a struggle ahead. Two bodies lay on the sidewalk, one draped over the fence like laundry. Julian was fighting his way out from under a forth, pistol in hand. It was at slide lock but judging by how little the fourth man was moving, which was not at all, it did the job even out of ammo. He came to his feet, favoring his right leg, stripping and pocketing the empty mag to replace it with a fresh one. He did the same for his rifle once he pulled its stock knife out of the chest of one of the downed men. With a wipe of blood from his face he gave me a sarcastic smile.

"Oi, you get it now?"

I couldn't argue with success. The bayonet was not dead, yet.

"Yeah, now pull it together. Maddy is pinned down."

The rate of fire had not decreased.

"Off we go, then."

Julian chambered his first round on the rifle and moved, I fell in beside him, we stayed in the sidewalk under the trees, following it back out to the main path. The sidewalk was overgrown and covered in trash and debris, making footing tricky. Lights pulsed through the trees. Beyond the short woodline I could see the front of a large building with a sign that barely still read *Jocco's Mardi Gras Madness*. In front, a dozen of Heller's men were formed up behind what looked like riot shields, only with a more streamlined shape. One man held the shield in a crouch while another stood over the top of him, firing up at the roof of the building Madeleine was on. She was firing back but whatever the shields were made of, it wasn't getting through. Three more men were forming to the rear of them, a tight perimeter of shields. The three facing us opened fire with handguns at the edge of the shield. A hard way to shoot accurately, but it forced both of us to cover behind a stack of salvaged light poles.

"Maddy, ideas?"

I could hear the impacts of fire when she responded.

"Search me, let them run out of ammo?"

I rolled my back off the poles, finding a small sliver to look through. Julian was firing over the top but even his larger caliber was having no effect on the shields and their formation didn't leave any gaps to shoot through. The lights and music made it more ridiculous than dramatic. Or I was desensitized to the violence of it, either, or I suppose. I could see the formation, and I could also see three more men moving out of the building, two with shields, one was toting a large bullpup style rifle.

"Shit."

"Oh, *va te faire cuire le cul!*"

Julian shouted, crouching back down. He saw the rifle, also.

"Bets on who they use that on, first?"

With only a glimpse I knew what it was, a 50 caliber anti materiel rifle, either a Barrett or a Lynx. I wasn't sure on the type but I knew it had to be loaded with an armor penetrating round, probably incendiary. Since what me and Julian were hiding behind wasn't even actual armor, and Madeline was using mostly the defilade of the roof angle as cover, we were all screwed.

To make things worse, I could hear the howl of a diesel engine. I'd heard the same pitch before and was mostly convinced it belonged to one of Virtua's MRAPs. If they pulled an armored vehicle into the fight, we were certainly going to lose. The gunfire stopped at once. Julian started to go back over the poles, I grabbed his arm, pulling him back down.

"Wait."

It was silent, well, except for the ever-present sounds of the summer night. The insects couldn't be bothered enough by our gunfight to move on. My headset amplified sounds that weren't gunfire, so I could hear the brief shuffling of boots on concrete and the creak and scrape of gear, but nothing else. The diesel sound was growing louder. Using my small peephole I looked as far to the right as I could, headlights were pushing up the pathway from the east. It was one of Virtua's MRAPs. The last one I had seen was deep black, this one was desert tan like it had just come from the middle east. The same front bumper that sat low in the front to protect the undercarriage. The entire body was a series of extreme angles, intended to redirect fire and explosions. A short, sectioned windshield sat atop the sloped hood at a severe slant. The vehicle was wide with high ground clearance. This one had a protected turret sitting middle of the roof, same angled armor. I was having slight flashbacks of my warehouse in Atlanta. Friends died that night.

The truck stopped next to the formation of shields, the turret slewed around, twin barrels elevating to the roof Madeline was on. I doubted she was still up there. Hoped she wasn't.

The men on the ground repositioned, all of them turning their attention to me and Julian, using the cover of the MRAP to protect their backs from the rooftop. Somewhere

in the phalanx of shields was the 50 caliber rifle, waiting
for a point to shoot us through our improvised cover.
"Goddamn, boy, you are a serious pain in my ass."
It was a voice piped through the MRAPs broadcast speaker,
but I would know that voice anywhere.

Martin Heller.

I had to yank on Julian to keep him from going over the
poles. I had to do the same to myself. He was less than 25
yards away, but he might as well have been on the moon. I
was working on a plan, trying to think of some way to kill
him. I didn't even need to live through it if I could be sure
he didn't either, when the ground shook and it felt like the
world was dumped on its end. A brilliant flash, like a
mallet to the side of my head and my chest. The stack of
poles collapsed towards us. I rolled away from them as fast
as I could, my vision narrowing to pin points. I was
recovering from the blow when it happened again. And
then again. God was pounding on us from the sky with a
hammer.

31

"Jesus, here comes another one."

Toomby was keeping track of random vehicles that pulled up to the other entrance gate north east of them. Cars would pull as far forward as they could, sit for a minute or leave immediately. Occasionally they could see the driver make a call, get no answer, and then leave. After half a dozen cars, an SUV drove out of the park and pulled to a spot directly in the middle of the parking lot. It doused its lights and sat. Card could see a driver and a passenger, both watching with NVGs on. The sniper on the roof near the foot gate was watching as well.

"Money on Madeline."

Card said with a chuckle.

"She did this before, you remember that Virtua safehouse in Seattle a few months ago?"

Toomby stifled a laugh.

"Shit, yeah, she called every pizza and Chinese place in delivery distance, they were going to the door for over an hour. She prepaid for the food so those assholes were taking in pizzas and Mu Shu nonstop."

Card shifted his attention back to the park. They had moved to a new position, one man moving while the over covered, now they were laid in at the edge of a service road, 150 meters short of the foot entrance, a clearing across from this was piled high with the bones of buildings and amusement rides that had been destroyed. To the left and behind them was the remains of a water slide ride. Toomby had considered using it to get high, but it would be an exposed position and no matter where they went in the park, they could only keep a crosshair on two of the snipers at a time, so staying low gave them additional protection. As it stood, Card was more worried about them having a drone of their own. Anything overhead with thermal and they would be made.

"Breathtaker, Vicious."

Toomby slapped Card on the shoulder.

"Why doesn't he ever talk to me?"

Card ignored him.

"Go ahead."

"We are at the northern most service road. We have line of sight on the lot and Red One. No contact with Knight."

That didn't make sense to Card. Madeline didn't have a way to re-fill the radios, so she would still be using the old channels. It should have been simple for Tellison to make contact with her. Card considered trying to do it himself, but it would take too much attention off of what he was doing.

"Roger, Vicious. We are at designated Blue Three. We plugged our location in. Line of sight on lot and the foot gate. No new movement."

Toomby was reading his mind.

"Chief couldn't get her on the net? Like, is she ignoring him, or?"

Card shook his head. He didn't like the drama. There was no place for this sort of drama on the team. Regardless of what Madeline had done, they all ended up in the same place, at the same time, with the same mission. The complete waste of time fighting and still ending up at the same place was not lost on him.

"Don't know, Will, but Chief seems to be losing it over this."

Card had realized it as he said it. Tellison was the coolest dude he knew. He was also the coldest dude he knew. Both were usually traits that made Tellison an effective leader and an even more effective shooter. Now, his feelings towards Rushing and by extension, Madeline, who he never wanted on the team to begin with, were beyond clouding his judgment. The man's energy was dark.

"Yeah, Tony. The asshole that cut up the Colonel seemed to make it worse. He's hiding it pretty well, but he's not thinking like the old Chief."

Card had a response for that, but he was interrupted by gunfire. Close, to the South. Toomby ducked under the cloth to look at the tablet.

"Priest is engaged, just put down two on the south service road. He's moving fast into the park. Rushing is moving as well, west sniper is down."

Card absorbed the information. A few seconds later, the SUV made a tight turn and headed back towards the park. More unsuppressed fire. It sounded like a short .308, maybe a FAL. It figured to Card that the priest would use a FAL. He could hear suppressed fire as well, further off.

"Breathtaker, Ruckus, go kinetic."

Card already had a good sight picture on the sniper near the gate, so he took his shot less than a second later. One round of 77 grain Open Tip Match left the end of his Surefire Socom II suppressor traveling at 2500 feet per second, it only had to cover 60 meters, which was practically instantaneous, making contact in .078 seconds. The sniper was sitting cross legged, laid in on his rifle set up on a tripod. Card hit him in the side of the head. His head snapped to the side but he didn't go over, he just slumped forward on his rifle. Toomby was tracking the SUV, it was accelerating, Card pivoted left and depressed his gun, dialing out quickly on his scope. The SUV turned to the north, driving mostly directly away from them. Card tracked up from the tail lights to where the driver sat. The first round was going to shatter the back window, but because of the unpredictable deflection caused by rear glass, Card couldn't be sure of a hit. Toomby knew that, so Card expected him to service Card's target as well as his, and he would do the same. His shot broke, the window shattered, Toomby fired just as his trigger reset for the next shot. The rifle hopped on the bipod, the crosshairs came back down almost where Card wanted them. He pressed again. The SUV veered to the left, then to the right, coasting out into the parking lot until it rolled up onto an island and stopped.

"Let's fold it up, Will."

Toomby tucked the tablet away and slung his bag on his back, Card was on his feet, but he let Toomby take point with his more maneuverable rifle. Suppressed shots from the north, triple taps, which was how Tellison shot everything. They jogged towards the pedestrian entrance. Card knew there were at least two of the guards they had marked with the drone somewhere under the canopy that held the park ticket kiosks, the old security office and other front of house services. When they were 30 meters away, one of them ran out of an opening door, Toomby hit him multiple times, the body armor caught most of it, the rest took his jaw off and caused him to career into a support pillar. The second man was right behind him, Card rolled his rifle 45 degrees and lined up his offset Aimpoint, one round to the head and he was down. Toomby was shooting with his rifle's IR laser. Card didn't have an IRL on his rifle, so co-witnessing with his NVGs was his only option.

"Nice, Tony."

Toomby said, he had been half a pound of trigger pressure from catching the second guy. They passed the bodies, moving under the canopy, hooking left into the park, then right onto the main pathway. Three guards were moving away from them. Card didn't like shooting guys in the back, bad karma, but he liked it less when he had to shoot them in the front while they were shooting at him, so he watched his red dot bounce for a good placement and pressed. Toomby fired at the same time, they both raced to the last man in the middle, he was mid spin to fire to the rear when they shot him off his feet.

"Breathtaker, light contact to the north, we are direct to the warehouse, ETA?"

Card matched what he saw with the map in his mind. They were bounding down the main path, watching the hundreds of angles for more bad guys. He knew the path would curve to the west and then start to hook gradually south, there would be a right turn at that point that would lead to the warehouse.

"Five mikes, barring contact."

Card put his support hand back on his rifle. Toomby signaled he was set, so Card sprinted past him, watching the front of a large gift shop building on the right. He identified a pillar that looked like it would at least serve as concealment and shuffled his feet to stop. A simple wave to Toomby that he was set. As soon as Toomby hoofed it passed him, the park lights came on like he'd hit a tripwire. Toomby went straight to the deck. Many of the pathway streetlights were missing, but any bulb that still worked came on. Brash colors and music from some of the rides. There was a swing ride off to Cards right that started spinning. It was unreal.

Toomby was back on his feet, the gunfire in the distance, somewhere ahead on the path around the curve. Card could see the occasional muzzle flash from the priest. He was putting in heavy work.

"Breathtaker, are you in contact?"

Toomby set into a new position, Card responded to Tellison on the move.

"Negative, Vicious, not us at the moment."

Card set into his new position, he could see the right turn ahead. Just beyond it, a formation of men with shields were engaging in two directions. They were dispensing a great amount of fire towards the roof of a small building. Card was pretty sure he found Madeline, Rushing and the priest. He could also see that there was no way they were going to make that left without getting involved in the same gunfight. He could recommend to Tellison that they assist, but he was sure to say no. Card couldn't sit with not trying.

"Vicious, Knight and friends are pinned, advise we assist."

Tellison fired right back, a clear edge to his voice.

"Breathtaker, negative, move to Red One."

Toomby looked back at Card and held up a hand *what did you expect?*

"Vicious, Knight's position is in our line of travel, we have to move through that position to reach Red One."

A short delay, Tellison was probably confirming with Finn via the drone.

"Breathtaker, find a way around."

Well.

"Vicious, Ruckus, advise we assist."

Card had no doubt that Tellison would have interrupted Toomby if he could have.

"Negative, Ruckus, do you guys have problems hearing, or just following orders. Find a reroute and move to Red One, now."

The level of gunfire was growing in intensity. Card heard something else, it sounded like a vehicle, a heavy vehicle. He moved up to Toomby's position.

"Pull up the drone, Will."

Toomby didn't hesitate. He let his rifle hang on its sling, rolling his bag around to pull out the tablet. He woke it up and checked the feed. The drone was loitering with a wide view of the park, but the firefight was evident with the oppressive glow from the park lights. There was an MRAP pulling out of the overgrowth under the northernmost rollercoaster. Card recognized its profile, it was a Virtua built *Sovereign*, Category I MRAP, V shaped hull, low signature armored cab, troop capacity of ten with a crew of three. It could be configured for anti-air, or traditional manned or remote weapon systems. This one had a manned twin 50 caliber turret.

"Vicious, Breathtaker, we have red armor."

Tellison had to be watching it as well. The Sovereign was moving to the firefight. Madeline and the others may have been able to hold out and work a win against ground forces, but they were not equipped to handle the MRAP. They were.

"Roger, Breathtaker. Continue movement to Red One."

He was going to let them die. Card looked at Toomby, the screen of the tablet lighting his face. He looked pissed.

"Fuck em'"

Toomby pulled up the administrator window and punched in the override code. But control wasn't transferred instantly, Finn would have a five second prompt where he could cancel control handoff and lock them out with a code. He didn't.

"Okay, Tony, let's kill some shit."

Card maintained security while Toomby crouched behind him, steering the drone out of loiter and waking up its weapons. He tapped the group of shielded troops, selected a Spike missile and put it as priority for launch. He selected a second Spike and designated it for a five-meter impact just outside their perimeter in the direction of the MRAP, where they would likely run for cover. The impact delay would be two seconds. Then he zoomed in on the roof of the MRAP, designating dead center of the turret. He tasked two of the Air KAP missiles with a delivery delay of one second and added them to the order of fire. "It's gonna be danger close, dude."

Toomby said, hitting the execute command. They had no way to warn them, so all they could do was hope their cover was good. On the screen, Madeline was dropping off the roof on the far side of the building, at least she had a solid position for what was about to happen.

The NAVAIR Spike missile was an ingenious solution to weight and cost of traditional anti-tank missiles. It was five pounds, 20 inches in length and carried a one pound Explosively Formed Projective warhead. It was intended for light vehicles, slow aircraft, and troops, to be cheap and portable for drone launch, or carried by troops in the field. The Roci's Spike missiles were the latest version, with an improved EFP warhead that was *smart* programmable for vehicle or troops. Toomby had set it for troops, top direct. Since it was dark, the Spike could not use its optical guidance, so the drone was guiding it in via laser assist. The rotary launcher spit out one missile, then the second according to the strike delay, both deployed stabilizing fins, their rockets ignited then they shot towards the earth at 600 miles an hour. When the first missile was three meters from the ground, the warhead's detonators fired to create a wide wavelength explosion, shooting multiple high velocity fragments within a five-meter blast radius. The second missile detonated right behind it, though to Card it sounded like one explosion. The perimeter of shield wall was smashed flat to the ground by multiple copper slugs moving at over 2000 meters a second. The explosive damage was so devastating, it created a blast radius of Kevlar, weapons and body parts that would spread over half an acre.

One second behind the last Spike missile detonation was the first of two Air KAP missiles. The Air Kinetic and Anti-Personnel missile was the newest in compact kinetic energy weapons. The 22 inch missile body housed a 15 inch sabot round that would be fired from the missile body just prior to impact, carrying its own rocket engine that would accelerate it to mach six, using kinetic energy to penetrate and destroy light and some heavy armor targets. The Sabot tungsten carbide dart had an explosive collar near the tail of the dart that would detonate in a 360-degree radius as the round penetrated its target, sending hundreds of steel 20 gauge spheres outward on the horizontal plane. It was essentially the Spike on steroids. 20 feet from the top of the MRAP, the first missile fired, the sabot round reached maximum speed just prior to impact. Since it was a smaller round as far as traditional kinetic sabot went, had it hit the Sovereign from the side, there was an even chance the hybrid aluminum and polyamide angled armor would have stopped, or seriously impeded the kinetic dart. Since the invention of armor vehicles, weight has been an issue and weight savings was usually achieved by having thinner armor in the least likely places to be hit, which traditionally had been the top. Since the Sovereign's turret was an open top, it didn't matter anyway. The MRAP had started to back up after the second Spike hit, but it didn't matter. The Air KAP dart cut right through the gunner and exited the vehicle through the floor, discharging its shotgun-like payload into the troop compartment as it did. The second sabot had been course corrected for the reversing vehicle, but missed the turret opening anyway, punching through the armor directly over the driver's seat. If he had lived through the first round, he didn't have time to realize it before the second round vented him and his entire seat through the bottom of the vehicle.

Card and Toomby were moving, just after the last round hit. The initial explosions weren't the bright fireballs everyone expected, more like grim clouds of fast moving air, debris and violent bits of steel, bone and blood. Card always wished they were fireballs, they looked cooler. But there were secondary explosions, the fuel from the MRAP ignited and small arms ammunition was always good to cook off when hit with high explosives. Danger close didn't begin to describe how close they had been to the explosion. Toomby had a bloody nose, which was better than a chunk of steel that had missed him by a few feet and splintered a pillar near their position. They headed directly for Madeline's last position. Tellison was yelling over the radio but they had a silent agreement to ignore it. Madeline came around the side of the small bathroom building, her rifle shouldered and pointed in their direction.
"Blue on blue!"
Card yelled. She went into a high ready, then depressed off of them when she recognized them.
"Christ, was that you?"
Toomby moved passed her to pull security at the corner.
"It was."
Card said.

"Against orders. A lot of shit has gone down today. Who was that on the PA right before we blew everything up?" Madeline grinned.
"Martin Heller. I think you cunts just killed him."

32

Heller wasn't in the MRAP. I was pretty sure of that.
There was a body burning in the passenger seat, but it
wasn't him. The driver was mostly outside of the vehicle,
and it wasn't him either. The troop compartment was
engulfed, but the flames were not burning anything but gear
and whatever else was flammable. I felt the heat at my
palm and yanked my hand off the passenger hatch.
Reckless. I had jumped over our cover as soon as I could
see straight and ran directly to the vehicle, convinced
Heller was in it. Julian had yelled for me to get down and
when I ignored him, he shot a survivor who was trying to
collect himself enough to do anything other than stay on the
ground, which would have probably included shooting me.
A second poor bastard was shot by Madeline and Card as
they moved in from the other direction, seeming to move in
freeze frames of the red and green pulsing lights of
something called *The Kings Retreat.*
"Bullocks, Rushing, get back!"
Madeline pulled me away from the vehicle. I couldn't
think straight. I shrugged her off, scanning for Heller. He
was there. I could feel him. I could smell him. I choked
back my anger and it came right back up.
"Get back!"
She pulled on me again, but this time it had nothing to do
with the fire. A quick pattern of rounds passed through the
air I had just been in. The shooter met with fire from the
two SF sergeants and he was done.
"North warehouse."
Card said.
"They moved the van there, if he's here, he's there."
Madeline led me to cover, I followed. She and Julian
pulled security while Toomby got the tablet back out. I

figured it was a drone that saved us, and Toomby was flying it. Card was on his radio, talking to Tellison or maybe the Colonel. When he spoke I knew it was Tellison. "Chief and Finn are staged on the warehouse. We need to move to them."

Card didn't look happy about it. I'm sure there was a story there. I couldn't wait to hear it.

"Well."

I said, checking my rifle.

"Let's go, then."

"Right, I'll take point."

Madeline said, leading the way. We moved through the destruction, fire and twisted metal. Parts that used to sum up to complete people. The ground was awash in blood, oil and diesel. Unrecognizable burning bits, torn fabric, armor and weapons. The MRAP sagged in the middle, all tires tilting towards the center, as if drawn towards the earth by an omnipotent power. I didn't know what the drone rained down on them, but I had a sense of what it was like to be a sandaled dirt farmer fighting Americans in Afghanistan.

The pathway to the warehouse was clear of bad guys, if there were any left. It curved gently to the right, past the entrance to the big rollercoaster to the right and another, watching over the park like a Geiger-ish visage. The park lights faded away, only a lone blub lit the warehouse from the approach side. They were coming up on the bottom of the L. It was a massive building, so there wasn't much surprise as to why Tellison was waiting. Going in with two men would be difficult even if they didn't expect hostile visitors. Two-thirds of the bottom wing were canopy storage stalls. I had no idea what they were intended to cover, but they were empty now except for random storm

debris, standing water and rotting foliage. I pulled my
NVGs back down to check shadows. It looked clear.
Madeline already had hers back in place and had cleared
the shadows before I did. Card reached forward and
squeezed my shoulder.
"I got right, just keep your eyes on the building. Toomby
has the roof. Don't try to see everything."
"Oh, Toomby has the roof? *Branleur.* I'll take the rear,
then. Watch the dead bodies."
Julian said.

We worked past the edge of the lower wing in a wide arc,
working the angle. In the corner where the two wings met,
there was a short staircase set against the wall leading to a
pedestrian entrance door. I could see Tellison and Finn to
the right of it, in a sloped depression that allowed freight
trailers to back to the roller door above it. They would be
all but invisible if not for seeing them in white phosphor.
"Eyes on, count four."
I could hear over Card's radio.
"Four."
He replied.
"Stack in on us, we are breaching."
Card tapped my shoulder and moved passed me, Toomby
right behind him. They had unit cohesion. Me and Julian
were just tagging along.

Second string, again.

Madeline fell in behind Finn, then Card, then Toomby.
Tellision looked at me.
"You and the holy father can work around to the front,
watch for squirters."

Julian looked at me, then Tellison. Incredulous.

"Is he serious? Are you serious?"

"Dead. Stay the fuck out of our way. Madeline, get your shit together or I'll put you on the short bus, too."

I wasn't going to get in a pissing match with him. Time was bleeding away. Anyone inside the warehouse was likely either about to flee, or about to fight back. We could argue later. I turned to move around to the far side of the building, Julian moved with me. Finn moved past Tellison and taped something against the door without standing in front of it, then backed back into his position, reeling shock cord out from the charge he set on the door. We made it to the side of the building before Finn blew the charge. It was loud and caused no small amount of shouting from inside the warehouse. I broke into a run, Julian was right beside me.

"How many men does he have?"

"A lot."

The first sounds of gunfire reverberated through the sheet metal walls as we rounded the corner to the front. At first it was controlled, professional fire. Then the bad guys started shooting back, professional as well, at first. Then it was a cataclysm of ballistic madness. What started as men, and at least one woman, engaging with rapid semi-auto fire became a torrent of fully automatic fire as the breach was resisted, and the breachers fought through an improvised ambush.

The front of the building was deserted, nothing more than a forsaken bit of concrete that used to be a parking lot. There was a guard shack and the remains of a striped gate arm laying on the ground, long since run over hundreds of times. The patch of grass between the building and the parking lot, dotted with picnic tables, looked like something out of the Jurassic period. There were no windows, only a pair of roll up doors for vehicles and a single pedestrian door at the far side of the building.

"I don't suppose you have one of those fancy stick bombs like the boy band kid?"

"I don't."

The fusillade of gunfire had not relented, if anything it sounded higher.

"You think they need our help now?"

Julian asked, heading for the first door. I was genuinely worried, moving to help him get the door open. He moved to the far side, we bent down to lift at the bottom since neither of us could find an access handle. It didn't move. We moved to the second roll up door. Same result. The gunfire continued, I thought I could hear the fight snaking through the building, it could have been my imagination.

"Not this one."

We were moving for the pedestrian door when the metallic clanking of a chain caught our attention, it sounded like it was being drug against the first roller door, barely audible over the gunfire. We both heard it, turned. The door was coming up. Amber light poured out from underneath.

"Well, we'll do this, then."

Julian went into a crouch, I sidestepped and did the same, waiting. The higher the door went, the louder the gunfight. An engine revved from inside.

"I'll get tires."

I said, though I had a suspicion whatever was coming out would be armored, tires and all.

"Driver."

Julian said. The door neared car height, then SUV. Then it locked to the top. Nothing. A loud rev, a shift into drive and an SUV lurched out. I was early on the front tire and corrected. Julian pounded the driver's side window and to my surprise, it splintered, and the driver jolted from multiple hits. I managed to kill the tire, not that it mattered. I worked my IR laser up, targeting the front passenger, Julian kept on the trigger, raking the back windows. The SUV continued forward, clipped the curb of an island and flipped up onto its side. Coming out directly behind it was a second. I was prepped to do a repeat, but three men moved out of the door on foot just before it nosed out, they were mere feet away and demanded attention first.

Stimulus to thalamus, signal to amygdala, suppression of startle response, selective sectioning and exploitation of time.

I saw the first man move like he was fighting gravity, his muzzle was coming down and around. The IR laser jumped twice across his face and I was tracking to the second man, I spared only enough time to press once and then I was on to the last. Julian had already put him down and had sent a round into the middle man fractions of a tenth of second behind mine. The SUV was completely out of the building, veering hard away from us. The back window shattered from outgoing fire, the air snapping loud around my head. I dove low, Julian launched to the right, shouldering into the side of the building. He was following the SUV with fire until his rifle went dry. I picked up his slack, hitting the rear and then the shooter in the back, but the SUV smashed through the exit gate, wheeled hard right and accelerated away. I resisted the urge to pursue on foot because it was a stupid idea and I couldn't run that fast. "Damn."

Julian said, fighting a new magazine into his rifle. He
patted his pockets, it must have been his last.
"In, then?"
I asked, reloading mine as well.
"No place I'd rather be, but you lead."
The interior looked dark, so it only made sense for me to go
first. Tellison wouldn't want us coming inside.

Fuck Tellison.

I worked the edge of the door wide, rifle high, thumb ready
to fire my IR. A service bay was revealed to me as I
moved, the dim security lighting that trailed the walls near
the floor was amplified by my night vision, making it seem
much brighter than it was. There was a Ford van like the
ones the Russians had backed into the center of the room,
parked underneath a service lift that was raised all the way
to the ceiling. Someone was behind the wheel, he looked
up at me, his eyes shining dimly under IR. My laser cut up
to the windshield, I held high on his head, knowing the
round would deflect down. He started the engine, the
headlights kicked on. For older night vision this would
have been a problem, but modern night vision, especially
the latest in white phosphor tubes, was all but visible-light
safe and had incredibly fast auto dimming. All I noticed
was two bright halos of light, but I could see right through
them to the driver. The laser settled. Safety off, press,
press, followthrough, safety on. I swept the van, waiting
for another occupant but it was just the driver. Julian
moved to my right, scanning the other bay. The room was
strewn with empty crates, rolls of plastic, hard sided cases
that had once held weapons or other equipment, but no one
else. The rear left of the service bay had the only door, we

moved towards it. The building shook, a sharp clap rolled through the building. It sounded like they hit the building with the drone. The gunfight beyond it sounded like someone turned a volume knob down, but it was still involved. I reached the door, Julian grabbed the inside handle, gave me a nod and pulled, opening it as he moved out of the way so I could move through. The hallway was softly lit like the bay, lights at the base of the walls. The overhead fluorescents were empty of bulbs. There were doors on the left and right side of the wide hallway. Wooden with ¼ glass windows, offices. Julian stepped beside me, I covered across him, he covered across me as we moved. The total hallway was maybe 60 feet, not the full length of the building. Double doors ahead, identical to those we had just moved through. The Gunfight grew louder. I was pissed that I had no way to talk to them. We were almost to the doors when one of them bumped open.

The figure that moved through it was wearing armor, armor I had seen before. I remembered a description of the suit; *Custom fitted inorganic nanofiber with Aramid woven polymer plating.* It was Virtua technology that gave the wearer enhanced protection from head to toe, while augmenting their strength and reflexes slightly. It also came with a multi spectrum visual suite built into the helmet. There were two versions of the suit, at least there were when I learned about them from an asshole named Wesley Kurges, a now-deceased Virtua employee who had helped kill friends of mine. The suit I was looking at was the light model, more for speed than protection. Even then, they offered more protection than the traditional plate carriers and helmets the other men had been wearing. The last time I faced men in those suits, they had advanced rifles as well, caseless ammo and minimal recoil with superior ballistics. This guy was carrying what looked vaguely like a shotgun, but with a rectangular box beneath the barrel, starting just behind it, running back to the grip. He was bringing it up. Julian hit him twice in the chest, no reaction. I hit him three quick times in the chest on the way up to his head. I knew the armor was weak at the visor and the joints. The shotgun-like rifle fired, loud. Hot pain at my arm. Julian was wide so it missed him. He had done the math and shot him in the face the same time I did. He flipped onto his back, but his forward momentum was still there, he slid feet first between us.

"Head and joints are weak, everything else isn't. I've fought these assholes before. This is the light armor suit, they have a direct assault model, too."

Julian started to reach for his weapon.

"Don't bother, they only work for the user."

Julian kicked him out of frustration.

"*Pine D'huitre.*"

The French really did have the best insults. He called him an *oyster dick* and I had to laugh in spite of the situation.

"Moving."

I said, continuing to the door. He was right beside me. The doors had closed after the ninja man came through. The gunfire had throttled down more, but the fight was still on. We stopped at the doors, I thought of the shape of the building in my mind, spatially I knew we were just left of dead center of the wing. If the floor plan made sense, the other side of the doors would either be a large bay with doors or a hallway to the other wing to the right, or an enclosed hallway with doors or a hallway to the front and left. Either way, they had more directions to worry about than they had eyes to watch them.

"Probably a hallway intersection, either that or an open bay ahead, hallway right. Or I could be wrong about both."
He smiled.
"Men to kill, Rushing."
I reached forward to grab the handle, letting Julian take point this time. The sound of gunfire elsewhere in the building seemed to have stopped. He stepped back, ready to move through the door as soon as it was wide enough to do so. Then the door was exploding back towards me, both doors forced free of their hinges, the handle twisted free of my hand after pulling me onto my back. Julian ricocheted off the brick wall, skidding onto the floor next to me. His rifle clattered behind us. It wasn't explosive. It was a man in a suit.
"T-this the other one?"
Julian coughed.

33

Card set into the stack. Tellison took the time to give him a rueful look before directing his attention back to the door. Finn's charge was set; an Alford Dioplex 40mm linear charge, pre-cut to eight inches. The charge was long enough to defeat almost any common door at the locks. Finn attached it to the door with breachers tape, made the connection with his shock cord and wound it out until he was back in his position in the stack. He connected a center punch initiator and waited for the squeeze up. Everyone squeezed ready. Finn punched the charge. The three-millimeter tube of shock cord, lined with HMX aluminum powder, sent an explosive signal at over 6,500 feet per second to the C4 Dioplex charge. The 40mm charge was capable of delivering a linear explosive penetration to over one and a half inches of steel. The door was a 16 gauge steel full flush security door with handle and dual deadbolt locks protected by an aluminum latch guard. With the charge placed directly over the latch guard in line with the door seam, it exploded through the guard, cutting through the handle and deadbolt latches. The shockwave was around five PSI, which was a little north of safe but not the danger zone of seven or above, Card still felt it in his fillings.

Tellison moved forward, gripped the twisted handle and yanked the door open, flowing through the opening. Finn was right behind him, Madeline on his heels. Tellison took fire as soon as he hooked the corner into the room, a round struck his primary hand, severing his pinky and blowing off the bottom part of the pistol grip on his rifle. He acted like he didn't notice. They all pushed into the building, moving along the walls where furniture allowed. One man was dead center, the man who had shot Tellison, and in turn, Tellison shot him in the neck and head. Finn and Madeline picked up the same target. The first hits to his torso had no effect, headshots only. Card guided his RDS to man number three, his rifle at 45 degrees, three quick presses and he went down. All three men were wearing Virtua's advanced body armor. They had learned a lot about it from a suit they had recovered on a previous operation. It offered much greater protection than anything they were wearing, which made the fight even harder.

The room they were in was cots, couches, cheap folding tables and evidence of men living in sequester. Junk food, fast food and empty cans and bottles massed in trash cans. Empty ammunition boxes, random gear. The room had two doors, one at the far wall adjacent to the entry door and one centered in the wall opposite the entry door. Tellison drove the train, pushing to the opposite door. It opened before he reached it, an entry team moving professionally through, running the walls short in a limited penetration. The firefight was close and violent. Tellison rolled his selector to full auto and hit the man closest to him as he opened fire on Finn. Finn was tracking the second man; his shots went sloppy as he was hit in the plate carrier. Madeline targeted him as well, Card and Toomby hit the third man as he went wide with a burst of fire. Anything not nailed down in the room seemed to burst into the air. Drywall dust, empty food containers, shattered florescent bulbs popped as errant rounds hit the overhead lights. Finn rolled backwards from the impact, Tellison pushed forward, over the first man, he dead checked him with two more rounds and set up on the door.

"We good?"

Tellison asked, his tone as neutral as it would be ordering dinner. Finn checked his carrier. The rounds had punched through two of his magazines, hit his plate and punched him in the chest on the other side with rear plate deformation deep enough to crack his ribs. His armor had stopped the rounds, but just. He tossed the damaged magazines to the deck.

"Good, Chief."

He coughed. Everyone else repeated the same. Card watched the door on the far side of the room. It didn't move. Ammunition was topped off. The biggest problem was that they did not know the floor plan. You have read and no-read buildings. This was a no-read. There were certain floor plan layouts you could expect in residential and even office buildings or common public access buildings like stores or restaurants. But industrial buildings were built to suit and could mean the interior made sense or didn't. The room they were in was a break room, a large one. The two doors most likely led to work areas, deeper in the building would be the offices. It would make administrative sense to put the offices closest to the parking lot, for the administrators anyway. Both of the doors could have led to a large open room, or to two different rooms. Knowing which would have made the decision easier.

"This way."

Tellison said. They wouldn't be splitting up. Card fell in, the door led to a hallway, there was a closed door to the immediate left, a double door that would swing in either direction when pushed. To the right was hallway, concrete and only lit by floor security lights. It was a wide hallway, which was better than a narrow one, they would be able to get more guns in the fight. They couldn't afford to lose momentum. Tellison underhanded a flashbang into the hallway, shielded his NVGS and waited. One and a half seconds later it popped, nine explosions of blinding light and deafening sound less than a second apart. Tellison flowed through the door at the last flash, Card was right behind him, hugging the right wall as the Chief pushed to the left. They were in immediate contact. Card tracked the shooters, head shots on the move was difficult in the best circumstances. Worse when the heads were connected to armored bodies shooting back, worse still in a confined space. Finn pressed up between them, working controlled burst of full auto. In normal circumstances, full auto didn't serve a purpose outside of reacting to an ambush or providing support by fire on an objective. Its uses *in* CQB were small, but these were not normal circumstances.

The hallway ended where the dead bodies began, opening up into a large storage room with floor to ceiling shelving facing them, electronics racks and food storage freezers for the park. The lighting was just as bad, but everyone in there was using night vison so it hardly mattered. Card picked up movement as he hooked the corner. The other door from the break room was at his back. One man, moving behind a forklift. Card put one round into the forklift's propane tank, blowing the man down and clearing the forklift for safe cover, Tellison was involved to the left. Madeline Finn pushed in besides Card, all three working to put down two more shooters as they emerged from between a row of cold storage freezers. Card could feel the crack of rounds barely missing him. He worked his sight picture as fast as he could. Felt the bolt carrier lock back on an empty magazine, he guided his rifle out of the way with his support hand, drawing his side arm with his primary.

Under NVG he had no way to aim the handgun, he lifted his chin to see out underneath his nods, picked up a sight picture in the dim lighting and went through half the magazine. He swapped for a fresh pistol mag, holstered, and then reloaded his rifle as they rushed forward to cover. Tellison and Toomby found cover behind a pallet of cement bags. They were all under fire from Heller's men moving from position to position amongst the shelving and freezers. Their caseless rounds were being stopped by the forklift body, but Card could hear them pinging and slapping deeper into the frame. The counterbalance at the rear was the best cover, Card had to settle for the frame near the driver position. Card pushed his back off the forklift and leveled his rifle over the driver's seat, the first man he saw was leaned out around a freezer. Card doubted he could punch through it. A house refrigerator was not much protection, but this stainless-steel monster had both gauge of steel and depth on its side. Card rolled his rifle back to his magnified optic, it was set on its lowest magnification. Card had enough ambient light to see him as he popped out again to fire. He found his point of aim, breathed and watched his head snap back. More men were coming into the room from somewhere beyond the freezers. The already high rate of incoming fire increased to deafening levels. They were working to change firing positions as often as possible. Card looked over to Tellion and Toomby. The incoming fire had eaten away half of the cement pallet. Some of the bags had hardened from moisture, but others were still mostly powder and were throwing up a cloud of dust with every hit. The cement poured freely to the floor with each hit. The next closest hard cover was a few yards on the other side of the forklift, a shelf stacked with odd parts for the rides and a small pallet of red brick. Beyond that, wooden crates, empty shelving and then the freezer farm they were being engaged from. It was bad.

It got worse.

Four more men moved into the rows of freezers, ignoring them as cover. Card could see a handful of men move by behind them, carrying bags. The disappeared into the row of freezers and where gone. The four were wearing bulkier versions of the advanced armor, like aerodynamic attempts at bomb disposal suits but with much more mobility. They carried large rifles. Card had seen something like them before, the future of crew-served machine guns. It fired a larger caseless round and had either a 200 round box magazine or a backpack feed of 800 rounds, at least the one Card had seen did. This one had a magazine that looked somewhat larger, somewhere in the middle capacity wise. IR lasers danced around the room, appearing, moving to targets, bouncing under fire and then disappearing. Two of the heavies went to a crouch, the other two stood over them. IR lanced out from each rifle, they were taking hits from everyone, to no effect. The machine guns opened up with a dominating rate of fire. Two guns were slewed to Tellison and Toomby, the others to the forklift.
"Finn, the fucking drone!"
Tellison yelled. Card barely heard him. Toomby still had control of the drone. He wrestled his pack off his back, pulling out the tablet. The Roci had two Air KAP missiles remaining, they weren't intended for what they were going to use them for, but the designers knew their customers and had expected unorthodox uses of their weapons if the need ever arose, and it did. Toomby brought the drone out of

loiter, driving it directly over the warehouse. It had a solid lock on the tablets location as well as their friendly transponders, which were accurate to within a meter. Toomby selected one of the remaining missiles and tapped to open its deployment options.

"Tony, how fuckin' high is this ceiling?"

Toomby yelled over the crew serve guns. He and Card were snipers primarily, distance estimation was second nature. Toomby already had an idea in his head but he wanted a second opinion.

"16 feet!"

Card yelled back, ramming his second to last magazine into his rifle. The heavy guns were talking now, conserving ammo as two of them reloaded. They would rush them soon. Toomby set the Air KAP for secondary detonation at 13 feet. There was a chance that it wouldn't detonate if the sabot was too damaged coming through the roof, but it was going to do enough damage on its own that it was worth the risk. At three feet off the deck, it's was going to cut them in half, Card hoped. An improvised bunker buster.

Toomby tapped a spot on the roof for the point of impact. The heavies were 15 meters away. Card figured they would survive or they wouldn't, and if he didn't, he wouldn't know he didn't, so he was cool with it.

"Get small, incoming!"

He tapped to fire the missile, then turtled up as he yelled.

"Cover up!"

Tellison was leaned around the far side of the cement pallet, fighting back a flank from two of the light armor shooters. Finn was leaned out the other side of the forklift, protected only by a slight angle from the crew serve guns. Card reached across Madeline and yanked him in. The Sabot hit the roof, it was like being inside a rung bell that was hit with a hurricane of anvils. The shot performed as asked, detonating three feet from the floor. It vaporized the heavy standing to the rear left, blew over one of the ceiling height shelves, severed a second heavy at the waist and cut the head off of another just below the lip of his helmet. The last heavy was shielded by the blast by his friends, at least until the round impacted with the cement floor a fraction of a second later. The kinetic force sent concrete out like a shotgun in all directions, peppering exposed men, and the cover the others hid behind. One of the freezers sparked as it was blown clean through. The heavy guns were silent. Tellison had pushed back the men trying to flank, one he felled, the other was killed by the sabot, or the collapsing shelf. Maybe both. The blast pushed the forklift into them, all three put their backs into it in a mostly vain attempt to keep it from going over. If it was going to be blown over, they wouldn't have been able to stop it. Tellison and Toomby were covered in concrete dust, most of the pallet had been blown into them. Toomby was rolling to a seated position, shaking his head. His NVGs hung from their battery pack, the mount had been sheared off his helmet, along with a large chunk of its Kevlar dome. Card could see his hair through the hole. Tellison was already up in a crouch, reengaging the remaining shooters. There numbers were considerably thinned, it looked like all the heavies were dead. Madeline and Finn were up, IR lasers looking for targets. The dust was thick in the air. Card could smell explosives and blood. His headset was dead, maybe the overpressure from the blast killed it. It still worked as ear protection but he wouldn't be able to use it for the radio.

Tellison worked through his magazine, dumped it and had in a fresh one in a practiced reload. Card could see his pinky dangling from his hand, held on by a strip of skin. Tellison was still unaffected by it and hadn't had any time to treat it. Toomby ditched his helmet, coming to a crouch and then to his feet.

"Push forward, bounding!"

Tellison yelled. Card and the others immediately worked to suppress the remaining opfor in the room. The Chief and Toomby made it to the edge of the collapsed shelving, the top shelves had been stacked with gift shop back stock, there were stuffed animals, T shirts and novelty mugs everywhere. Card could see at least three remaining shooters, all working a stonewall defense from the back of the room at the last row of freezers. He leveled his rifle over the forklift, rolled back to his Leupold, flipped his NVGs out of the way and drove the reticle to the first man. He just ducked back in. Card settled the reticle on the spot he had last seen his head and waited. He popped back out after reloading. Card put a round through the center of his visor, confirmed he was down and moved to the next shooter. He was firing from between a toppled freezer and a pallet mover. He was the smart one with his choice of cover, Card only had four inches of a gap to work with and he was only exposing the leading edge of his head when he popped out to shoot. Card settled and waited. As soon as he saw his IR laser ignite, he pressed. One more down. The last man was moving. Tellison hit him on the run but his armor stopped it. Toomby hit him in the neck at the base of the spine. Brainstem stop, he went down like his soul had been snatched out from behind.

Card became aware of gunfire elsewhere in the building. It was close.

"Set, move up."

Tellison yelled. Finn and Madeline moved. Card checked his rifle magazine, he had maybe five rounds left. He clicked it back in and took up the rear.

"Magazine."

Card said as he reached the others. Madeline handed a magazine back blindly. Card took it, racked out the chambered round, swapped in the new magazine, hit the bolt release then placed the extracted round into the removed mag and tucked it in a pouch. His gun wasn't zeroed for the specific ammo in the borrowed magazine, but it would be close enough for the work they were doing and if he needed to go long range, at least he had a few rounds of Black Hills left. There was a bright light source at the back of the room, it was in the corner of the wing at the edge of the exterior wall. The freezers blocked their view. They could reach it by going around either side of the long row.

"Both sides on three."

Finn set up to take point on the right, Tellison on the left. He said the count and they moved. The other side of the freezer revealed a transparent tent, filling up the corner of the room. It was some sort of a clean room around 20 feet by 20 feet, with an air lock barrier that could decontaminate those moving in and out of the room. He saw medical tables, glove boxes, centrifuges, lap tops, medical cabinets and in the center of the room, the tank that had been in the van. There were half a dozen roller chairs in the lab, two seats were occupied, bodies dressed out in bright orange suits that covered the entire body. Card imagined they would be bulky and inflated with supplied air from the

SCBA tanks on their back had it not been for the blood. Both were deceased, probably shot. The suits were defeated, air leaking out of them gently fluttered papers on the table.

"What am I looking at?"

Tellison asked. Before anyone could venture a guess, Toomby caught movement to their left and spun to engage. A dark figure in conventional armor was moving along the flanking wall, heading in the direction they had come from. Toomby was thinking ahead. He lowered his sight picture and fired into the man's legs, causing him to skip across the floor like a stone but not killing him. Gunfire erupted from elsewhere in the building. Tellison pointed at Madeline and Finn.

"Go find them."

They didn't get a chance to move on the order. Something flew into the room and bounced off a shelf. It hit the floor and rolled between them.

A grenade.

34

It was the heavy suit. He seemed to be alone, or at least he would be when he killed the two of us. Julian was on his feet first, he drew his handgun and went for the head, five shots sounding like one. There was no effect except for the heavy to reach behind him and draw a large rifle from his back, it looked like a heavy machine gun except it didn't look like it was belt fed. If we let him fire, we were both dead. I pushed my rifle out between my knees, no time to recover to my feet. It was all but impossible to get a cheek weld on a rifle when laying on your back, but I didn't need one. I rushed the IR laser vaguely to his head and started firing, Julian trusted that I wouldn't hit him as he advanced, I thought it was beyond suicidal to engage the heavy in hand to hand combat, but I didn't have time to raise the issue with the priest. My fire was having no effect except to damage the helmet visor and maybe give the wearer a headache. I hit bolt lock on an empty magazine, Julian hit slide lock on his handgun, he didn't break stride. The heavy rifle swung towards him.

He slammed into the heavy, a hard strike with his handgun to the neck line. He was swatted away by his support hand, then the rifle swung towards him. Julian ducked under the first burst of fire as I recovered to a knee, he sidestepped a burst of fire that pulverized the brick where he had just stood, his left hand pushed up against the rifle while he stabbed the pistol repeatedly at the armor over the elbow joint. The heavy reacted, torqueing towards him, Julian followed the momentum, stabbing rapidly under his left arm. The heavy shot backwards like he had been propelled by a rocket, Julian was just able to duck under a second burst of fire, he lunged to close the gap and get inside of his arc. I had a fresh magazine loaded, but Julian was moving in and out of my line of fire. I waited for an opportunity. The heavy smashed Julian in the chest with an outward swat, slamming him into the opposite wall once again. The rifle leveled on him, my IR lined up with the rifle's magazine I inched up to where I imagined the chamber would be and I pressed, at five yards there was no way I could miss. The box machine gun clicked on his trigger press, the upper receiver exploded. He looked down to fix it, I traced the laser up to his helmet but Julian was already in the way again, he slid in low, stabbing to the knee, then the armpit and then he went for the neck once more. The heavy dropped the machine gun and picked up Julian, throwing him hard into the celling as if he were weightless. I let off quick rounds to the helmet. The heavy picked up Julian by his jacket and threw him in my direction, he hit me at the knees, sending both of us tumbling back further into the hallway. I lost sight of him, scrambling back to my knees, the heavy was on me before I could raise my rifle, he swung a right hook, I got just outside of it, the clenched fist hit the wall instead with a crack of force and brick. He was so close he was blurry in my night vison view, but I didn't want to risk the time it would take to push them up. I was on my feet, firing for the neck and head. The heavy closed again, I ducked another swing and was able to side step a high knee, but not a following downward swing with his other arm. It hit my shoulder and carried down into my rifle, splintering the buffer tube at the receiver, the spring and buffer shot out of the severed tube. I immediately released the disabled rifle, going for my handgun as I arced wide outside of his next swing. I was going to be beat to death and there was little I was going to be able to do about it. If I couldn't kill him with guns, it was going to be impossible to do it in a fist fight. He turned on me, braced to rush me. I heard a shot from the hallway.

The heavy paused, faltered and then fell forward. His helmet was deformed at the ear, it hadn't been pierced, but the depression in the side of the armor was deep enough that if he was still alive, it could be coloring books and crayons for the rest of his life. I jerked my head in Julian's direction, he was laying across the body of the light armor attacker, using the dead man's firing hand to work his shotgun. When he saw the heavy was down, he lowered the shotgun and rolled onto his back, coughing through a laugh.
"*Merde*, I can't do that again."
I fought to catch my breath.
"I don't think I can, either."
I untangled myself from my rifle sling and left the destroyed gun on the floor. Julian was working his knife into the armor at the wrist of the body next to him, he cut away the man's glove and then worked on a bracelet that had been under the material. He was able to stretch the band off his wrist. I collected myself and moved over to him, grabbing his rifle to return it to him. He held a small black band that had an oval hard plastic bubble on it, it had a small screen and three small buttons. The middle of the screen had a green light. Julian moved the bracelet away from the shotgun and the light turned red, moved it back and green again. The arming distance was about six inches.
"So that's how that works."
Julian handed it to me.
"Got my own gun, mate."
He picked up his rifle and checked it for damage. I slid the bracelet onto my wrist and then picked up the strange

weapon. It was roughly the length and size of a traditional shotgun, a pistol grip with a shoulder stock, a red dot optic mounted on top of the receiver. On the left side of the receiver was an ammunition selector, it didn't tell me what was loaded, just that I had two types to choose between. It was currently shooting a traditional shot, something similar to 00 or 000 buck judging by how it behaved when the previous owner had shot at us. It reminded me to check my arm where I had been hit. High on the outside of my left tricep was a clean gouge where skin had once been, it was bleeding but didn't look like it was going to cause anything more than a scar.

I bent over the body and checked his gear, his carrier had elongated pouches, two of them had long rectangular magazines in them for the shotgun. I pulled one out, it was heavy for its size, markings on the side read *00 buck, controlled flight/AP sabot,* it declared it had 15 rounds of each. The other magazine was marked the same. I tucked both in my gear, then checked the rifle so I knew how to reload it. Human ergonomic needs don't change even when gun design does, so the magazine release was more or less where every magazine release was, close to the trigger for activation with the shooting hand. I swam into the shotgun's sling, took a breath and turned to Julian. "Ready then, I guess."
A curt nod from Julian. He coughed, spitting out blood. "Think my ribs are broken."
"All of them?"
"I think the number is academic at this point, mate."
We started down the hall. I had heard the last muffled shots a few moments ago but now it was silent. Either Madeline and the others had won, or they had lost. I was

overcome with a shock of fear for her at that thought but couldn't be bothered to dwell on it, I had to go find out for myself.

An explosion. It was muffled by the walls and distance, but my mind immediately linked it to a grenade. The doors at the end of the hallway dumped us out into a large office space, cubicles. There was a door center of the left wall and a door in the left corner on the wall opposite of us. I checked my mental map and motioned for the door in the corner.
"That way."
We moved as quick as we could check the cubicles as we passed them, reached the door and worked through it, coming out into a large warehouse space. It looked like it had once been an orderly room of shelving and cold storage, there were a few long tables for work, pallet jacks, crates and smaller storage lockers. Now, it looked as if it had been the scene of an intense fight, because it had been. Freezers and shelving had been blown over, debris, chunks of metal and concrete, blood and bodies littered the floor. I could hear yelling on the other side of a freezer that had been blown backwards, stopped by an identical row behind it. There was a brighter light source over there. We moved to the left, there was a set of double doors against the wall, leading back into the very edge of the building against the building exterior, into some room we hadn't been in, so we watched the door as we moved around.

Tellison was the first to see us, his rifle up. Recognition. He lowered it. He was on a knee, watching that same door. Card and Toomby were next to Madeline, crouched over a body, working. A plate carrier had been cut away.

Discarded chest seal packaging, bloody Kerlix. Madeline and Toomby had their hands on his torso, his shirt cut away. A tourniquet had already been applied to both arms and one leg, as high as possible and tight. Card was working on his head, and even though I couldn't see his face, I knew it was Finn.

Tellison was wounded as well, just then getting a chance to treat it. He examined his hanging finger, severed at the second knuckle, like it was a simple curiosity. He seemed to consider his options and then grabbed the hanging finger with his other hand and yanked. He didn't yell, but the look on his face told me how much it hurt. He stuffed the finger in a pocket, his face reset to its normal placid look and he was on the radio. I could hear his transmission because someone's radio was broadcasting out loud.

"Foundation, Vicious, status?"

A short pause and then a reply.

"Vicious, we are in position. Be advised that law enforcement is entering the park from the east parking lot. You need to exfil, now."

Tellison shook his head like the woman on the other end of the radio could see him.

"Negative. We have to process Red One. I need you to run interference. What is Poirot's location?"

Poirot had to be Hijazi. I wondered how Agatha Christie would feel about that.

"Poirot is on scene, but NOPD is in lead."

Tellison concentrated, thinking. He glanced at the room in the corner, it looked like an isolation tent, like something used to quarantine air and environment from the rest of the room.

"Foundation, inform Poirot we have a CBRN risk on site. I do not advice entrance into the park. This is real world, Foundation. I need you to move to our location, we need Level A suits. I have a clean room on site with unknown risk inside."

"Roger, Vicious, I will relay."

"Foundation, as soon as you do, I want full electronic and communications jamming. Black Hole."

"Roger, Vicious, we are moving to your location now."

CBRN was military speak for *Chemical, Biological, Radiological and Nuclear.* My eyes darted to the clean room, looking for any signs that the fight had compromised it.

"Tellison, we need to get Finn to the hospital or he's going to die!"

Tellison glanced in her direction, seeming to just realize the state of Finn. He looked at me.

"Any vehicles out there?"

"Van, there's an SUV but it's on its side."

He looked back to Madeline.

"Rushing can lead you to a vehicle, Card, Toomby, get him evac'd."

They had dressed his wounds, but not stopped the loss of blood. He was on the clock, and the clock had already been running for a while. I didn't know exactly what had happened but by the look of the room, Finn had jumped on a grenade, and saved lives doing it.

But who threw the grenade?

"We still have hostiles in the building, someone threw the grenade."

Tellison nodded.

"No shit, freak show. Why do you think I'm watching that door? This building is too big for us to clear with our numbers. My advice to you is to take the route you used to get in here, to get Finn out. We are going to hold this position, whatever is in that clean room, it's what we came for."

"Heller?!"

Julian asked, moving towards the watched door.

"No sign of him, mate. He may have gotten away."

The SUV that made it out. Heller would have no way of knowing the number of men making entry when they blew the door, he would have taken whatever they were working on in the tent and fled. We had just missed him.

"We are moving, Chief."

Card and Toomby had Finn tied down to an improvised stretcher made out of a crate side. They shuffled him towards me. Against my desire to go for the unknown door, I hefted my shotgun and led them back the way me and Julian had entered, searching for threats as fast I could.

We made it back out to the service bay without incident. The van was where we left it. I pulled the dead man out of the driver's seat. Keys were in the ignition. Card and Toomby slid Finn into the back, Toomby jumped in with him. I shut them in.

"The two of you did all that?"

Card asked. We had gone back over our exact route and he had seen everything.

"Took out one of the big guys?"

"Yeah, we didn't have missile, so we had to do it by hand."

He stepped into the driver's seat and started the van.

"Thank you."

He shut the door and pulled away. The van drove out of the parking lot. A white 18-wheeler was pulling into the lot. I turned and moved back inside, going back to the warehouse. There was still an entire wing we hadn't been in, but if there was anyone in there that wanted to fight, they had already come out and been killed.

When I returned, Madeline was pushing a restrained man out of the unknown door. He was wearing an orange suit like the two bodies in the clean room. It was zipped down to the waist and the air tank removed. He was a small man, bookish in appearance with broken wire frame glasses barely clinging to his face, his nose was crooked from what looked to be a serious blunt force trauma to the face. Tellison and Julian followed behind. I took in the room while they found a seat to put the prisoner in. There were no other survivors as far as I could tell, which made sense. When you have to shoot them in the head our cause severe trauma to stop someone, they tended not to live through it. We were alive, just barely, because of a collective skill, certainly not because of our equipment. The men with advanced armor had been kept in the warehouse to protect whatever was in the clean room. Had they been sent after us in the park instead, we may not have made it this far. Having them boxed in and unable to maneuver was how we won.

"Roger, Foundation, we have one in custody. I am coming to you."
Tellison looked at Julian.
"Watch this room."
Julian cocked an eyebrow at him.
"I don't work for you. Watch it yourself."

Madline intervened before it became a fight.

"I'll watch the room, Chief."

He considered her for a second, then pulled the small man up in an escort hold and started for the parking lot. I had no desire to go with him, so I didn't.

"Where did you find him?"

Julian pointed to the now not-unknown door.

"Storage room, he was hiding in the corner behind some boxes. Had a pistol but he-"

Julian coughed. More blood

"Tossed it and gave up."

I walked to a workstation near the clean room. It was covered in the normal desk fare, paper, pens, a laptop, empty paper cups and food wrappers. I selected a piece of paper at random and started reading. Stopped when I couldn't understand what it was. Viral programming guidelines, testing parameters. Another bound file was about clean room procedures. Another was a test report on something called *Kolyma Smallpox Viability*. I picked up another, it was a report translated poorly from Russian on something called the *Pokhodsk Smallpox Incident 1893*.

So. Smallpox then.

Julian joined me at the table.

"What do you suppose they want with the cold?"

"What?"

He held up a large text book, it was a history of the common cold. I was immediately uneasy with the implication.

"How much do you know about smallpox?"

I asked, showing him what I had found.

"Enough to fill this sentence."

"Same."

Julian set down the text book.

"Pretty good odds that arse in the orange suit knows, though."

We both turned to the noise behind us. Men, moving. Julian sighed and readied his rifle. I did the same. They were coming from the back entrance, the same entrance Tellison and the others had used.

"FBI!"

Someone yelled. A Hijazi someone. I saw him and lowered my rifle. Julian trusted that I knew what I was doing and did the same. Hijazi was leading a pack of officers dressed in multicam and plate carriers, rifles at the high ready as they swept the room. He was at odds with their attire, dressed in a navy blue three-piece.

"These are my men."

He said to no one or everyone as he quickened his pace to reach us.

"Agent Hijazi, this room isn't secure."

An officer said as he moved away from them. He waved them off.

"I assure you, commander, this room is secure. Mr. Winter, um ...Father? You should go."

He shooed at us with his hands.

"Seriously, Mr. Winter and friend, you have about a ten second window before the wrong people are in this room and you cannot leave."

We looked at each other and took the advice, heading out to the west parking lot. We ran into Tellison in the service bay, he and another man, Porter, were dressed out in subdued green chemical suits, making the awkward walk back inside, avoiding all the sharp objects.

"Hijazi is in there, with a lot of local cops."
I said as we met. He didn't stop to talk, just gave me a slight nod and passed us. We made it out to the parking lot. The 18-wheeler was in place, leveling feet set into the ground, expandable compartments extended. So, they would be staying for a while. The door we approached had a keypad. I didn't know the code, so I knocked. A brief delay and a light on the keypad turned green. I figured that meant it was open, so I pulled the handle and we moved up the extended steps. It was like walking into a high-tech control room for NASA. Except for the blood on the floor. It wasn't new blood.

Madeline sat in a swivel chair, pouring a bottle of water over her head, grime and blood streaking off her face. She was working her jaw like she was trying to pop her ears.

"Mates."
She said with an exhausted tone. I expected to see Colonel Solomon, but the only other person in the trailer was a blonde woman built like a small powerlifter who was leaned over a console talking to someone with a broadcast mic on the panel.

"Roger, Vicious, we have video feed."
She tapped some keys and all the screens in the trailer showed a feed from Tellison's helmet cam. It had a diffused look since the camera was inside the chemical suit, but it was clear enough for the purpose.

"Copy, I am entering now."
He was moving into the clean room through its airlock. Apparently, no one was questioning who he was or what they were doing there, then I remembered that officially they were all law enforcement with credentials.

"What the hell happened in here?"

The blonde turned to look at me and I couldn't help but notice how beautiful she was, a turned-up nose, an oval face with ample lips and piercing eyes. She was tired, angry and annoyed by my question.

"One of your siblings tried to kill all of us."

She turned back to the console, not waiting for me to start a conversation about it.

"Just learned about that bit myself."

Madeline said, drinking the remaining water in her bottle.

"That's Gianna...there's water in that little fridge there."

She said, pointing to a refrigerator under the console desk we stood next to. I suddenly realized how thirsty I was and helped myself.

"Ammo?"

Julian asked, pulling empty magazines out of his pockets. He knew we weren't done fighting, and he wanted to get right back into it. Gianna turned again, looking at Madeline, who tilted her head at her as if to say *well, tell him.* Gianna pointed towards the back of the trailer.

"Lockers on the right."

Julian headed back. I found a seat next to Madeline and sat down. She put her hand on my knee.

"Glad you made it."

She said, making eye contact. I put my hand on hers.

"You too. How's Finn?"

I doubted they had gotten to the hospital yet, but I wanted to know.

"He jumped on a fucking grenade, Rushing. Shit you read about, maybe see in a show. Never seen it, never want to see it again. That arsehole we have locked in the back tried to frag us, Finn jumped on it without a thought like it's something he always wanted to do. Saved all of us."

She had a pant leg pulled up, a fresh dressing in place.

"I've fixed mine, how about you?"

She stood, tearing at the material around the wound to my arm.

"What did this, then?"

I held up the shotgun.

"finders, keepers."

A light laugh. She dragged a trauma kit across the console by its flap, dug into it to find what she needed and started working on the wound. My attention was back on Gianna. The camera feed showed Tellison inside the clean room, he was examining everything for the video's benefit. He was handling a cylinder, it was opened, and looked like it was designed to transport vial samples.

"I believe this is our cylinder, no vials inside."

He set it down, moving to a medical centrifuge. He opened it slowly, taking care to hold his hand on the lid when he hit the release so it couldn't spring open under its own power. There were only two vials inside. He slowly removed one and read the label, showing it for the camera.

"Kolyma B."

He checked the other.

"Also Kolyma B. Do we know what this is?"

Gianna keyed the mic to respond.

"I'm checking now."

"It's probably smallpox."

35

"Say that again."

Gianna's head shot around to look at me like I had pulled it on a rope.

"Smallpox. There's a table near the tent, clean room or whatever, there was a report there on a Smallpox outbreak in the 1800's Pokhodsk is a village in Russia, Siberia I think."

My obscure world geography was a little spotty. She turned back to the monitor. Tellison was examining more vials from a different centrifuge. They were all labeled *Rhinovirus K+*. The common cold.

"Image clear?"

Tellison asked through the speakers.

"Yes, we are getting good video. Continue."

Gianna responded. He continued to film the room. Another centrifuge was opened, only two vials were present. He removed each, one at a time and filmed them. *GM-SNP Group A, GM-SNP Group B*. I wasn't going to be any help on that one. Next to that centrifuge was the last one on the table, this one was different, it was inside a small glove box. He slid his gloved hands into the gloves set in the glass and got the camera as close to it as he could, he opened it in the same careful method, his hand slipping slightly on the release button. This one held eight vials in 12 available slots. He checked the labels, they all said the same thing. *Resolute*. It could have been called *Pink Polka Dot* and that room would have given it an ominous connotation.

Tellison moved on, filming all the equipment in the room. Size, positioning and then serial number plates if they were present. The final object in the room to examine was the large tank. I didn't know what it was, but Tellison apparently did.

"This is the incubator from the Slidell location, appears Russian in manufacture."

Tellison moved a trackball on the control panel keyboard, the screen woke up. It listed a number of options as well as meters of conditions inside the tank. Everything was in Cyrillic. That was weird. Not that a Russian incubator would use a Russian language, but that it would only use the Russian language. Nearly all scientific equipment would also have English on corresponding keys on a keyboard as well as controls, meters and text on the screen.

"Foundation, is our Russian speaking guest with you?"

I guessed that would be me.

"Roger."

"Can you ask him, pretty please, to walk me through this keyboard?"

My Russian reading was even rustier than my Russian speaking and I didn't like Tellison, but hey, do it for the team I was only on when it was convenient to him. Gianna moved slightly so I could sit down at the console and lean in to see the screen.

"Just press this to broadcast."

She said, tapping a button on the console mic. I put a finger on it and started reading what Tellison was seeing.

"Ok, apparently the tank is saying it's finished its cycle and is safe to be opened. I don't see a prompt for a lock, maybe it doesn't have one."

The camera view widened on the tank as Tellison stepped back and shuffled sideways to the door set in the side of the cylinder. There was a depressed handle, probably so some fluttering lab coat wouldn't snag on it and pull it open. He wedged a gloved hand into it and pressed. The tank beeped and the door rose on hydraulic arms. Since the door ran almost the entire length of the cylinder and most of its height, Tellison had to step back to let the door all the way up. Inside were three partitioned chambers that would be completely separate when the tank door was closed. Each chamber had an articulated robot arm at the back, each with slightly different instruments attached. Set into the partitions were sliding drawers that looked to be automated as well so one industrious little robot could pass something to the next without cross contaminating. The last partitioned station looked like it was to combine something with a compressed gas. Small tanks were present, attached to a mixing chamber. Each chamber had an autoclave burner below it, I imagined, to sanitize the chamber before it was opened. Whatever it was designed for, it was dangerous. Bioweapon dangerous.

"Foundation, do we have any information on what I am looking at?"

Since I wasn't needed to translate, I got out of the way. Gianna moved back over but didn't sit, she seemed to like standing pensively over the console instead.

"Negative, but I think our guest might."

"Roger, Foundation. I'm going to finish footage and then exit."

Tellison and Porter returned 15 minutes later. I was sitting in the small crew area with Julian, who had reloaded all his empty magazines while we waited. Madeline had called Elvis, who had spent the entire evening lounging in the Tahoe, probably playing Candy Crush on his phone while we assaulted the park. She had him bring the Tahoe to the trailer. Tellison was beyond pissed that the Russian was free, or maybe free to breathe air, but he wasn't in a position to argue given the circumstances. He restricted Elvis to the table we sat at, and he was sitting with us, watching cat videos on his phone and laughing with a snorting laugh that was so annoying you would think it was designed for psychological warfare. After a conversation with Gianna, Tellison had Porter take their prisoner from the rear and put him in the briefing room. Before he went in, he came to the table and spoke to me.

"Me and you, we have a conversation coming, but I don't have time for it right now. I'm going to forget how bad I want to have that conversation, but I will remember later. I would like you to join us when we talk to this asshole. So we are clear, the only reason I want you in that room is because you know more about Russia and Russians than I do, and this clearly has a link."

I thumbed at Elvis, who was oblivious to our conversation.

"Hes *actually* Russian, you know that, right?"

Tellison glanced at Elvis, then back to me.

"No."

He turned and walked down the short stairs and into the briefing room.

"I don't think he likes you."

Julian said with a sarcastic tone.

"No, he doesn't. But he doesn't like you, either."

I said as I stood up, pushing a half-eaten bag of almonds to Julian. I went down the same stairs and into the briefing room.

The man from the orange suit was named Steven Vic. Doctor Steven Vic. He had enough acronyms after his name to use the alphabet twice. He was an MD from Johns Hopkins, a PHD in infectious diseases from Harvard and had been the head of the Center for Disease Control and

Preventions Emergency Preparedness and Response division after serving as the Assistant Deputy Director for Division of Health Emergencies and Communicable Diseases for the World Health Organization-Europe. Of course, before that he worked as a researcher and field investigator for both the WHO, CDC and on contract with United States Army Medical Research Institute of Infectious Diseases, working in their Special Pathogens Lab. More recently he had been arrested for possession of child pornography, soliciting a minor, resisting arrest, bribery and assault. He had managed to only serve one year on a federal charge for transmission of electronic child pornography and everything else went away, including any and all medical licenses he had. He was 62 years old, divorced and had two kids who probably didn't talk to him anymore.

He didn't tell us any of this, Gianna pulled it all up. It was on the flatscreen in the briefing room as we sat in the repressive silence of the sound proof room. It was still sound proof even after multiple impacts to the glass from a firearm, which I wanted to ask about but figured it could keep. Tellison stood up after a few minutes of letting the doctor examine every fiber of his pant legs to avoid eye contact. He had glanced once at the monitor and only once. Tellison stood behind him and forced his right hand onto the table. Before anyone could react, and certainly before the doctor could try to resist with his anemic frame, Tellison slid a pair of surgical shears onto his pinky finger at the second knuckle and cut his finger off.

So that set the tempo, then.

Madeline stifled a gasp, not that anyone would have heard it over the doctor's scream. Gianna winced but said nothing. I had seen worse, much worse. I had actually done the exact same thing to someone once, but it still seemed an aggressive way to start things off. Tellison let go of him and let him cradle his hand, he let him suffer for at least a minute, then forced his hand back onto the table and stabbed the pinky with a syringe before handing him a roll of gauze.

"That was bupivacaine, should help with the pain. But that's the only time you get it. If I have to cut another one off, you will ride it."

Threat delivered with indifference, he let it hang for a minute before he spoke again.

"I want you to start talking at the beginning, and I want you to walk us through everything you think we want to know." One look at Dr. Vic and you could tell he wasn't going to resist. Small frame, hawkish nose that didn't fit with his doe eyes, a nervous habit of fidgeting with his glasses, even though they were too broken to really serve their purpose. When he spoke, his voice cracked constantly under the stress. He stuck me as a man who was probably arrogant in his own environment, which he certainly wasn't in.

"In the 1980s there was a Smallpox outbreak in Pokhodsk, a village in Kolyma, Siberia. The outbreak killed almost half of the Yukaghir people who lived there. The others buried them as deep as conditions allowed, which was not very deep. Climate change or Global warming or whatever you choose to believe was taken seriously as long ago as the 1990s. The Russians were concerned that if the permafrost thawed too deeply, the bodies would be exposed to the air and risk further infection, either that or they were shopping for the strain of Smallpox. Either way, a team from Vector, it's like the Russian CDC, went to Pokhodsk to investigate. They did not find significant cause for concern, publicly. In reality, they exhumed every body and took them somewhere else. Except they didn't get *every* body. They missed a gravesite entirely and had no way of knowing that because they didn't have an accurate count of how many there were supposed to be. Last year, my team recovered the bodies they missed and tested each for viability of the Smallpox virus. It has never been seriously believed that a virus could lay dormant in those conditions and be made viable. Well, people who believe that are idiots. I recovered adequate amounts of Variola major and minor, the minor we discarded. From there it was a simple matter of making it more effective as a virus and giving it a specific target to infect."

Tellison interrupted him at a reasonable place to do so.

"So, it's Smallpox in the clean room?"

Dr. Vic was visibly upset at being interrupted, he seemed to have forgotten about his finger completely when he was patting himself on the back for his genius. That attitude would get worse.

"Uh, yes, but that's not what I built. I can't expect you to understand everything, but I will do my best. The human Rhinovirus is far more contagious then Smallpox, even if the stakes aren't as high. Rhinovirus is smaller, only 30 nanometers, which helps with infection. I used CRISPR, which I had a small hand in helping develop, to edit the Rhinovirus at the protein, creating a hybrid of Smallpox that is only 60 nanometers in size as opposed to the normal 300 nanometers. The size reduction was possible because we only needed enough information to give the hybrid a specific mission and the other genetic coding could be discarded. Smallpox is a double stranded DNA virus, plenty to work with. Since it's already naturally invasive and has the ability to evade human immune systems, just like Rhinovirus, I didn't need to include extraneous programming to make it more infectious. I edited the SNP, sorry, the *single-nucleotide polymorphism* to target specific genetic markers, which was easy since SNP does that anyway. I named it *Resolute,* which is a fitting name."

He said the last sentence with a smug face, like we were supposed to know why it was a fitting name. If I was understanding him, he created a Smallpox strain that could target only specific people, or types of people. Tellison was thinking the same thing.

"So, it will only effect people you want it to?"

"Yes."

He said with the same smile.

"My employer asked me to program six variations, five different genetic markers and one specific hereditary bloodline. In reality, I created six lethal strains of *Resolute,* not just one."

The fact that he talked about it like he created a new recipe for apple pie made me what to cut a finger off.

"Who does it target?"

Madeline asked, burying her own desire to cut off fingers by her look. Dr. Vic was beaming at talking about himself. He had to have had an entire team, but it was all *I* this and *I* that. He didn't know that *I* wasn't in *team.*

"I doubt anyone here would understand the genetic markers if I explained them to you and as for the hereditary targeting, I only know what their anthropological DNA looks like, not who they actually are. Your surname isn't in your genes, after all."

A smarmy laugh at his joke. Now I wanted to take an entire hand.

"What are they going to do with it?"

He talked through his laugh as it subsided.

"Do you make a weapon and not use it? They are going to use it."

He threw his hands up and glanced around like anyone in the room would agree with him.

"Jesus, can we just fucking kill this guy?"

Gianna said in disgust. She had overcome her initial pity for him, that was for sure.

"You cooked it up today?"

Dr. Vic nodded like we were idiots.

"I perfected the process in Russia. It is *science*, not baking. Once I had the smallpox supply, the combination protocol only takes a short time."

"When, where?"

I asked before anyone else could. His demeanor changed, annoyance on his face.

"Well, I don't have those details. My role was to create *Resolute*, not deploy it. That sort of work is best left to...others. You can ask Mr. Heller, if you wish."

Hearing a frank admission that Heller was involved felt cathartic. I knew from the first moment, even with the doubt from others.

"Where is he?"

Even I heard the acid in my voice. Dr. Vic wasn't as helpful as I wanted him to be. Since he wasn't talking about himself or his work anymore, his tone was reserved and noncommittal.

"I don't know, he's a boorish man, really. Very violent-"

Madeline slammed her fists on the table.

"You created a super virus to kill specific people, you absolute cunt!"

He held up his hands again.

"I create. *Resolute* is my crowning achievement. Its use will cement my rightful place in the history of gene research. I'm the first to do it. Not some banana republic dictator, not a nation state. Me. Dr. Steven Vic."

"Dr. Vic."

Tellison said.

"I really, and I can't stress this enough, *really* want to shoot you right now. If the next sentence out of your mouth is not helpful information on the location of this virus, or Martin Heller, you will serve no purpose and I will shoot you. We are beyond laws here, we are beyond your constitutional rights."

The doctor weighed his options. He was a survivor, which meant he would do anything to survive. But he was weighting that against the legacy he intended to establish. If he gave us anything, it wouldn't be the full truth.

"Well, you have to understand that you interrupted the final step in the process. If not for your attack, all strains would have been prepped for dispersal. We were only able to complete C through F. Not a terrible loss, as A is the bloodline strain, but B covers the largest demographic."

Tellison set his sidearm on the table to underline his point.

"Sorry, I mean to say that I only know the targets and the delivery system, not how they intend to deliver. As for Heller, I only know he is staying somewhere in New Orleans, that awful French Quarter. This amusement park was our only lab."

"How long have you been here?"

I asked. He seemed distracted by the question, and Tellison annoyed that I was jumping in.

"Um, Uh, a few weeks."

I could find him. I stood up and left the room. Madeline followed me out.

"Rush, what?"

"If he's in the French Quarter, I can find him. I'm going." I pointed to Julian, who could tell who I was talking about and was already standing up.

"We are going."

She frowned.

"Rushing, we need to find these blasted weapons. Heller can wait."

"Find Heller, find the weapons. Find the weapons, lose Heller. Maddy, you know he's going to escape again. I would hope you of all people can understand this."

She took the personal comment in stride. It wasn't an attack against her motivation and she knew it. I hoped. "One man versus who knows how many? Do you want to help me save lives, or do you want to kill one man?"

I wanted to kill one man.

Because that one man killed my entire world. I held onto that anger, it slipped away from me the harder I tried. She was looking right into me. If she could set aside her hate for Heller for a greater good, who was I to not do the same?

36

Eight hours before Resolute

Their delivery system was very low tech and brilliant because of it. Each finished strain of the *Resolute* virus had been produced in 120-gram batches, and then mixed with nitrogen. The nitrogen was then evenly distributed into 12 tennis balls per strain. The tennis balls were specially made, with a thicker rubber membrane than a regular ball. A tennis ball had an internal volume of around four cubic inches and was normally charged with a collective 26 PSI. The specially made balls could handle three times that pressure, ensuring a high-pressure release of ten grams of *Resolute* per tennis ball when they were pierced with the sole intention of deploying the weapon. They went so far as to order thousands of the balls for a fictitious charity in India to complicate the investigation that would come. The balls had been filled and sealed in a sterile environment so that they would pass any inspection and not alert any potential detection. The tennis balls were bagged in store packaging, 12 to a bag, with one man each to disperse them according to the plan. Only four strains made it out of the lab, so they only had to find four men, maybe. Dr. Vic didn't know who they were, only what their targets were. He was adamant, and upset, that only four stains had made it out.

Detroit, Michigan.

San Francisco, California.

Franklin, Tennessee.

Colorado Springs, Colorado.

He would have met them and delivered the deployment bags himself if not for our attack on the park. As it stood, he failed his emergency plan of killing the two technicians and destroying the clean room with the grenade. He managed to kill the techs but couldn't figure out how to work the grenade until he was pissing himself in the storage closet. Dr. Vic explained what he knew, and that was that the choices were based on political leanings and demographics. At some point, someone had done an assessment to choose targets where genealogy and party affiliation crossed. Franklin, Tennessee was in the most conservative county in the nation, I remembered that from the last election. San Francisco was the polar opposite. Gianna had checked for the soonest flights to each originating in New Orleans. Hijazi, who had finally pulled himself away from the crime scene and came to the trailer, had taken that information and ran it up the Joint Terrorism Task Force to alert all airports about the tennis balls. He could have kept it to airports in driving distance, but if you want to rest the table, dumping it over was the fastest way to clear it.

Gianna was mapping casualty projections based on what they had learned from Dr. Vic, he had to *dumb* it down for them, but in the end, he told us. Strain C targeted those with something called HERC2 in chromosome 15, for brown eyes. Strain D targeted those with Hemophilia. Strain E targeted those with blond hair and Strain F targeted a specific hemoglobin gene mutation in chromosome 11 that led to sickle cell disease.

Hitler couldn't have thought of a more atrocious weapon. They could have programmed it to wipe out an entire race of people if they wanted to. The only good news, if there was good news, was that all strains were programmed to self-destruct after a set number of replications. That meant that the strain would only kill a certain number of people before it died out. I didn't understand the math needed to program a virus to kill within a ballpark number, but Dr. Vic did, and I wanted to kill him for it. He was the architect, and he was valuable alive even if he refused to produce a vaccine, though he said it would be over before enough could be produced to help anyone. The existing stockpiles of Smallpox vaccine wouldn't be effective against it, nothing would. If someone lived through exposure, it would be a literal miracle.

The wheels of law enforcement were rolling. They wouldn't stop them, I was convinced of it. I couldn't be an optimist. No matter how much manpower they threw at it, it wouldn't be enough. They say optimism is the key to happiness, but optimists were also the same people who got hit by trains. I was a cautious realist, and I had never been hit by a train, so it was working out pretty well so far. Virtua was too smart for their men to be caught. If they were flying, it wouldn't be commercial. Gianna was checking private flights as well, but a flight plan could be ignored or not filed at all and transponders turned off. Our concern was New Orleans, since we were there. The hunt originated there, and if the delivery men were compromised, they may release in New Orleans. I was crashing. It was nearly 4AM. Julian and Elvis were asleep. I was hanging on but was not serving much of a purpose. I decided to catch a nap while smarter people decided where to search for a single soul in over one million people in the metro New Orleans area. I rolled onto one of the bunks and was out immediately. I didn't dream, I drowned.

Madeline woke me up, brushing back my hair. I opened my eyes, no idea how long I had been asleep, it felt like forever and just a few seconds. It took me a moment to collect myself.
"What time is it?"
I asked, my throat dry.
"Six, seven? Just late enough to now be early."
I couldn't argue with that. I swung my feet to the floor, I wanted water. Madeline handed me a bottle, reading my mind.
"So."
She paused, blowing out air.
"Colonel Solomon is on the way, against medical advice, I'm sure. Finn is still in surgery. Card and Toomby are already here, getting a wink in the back."
She paused again.
"Rushing, there's something you need to see. I can't make sense of it, but, well, just...just come look."
Her tone was cautious, like she thought she knew something but couldn't say what it was for fear of being wrong. I stood up and followed Madeline out of the command trailer. The lot had gotten busier since I was last there, more police vehicles, a crime scene van and a small group of men in Tyvek suits processing the SUV we took out. We moved back into the warehouse, following the hallways back into a breakroom. It was my first time being in it, but this was the room that Tellison and the others had made their entry. The violence was long since over but the evidence of it would never really go away. Every body we

had made was laid out on the floor, a neat row and column formation of dead bad guys. Each was covered in a sheet. Madeleine moved to one in the top row, gave me a glance and then pulled it back.

Ok.

I was looking at myself.

He wasn't a twin, but the resemblance was stronger than if we had been brothers. Only his head was visible, and there was a neat hole in his forehead from a 5.56, the wound was discolored, and the surrounding skin had been peppered by spalling from the helmet. I didn't need to look at the back of his head, I already knew what it looked like. Having a twin was something I didn't have. I didn't know much about my mother, but if she had another son, he would have had to been older. This man was younger than me, maybe by as much as five years. I would have remembered my mother being pregnant before she abandoned me when I was eight. I yanked the sheet off of him, he was wearing the light armor, like most of the other bodies. I figured out how to release the wrist collar, so I could get to his glove and pulled it off of his right hand. No finger prints.
"They are all like this."
I considered it.
"No, they aren't like me."
She walked around so she could look at me.
"How do you know?"
"Because if they were, we would all be dead."
I let it sink in. Madeline knew me at a personal level, but when we met we were enemies. She was lucky to not stay in that category. She also had only once gone against one

of my siblings, the same who killed Pepper and beat her halfway to dead. Madeline attributed my skill to her personal bond with me and maybe never consciously considered that my skill was not due to a personal occupational dedication, rather it was because I didn't have a choice in learning to be who I am. If this man was the same, if the others were the same, they may have killed two or three, but we wouldn't be having this conversation.

Madeline nodded. Perhaps remembering that.
"Right."
I pulled the sheet back over him.
"Is this the only one?"
"That looks like you, yeah, but there's more."
Oh, I couldn't wait. Madeline led me to an improvised work center. A rolling cart with computers. I wanted to question to wisdom of doing all of this inside the actual crime scene, but I wasn't the defense attorney who would use it against them, so the concern slid away as quickly as it had developed. There was an older woman with a NOPD Crime Scene Unit jacket was sitting on a stool, working through pictures that had been taken. Madeline gave her a gentle tap on the shoulder.
"Can you show us the video?"
The tech looked back at her, smiled and then started clicking away on her laptop until she found a video. She looked at me and did a double take.
"That's why I'm here."
I said. She considered me for a second, mumbled something about *I'm too old for this shit*, then started the video. It was a full color security camera video of an open-air market. It looked like a fish market. On the video, the guy who looked like me could be seen standing at the edge

of a stall, he had a small knife in his hand and a tennis ball. He cut the ball, I could see the air come out with enough force to ruffle his shirt. The scene changed, now he was standing in a crowd of people moving through a tight space between stalls. He cut open another tennis ball. This repeated, over and over again. 12 times.

It already happened.

Madeline read my mind.
"Kaynda, can you show us the data?"
The technician mumbled something else and pulled up a program she used to analyze the video. It was all code, but the program made sense of it. The video was dated 12 hours in the future.
"In case you were wondering."
Kaynda said.
"You can't do that without a time machine. That damn MHPA law made editing organic time stamps on video a federal felony and opened up software and video companies to prosecution if their products could be easily edited. The coding is so good these days, it would take a smart person to make this."
Virtua was a trillion-dollar company, but I didn't think they could afford a time machine. This was ready made evidence. My stress went down, a little.
"Now if y'all don't mind, I have work to do."
Madeline led the way, walking to a corner of the room. She talked in a hushed voice, dozens of officers and detectives were coming and going. The random camera flash of evidence recording. Cop banter. The smell of coffee and donuts was mixing with the smell of explosives and blood.

"Do you have any idea why he looks like you?"

I didn't.

"I mean, everything is a roll of the genetic dice, but I don't really do coincidences. I can't explain how weird that is."

She nodded.

"This is Heller, this also explains the plain man's car being in your name. Why would he go through all this trouble to frame you?"

"He didn't, but why not take the opportunity when you are already going to kill a few hundred thousand Americans? He had to know I wouldn't stop trying to find him."

It made sense to me, but there was more to it. There had to be more to it. I couldn't connect all the pieces.

"We are exposed now, so I guess we get to see just how deep the hooks are in."

She wasn't wrong. There was no lid on the crime scene. Hijazi couldn't cover up a fight this large, complete with drone strikes, if he wanted to. Solomon's unit had been decimated and it would probably get worse.

"How bad is it?"

I asked. I didn't think Solomon or Finn would have been in the hospital under their real names, but you never know.

"I don't know all the details, Rush. That hasn't changed, but no, they aren't in on real names, both are on solid legends, too bad they'll have to burn them now. But we…he's cut off from the system completely, you know that. Losing this many people. Someone attacked the truck yesterday, I still don't know the story on that, people died."

The violence of the past few days was not lost on me. I didn't have time to absorb it, because I was convinced there was more to come. Time to think about that later. I considered the room of bodies one last time before we walked back to the trailer. I had a passing thought that I should check the other faces, see if I recognized anyone. I didn't, but if I had, I would have recognized quite a few.

37

Resolute

"I'm only going to say this once. The infighting stops. Rushing, you have a problem with Tellison, Tellison, you with Rushing? I don't give a shit. We are clearly on the same team. We are combat ineffective, but we don't have time to be. I have at least four unknown men that are *right now* moving to targets to release a viral weapon we have no means of combating. We don't know their timeline, but we did recover staged evidence videos they have already prepared for the suspects, or who they want us to assume are the suspects. Each video is dated less than 12 hours from now. That means we have time to stop this. Because of the timeline, I am assuming that. Because of the videos we recovered, we have a strong likelihood of knowing the specific location for the attack in each state and those people outside this room are either going to work to stop it or allow it to happen and we have no control over that. What we do have is everyone in this room…"

Colonel Solomon paused to look at everyone. Me, Madeline, Card, Toomby, Tellison and Porter. Julian wasn't allowed in, and Elvis was asleep.

"…And that is enough to guarantee we stop these assholes. We are expecting a single belligerent to deploy the virus, but they may have security with them. We cannot act as a unit, we must split up and go after each of them at the same time."

Solomon was visibly in pain. Just standing and talking had him sweating. His arm was in a sling, hard for a guy who talked with his hands. Every time he wanted to enunciate a point with his hands, we got a chicken wing and an arm waving around.

"Solomon, Heller isn't going to go with the original plan."
He looked at me like I suddenly existed.
"You have some information we aren't aware of, Mr. Winter?"
"You mean besides not being retarded? Look, Heller has a history of being a survivor and a problem solver. He did not plan on us finding this place. He didn't plan on losing a few of his weapons. If we interrupted his plan, do you honestly think he's going to continue as planned? You don't think he has alternate targets? You think he remembered to take the finished strains but forgot the videos?"
Solomon clenched his jaw, I had struck a nerve.
"What I think, Mr. Winter is that you have blinders to anything that isn't killing Martin Heller. Oh, I want the same thing, but not at the cost of innocent lives."
I leaned forward on the table. It felt like we were the only two people in the room.
"Find Heller, find the men. You want to go off on what could be a wasted effort? Have at it. I was going to do the same thing at first, would have been right there with you, but then I got to thinking; why was the car in my name? Why is there a dead asshole in the warehouse who looks almost exactly like me? Why did someone, who is probably one of my siblings, come in this very trailer and kill your people, nearly kill you? What did that person take? Here's the conclusion I've come to. Virtua is at war with The Children, and its Martin Heller is shaping this attack to set them up."
I got an actual *pffffit* out of Tellison.
"Those are your people in there, sport."
I leaned across the table towards Tellison.

"We both know they aren't. If they were, you'd be dead. Everyone would be. I have no doubt that you are good at what you do. But I know my siblings. Me and Maddy already had this conversation, had it been my siblings in there, you'd be deceased. Sure, you could have gotten a few of them, but that many? No. Not with our numbers, not even with me. I'll forgive your ignorance, but this is the last time I will."

He wanted to hit me. Maybe shoot me, there's a nuance between the two looks and it was sometimes hard to tell the difference.

"Okay, Colonel, this asshole has to go."

Solomon's eyes flashed.

"Is that right, Chief? Didn't I just get done talking about this? We are wasting-"

I stood up, the irony of having done the exact same thing a few hours ago was not lost on me.

"No, Colonel, you are wasting time. Have been for days. I can find Heller, feel free to do whatever it is you are going to do, but you are going to do it without me. Consider this an official reversal of expectations."

I hit the button to unlock the door and exited the room. Julian was already standing, ready to go. Elvis, apparently was coming too.

"Took long enough."

He said, leading the way out of the trailer. The sun was creeping into the sky and it was already in the 90's. With all the standing water in the park, mosquitos were hovering in all the shadows, looking for an easy meal. We didn't have a car, which made our exit a little less dramatic. Elvis was laughing about it. I was considering having Elvis use his phone to call for a ride share when Agent Hijazi walked from the warehouse, he saw us and strolled over.

"Hello, Mr. Winter, other people I don't know. Are you leaving?"

I nodded.

"Yeah, and you are giving us a ride."

He held up his hands in surrender.

"Well then, I was headed back into the city anyway, I would like to get some sleep at some point today, so I would be happy to give you a ride a convenient location, but only if it's on my way."

Hijazi pointed at the shotgun I was carrying.

"You can't keep that, you know? Its evidence."

I held it up.

"You gonna take it from me?"

Hijazi's mouth twitched. I let him stew for a second and then handed it to him.

"I'm done with it, anyway."

We started over, Hijazi ran the shotgun over to an agent and then met us at the car.

"Rushing, wait."

Madeline trotted out of the trailer, she ran to her Tahoe, grabbed something from inside and ran over to me. She handed me one of the burner phones and pulled me out of earshot of the others.

"My number is on the back. Call me if you get anything, as soon as you get it. Solomon is arranging for us to chase down the target intel."

She was distressed.

"I can't believe you are going to go after Heller when you *just* agreed stopping these bloody terries was more important."

"Did you not hear me in there? There's more to this than an attack. We are in the middle of a war between my alma mater and the most powerful defense contractor on the fucking planet. You remember Atlanta? That has to have been when it started. Rose was running against the School, Heller working for her. That monster, Heiger, you remember him, the one that almost beat you to death, me to death? He's not one of ours. He's not from the same school I went to. What if Virtua decided to make their own Children?"

The thought that the man who looked like me was some sort of clone or designer baby occurred to me and it was both absurd and plausible all in the same sentence. Madeline pushed the air at me.

"Rushing, that's not a right now problem, is it then? Thousands or more lives are at risk and we need the help." I pushed back.

"Oh, I'm going to help. You honestly think Heller wouldn't change the plan after what we did here? He's going to either wing it or go with an alternate plan. Either way, catch him, we have a better chance of stopping these guys by getting Heller than going off of stale intel and hoping to get it right. You have the manpower you need to run down the targets, I'm going after Heller right now in case you are wrong. For all we know, they were on planes an hour after we hit this place and nothing we do here will stop them."

Her resolve cracked a little. I was getting through to her, but barely.

"What if you can't find him?"

"I can. You can trust me on that. If he's in the city, I'll know where he is. Now we are wasting time. I'm going." She grabbed my arm before I could turn away. Frim, then softer.

"Rush, be careful."

I smiled.

"Maddy, we are not careful people."

The drive back into New Orleans was silently uncomfortable. Elvis tried to start a conversation with Hijazi, but he didn't want to talk to him and said as much, so he crossed his arms and pouted for a minute before going back to his normal dopy behavior. We were going to have to go into the French Quarter, and blend in, so our current attire was out. As much as I felt the clock ticking away, I knew a shower and a change of clothes would help us blend in. Hijazi drove us directly to my house. As much as I didn't want Elvis knowing where I lived, I had no intention of living there any more when this was over, and one way or another, it would be over soon.

I let us in to the house. It was as I had left it, what seemed like a lifetime ago. I showered quickly and dressed in jeans and an Adult Swim T-shirt. I could risk my 1911 in an appendix holster and four spare magazines at the waist, anything more would print too much and law enforcement presence in the French Quarter was bound to be higher than usual and I didn't want questions. Julian took me up on the offer of a shower, but not on the offer of clothes. He showered and put back on his soiled suit without any obvious thought as to how dirty it was. Elvis was as clean as he had been when we met; besides his time restrained in a chair, he hadn't so much as broken a sweat nor helped in any way besides the introduction to Anton. I knew he was with us because he was told to be, to get Anton to Heller, and to get Julian to Anton when it was over. Despite his fresh appearance, Elvis took a shower anyway, and not a short one. While we waited and ignored his signing, we sat in my sparse living room.

"I have to ask, Julian, what's with the suit?"

He considered the question.

"I was wearing this same suit the day Heller murdered my congregation."

He removed his jacket, showing me a rough patch job he had done on the inside of the upper back of the jacket. It covered a bullet hole. He put the coat back on.

"It's an armor of sorts. I'm not stupid enough to think its bullet proof, it's clearly not. But it is my armor of faith that keeps me righted. I will always be a priest, even if I'm never accepted back into the church for what I've done and what I will do. When Heller dies, I want this to be the last thing he sees."

I wouldn't question another man's resolve, at least not his.

"And you? How did you come to be here?"

"The short version? Heller was ultimately behind the man who killed the woman I love...loved. The way I see it, the way I rationalize it, four people are responsible for her death and he's the only one still breathing."

Julian studied me, he moved closer on the couch, seeming to soften. It was like watching a king of killers become a priest. It was the first time I could actually see him as what he really was.

"Revenge then? I can't talk to you of revenge, or out of it. I can see your drive because it's the same in me. I wonder though, if she would have wanted this for you?"

I had to laugh. It sounded sad.

"Are you trying to take it from me?"

His nostrils flared, eyes narrowed.

"Is it really yours to take?"

When he saw my reaction, he raised his palms.

"In spite of my actions, the lives I've taken since putting on this collar, I am still a man of God. He guides me, and he will guide you, if you let him. If God wants us to kill Martin Heller, he will put him in our path, but we do not get to take anything without His permission."

I leaned back, suddenly very tired. Physically and mentally.

"I'm not going to argue theology with you."

He seemed amused.

"Theology is man's poor attempt to explain faith. Have faith in His plan, even if you don't like its results."

"Okay, we'll see how that goes."

"Yes, we will."

Elvis was out of the shower and had helped himself to the clothes that I had offered to Julian. They fit a little loose on him, but he didn't seem to mind. I wouldn't offer him anything else to wear even if he did.

"Ok, we wasting time, we go now."

Me and Julian looked at each other. Elvis tucked his handgun in his pants and headed out the door. I followed. Julian hoisted a covert rifle bag I had given him, a sling design that was in sporty colors to disguise its real intention and followed me out. I didn't want to risk long guns in the Quarter, but Julian refused to leave the rifle behind. The bag would fool the untrained, but it was marketed to the types of people who would usually be more attentive and certainly recognize it for what it was. A causal person might assume it was an instrument or a tripod bag, a gear-centric cop or agent would know it by brand for what it was.

I started my car, Julian and Elvis got in and I pulled away. The drive to the French Quarter was short. I picked up Magazine street and pushed into the late morning traffic, a left on North Peters until it merged with Decatur street. The sidewalks were full of summer travelers, walking, taking photos, day drinking and drifting in and out of the street side stores. The closer we inched to Jackson Square, the louder the brass and the brighter the colors. Across the from the Square was a grand set of marble stairs that led up to the embankment that ran the length of the Mississippi bank in that part of the Quarter. The stairs were set back into the embankment, forming an angular semi-circle that was perfect seating for tourists to watch street performers who took advantage of that wider section of sidewalk and used it as a stage. There was a group of young men and older boys performing. Comedy and acrobatics with a bit of parkour off the generous concrete bollards. The crowd was large for so early in the day and everyone looked well entertained. Elvis was rapt with amazement as we passed them.

"Do you see this? Did you see that flip?"

We moved past Café Du Monde and the attached stores, then followed the split back onto North Peters by the Joan of Arc Statue. I found a street spot that was opened and swung in.

"Okay, I need to meet someone, so act like a tourist." Julian removed a white collar from his pocket and slid it into his Collarino shirt, completing the uniform. I hoped his outfit would grant him less suspicion. Elvis was acting exactly like a tourist, so he would be fine. We gathered on the sidewalk, I scanned the currents of people, looking for a Traveler.

New Orleans had always been a colorful place that attracted colorful people of all social classes and types.

From pirates to pimps, thieves to gamblers, street hustlers to the entrepreneurial homeless. A more recent population was the Travelers. Sometimes called street kids or gutter punks, they were urban walkers who carried what they owned on their back and almost always had a pet dog, or the rare cat. Men and some women in all age groups. Dingy shorts or pants, leather, beads, dread locks or just matted hair. They were weathered from the street because that's where they always were. They were a problem for the city, because they scared the more timid tourists when begging for money, even though most of them performed one act or another for donations. Many were musician's. Because they were usually hassled by the police, they were a tight community and groups of them could regularly be seen in conversations or hanging out together around the Quarter. The Travelers were an exploitable network. I realized that as soon as I moved to New Orleans and made it a point to befriend as many of them as I could. We couldn't search the entire Quarter for Martin Heller, but if he had been there, or was there, the Travelers would have seen him.

I spotted a younger couple, each with a dog, hiking packs and bed rolls on their back, leaning against a wall outside of a metal and punk T-shirt store. I crossed the street, as I got closer I recognized them.
"Hey, mike."
The young man turned to look at me and a smile lit his face.
"Hey dude! Man, good to see you."
Mike was hardly 20, was a charcoal artist and an attempted ex-heroin user. He had bright beads worked into long dread locks and a ring on every finger. He also played the

banjo, which was his primary source of income. His Jack Russel was named Wishbone and did backflips for money.

"Same. Hey, can I ask you a favor?"

He nodded enthusiastically.

"Anything for you, dude. What do you need?"

"I'm looking for a friend. He's somewhere in the Quarter but he doesn't have my number and I don't have his. I was hoping you could put the word out and see if anyone has seen him?"

His head bobbed. He lit a joint and burned it down, then passed it to the woman.

"Sure, what's he look like?"

"White, early 60's, hawkish face, close cropped hair, he's got a fake right foot, limps a bit. He's got some other friends with him, dudes that probably wouldn't understand you guys."

Mike bobbed through another hit of his joint.

"Oh for sure, I've seen that guy, major asshole. Let me pound the drum, dude, and see what comes back. You gonna be around?"

"Yeah, we are gonna grab a bite at the River Bottom."

More head bobbing.

"For sure, for sure. I'll get ya word, dude."

I handed Mike a 20.

"Thank you, man."

"Thank nothing, bro."

Mike would spread the word across the Quarter faster than I could drive the same distance. I led the others to the River Bottom bar to wait.

The River Bottom didn't stand out from many of the bars in the Quarter. It was mostly bar top, with simple tables and

24 an hour alcohol service, random liquor advertisements where posted on the plaster walls and the music was loud. The kitchen did New Orleans bar food, so we ordered to blend in, seated at a high top against the wide street opening. I found myself wondering if the ancient row of French doors that opened most of the front to the street could even be closed. The sidewalk was a flow of conversations and colors. It was what I loved about New Orleans and now, somehow different. The ignorance of those teeming by, who had no idea how close they were to being killed by a tailored virus, seemed to bother me. I didn't envy them, Ignorance is a wonderful place to be when it costs you nothing, but there was a cost here.

We sat and let the sand run out. Every tick was one less moment to act. I was confident in my decision, I was convinced Heller was still there even though I had no actionable information to prove it. The end was near, one way or another. Out food came, but no one much felt like eating except for Elvis. He helped himself to all the fried shrimp and boudin balls in the basket. I was relaxing as much as I could when my phone rang. Since only Madeline had the number, I answered it.

"Maddy?"
A pause.
"Rushing, we were too late."

38

I didn't know what she was talking about until I caught the bar TV out of the corner of my eye. It was a breaking news banner. The bartender was on the phone and had been flipping channels to find what their caller was telling them to watch. The scene was a wide shot, taken from a height like a parking garage or balcony, it was looking down on a grass field and stage, some sort of summer concert. People were fleeing, but at that nervous trot speed people used when they didn't know what they were running from. First responders were running the opposite direction, to help.

The concert was a large one, a central area with multiple stages just far enough away from each other so the sound from one wouldn't bleed into the other. Hundreds of people were already down, some sitting, most laying. A few had loved ones trying to care for them, but many were simply alone. The number of infected who had paramedics helping them was tragically low, even if they would be able to do nothing to help them. It didn't look like any were dead, but they were dying. I didn't know much about infectious diseases or viruses, but I did know that onset of even the deadliest viruses was not this fast.

The scene was unfolding in Birmingham, Alabama at the Great South Summer Concert Series.
"Where?"
I asked, hoping Madeline was talking about the same thing I was watching.
"Salt Lake City airport and on flights that originated there when it was released. Casualties are light at the moment, thank god. We think this is one of the more specific strains."

"Maddy, I'm watching a news report on an outbreak in Birmingham, Alabama. Much higher numbers. This thing is moving fast."

"Shite, ok, I'm in the air, headed for Tennessee. It looks as if flights are being grounded so I don't know where I will actually be in the next ten minutes. The others are in the air as well. The doctor is still ours, we haven't handed him off yet."

Whether she was going to admit it or not, there was nothing we could do to help anyone now. The virus moved fast. Once it was released, no one it targeted could be helped. I had no doubts that the other two strains had reached alternate targets as well. It had been over 12 hours at that point since Heller escaped the park. 12 hours was enough time to get anywhere in the US by air, and six or 700 miles by car. It was just beginning.

"Maddy, anyone on a plane is going to be quarantined. I am close to finding Heller. I will get you the other targets."

She sighed.

"It's gonna be too late, Rush. Our only chance was the park and we blew it. I should have listened to you."

As much as I wanted to agree with her, we were both wrong. They couldn't stop the attack, and me finding Heller wasn't going to prevent anything.

"It's not your fault, Maddy. It's not mine, either. Just get back here as soon as you can."

"Right, see you."

She ended the call. I put the phone back in my pocket and watched the TV. Now it was switching back and forth between the scene in Birmingham and the scene in Salt Lake. It had already made it out of the airport and into a school and a shopping center. I stood and walked out onto the sidewalk, looking for Mike or any other Traveler I recognized. It was the first time I could remember where I stood anywhere in the Quarter and didn't see at least one of them. Heller could already be gone, the attack was already happening, there would be no reason for him to still be in New Orleans. My anger built, slowly. I was so used to being angry that it took conscious thought to recognize it. I didn't think I could be any more angry. I was wrong. I took a deep breath and willed calm. I turned back to the table. Elvis was watching as well. His demeanor had totally changed. He was subdued, his eyes wet. He was mourning people he didn't know in a country that wasn't his. I was struck with how at odds it was with the impression I had of him.

"Rushing, he's not going to be here much longer if he is still here."

Julian said, reading my mind.

"No, he isn't. But if he is here, they will find him."

Ten minutes later, an older man wearing a chimney sweep hat, leather vest and brown T shirt that had been stretched a size larger by sweat and life walked by the bar. He glanced around, saw me staring and walked to the edge of our table. He smelled like earth and patchouli.

"Rushing?"

"That's me."

"Oh, hey man, your friend is staying at the Baroque on St. Ann."

I knew the place. It wasn't far. I gave the man a 20. He thanked me with a prayer bow that so many of the Travelers did and mixed back into the street traffic. We did the same, heading west, inland on St. Phillip.

"How did they find him so quickly?"

Julian asked as we set off.

"They are on the streets, it's where they live. We pass by going from one building to the next, we see what we see on the way, the Travelers see everything that passes by from one fixed point. They watch people to find who they can talk to, beg from, get food from. Heller sticks out more than he would like to someone like that."

The architecture breathed. Wrought iron balconies, plater and clap board walls in bright colors. New Orleans was a unique combination of many eras and styles. The Creole, Classical Revival and Victorian doors, Italianate corniced windows mixed with the softer look of the arched Neoclassical. The East to West streets on the East side of Bourbon street were mostly stores, restaurants and museums. The South to North were bars and homes; Creole cottages and townhomes, Gallery style houses, shotgun houses and the occasional California bungalow. Hotels of all types and sizes were mixed throughout, some were converted from old homes and mansions, others from warehouses, horse stables or boarding houses. New Orleans was very protective of its historical architecture, so building anything modern became more difficult the deeper in the Quarter you went.

Which was why the Baroque hotel sat further west, across Bourbon street where the bars were less and the properties were mostly homes, apartments, condos and corner stores and other general businesses. There had been a controversy over the hotel, though it had happened before I moved to the city. A developer had purchased the old Inn at St. Ann and all the properties on that corner of the block and gotten permission to build modern. The city relocated two of the homes, everything else was demolished after what could be sold was picked away and built a ten story building that was an alabaster spire with iron facades and the marble balconies, pillars and adornments common with baroque architecture. It could be seen from nearly anywhere in the Quarter and its modern restaurants, bars and a night club made it a favorite for more wealthy visitors to the city. The second floor housed the club, bars and restaurants. The top two floors were executive suites and the roof of the hotel boasted a helipad. It took up a quarter of the full block it sat on, right where St. Ann met Burgundy Street.

Our walk was quick, a left at Lafittes Blacksmith bar, which was little more than a leaning shed that used to be a blacksmith shop and was arguably the oldest bar in the US. It was a favorite spot for college kids from Tulane and Loyola. Even at that time for the day, it was young men in T shirts and women in tank tops and shorts, drinking grain alcohol drinks in fun colors while standing in the summer sun.

At Marie Laveau's, we turned west again. The hotel was a two block walk from there. Most of the tourist traffic evaporated; the risk of standing out had increased. The streets were tight and mostly one way, making overwatch of approaches to the hotel difficult for anyone wanting to. We kept to the edge of the buildings, using the signs and balconies to cover while watching faces and people of those who were moving on both sides of the street. At the South East corner of the intersection before the hotel there was a bar. We crossed the street and bought sodas so we could stand just outside the bar on the sidewalk and not look too suspicious. The front entrance of the hotel was set back from the street in the center of a circular drive

underneath a massive marble overhang. It may have been
fake marble, it was hard to tell. The drive was wide enough
for limos and executive sedans to sit and still have two
lanes of traffic. The entire parking row was occupied by
four Audi A8 sedans. They were silver because of course
they were. Virtua had a thing for silver. Four sedans
meant Heller still had manpower. I was counting on at
least 15 men. It could have been less or more, but 15
sounded like a reasonable number.

"I can go in."

Elvis said, breaking my concentration.

"What?"

"He does not know me, I never meet him. I go in, find
out."

He had a point, if he was telling the truth. Finally, Elvis
was going to be useful again.

"Okay but try to keep a low profile."

Elvis straightened up, he actually seemed happy to be
useful. His demeanor had changed since he saw footage of
the attack on the news. I didn't know him well enough to
figure out why. He jogged across the intersection and
made the walk up the gentle incline between the massive
columns supporting the canopy. He wandered like he was
lost, gave an idiots grin to the valet and walked through a
set of double doors next to the main revolving door.

"Think you can trust him?"

Julian asked, watching with me.

"Not sure. His people want Heller. They want you, too.
He's here to make sure both happen."

A nod of agreement.

"I have no intention of going with him when this is over."

I patted Julian on the shoulder.

"I have no intention of letting you, Father."

Elvis came back a short while later, smoking a cigarette and drinking out of a plastic cup so big it came with a necklace strap. Some sort of frozen daiquiri. Even in a place as classy as that, you could get a feed bag drink. "Okay. Very *bezopasnyy*. Hotel security is many, but not armed. They all dress in black suits, they have red pin here."

Elvis tapped were a lapel pin would be on his chest. "Heller is on top floor. Some of his men in the bar, five. Others upstairs. Luggage man, how you say, *bell boy* say he has 12, maybe a few more. They rent entire top floor. Need special key to go to top, or go to just under and take stairs but still need key. Security room is on the first floor, door behind counter leads to it. They say they ask for luggage carts to be brought up later, to leave."

I was impressed with how much he'd learned and once again it occurred to me that Elvis was smarter than he let on. If you are stupid, you can't pretend to be smart. If you are smart, pretending to be stupid usually requires constant attention to the act. Smart will slip out, if anyone is paying attention. He had more.

"Maid say, some men have suits like she see on TV, armor. Those men don't leave their room, across from Heller's room. She think four or five of them."

"Sounds like his own little QRF."

Julian said. A Quick Reaction Force. Heller's personal bodyguard, he was clearly important enough to Virtua to have one. And if one of my Siblings was really hunting him, he would need it. Elvis continued.

"Very secure, they probably expect you."

He was right. And getting to the top floor was going to be a problem, at least it was until Elvis produced a key with a beaming grin.

"But I get key."

"How in the bloody hell?"

Julian asked. Elvis responded.

"Capitalism. Everything for sale. Communism, everything already yours."

There was only three of us. They could leave at any time and stopping them would be fantasy. We needed a way to keep him in there until more help arrived. I called Madeline again. It rang and rang. I ended the call.

"No lift from them, then."

Julian declared with a sarcastic tone.

"No, I think it may be just us."

I was trying to think of a plan that wouldn't get us all killed when I noticed a woman walking in our direction from the hotel. She was on the opposite side of the street but her attention was on us. We were the destination. She was dressed in a flattering black dress, four inch heels and a windblown look that complimented her oval face well. When she crossed I could see she wore a small red nametag. She worked at the hotel. Her heels tapped to a stop in front of us. Customer service smile.

"Mr. Winter?"

"That's me."

She handed me a note.

"A gentleman at the hotel asked me to deliver this to you. Have a good afternoon."

She executed a practiced turn around and headed back to the hotel. Life's little surprises. I opened the note.

Join me at the bar, boy, we can have a parlay.

Just you.

-Heller

"Who's it from?"
Julian asked. I handed it to him.
"Heller wants to have a talk."

39

I took a minute to talk to Julian and Elvis, and then I made the walk to the hotel. I didn't know how to make an intimidating entrance that didn't include gunfire, so I just walked through the door. I didn't use the revolving door because no one looks cool going through one of those. I went through a normal door. The lobby was a white marble strip that led to the main desk, with black carpet to either side. On the left, past a lounge of pillars and red furniture was the bar. Above me, an impressive oil mural of the Birth of Man intended to look like the underside of a cupula. It was painted in grays and blacks with hints of red, keeping with the theme of the hotel. The ceilings were high, with dim lighting from sconces high on the marble pillars. Day light from the street peeked through the occasional gap in the flowing red drapes adorning every outside facing window.

Heller was in the bar, seated at the short end near the far wall so he could watch the lobby. He had five men with him, spread out but close by. The rest of the bar was empty. He was about 25 yards from me when I saw him. I had no doubts that I could hit him with my 1911 from that distance, but this is where an emotional attachment to the 1911 would fail me. I had nine rounds and six men. Heller didn't appear to be wearing armor, but the others had the unmistakable lines of soft armor under their suits, which meant headshots or getting around the armor to incapacitate them, and the latter would require more ammo. I worked the scenario in my head as I closed the distance; Heller first, two rounds. Man number one would be just behind him and the first to see me draw, two rounds. A shift of a few degrees and man number two would take two rounds.

At that point, the others would process what they were seeing and react. Man three was far to the left, I could move to one of two pillars for cover, but he would be moving either to cover or to flank me, three rounds for him just to be safe. A reload from concealment would eat up close to a second, by then I would be under fire. Working from either pillar I could expect to have line of sight on Man four, but Man five was certainly going to cover down on the corner pillar he was standing next to and no matter which pillar I chose to use, he would have line of sight on me when I engaged Man four. I scattered the pieces in my mind and ran the scenario again and again, but no matter my choices, the reload time would get me killed. I also had no doubt that Heller had more men close by who would respond quickly. I would get Heller but die in the process. I considered it anyway.

Heller made eye contact with me as I stepped onto the carpet. A few more feet and I would pass by my cover options and be in the wide sea of tables. He smiled and waved me forward. He chose his seat so no matter which I chose, I would have men at my back and it would seem natural. I resisted the urge to shoot him in his arrogant face with every step I took. I worked the scenario again and the outcome was the same. I was close enough to see his eyes and I didn't see arrogance there, I saw exhaustion and maybe a hint of fear. He was in control of this room, but his worries were outside those walls and they were weighing on him. My last chance to engage while still having mobility vanished and I was committed to sitting down. I took the bar corner seat, sitting to his right with him on the other side of the corner. This was the first time I had ever been in the same room with him. His confidence radiated out from a callous demeanor. A man who had been killing people all over the world for decades was not going to be a common sort of man. His confidence wasn't based just on success in life or in profit, nor on social position or status. It was based on the absolutes of violence. We were much the same in that, but he existed on the wrong side. I did once, too.

"I have to give you credit."

Martin said, brushing the crumbs from his hands. His mostly eaten meal of a club sandwich and fries pushed away from him on a plate. There was no bartender or server to fetch the plate. Martin had obviously sent them away.

"I have been underestimating you since Atlanta and you have been a considerable pain in my ass ever since. If Stewart Garitty ever produced a more effective fighter, you probably already killed him."

He knew about Garitty, the man who created the School, the Children and had created me. He saw it on my face. "Still haven't pieced it together, have you? No surprise, it's not like there's been much evidence of it."

He wiped his mouth with a napkin and dropped it on his plate. I ran the scenario once again. I could pull and get him under the corner of the bar, two rounds to the stomach then one to the head as I came out. The man behind him next. I would get the number two man, but certainly be at reload by then and shot in the back shortly after I got the gun loaded again. Every second at the bar, my anger built and the urge to preserve my life was being outweighed by my desire to kill Heller. My hand moved of its own accord, drawing at the hem of my T-shirt to clear it from my draw path. Heller's hand shot out and collapsed on mine before I could drop it from the bar to draw. His grip was strong.

"Don't, boy. We can have a gunfight later, if you want. But right now, I want to talk to you."

His movement had been fast, especially for his age. It shouldn't have been that fast at all. His eyebrows went up at my realization.

"Mr. Grimm trained you, right?"

Mr. Grimm had taught me to be fast. To slow things down in a way the average person could not. To exploit fractions of seconds.

"Yes."

The arrogant smile again.

"Who do you think trained him?"

He let it settle. Let me read him to tell he was being honest, then he continued.

"People like us, we aren't born. We are built. I was built before you, long before. The men who built me, were built by others and so it goes, back longer than even I know. The School is older than you think, older than Stewart Garitty. He created what it is now, he aligned it with Virtua, but it didn't start with him. No, it didn't. But that's a footnote. What's important, why we are sitting here is this; the School has to be stopped. It's a selfish desire of mine, that aligns with my employers."

"So, they turned on Virtua, huh? Because Virtua wanted to cut out the middle man and build its own Children?"

He laughed.

"Is that you call yourself? Ha. Yes, Virtua has done exactly that. Although the recipe must need some work based on their performance at the park, doesn't it?"

I didn't bother answering. Me sitting there was the answer. He leaned in.

"Here's the deal, boy. Have you been watching the news? Birmingham, Salt Lake, Seattle. Phoenix in the next few minutes. Fatalities will be high and unavoidable. But New Orleans could easily be added to that. I'm going to walk out of here, and there's nothing you can do about it. If you try to stop me, we will release here. I'm not trying to negotiate with you, I'm stating the facts."

"Why?"

I responded. He caught the *why* I was asking.

"Why? Why not? Virtua has a plan to create an America, hell, a world, where people like you and me don't exist. Where we don't need to exist, where we *can't* exist. I won't get to live there, but I will do everything I can to guarantee it happens. Have been for the past 20 years. In a few months, an election cycle will begin, and that election will be the first concrete evidence of what we have been working on. We are going to change the world so things like this don't…can't happen."

"If you live long enough to see it."

He got the threat, and knew I wasn't talking about him.

"You pieced that together, at least. Yes, the School doesn't take kindly to its own doing whatever they want, you know that as well as I. I'm being hunted, as I imagine you are. But do you know what is hunting you?"

The attack on Solomon's command trailer came to mind. Heller didn't seem to be aware of it.

"A ghost with knives."

His eyes grew briefly.

"Tell me you killed him."

I shook my head.

"Never met him, but he made a go at friends of mine, didn't succeed.

"Then he wasn't trying. That man is an *Elite.* When you create people like us, ask yourself, what do you create to make sure they stay in line, or at the least, can be killed for

getting out of line? You build something with only one
purpose, to hunt and kill *us*."

Was it fear I saw on his face before he hid it away?

"Heller, I'm pretty confident there isn't much more they
could do to make people like me, us, I guess, any more
effective. Any two Children fight, it's even odds who
wins. Unless one is old and out of practice and the other is
me."

He bit his teeth together, a snarl of sorts. He caught my
barb but brushed it off.

"We were taught to blend in, to fight and kill if necessary,
but to work in the shadows. While you were learning
languages, or chemistry, the Elites were being taught to
kill. When you were learning disguises and etiquette, the
Elites were being conditioned to kill. When you made it to
advanced weapons training, the Elites were already killing
live targets as part of training. They aren't special because
they are like us, they are special because they only exist to
kill us. You have many deceased brothers and sisters
because of Elites."

I didn't doubt he was telling me the truth. There was
always rumors of something like what he was describing,
and if they were as effective as he claimed, a reason they
were only rumors. Anyone who met with one wouldn't
live through it to survive and confirm they existed.

"Why are you telling me this?"

Martin became reserved. His men shifted nervously. They
were under him on the food chain but didn't like the fact he
was talking to me, and freely.

"We come from very different generations. You remember
Mr. Topp? Word is, it was you who killed him. Anyway,
me and him were school mates. Topp was a monster,
because he was raised to be. So was I. We are the violent

past of the School. Blunt instruments gives you blunt trauma no matter how you use it. Your generation were refined to match the world. Extreme violence was becoming less of a viable tool. The newest generation are about less direct action and more conspiracy and subterfuge, taught to be puppet masters and killers if they must. Even If I hadn't gone against the School, I would be on the list. Virtua used their services to set most of this in motion, back when we *Children* as you call them, were strategic, not tactical. From the outside, it's the same organization. But it isn't. Virtua was the customer. But a king is the customer of a bootmaker, does that make him any less of a king? The School doesn't want to make boots anymore. They want to fade back into obscurity. Look, boy, I don't know how old they are, but they are older than these politics, maybe older than this country. They play the long game. Viruta is making their own now, and the School wants its intellectual property back."

I had been right. I didn't know the whole story, or the motivations, but I had seen the split. The School was going to clean up its mess. I wasn't at war with just Virtua, or the School. I was at war with both while they were at war with each other. Heller wanted to turn me on the School. He had baited me with the car registration, stacking the deck in case I was involved in trying to stop him. He sensed my desire to know who and what I was. Maybe because he saw some of himself in me. Maybe he had searched for who he was before the school got ahold of him and wanted the same for me. Or maybe he already knew and wanted me to find out for myself.

"You want me on your side, Heller? Is that it? Because that's not going to happen."

He waved off the thought.

"I'm not so stupid to think that we are going to leave friends, boy. But I am leaving, and you are not going to stop me. I decided to do you a favor, a selfish favor. I'm going to give you a thread, and if you are alive at the end of this, you can pull on it. I am a monster, Rushing, but I didn't know what sort of monster I was until recently. I am the worst that could be created. Even now, innocent people are drying because of actions I either took or supported. It is for a greater good, I honestly believe that, but I guess my point is that I had a choice in being who I am. You didn't."

He stared at me, letting his words work their way through my thoughts.

"I'm not remorseful, or nostalgic. I'm just going to give you a chance, if you want it. Now, I'm going to finish my drink and go upstairs so I can finish packing. You are going to fuck off somewhere else and let me leave, or I'm going to release the virus here."

I had a bet to make, and that bet was that he didn't actually have the virus and he didn't know we had Dr. Vic. Four attacks had taken place already. Four strains made it out of the lab. The TV above the bar was showing reports from Phoenix. The downtown baseball stadium, and MLB game. The casualties did not look heavy, one of the more specific strains. Birmingham, Salt Lake, Seattle and Phoenix. My bet was that those were all of each strain they had to release and Martin had nothing in reserve.

He slid a key across the bar.

"That's for a post office box, package store a few blocks from here. Now go, before I change my mind and we both die in this bar."

"Be seeing you, Martin."

I said, taking the key and standing. His guards tracked me as I left but made no attempt to stop me.

I went out the front door and crossed the street back to the bar. Julian and Elvis were where I left them, sipping on sodas. Julian handed me my phone back.

"Well?"

He asked, watching the hotel.

"He's in there, he says if we try to stop him from leaving he will release the virus here."

Julian took his eyes off the hotel, looking at me.

"You think he will?"

"No, I think it's a bluff. I don't think he has the virus and if he does, it isn't here."

Julian didn't see totally convinced.

"Four strains, four attacks. Two strains never made it out. I don't think Heller knows that we know about any of that. Dr. Vic was supposed to blow the lab. I'm betting one of Heller's men was supposed to kill the doctor. No one knows that Solomon's people even have the doctor, not yet."

"Right, then. I did what you asked. Your Madeline took a bit to get ahold of, but she arranged it. What's the plan now?"

I thought about it. I was taking a risk with assuming Heller didn't have the virus. But I also knew that if he did, he was going to release it anyway. You don't go through the trouble to create something like that and not use it.

"We are going in."

Elvis choked on his soda.

"What is this *we*?"

He looked around for other people, either as a joke or seriously. I knew his help ended with the low risk recon he did for us. Which was fine.

"You can stay out here if you want, Elvis. We aren't letting him leave."

40

Heller may have thought I wouldn't come after him, but he wouldn't bet on it. He would still have men in the lobby, and he wouldn't just protect access to his floor from the floor itself. He would have men on the stairwell and probably other floors as well. The hotel had four elevators, arranged in a grid, but only one of them lead to the top two floors. Guarding it would be as easy as leaving a man on it, but more likely just at the door at the top. There were four stairwells, one in each corner of the building. That was at least five men spread out. A maid had told Elvis that at least four or five of Heller's men were set up as a QRF. It was likely the room they were in was directly across from the room Heller would be in. The maid said that room was the North East, which put Heller on the North West. If the maid was right and if I was right. If there was still five men in the lobby, that added up to all of them, but that wouldn't be the case. So, Heller was going to be in the room with whatever was left over. Having them spread out reduced their effectiveness and gave us a chance. Since it was early afternoon, the second-floor club and bars wouldn't be open, probably the only bars in the Quarter that weren't, which would cut down on innocent people.

Julian and I crossed the street, walking North on Burgundy. The Hotel's side exit was a few yards up. We still had to go through the lobby but weren't going to be dumb enough to walk through the front door. I didn't know how many people were in the hotel and assuming Heller wouldn't endanger others, so he could escape would be stupid. He would go as far as to take hostages if he had to. Our closest help was Card and Toomby, who Julian was told were behind us by almost an hour. Too long. Heller would be gone by then.

We reached the door. Julian recited a number from memory, I dialed. It rang once and was answered.
"I'm in position, ready to go."
Gianna said as she answered.
"We are advising you wait until we have additional support on the ground."
"There isn't time."
I said, watching the hallway that lead to the lobby through the door.
"Tell Solomon to let this happen or get his ass out here and back us up. We are going in, regardless."
A pause on the line, then she replied.
"Okay, in ten seconds."
I hit end and pocketed the phone. Gianna was nearby with their command truck and was about to jam every form of communication she could. If nothing else, it would keep the lobby guards from warning Heller. We didn't have suppressors, but nine floors away worked just as well. The police would be called, but only if someone used a cell phone or a landline outside of the jamming area. That would buy us some time.

Ten seconds came and went.
"Ready?"
I asked Julian. He zipped his rifle out of the bag, letting it fall to the ground.
"In we go."
I opened the door and he pressed in first, moving down the hallway at a high ready. The hallway would put us in the expansive lounge opposite the bar area, on the other side of

the marble strip that lead to the front desk. It would be a center fed exit, so men could be on either side of us.

I fell into step besides Julian, covering the distant corner to the right while he covered to the left. Just before the exit, the first man was visible, walking from right to left, from the elevators to the left of the front desk. He didn't see us. He didn't see us. Then he did. Julian fired once and I was glad for the improvised ear plugs he recommended. His short barreled .308 in the hallway was like a flash bang. The man lost his feet and fell sideways away from the impact. We kept our pace. I heard a scream and a door slam. The second man met us at the mouth of the hall, I center punched him twice, Julian shot him once in the head. We split up at the exit, getting out of the hall. I caught the view of a few guests fleeing out the front door and some poor fool who tried to flee with the revolving door, missed the exit, and had to ride it around a second time to make his escape.

"Looks clear."

It wasn't. Two of the hotel security came out of the rear offices, they had batons, saw guns and dropped them.

"Back where you came from."

Julian said, covering the bar area as we moved to the elevators. They didn't need much motivation. I hit the call button and waited. The first elevator down wouldn't take us to the top. I held it. The second elevator opened. It would. Julian stepped in, pried the key panel apart with his rifle blade.

"Which wire, mate?"

I shrugged.

"All of them."

He grabbed a handful of wires and yanked. The elevator made a weird noise. He took his foot off the door. It stayed open.

"Well, that's that, then."

He crossed over. I took my foot off the door and hit the button for the 8th floor. The elevator started up. We rode unopposed. We backed into the elevator and crossed cover, waiting. The car came to a stop with a ding and slid open. I was looking in the direction of the exit from the elevator bank, so I moved first. The hallway went in either direction from the bank exit. Julian popped out right while I went left. Empty hallways. The same black carpet. The walls were a muted gray with white floor and ceiling trim. Each door room was red, the number in black. I felt like we were in a hotel designed by a guy who had read about vampires and confused them with drag queens.

"Clear here, moving."

I said. Julian walked backwards to me as I moved into the hallway.

"Big gun up front, mate."

We spun like it was choreographed. He picked up the lead and I covered our rear. The size of the building didn't change the basics of how a hotel was expected to work. Each room needed a window, so even the rooms below the penthouse floors were huge. There was enough square footage on the floor for twice or three times as many rooms if they were the common size. According to the sign posted on the wall at the elevator bank exit, there were only 18 rooms on this floor. Big rooms. We reached the end of the hall quickly, a T intersection. We cross covered and then popped at the same time.

"Clear."

"Clear."

Each direction in the hallway would lead us to corner mini-suites and stairs. We went left, as planned. I opened the stairwell door, Julian flowed in. It was a closed stairwell, open to go down, keycard needed for the door that would go up. I keyed it and yanked it open. Julian arced around to see up to the mid-floor landing, I was right behind him. Two men on the stairs. I was hoping for just one. One could be done quietly. Two, not so easy. They were talking, trying to troubleshoot why their radios weren't working. Julian unshouldered his rifle, handing it back to me. I holstered and gripped into it. He went low and quiet, they were standing parallel to the stairs, but if either of them glanced down, they would see us. He crept up the stairs on all fours, their chatter masking the light sounds he made. I covered the man on the right, ready to fire as soon as Julian moved. He stuck to the outside wall, just below the left man. Just as he moved, the right man saw me out of the corner of his eye, he spun to go up the stairs, my round hit him, but it was a glancing shot. Julian shot his man repeatedly in the back and pushed passed his falling body. I moved to follow. He caught the ankle of the fleeing man and yanked him flat on the stairs, he stabbed his gun into his thigh, fired, back, fired, neck, fired, each stab used to pull him higher as he scrambled over the man. He sucked up to the far wall on the landing, looking up the stairs to the next landing. I was right behind him. We pushed up to the exit to the top floor.

"They know we are here now, you ready for this, mate?" Julian asked. I keyed the door.

"Yeah, you?"

"On ne vit qu'une fois."

I pulled the door. Julian followed his rifle out of the stairwell. The penthouse floor had the same central hallway as the others. The elevator bank would be in the middle, but only for the single elevator that could move to the top floor. The doors to each of the four rooms were near the elevators, those rooms on the same side as the elevator having their doors set slightly wider to accommodate its interruption in their floor plan. Heller's room would be on the left as we rounded the corner. We would need to move half way down the hallway to reach the door. If they were moving to escape, they would have tried the elevator first and would now be moving in our direction to use the stairs. Quick math in my head on the time that had passed. They would probably be moving our way at that moment. I heard nothing on the thick carpet, probably wouldn't have been able to without the ear plugs.

Julian reached the turn, keeping as far away from the corner as the narrow hall would allow. As soon as he cleared the angle by a few degrees, he was on the trigger, firing uninterrupted as he moved across the intersection to the other side of the hall. I pushed into his place. Julian called out to me.
"Used to be four, now three."
I gave him a nod, we both peeked out on our respective corners. One man was down closest to us, three more were just moving away from the elevator bank and suite doors to move on us. Just dress suits with soft armor. Julian's FAL would most likely punch their armor, as most concealable armor did nothing for heavy rifle calibers. I couldn't, not with .45 ACP. Head shots it was. I drifted my sight picture onto man number two as the first man was put down with a quadruple tap from Julian. Man two went down with a quick press, the round hit just above his nose, cut through the nasal cavity and struck his brainstem right between the

Pons and Midbrain, severing all Central Nervous System signals. He bowled sideways and backwards, dead before he hit the ground. I knew the hit was going to be a good one and had already shifted to the third man, he was dodging the falling body of man two so I had to track a moving head forwards and sideways. I fired the same time Julian did; a .45 to the high cheek, multiple .308 to the chest. He fell against the wall, his rifle clattered to the floor. He made a wheezing sound as he slowly slid down the wall on his face, struggling to unholster a handgun at the hip.

"Don't be so dramatic, mate."

Julian rolled his rifle around as he moved by, his buttstock blade entered the top of his head. His slow slide ended, gravity did its thing and he was dead on the carpet.

My headcount told me we had between four and seven men left to deal with and some of them would have the advanced armor. We were almost to the first set of room doors. The door on the left, the one I thought was Heller's, opened. A pair of black cylinders flew out, tossed low towards the carpet. I watched spring loaded spoons fly off of each. They rolled through the air in slow motion, I caught the label as it turned away from me.

"Flash bang!"

I yelled. We stopped, closed our eyes. They detonated. Even with my eyes closed, the flash was blinding. I opened them and moved, one man appeared in the hallway, he was shouldered into his rifle and pressing towards us, the rifle jumped at each round fired. I stepped into the wall, he was tracking me. The air rippled and cracked. I pressed until my gun ran dry, Julian landed multiple hits. Magazine out, clear from under my shirt, magazine in, slide release, press out for sights. The next man out of the room went from in focus to blurry as I found my front sight. I fired, Julian fired. He danced and spun, hitting the door frame hard before collapsing into it. Julian was in the middle of a reload on his rifle when the wall of the opposite room exploded.

There isn't much to interior walls. Wooden studs, sheet rock, wiring, outlets and occasionally insolation. With enough weight and a head start, the average adult male could run right through a wall or make it most of the way through. Wearing a suit of advanced armor with microhydraulics to increase strength and reflexes, going through the wall would be like punching through wet paper. Julian was closest to the breach, his FAL barked in a full auto burst, I shielded my face from the flying sheetrock and debris, recovered to push my sight picture right to engage. Julian was blocking my shot. The opposite room door was kicked clean into the hallway, a second armored man. I heard and felt the wall behind me explode out into the hallway.

Julian reached the end of his magazine just as the first man through the wall got into arms reach. He had come through the wall on the shoulder, he was trying to bring some sort of SMG to aim when Julian hit him with an uninterrupted burst, it started low and followed the muzzle rise up, Just as I was tracking the man through the door, Julian rolled his rifle underhand, the spike drove up and under the armored helmet and was just long enough to punch the roof of his mouth and enter brain mass. I fired, pressing as fast as I could work the trigger. I could see his head bounce beyond my sight. The first two rounds didn't penetrate, and I needed to finish him and turn to deal with the man coming through the wall behind us. Julian let go of his rifle, used the falling man as a step and pushed up, kicking off the wall, grabbed the falling man's neck and used his weight and momentum to spin around to the rear, his handgun cleared its holster, arcing away from his body until he told it to stop, he fired. The man was already firing, I watched a spray of blood from Julian's neck splatter onto the wall. He came back down to his feet, his aim had been good, the man only managed to fire a single burst before being shot through his visor. A fourth man was just behind the last to come through the door, he was close, his rifle was already shouldered, making a small correction of degrees to fire. I tracked through the recoil of my last shot, the first man through the door was falling out of the way. I found my sight picture as the slide locked forward on the next round. I pressed, my first round hit low on the neck, the second hit roughly where the jaw would be behind the armored mandible of the helmet. The first round punched through, the second was stopped by the armor but it was enough to throw his first burst wide, missing me by inches.

I was at slide lock.

Magazine out.

He stumbled.

Index reload.

His back hit the door frame.

Reload moving out from under my shirt, up towards the waiting magwell, gun canted slightly and pulled in halfway to my chest.

He swung the rifle back towards me.

The magazine slid in hard, pushing the entire gun up into my thumb resting on the slide release.

He corrected his aim.

I pounded the trigger, the first rounds fired from the reloading position, driving the gun out.

He fired.

I fired. Eight rounds as fast as the gun could cycle.

My slide locked back on another empty magazine. He slid down the floor next to his friend.

A five second explosion of savageness from the flash bangs to the last man being put down.

I was working my next fresh magazine into my gun, Julian had to put his foot on the man's shoulder for leverage to pull his rifle free. Once he did, he stumbled. The wound to his neck was bleeding. It didn't look like an artery hit, but it was certainly in the neighborhood of one. He considered the rifle, then dropped it on top of one of the bodies. He couldn't keep pressure on the wound and work the rifle at the same time. Julian reloaded his pistol and gave me a nod. I took the lead, heading for Heller's door. It was just barely open, stopped from closing by the hand of the last man who had come out of it. I could hear Heller talking loudly inside the room, yelling at what I hoped was his last man. I looked to Julian before I pushed for the door. "You good?"

He was visibly in pain, a hand pressed tightly on his neck, blood breaking through the seams of his grip.

"I'll make it, let's finish this."

41

I pushed through the door and ran right into one of Heller's men. He was close, bringing a handgun up. I stepped inside his reach, trapping his gun hand under my arm. He was pressing the trigger, firing into the hallway. I shot him multiple times from close retention, my 1911 held close to my chest. It pounded his armor, I twisted and drove an elbow down to collapse his arm, snaked my wrist around his forearm and stripped his gun, shifted aim with my gun and fired low, into his pelvis and leg. I reached up and yanked his head back, driving the muzzle up under his chin and fired my last round. Blood splattered my face. I pushed him off of me, Julian was in the door, moving past me. Automatic fire raked the room; Heller was firing blindly through the wall of the master bedroom as he moved deeper into the suite.

"I'm here for you, Martin."

I yelled, reloading. He responded with another magazine of fire. Julian moved for the room first, one hand on his neck, the other keeping his pistol in front of him. He ignored the puffs of paint and sheet rock as rounds exited the wall, glass mirrors shattered, the lights flickered and the door was beat all the closed by impacts. He kicked it right back open and went right, I followed, going left. The bed room was massive; a California King bed set in the center against the back wall looked small in comparison. A city view to the left, a hallway and closets to the right. The lighting was dim, the walls a deep purple with red carpet and black furniture. More fire, this time from a doorway in the hall, Julian pushed along his wall to the corner, I pushed out across the fire until I was past the hallway opening, then turned for the wall. We met on opposing sides of the hallway entrance. Martin was reloading, I could hear the scrape of a magazine.

"Hello, Martin. It's been a long time."

Julian said, crouching next to the frame.

"Who'd you bring with you, boy?"

"My name is Julian Whent."

Martin was as sharp as ever.

"Ah, the church in Araouane. You were really hanging your neck out there, Catholics in the heart of jihadi country. Very biblical, a bit too far south for a crusade though."

Martin chambered a round on his fresh magazine.

"Oh, didn't I kill you, Father Whent?"

Julian felt along the wall, coming up into a slight crouch.

"You tried, Martin. Why don't you come out and try again?"

A laugh and a burst of fire. The doorway splinted near my head.

"I'm just going to bide my time until my men get here, if you don't mind."

"They aren't coming, Heller. We've killed them all, you can't call anyone. This is it."

I said, risking a peek into the hall. He was near the end, in what was probably the bathroom. Judging by how deep the hallway was, it was a large bathroom. A second burst of fire. The cyclic rate was high, it sounded like a machine pistol. He wouldn't have much ammo left in his reload after that.

"You want me? Come get me, boy."

Julian moved his hand on the wall again, he seemed to be homing in on Heller. There would be a lot of open room between him and the wall and there could be furniture or other objects in the way as well, but it was worth a try. The other option was to run him out of ammo or breach the room and risk all of us dying on the bathroom floor. Heller didn't have more men coming, but someone would eventually get the police and they would come and their clock was ticking down to exactly that happening.

"I'm going to push, keep him busy."
I said, bringing my gun up. Julian gave me a nod. If you don't have cover, accurate gun fire works well enough. I drove into the hallway on the trigger, each round going through an increasing angle on the bathroom door. Julian took one step off the wall as I moved, settled his point of aim where he thought Heller likely was, and fired. He was still firing when I reached the near side of the bathroom door. Heller had returned fire, but either taken a hit or ran out of ammo. I dropped magazine and reloaded, reminded again how long eight rounds lasts. Julian was behind me. I listened to the bathroom; nothing.
"In?"
Julian swapped magazines.
"In."
I cut the angle. It was a deep corner fed entrance, ornate double sinks and a salon mirror to the left. Directly ahead was a massive tub next to a hot tub, in the right corner was a standing shower the size of a small convenience store and directly to the right was Martin Heller swinging a slide locked Glock 18 like a cleaver at my head. He was fast, but I was prepared for his speed. I sidestepped, blocked the blow with my support hand and shot him in both knees, Julian was right behind me, he stabbed his pistol blade into Heller's extended arm and then shot him, yanked it free and gut shot him multiple times, just under his armor. Martin staggered away from us, disarmed, out of ammo and defeated. He sunk down to the edge of the smaller tub,

palms up with his forearms on his thighs. He made no attempt to treat his wounds, nor did he seem to notice what had to be extreme pain.

"Well then…"

He strained.

"I underestimated you."

He said looking at me, then he looked at Julian.

"And you. Huh. I didn't even know you were alive until a few minutes ago, so I guess I underestimated you, too. I suppose this is the part where I apologize, or beg for my life or-"

Julian looked at me while he was talking, looking for permission. I gave him a nod.

"No, Martin, this is the part where I kill you because God forgot to."

Julian shot him once in each eye, he fell back into the tub. It was over.

Martin Heller was dead.

I expected to feel something, but I didn't. In the place of anger there was nothing. Or I had been mad for so long that the anger being gone felt hollow.

Julian lowered his gun. He turned to me, a blank look on his face.

"What's it supposed to feel like?"

I asked.

"Peace is what we want, Rushing. It isn't always what we get."

It was hard to disagree with him. Julian was council to his own feelings. For so long I had been wanting this moment to come and when it did, I gave it away. It wasn't that

Julian deserved it more than me, it was that he was a better man than me, and Martin deserved to be killed by such a man.

"*Ni figa sibie!* Wow, guys. Really *afigenna,* yeah?"
Elvis surprised both of us, and had both guns pointed at him. He raised his hands in a startle. We lowered our guns.
"Police come soon. We go."
He motioned to the hall with his head. We followed him out without so much as another look at Martin Heller. Through the master bedroom and into the living room, which was full of Elvis's *Vor* friends including Anton, Ulf, the Ogre from the service hallway at the Biloxi casino and the man I had seen in Anton's room on the balcony. They were spread out around the room, as far from each other as possible. Anton held a pistol; the others had modernized AKs. It would have been a challenge to get all four, but not impossible. It only became impossible when Elvis put his gun to the back of Julian's head.
"Guns on floor, no fight, yeah? Be quick, we must go."
I knew the issue with turning Julian over would come up, but I didn't expect it to be so soon. Elvis had been talking to Anton the entire time, through text I imagined since I never saw him talking on the phone. He told them where we would be, knew we had found Heller, it only made sense for them to come. It was a more economical use of time on their part, anyway.

Anton wore a huge smile, cigar bit between teeth. We set our guns on the floor. Anton's men relaxed and closed in a bit.
"Go, find it."

Anton said with a clap of his hands. Ulf passed by us, going into the master bedroom. The sounds of rummaging in drawers and objects being thrown around the room could be heard as soon as he went in. Anton turned his attention to us. It wasn't lost on me that he was perpetuating a stereotype by wearing a track suit.

"Please, come. Sorry, Rushing, but I couldn't trust you to do the right thing. I also needed what was promised to us." He motioned for us to stand in the middle of the room, so we did. Too far away from furniture, too far away from Anton's men. We could move on them and win but it would require having a telepathic link with Julian. We thought alike, but not that alike. I waited and kept running scenarios each time something changed.

"You see, Heller was supposed to share. We smuggle in his Smallpox, he makes it, we get the, uh, how you say, the *recipe*. He could not have done it without us, or our machine. We it stole from Vector, we lost many man getting it. So, two birds, one Kalashnikov, eh? We come, get our priest and recipe."

Anton was very pleased with himself, and the Russian mob helping Heller in exchange for the *Resolute* virus was an easy choice to make. Either on behalf of the Russian government, or more likely to be sold to the highest bidders. Having that code for building that virus meant you could kill specifically and easily.

Ulf was still trashing the room. I wanted to ask if he knew what he was looking for. I would hate to think that he took *recipe* literally and was back there looking for a cook book. "So, enough talk. Rushing, please step back. We deal with priest, and then you can go."

The crashing sounds from the room stopped. Ulf walked back into the room, a laptop in tow. Anton smiled and welcomed the laptop like a long lost friend.

"Ah, thank you, Ulf."

I needed to buy time, for what, I wasn't sure, but more time meant more options.

"You sure that's it?"

Anton gave me a sardonic look.

"Please. I saw this laptop in Russia, see this *Harvard* sticker. Prick doctor, this is his."

Dr. Vic. Well, that removed any doubt about him having the right laptop.

"Besides, *Velns,* why you care, anyway? The priest owes us a debt. I consider yours paid, but I can easily put you on the carpet next to him."

Elvis was moving, he threaded between the four of them standing behind them, slowly so he wouldn't draw attention. I couldn't figure out what he was doing, but he made it easier for me to shoot him, too once I figured out a way to get a gun. Anton's men were still positioned wisely.

Julian looked at me, peace in his eyes.

"It's okay, Rushing. If this is God's will, then I am okay with it, mate. This isn't yours to fix."

Elvis put a finger to his lips. He reached behind his back, a gun appeared in his hand.

"Okay, enough of this, priest, on your knees. I let you pray to your god, a quick prayer, then we will make eve-"

The front of Anton's face deformed and exploded out. The closest man to him, Ulf, reacted first but was shot through the head before he could do anything. Julian rushed the ogre, I moved for the last man, I managed to push his rifle burst intended for Julian up into the ceiling, and thcn Elvis shot him as well. Julian rode the ogre to the floor with a thumb in each eye. When he pulled his hands free, Elvis shot him as well.

"Oh, my, this is disgusting. Did you have to put thumbs in eyes like *shar dlya boulinga*? So gross."

We recovered our guns. Elvis tucked his away.

"Friends, yes?"

Julian hesitated to holster his gun, only doing so when I did.

Elvis shook my hand, then Julian's like he was meeting us for the first time.

"My name is Elvis Igoshin, *Federal'naya sluzhba bezopasnosti Rossiyskoy Federatsii.*"

Julian didn't speak Russian, so I translated.

"He's FSB."

Elvis nodded. His demeanor had changed, he wasn't *as* dopy.

"Yes, KGB two point oh, yes? I've been, you say, undercover? Two years working with these *pridurki*. To get to top. They make deal with Heller, FSB want it, too. But watching people die, I'm not giving it to anyone."

Elvis held his gun out to the side and fired, the window spidered. He picked up the laptop from Ulf's body and walked to the window, kicking it out of the frame onto the street below. He held the laptop out the open window and dropped it with a smile.

I watched in disbelief.

"What?"

He asked when he saw my face.

"You don't think this break it?"

Ten minutes later, all available law enforcement collapsed on the hotel. We had been gone for five. We walked to Bourbon street, to *NOLA Po'Boys*, right next to the New Orleans landmark *Clover Grill*. Elvis wanted New Orleans food, and he deserved it. I wasn't hungry, Julian wasn't either. We sat with him while he ordered three different types of po'boy, so he could try them all. Madeline called and said that Card and Toomby were at the hotel. I told her where we were. Card and Toomby showed up a few minutes later. They sat with us for a minute, learning what happened in hush tones then decided to order themselves, taking their own table. The single TV in the eatery was set to a global news channel. Everyone in the room was watching it, though the streets were much more empty than they had been 24 hours ago. Fear was setting in and people were not going to want to be in public places with crowds for some time.

Around an hour later, Madeline arrived. Tellison was also back from his flight but did not bother to come by. She joined us at the table, not wanting to eat. I filled her in as well and then we just sat and watched. The hours ticked by.

Birmingham, 3,200 dead and climbing.

Salt Lake, 800 dead and climbing.

Seattle, 320 dead and climbing.

Phoenix, 75 dead and climbing.

The talking heads and experts were on the interview circuit. Mostly speculation, but what was becoming obvious was that the first generation of the virus was fast acting, intended to draw first responders in and increase the odds of infection. After that, the symptoms took time to develop, so people would escape quarantine before it was established and spread the virus further. Every minute it would infect any it was programmed to who had the misfortune of breathing the same air as a carrier. All non-government flights were grounded. Smaller outbreaks were being reported at the destinations of flights from Salt Lake City. One flight had crashed, both pilots were infected, there were no survivors. That death was preferable to the virus. Smallpox was a painful disease. The hybrid was painful and fast. Once symptoms presented, death would occur in four to five hours. Smallpox vaccines were being used on the latest victims to present with systems, but with no effect. It would be after midnight before we peeled ourselves away from the TV and went to meet with Colonel Solomon and the others.

Gianna had parked their command center among a small sea of 18-wheelers at a truck stop near the airport. We made our way there. Solomon was waiting, Tellison, Porter, Hijazi and Gianna with him. They were gathered around the central consoles of the command area, when we arrived, everyone piled into the briefing room. This time, Julian and Elvis were allowed. Elvis officially introduced himself and explained his role. He also explained that the FSB would deny any knowledge of knowing about the virus, Virtua's involvement or any of Heller's actions inside their country, which was expected. Elvis sank back into the corner after that, watching cat videos on his phone,

only with it muted this time. Solomon looked the same.
Sweating. In pain. But also relieved that they had stopped
at least some of the attack and they had all of Dr. Vic's
research, as well as Dr. Vic, to create a vaccine to combat
the virus in the future, even though Dr. Vic assured them
that Virtua had no intention of another biological attack.
The problem with weapons though, is that once they are
created, they belong to anyone who can get them. Dr.Vic's
Resolute was the most effective biological weapon ever
created, it would be sought after by anyone who learned
about it.

"Current death toll is North of 5,000 but expect that to rise.
People are dying faster than they can be counted.
Birmingham and Phoenix are the worst, it's biblical there.
They are censoring footage from the stadium. It looks like
half the people in attendance died before they made it out
of their seats. We had no idea the gravity of what we were
facing, and now we are in no position to stop something
like this from happening again. Counting the people in this
room, except for our guests, we are at 16 personnel total."
He let the number sink in. I didn't know how big his unit
had been to begin with, but 12 wasn't enough to fight a
secret war across the US, let alone the world. Those who
knew what the unit used to be, were solemn. I recounted to
Solomon and those in the room what Heller had told me. I
explained that things were more complicated than them
against the corporation, they had to protect themselves
against the School as well if they got caught in the middle
and Heller offered me nothing to explain what the School
actually wanted at the end of everything.

"He knew he would die in that hotel, I suppose he wanted to sew fear in you before he died."
I said, after going over my conversation with Heller. Tellison scoffed regularly throughout my talking. I ignored him. Where I was once mad at his attitude, I found only indifference. I couldn't change his opinion of me or what I was and I wasn't going to try. With nothing left to say, I walked out of the trailer into the late night. It was quiet that far away from the city. It was eerie that there were no aircraft in the sky, no late night flights coming into or leaving the airport.

Julian joined me, Elvis behind him.
"What are you going to do now?"
I asked Julian.
"I have a congregation to rebuild, though I have to have a conversation with God before then, to see if he still wants me. Warrior priests have always been, but it's been a while since the Holy See has supported it. So, we will see if this is still my path. Regardless, Africa is calling me home and I will go."

As the sun peeked above the horizon, Julian was in a cab, his rifle wrapped in a pool towel he took from the hotel. He left me with a handshake and a hug. Elvis left not long after, picked up by an executive car with diplomatic plates. The others were still in the trailer, talking. I caught a cab at the gas pumps and had him drive me back to the Quarter to get my car, then I drove home. I was getting in the same time my Neighbor, Cyn was.
"You look like shit, dude."
She said with a smile.
"I feel about the same, I'm going to go sleep for a day."

She laughed.

"Me too. I'll be seeing you."

I let myself in, secured the door and sat on my bed. Pepper's 1911 in my hands. I unloaded it, then held it and stared at it, remembering her. If I tilted the gun just right, I could still see a trace of her blood between the frame and grip. Maybe it was someone else's blood. I didn't know. I did know that I was done with it. Everyone who had a direct part in Pepper's death was gone. Martin was the last. Revenge, retribution, whatever you wanted to call it. It was done. I sat and thought for what seemed like a long time. Finally, I took a simple black box from my simple night table and laid the gun inside. Then I took Pepper's St. Jude necklace off and placed it in as well. I put the box back in the night stand, then laid down and went to sleep.

When I woke, it was late afternoon. No one had come by. I watched TV for a few minutes, the coverage was and would be for a long time, about the virus. The death toll was nearing 10,000. It was a hard number to wrap my mind around. I worked it over in my head while I worked my body through a round of weights. Sweating in the yard, burning out the stiffness from the last few days. Heller had given me a key. I didn't know what it would lead me to. What I did know, was I didn't have a purpose at that moment. I didn't belong with Madeline and her team. I didn't belong anywhere. If what Heller had told me was true, there was a sibling out there who was going to eventually come for me. The *Elite* that Heller was afraid of. When I was growing up there had been rumors of them, but they were the boogymen in the closet, they weren't supposed to be real.

After my shower there was a knock at the door. Madeline. I let her in. She was showered and looked somewhat rested. She told me they were headed out of the city that night and she wanted to come say goodbye. She had time to eat, so we drove into the Quarter, once again she was able to find a spot for the Tahoe and we made it into the Oceana Grill without a long wait, going up the narrow stairs to the top side seating, near the bar. I only wanted Gator tail, so I got two orders of blackened with a double Blantons Old Fashioned. She kept it simple as well, water and a steak. The food came and went without much conversation. When we were left with cleared plates, she finally brought Heller up.

"Did he go painfully?"

It wasn't asked with hope, it was asked as a curiosity.

"Not intentionally, but yes. He knew we would never let him out of that hotel, he tried to bluff having the virus, threatened to release it. Threw every man he had at us. Honestly, if it wasn't for Julian, I don't know if I could have gotten to him."

She agreed.

"He's a good chap, that one. Sad to have him go."

"He did it."

I said. She looked into my eyes, thinking of how to ask the question on her mind.

"Why?"

"Because I didn't need to. I had beaten him, he had given up. He took a lot from me, from both of us, but nowhere near what he took from Julian. He walked away from his faith to find Heller, or maybe it was his faith that helped him, I don't know. I never had the option to be religious and I'm still pretty undecided on it."

A morose laugh.

"I'm British and Irish, mate. I was born to be undecided. What are you going to do now?"

I sipped at my drink. I didn't have an answer to that. I could feel the key Heller had given me in my pocket. It held some kind of truth and the desire to find out what it was, was growing.

"I need to find out who I am. Who I really am. Heller was one of us. I don't know why it never occurred to me. He baited me with that car registration, I have a birth certificate, I think. In a weird way, when he knew we weren't going to stop looking for him, he wanted to give me a clue. I have a mother out there somewhere, a father, maybe. I don't know anything about who I was before I was taken by the School. There's other kids being taken, right now. Other kids in a school somewhere being turned into what I am. Or was. They can be saved."

She reached across the table and placed her hand on mine. A soft caress and held it there.

"What about you?"

I asked.

"Oh, more to do. We are slim, no doubt. Gianna thinks that the cunt with the knives, an *Elite* you called him? He was after intel only. As to why he's been killing off our unit, we don't know. But the laptop and phone he swiped would give him actionable intel, we can follow behind and see if we can piece together what they are trying to accomplish. It's not a good feeling being against someone like that, but they are after the corporation too, and we can use that."

"Doesn't sound like much of a plan."

She had to agree.

"It's not, but we have to crack on. Figuring out what Virtua was trying to accomplish with this attack is our first priority. Stopping whatever that is. Solomon wants to go direct, start hitting them at the management level."

The conversation drifted to Pepper, as we both reminisced about the woman we knew and loved. How strong she was, her sense of humor, the fact that she was an amazing artist but hid her drawings like she didn't want anyone to know. How she loved being a cop and regretted ever leaving it and how she loved me and talked to Madeline about it, frustrated that I didn't see it. And when I did see it, it was too late. By the time the summer sun had gone, Madeline had to leave. I paid the bill with the last of my money and we walked down to the street. She offered me a ride, but I told her I'd rather walk.

"I wish you'd come with us, Rush. But I understand why you won't."

"Not now, something I need to do. But if you need me, you can find me."

She reached out and hugged me, tight and high. Her lips on my cheek, they lingered.

"I'll be seeing you."

She climbed into the Tahoe, and with a sad smile, she pulled away. I watched until her tail lights rounded a corner and then I started for the box that belonged to the key.

Epilogue

Heller's box had contained nothing but a photograph. A frontal shot of a large southern style plantation house. Two stories, Antebellum architecture. A wide veranda that wrapped around the entire house. I knew it did because I used to live there. It was the school I grew up in, where I was trained to be who I became. The photo was old, much older than me. On the porch was a young Stewart Garitty standing next to a much younger Martin Heller. A third man in the photo I didn't recognize, but if he was still alive, he would be ancient now. On the back was an address, fresh ink at odds with the old and frayed picture. The School.

I reached out to a man named Chester, an old not-friend from when I worked for Garitty. He had my money, which I hadn't touched for a long time because there was always a worry that Virtua could track it, or the School could, and they could find me. Chester had reached out to me months earlier, told me he had found a way to move it, and it was safe and tied to a new identity. It wasn't altruism on his part, his money was in the same situation, so it was of benefit to him to figure it out. He also told me he paid himself handsomely for his work. Chester sent me my new legend. While I waited, I said my goodbyes to those I knew in New Orleans, packed what little I owned into a storage unit, bought a new gun, then climbed into my car and drove non-stop nine hours to Colliers, South Carolina.

The school property was about ten miles south of Colliers, which wasn't a town so much as it was a name on a map with a church to match. The School property was 8,000 acres of woodland near Dry Branch, off a lonely state highway that was used by wildlife more than cars. The address on the photo brought me to a dirt turn off that punched through the dense trees. It showed signs of once being well maintained, but the forest was swallowing the road up and at times it felt like the road would swallow my car. When I finally broke out of the trees, I recognized the imposing fence line that I had seen for so many years from the other side. It was in disrepair, the once cleared grass fields were overgrown. Trees that were not there in my memories were growing unopposed. The guardhouse was home to owls. The gate was pushed aside. I drove through, looking for any signs of life. I drove up to the top of the gentle hill where the house sat. About 22,000 square feet of Southern Mansion built sometime in the 50's.

The main stairs gave no clues as to what waited inside. I parked. I didn't see any other vehicles. I drew my gun as a precaution and walked up the stairs, across the long landing to the front door. I turned the handle. Unlocked. I moved in. The entrance was as I remembered it, a grand staircase directly ahead, a hallway between the stairs that led to the rear of the house. The wing to the left was the school wing. To the right, the admin wing where we were never allowed to enter. A hint of childhood curiosity washed over me. The floors were covered in dust, but there were foot prints, small ones. The thought that there was a child, or children in the house made me uneasy. The foyer furniture was covered in sheets, the air smelled of sugar and tea. Fresh tea. Someone was living there, it even looked as they were trying to keep up the house, but it would be a lot of work for one person. I moved to the admin wing, where the adults had lived. The first door led me past bedrooms, then opened up into the dining room. Sitting in the corner, at the only set table was an old woman, patiently sipping tea as she watched a hawk hunt rabbits out the window. She glanced over as I entered, saw my gun, considered her own sitting on the table but instead of reaching for it, she smiled.

"It's been so long. I knew someone would come, I thought it might be you."

I crossed the room. She was old, her hair long since gray, dressed in a floral house coat with muted colors. Bifocals on a gold chain hung around her neck over a simple pearl necklace. I recognized her.

Mrs. Tinn had been in charge of the girls at the school, and occasionally taught the boys in classes about women. She had always been nice, except when given a reason not to be. When she was angry, she had been worse than Mr. Topp. I hoped I didn't have to kill her, too.

"Sit, please."

I sat. The table was set for one, a cup, saucer, napkin, silverware, small crystal vase with a flower and a small .380 with a suppressor. It was placed with a second napkin under it, folded so the grip sat off the table, making picking the gun up much easier. The table was covered in dust as well, everywhere that wasn't occupied. Her routine was so specific that dust sat on everything else. Mrs. Tinn studied me, a matriarchal smile on her face like a grandmother looking at her successful grandson. She motioned to my gun with her eyes.

"You can keep it if you like, but you won't need it here. I'm all that's left."

I set my gun next to hers, then folded my hands in my lap. She approved and relaxed a little.

"It's been so long since I've had a visitor. Oh, a nice man comes every few weeks with groceries and occasionally someone needs to come and fix the power, we are so far from town, you see? But an actual visitor, one of the children, no less, it's been at least a decade.

"You are here alone?"

I asked, looking for any evidence to contrary. She sipped her tea before responding.

"Always. This school and the other on the property was closed years ago, now. I was left behind because I wasn't needed at any of the others, and they needed someone to watch the property in case it was needed again, I suppose. If not for the weekly call, I would have thought they forgot about me a long time ago. There's a lot of secrets here, Rushing, but you know that."

"You remember me?"

I asked. She smiled.

"I remember all of my children. Between the two houses, I helped over 100 of you out into the world. I started after the war, my mother worked for the OSS during, served in France and Germany, she worked with Mr. Van Vleck. Mr. Van Vleck recruited me himself after we met."

"Who is that?"

She set her tea down.

"Oh, I'm sure you have so many questions. I'm old, Rushing. I'll pass soon enough, though I go to sleep every night expecting someone to shoot me in my sleep. I think my age is the only reason they haven't done it. Either that, or Mr. Van Vleck's grandson can't bear to order it out of respect for the old man. Mr. Van Vleck ran all the schools, he provided help to the OSS during the war. Your brothers and sisters helped beat the Nazis."

She laughed a sweet old lady laugh. Polite and quiet.

"How old is the School?"

She gave me a knowing look.

"Oh, very old. I wish there was some sort of family scrap book, but such things were never kept. It's as old as America, I do know that. The Van Vleck family has run some version of school since the 1700's. Mr. Van Vleck told me that himself. We had an affair, you see? Oh, he was older than me, but so wise and confident. He did such great things with you kids. His wife was a prudish woman. I only met her once, but she didn't deserve a man like Mr. Van Vleck."

She told facts and once shameful secrets like an old woman beyond the protocol of life. She was in the sunset and had nothing to hide.

"But the secret, oh the secret I'm not supposed to know. None of the teachers were supposed to know, where you all came from."

"I was a foster kid, in Idaho, I think. Stewart Garitty killed my foster parents and abducted me and others."

She shook her head with a smile.

"Oh, no dear. I'm sorry, but that was the model then. That's the secret."

I wasn't following. The model?

"The model?"

"They put a great deal of research into the way to make you, you see? Long before I worked here, they developed a formula. The science of the mind was new, but certain things were being understood. By the time your generation was being prepared, the Winter program was the most promising. From birth to you being brought here, everything was planned."

I was swimming. My mind was trying to reconcile what she was telling me with what I thought I knew. Were my memories even real?

"What are you telling me?"

She finished her tea. A pearl snap cigarette case appeared from her pocket. She set it on the table, carefully extracted a slim cigarette. A gold ladies lighter, from a time long ago. She gently lifted the hinge cover, struck it and lighted her cigarette. All of her movements were patient and precise.

"That you weren't born, Rushing. You were built, my son. They hired woman with certain *traits* to be surrogates. I'm not a doctor, or a scientist, you see? I know what I learned from Mr. Van Vleck. You were born and put into the program. Everything was tightly controlled, it followed a script of events. Anything you experienced as a child, was intentional."

I remembered my mother. A vague sense of a person who was there, in your life. But so much time has passed since you actually saw them, their face changed in your mind until you couldn't trust yourself. A *Flashbulb* memory was a concept from psychology where a significant emotional or monumental event would be burned into your mind, impermeable to time. But they weren't. The memory was susceptible to details being forgot, or to regret re-writing the events so you remember them in a more positive light or create memories of decisions you wish you had made to remember yourself and your actions more favorably. What I remembered of my mother, those flashbulb moments, were just scattered fragments of colors, smells, motions and words that I experienced or arranged myself, and I couldn't tell the difference.

I didn't remember my mother at all. I remembered the woman I wanted her to be and it turns out, even that wasn't true.

"My drug addict mother, the vague memory I have of a father, the foster home, the foster parents?"
She was nodding along.
"All part of the program, I'm afraid."
"So, who was my real mother? Where did I come from?"
She signed.
"Rushing, these things don't matter. Your mother was a combination of ideal genetic traits, as was your father. They were the *sum* of people, but not people, you see? The woman who carried you was paid to do so, she was a tool in the process. She probably carried many of you."
I was struggling to make sense of it. To make new connections of information to old memories. To search for clues in my mind to show that she was right.
"Where?"
Certainly, they couldn't fake locations. I remembered the foster home in Idaho, it had to have actually been there.
"Oh different places, the location wasn't very important to the formula. The place you remember was probably where you thought it was, or close enough."
"But I went to a school, I was in an elementary school with other kids. I wasn't taken until I was 12."
She touched my hand as if to console me for not seeing it.
"Oh, it was a controlled environment. Those other children? Your teachers, anyone you made contact with were because it was part of the formula. I don't know where they got those other kids, some of them were just like you. Was it a small school? Not many classmates, somewhere rural? I bet it was. The Winter program was

the first successful engineering, though later in life many of them did exactly what you did and went against the School. So maybe the short-term returns didn't justify the long term."

She gently ashed her cigarette, considering the hawks across the lawn. Every word unsettled me more. She was right, it was a small school, in a small town. 12 or 13 kids in my class. My name.

My name.

"So, I was named after the program, what about the other kids? I don't remember anyone else with my name."
She pursed her lips.
"Oh, no. That was actually a coincidence. Your names were random. So was the program name. No pattern there, no matter how much you want to see one. I see patterns in everything that aren't there, I was a Linguistics Cryptographer, at least that's what I went to school to be, to follow in my mother's footsteps."
She looked down at her watch, considering the time.
"It will be late soon, what more do you want to know?"
I had so many questions. I was so concerned with them that I didn't consider what she was getting at.
"Who are the Elites?"
Her face scrunched up like she had smelled something rancid.
"Well...They are the minders. Such a silly name for them, but men do like their hyperbole and I suppose they had to call them something. Mr. Van Vleck told me that it was expected that one of you would occasionally stray or become too old to be of use. We aren't monsters, you see? Many have been able to retire after a long career, but

some…some couldn't be allowed to. If one of you was ever arrested, well, we needed a solution to that problem, you see? Elites are only trained to kill. They aren't capable of functioning in normal society. They have no legend, no cover, no attempt to have them blend in. They are only sent out to hunt."

"From where?"

"Oh, I wouldn't know that, not anymore. Years ago, it was from here. Some of them were even teachers here, before they changed the program. Mr. Topp was an Elite. He possessed the mental capacity for it. We used to have to look for naturally occurring mental markers, the right personality, you see? But all of that changed with your generation, and those after you, it's less about the formula of upbringing and more about the formula of genetics. Science is truly wonderful."

She finished her cigarette, using a small corner of tea left in the cup to extinguish it.

"But that's not very important, not now. It's getting late, you see? This has become something other than what Mr. Van Vleck wanted. Its off the tracks. Someone has to right the ship, and I'm much too old to do it. That's why I hoped someone like you would come. I only have so much to offer, but I can put you on the right path, I think."

She mentioned the time again. The sun was getting low, but I still didn't catch the connotation. She deliberately slid another cigarette out of her case and lit it.

"What about the corporation?"

Her eyes lit up.

"A relationship was formed a long time ago. They were a customer…oh, I hope you don't mind my indulgence of a second cigarette, it's getting late and I wanted another one…anyway, they were our best customer because the ideology aligned. Until it didn't. Some of your brothers and sisters had worked for them for so long, when the split happened, they aligned with them. They wanted their version of the future versus our time-tested ability to shape the present. It's all but a war, now."

If she had been there for so long, cut off from the day-to-day, I wondered how she was so up to date, so I asked.

"How do you know this, if you have been here alone for so long?"

She became sad, maybe regretful. From her lap she held up an old cell phone.

"Oh, we ladies talk. It's all we have, you see? So many of us all around the world. Some just like me, minding an old ghost of a house, though not many. More still serve the greater good, working still with the children. I'm not so lucky. But you came, and I had hoped it would be you."

She pulled a small case from her house coat, gold with engraved initials, the finish worn from decades of use. She set it on the table, opened it and extracted a small gold pen that set next to a small stack of paper.

"You said *Idaho?* Yes?"

I nodded. She scrawled out an address, perfect cursive. Slow, deliberate.

"This is where you would have been. I'm not so old I have forgotten. So much to remember, and I think I remember it all."

A chuckle as she folded the paper cleanly in the middle and handed it to me.

"Now, our time is up. It's getting late and you really must go."

"It's not late."

I said, reaching the point where being polite was overridden by not understanding why she kept mentioning it. She shook the phone.

"Oh, I had to tell them you were here. I knew we would have time to talk before anyone could get here, but they must be getting close. I didn't want to, but I owe everything to Mr. Van Vleck, you see? I had to call. I'm tired, Rushing. This has been wonderful for me, but it's the end."

A spike of concern up my spine.

"How long?"

"Oh, they aren't close by, but they will be here soon. If you leave now, you will be gone before they arrive, but you must go, now."

She struggled against age to her feet, slipping her small pistol in her pocket. She hobbled over to a china cabinet, opened a door with care and moved a large serving plate. Behind it was an old combination dial. She spun in the combination and opened it. Inside, a throw lever.

"This part of your life is over, Rushing. But you have much to do. It has been wonderful to meet the man you have become, and I hope that you can either fix the legacy or destroy what it has become. I think the choice to do either will be yours in the near future. Goodbye, Rushing."

She pulled the switch down. There was an electric pop, the lights flickered and then a flame seemed to shoot from the ceiling and many spots along the wall, blue flames crawling towards whatever they could burn. She was burning it.

"What about you?"

I asked, motioning for the door. She smiled and waved me off.

"Oh, I will be fine. Go. Goodbye."

I left with one last look. Out through the foyer, down the stairs, into my car. The second floor was already engulfed by the time I got in. As I pulled away I heard a muffled gunshot.

Heller wanted me to pull on the thread. So, I did.

69115856R00309